The Harves
Xav

While there ..
humanity never ceases to try diffic...
arrangements. Xavier Lombard, a man of laconic
disposition not immune to beauty's seduction, hears
tell of hopes and sins, is visited upon by many faces
of Death, throughout moderates his own thunder, as
befits a guest in a strange place.

****

Some reviews of the previous titles:

No.3 in the Xavier Lombard Series

Also available in the same Series

The Lost Son

A Place of Gardens and Lilies

*****

The Harvesters

Eric Leclere

THE HARVESTERS

Alibi Books

First published in Great Britain in 2023
Alibi Books
London, England
www.alibi-books.com
info@alibigeneral.com

A catalogue record for this book is available from the British
Library

ISBN: 9780953556250

Cover Design © Doggo
Cover photograph © Margaret Leclere

Printed and bound in Great Britain

For Jeremy

"If you press me to say why I loved him, I can say no more than because he was he, and I was I."

Michel de Montaigne

ONE

Small mercies—The spirit never dies.

For two years now, every day between 5 and 7 p.m., Mrs Raspberry and her cat Pester could be seen inside the ground floor window of number 49 Cemetery Hill in Highbury. Being that it was a large south-facing bay window and Cemetery Hill uncoiled as a wide steep sloping avenue lined with semi-detached residences no higher than three storeys, come autumn and spring the dusk setting sun beamed on the woman and cat, illuminating their presence. Framed between heavy scarlet and black curtains, come what may, cold sleet or sweltering stillness, grey-haired, silk robed and decorously rouged Mrs Raspberry always sat poised in a high-back leopard-skin armchair, her cat Pester curled up on a crimson velvet vanity stool near enough for her to rest her deadwood-coloured hand on its tawny fur. One was eighty-one and the other seven. One day one had turned obstinate as the other had turned sweet-natured. And ever since at the same appointed afternoon hour the two never failed to show up in number 49's window.

There hardly could be imagined a more untroubled scene of contemplative tranquillity than Mrs Raspberry and her cat in the whole of London, so that while heading down towards the tube station at the bottom of Cemetery Hill, or be it while climbing the opposite way towards the church and graveyard at the top of the hill, well-disposed passers-by could and occasionally did feel moved to smile or wave graciously in her direction. By all means, some were so stirred by reason of being reminded of elderly relatives, or their own mortality.

1

Others, overwhelmed by their generous nature, merely wished to give an old woman a sign that she was still welcome among them. All the same, it hardly would have been a singular state of affairs if a few folks were swayed by a sense of gratitude, indebted to her for providing their afternoon with an image that evoked a time when miles still kept lovers and rivals apart and thresholds were spaces to pass from sight and vanish out of reach, gateways to all manner of unrecorded deeds. For although Mrs Raspberry never failed to ignore their warm overtures – and likewise Pester invariably growled forbiddingly at the sound of the front gate being pushed on its hinges – within an electronically connected habitat in which whereabouts were tracked and minds exposed to much distraction, the old woman and her cat provided an arresting sight. Certainly, seated all poised, rouged and robed in her window Mrs Raspberry appeared preserved from the agitation and swirls of instructions that dogged all and sundry in the course of their everyday activities. Such has forever been the privilege of the old. A day comes when age is clear to wander its way, to take a seat and reminisce about all that once summed up a life well done: births, funerals, weddings, separations, triumphs and defeats. And although such matters still punctuated most existences, a new rhythm and reality now influenced the very nature of existing.

For this was the time at which this tale took place: a time of great changes, a time of great challenges, a time unlike any recorded time before. The great changes stemmed from men's and women's ingenuity. Ever more wondrous communication and monitoring devices bonded humanity under an unseeable interactive cyber dome, tethered all minds to novel and untested arrangements. Where once each living soul was tantamount to an island – distinct from all others, set within their own shores, the sum of their own qualities and limitations – each now counted as a continent's fraction constituent, a scintilla within a digital effervescence, primed to provide at all times to digitized notifications and summonses. To look up at the stars or navigate the paths of passion no longer spelled distinct uniquely peculiar personal pursuits; to be, no longer was to endure, or leisure of your own, but to make good within a cross-connected information get-together. "We're going where no one has gone before. Safer and closer together; all as one," many cheered – "One size fits all and the mob visits each and every house," lamented some. Such environment, overseen by about a dozen or so dominant nations and transnational organisations, made for loud choruses of convictions pressed on young and old from beaches to mountain tops, an always-ringing information concert from the dawn to the dead of night, so that great changes had borne great challenges, for from the first men and women's ingenuity has always come a poor second to their zeal.

Thereby, afforded the means to instruct and audit all, a new elite advised a new generation that it knew better of all things than all generations which hitherto had passed; had all the answers; owned all the fixes. Former and present wrongs were to be remedied. Where inquisitions and persecutions once thrived, now they chimed of contrition and tolerance, set forth new sets of intransgressible rules designed to eradicate prejudices. Here some spoke of righteousness – others of oppression by another name. They who once enslaved people to promote their own homestead now sang with the confidence of former masters the virtues of mass re-education and repa-ration, picking out from among themselves and the formerly subjugated those they deemed most deserved to be put at the front of the queue. "Justice! Past wrongs must be righted; the better to heal and promote harmony in diversity," they declared – "Where is the fairness in shackling our children to a past which no living soul played any part in? Besides, nobody likes queue jumpers; two wrongs don't make a right," some whispered. Where once they felled forests, lauded the industrial revolution, slaughtered wild beasts for sport and built tall cities and empires, now they charged for drinking water, pressed for boycotts and restrictive taxes, microchipped pets and beasts and went on building cities and empires. Where once there were men and women only, now some denied the notion of genders, and academia and policy institutions were also found

3

to propose that in the affairs of mind and body smart and fit people were provided with unfair advantages such as required remedying too.

Such upheaval took some getting used to, spared none from its momentum. Providing that great changes bring about great challenges, likewise great challenges provide great potential for confusion. If the pursuit of the common good and ending discrimination called for the fostering of fresh discrimination and censorship, "let it be so" the chorus pledged. There were lists of words deemed good and lists of words deemed bad. There were banned words. There were prohibited pronouns, films, songs, images, statues, stories, and – inasmuch as they could be unmasked by judicious scrutiny of a person's conversation, demeanour or industry – outlawed thoughts, notions and longings. For all practical purposes, this profited many, unnerved scores more and the balance existed in fear of correction. Teachers, publishers, bartenders, train drivers, just about anyone, it hardly mattered. A frowned-on word could end a career; a suggestion lead to censure and public scrutiny; an opinion to social exclusion or arrest and detention. The elevation of social justice, diversity and accountability, some were adamant, warranted transparent and blunt instruments. And it followed that where once they celebrated the burning of books and people on public squares, they now divested and deleted books and people from places of learning, social platforms and stores, driving them into silent exile and oblivion. There were some who believed that, like previous great reassessments, this exaltation would run its course, spoke of growing pains. Others cited a new world order, the end of Western culture, a catastrophe equal if not greater than such as had befallen the Greeks millennia earlier. For it was true that while the prodigious technological advancements which drove the rearranging of human life concerned the entire world, the patients most receptive to the zeal-induced agitation which followed were places like London, Paris and New York, or all such western settings and lands which once had prevailed over earthly matters now determined by new eastern rulers with great designs of their own.

Such was the general situation at the time of this tale; not un-akin to simmering water within which each atom grows more and more agitated and restless by virtue of exposure to external heat. And Mrs Raspberry would readily have known none of it. But her advanced age had dulled little of her mental faculties. She never was without visitors, couldn't but have noted the younger generations' antics. Still, none of what she knew of it unduly concerned her. "Human nature doesn't change," she would say; "Winds of changes blown by angels are hardly novel and invariably herald thunder. At my stage of life I have too precious little time left to fret about such things."

This, it would turn out, were the words of an old woman who failed to grasp the scope of the changes around her. And in good time she would be disabused of the notion that her mind could afford to play such tricks as remain indifferent to the ways of the present. It would seal her fate and leave her stranded on Cemetery Hill. For had any of the good-natured waving or smiling passers-by called on any of her neighbours to query about the nice old lady sitting in the window of number 49 with her cat, they'd have been told that she was a crazy mean old woman – a fact nobody could deny after acquainting themselves with the note she had sent two years earlier to Audrey Pomeroy of number 54. And, had the same neighbours opted to produce on their personal communication devices the said note which Audrey Pomeroy had circulated two years previously on the neighbourhood's SafeHaven-Network for the edification of all, like they once used to click a flashlight they'd have there and then swiftly submitted the evidence:

'Dear Mrs Pomeroy, it is by no means certain that you shall outlive me. But then again, I started to die long before you, so most unfortunately it's highly likely that I shall perish first. If Hell does exist, there's little doubt that once released from this mortal frame I shall head straight there. You may like to learn that I have had most of the men I set my sights on during my long and full carnal life. So, if the devil is anything like a man, I want you to know that I'll make sure I'll make him mine, so that together he and I shall be waiting for you (and your litter) when your time comes. Yours most sincerely, Mary Raspberry.'

And to stress their point further, the same good neighbours may have gone on to state that the crazy mean old woman was also a racist who for two years now had turned herself into the bane of the neighbourhood by perching in her large bay window every afternoon between 5 and 7 p.m. for the intent purpose of causing nuisance to Audrey Pomeroy who lived two doors down across the street at number 54.

As often is the case with words from the street, speaking a little truth with great outrage helped spread a bigger lie.

It was fifteen years now since Mary Raspberry had moved to number 49 Cemetery Hill, a pleasant three-storey Victorian house with a generous garden graced with old oak and cherry trees. It had belonged to Mr Raspberry, a tree surgeon who had converted the property into three flats, retaining the ground floor and basement as his dwelling while renting out the two upper storeys. A quick courtship had led to marriage and her moving into her new husband's domicile. He was fifty-four, she sixty-six, and, more than a man of property – which was incidental since she had means of her own – he was a handsome fellow with a fit body, a good head of hair and strong hands who still climbed trees in the course of his occupation; and proud of it he was too. He was a good catch to enter old age with; while Mary Raspberry would never have settled for less, by then time had begun to catch up with her, setting up that stage of life when mind and body are no longer quite one and the same, start to move at different paces.

In the event, for all its pleasant promises, their union had lasted little more than a year. Perhaps Mr Raspberry had gone on climbing trees too long. A seizure while up with his chainsaw had led to his severing his femoral artery and dying of blood loss while still securely roped to the top of his tree; he may have been saved had he had the presence of mind to apply a tourniquet to his limb or the rescue service been able

6

to bring him down in good time to stem the blood flow. "Probably the best way for a man like him to go," his daughter from a previous marriage mused while on a brief visit from Australia for his funeral.

Mary Raspberry had considered moving back to Brighton in Surrey, her town of residence before coming to Highbury, but Cemetery Hill presented comforts and conveniences, not least the two upstairs rented flats which afforded her the right sort of cordial but formal social company. It was then that she had got herself a kitten for distraction, a male British Shorthair which soon grew into a rascally truant tom who by the time of its going missing seven years later had lost parts of both its ears and the tip of its tail, grown huge jowls, drooled and limped along. Always very fond of the animal, she never thought of taming or having it neutered as it clearly favoured the street to being confined indoors, oftentimes absent for long spells. Still, following its loss, she missed it enough to seek a new tom, a common tawny type of cat which she named Pester on account of its rumbustious character. It too soon had grown into a truant, unrestrained and unneutered, and five years had gone by with it, not unlike its predecessor, often returning home battle-scarred to stay put only long enough to lick its wounds. Now and then, a neighbour would complain about it spoiling their lawns, badgering their pet or killing birds. "What would you have me do?" Mrs Raspberry would say; "In China they eat cats. In France they declaw them. In America they bath and blow dry them. In England we celebrate their independence. What would you have me do?"

As it turned out, someone would not have her do anything, opting instead to take matters into their own hands. One February day, Pester had returned from its latest escapade a much-changed beast, bereft of swagger and testicles. "For goodness' sake," cried a disbelieving Mrs Raspberry; "Poor Pester. What sick degenerate did this to you?"

She called the police, fumed against the "criminal who castrated my Pester and must be caught and punished", and they, after attempting to explain that this was no police matter, that she should report the matter to the RSPCA – all in vain as she would have none of it – had reluctantly dispatched an officer to her home. The officer expressed sympathy, reiterated much of what was said on the phone, asked whether her cat was named Pester by reason of its being a nuisance, suggested it had been mistaken for a stray and advised that its ordeal would likely have been averted had she got it chipped. She hadn't. "There you are, Mrs Raspberry. Whoever interfered with your cat could have contacted you if you'd chipped him. The fact they let him find his way home after having had him neutered suggests they aren't a bad sort. They must have had cause to think he was feral-like—Quite an understandable error looking at his scarred face and all. There isn't much the police can do, Mrs Raspberry. It's all within the law really." "How can it be within the law to castrate somebody else's cat? This is absurd!" "If cause exists to think a tom stray or feral, it is indeed within the law, Mrs Raspberry. Like I said, it could have been averted if you'd had him chipped. Most folks microchip their pets nowadays, Mrs Raspberry. And not a bad thing it is too. As a matter of fact it is a legal requirement for dog owners; I believe the same may soon be the case for cat owners too. But don't quote me on that." She'd contacted her solicitor, was informed that he'd retired some years earlier and was put through to a young woman the law firm recommended. The latter, pointing out that she could only express an uninformed opinion as she did not have all the facts, echoed the police position, adding "Of course, were you able to provide evidence that the person or persons responsible were aware your cat was not feral nor a stray, you could have a legitimate complaint. But you'd have to know who they are in order to do so."

In the end, as she prepared to call at all the veterinary clinics within her neighbourhood armed with a photograph of Pester, Rose Pemberton of number 91 down the road – a retired ballerina and seamstress who had resided on Cemetery Hill even longer than she had and with whom she would exchange small talk whenever their ways crossed – cleared up the mystery. "Hello. Mary," she said after knocking at her door, the first time she'd ever done so; "I hope you don't mind my intruding but have you seen Pester recently? And if you have, has anything happened to him?" "Hello, Rose. Indeed—I have and something has happened to him: some deranged mind castrated him. What is it that you know?" "Oh. So it is your Pester. I thought so. Well, you see, two days ago I noticed that one of my dogs—Oscar, you know—Has a small tumour growing on his lower lip; better have someone look at it at once, I thought. The thing is my regular vet is booked solid for the next few weeks so I made an appointment at a new clinic on the Holloway Road, near the junction with the Seven Sisters Road, you know. Anyway, turns out it's benign, Oscar's fine. But while I was there chatting to the receptionist, she noted my address and remarked I was the second person from Cemetery Hill to visit their clinic this week. So I asked who the other person was. And she looked it up and said 'Audrey Pomeroy. Number 54. Do you know her?' 'Oh yes. But by sight only,' I said. 'She's only been on the Hill a couple of years. She's our local environmental activist,' I said, alluding to her making the national news last Easter when she took part in that lie-down protest on Waterloo Bridge together with her four teenagers; you remember, when they blocked the Easter holiday traffic? 'Well, she's a very nice lady,' the receptionist said, 'She brought this stray tom: a grumpy thing with a missing ear and scarred nose. It had been bothering her two cats and up to all sorts of mischief in her garden. She wanted it neutered.' Well, I said to myself—grumpy, missing ear, scarred nose—That sounds just like Mary's Pester."

Even though number 54 was a mere two houses down across the street from her, Mary Raspberry barely knew much about the Pomeroys; she hardly spent time in her window in those days. Yet, she recalled reading in the local paper about the 'Highbury environmental warrior mum of four teenage crusaders', who, if her memory served her right, was a Chartered Surveyor with an architect husband. Still, none of this mattered to Mary Raspberry when she set out across Cemetery Hill to confront Audrey Pomeroy, a woman in her late thirties wearing pink lipstick who opened her front door in a vest,

Lycra pants and trainers, ready for her regular early evening jog.

"You stupid woman! How dare you castrate my cat," said Mary Raspberry.

"Hello! What the—Who the hell are you?"

"Mary Raspberry. Number 49. How dare you mutilate my cat, you sorry excuse of a woman. I'm going to sue you."

Mary Raspberry was beside herself. And Audrey Pomeroy, none too pleased to be so confronted by an old woman on her own doorstep, in this soon rivalled her. A storm of words ensued and many things were said in the next few minutes. About Pester from Audrey Pomeroy: "If the cat's yours you ought to thank me for having him seen to at my expense and bringing it back here, you silly old hag!" – "You aren't fit to look after animals. And besides, your cat was a menace. He's been spraying and defecating all across my garden—Stinking the whole place up and endangering my children's health. When is the last time you gave him his shots, eh?" – "I reckon your cat's been contaminating the entire local feline population, you irresponsible woman. Go ahead. Sue me. See if I care. I had no idea that feral thing was a pet of yours. And now I do I'm not sorry. The law says I am entirely within my rights to have him done if he presented a health hazard to my family's wellbeing. Actually, now I met you, I feel sorry I didn't do your cat a favour and have him put to sleep to spare him further suffering in your miserable company!"

About Audrey Pomeroy from Mary Raspberry: "You're a liar. I've lived here for over fifteen years now. Most of the street knows my Pester; all you had to do is ask around if you had a problem with him. I'm two doors across the road from you, stupid woman. You did this deliberately. How dare you castrate my cat, Mrs Watch-Me-Care-For-The-World-By-Holding-Up-Traffic!" – And, after Audrey Pomeroy's four teenagers, drawn by the ruckus, had joined their mother outside their front door to sneer and smirk: "Let me tell you something: it's you who ought to be spayed, you high-minded nitwit. Instead of allowing you to go around mutilating animals and dispensing your misery onto the rest of humanity they ought to make it illegal for the likes of you to reproduce. There ought to be laws to prevent people like you from breeding! Think about it. Never mind the spite that leads you to mutilate animals—Think how much more agreeable the universe and space would be if you and your litter weren't around passing wind and judgement. You had no business with my cat, woman—You moron! Your expensive shade of pink lipstick may fool some into believing that you possess taste and discernment, but you'd only be fooling them. You aren't fooling me! Let me give you some words for your education, Mrs Pomeroy: 'But woman, proud woman, dress'd in a little brief authority, most ignorant of what she's most assur'd—Her glassy essence—like an angry ape, plays such fantastic tricks before high heaven as makes the angels weep.' You make the angels weep, Mrs Pomeroy. You're a fool. And far beyond help you are too. You ought to know your place. And I'm going to sue you."

Mary Raspberry had had little idea what she would say to Audrey Pomeroy prior to heading across the road towards number 54's door; too much anger fogged her thoughts. All that mattered was to let the woman know what was on her mind. And she was satisfied she had done just that when she returned home afterwards. She'd shown her teeth, was thrilled she still had teeth, chuffed at the way her mind had brought up the Shakespeare quote, not to mention the manner in which she'd substituted gender and pronoun without missing a beat. She'd known these words most of her adult life, from a time when she turned heads and lived in New York and was distracting a theatre producer-director who was putting on Shakespeare's 'Measure for Measure'. Teasing, she'd asked why he couldn't give her a part in the play: "I'm not just a pretty face, you know." And he'd laughed, pledged he would if she memorized the entire play. It was all in jest, but she'd resolved to make the joke on him, trusting her agile mind. Later, she could barely contain her glee at his amazement when she made him test her; she'd learnt the whole text by heart, all one hundred and forty-four pages of it. By then, all the parts were cast, but feeling duty-bound to keep his word the man had offered her a silent walk-on part, which to the relief of all she turned down after a mere two attempts at the role; her acting skills proved no match for her agile mind or power to drive men to distraction. Today, still ignorant of much of Shakespeare's work, she could still bring up most of 'Measure for Measure' on cue, now and again recited passages from it to herself as a means to keep her mind occupied, preferring this to solving crossword puzzles which after years of practice had become more tedious than challenging.

On this account, genuine concerns for Pester aside, she'd returned home feeling quite pleased with her performance at Audrey Pomeroy's door, particularly as she'd managed to keep her wits about her when the woman's four teenagers had turned up behind their mother to smirk and sneer. In fact, their appearance had spurred her on, five against one was no fair fight, and wasn't it a good thing that after all those years her knowledge of a Shakespeare play had come advantageously to her rescue.

Or so she thought. What occurred next was fast and brutal. Now she knew the culprit of Pester's misfortune, her plan was to call the young lady at the solicitor's. However, by the time she did, she had been visited by the police again, though not as she hoped on account of Pester. Instead, they informed her under caution that she was to be investigated for committing a hate crime, her offence being to have spoken and acted in a way which 'is perceived by the victim or any other person to be motivated by hostility or prejudice based on a person's race or perceived race'. In other words, the police had received complaints – dozens of them – that she had made threatening and racist comments, a serious offence which they were re-quired to investigate. "It's the law," they said.

As it happened, Mary Raspberry knew of mobile phones – she owned and used such a device to make calls – but had yet to use one to film, take photographs, or for that matter to explore the internet, with which she was still unacquainted at the time. Likewise, she had no idea that Audrey Pomeroy was – as the police put it – 'a woman of colour'; or to be more precise, 'a sixteenth woman of colour'.

"A sixteenth woman of colour? What on earth are you talking about? What colour? Have you seen the woman? She's grey. Wipe out the lipstick and she's the colour of a bleak sky on a joyless day."

"That may be how you feel, Mrs Raspberry. But that is not how she perceives herself. Or how her children perceive themselves. Complaints have been received and we must investigate. It's the law."

One of Audrey Pomeroy's four children, it transpired, had appeared at the door not merely to sneer at the old woman exchanging angry words with their mother; they had recorded the incident on their phone, so that while Mary Raspberry was back home still basking in her performance an hour or so after the fact, Audrey Pomeroy, ridiculing the charge that she had got Pester neutered knowing full well that it belonged to a neighbour, was posting the captured footage across several platforms for the world to see, charging Mary Raspberry with racism for 'comparing me to an angry ape under the cover of Shakespeare', suggesting she should be "spayed" and stating "There ought to be laws to prevent people like you from breeding!" 'I'm a sixteenth coloured woman and proud of it,' Audrey Pomeroy's comments concluded; 'This old woman probably thinks her age protects her, but she is a racist disgrace.' At once, without further encouragement, numerous complaints were made to the police, including four from the Pomeroy children who publicly declared having received offence and characterized themselves as *thirty twoth* of colour'. Almost overnight, most of Cemetery Hill's residents – even the previously gracious Rose Pemberton – had taken to shun Mary Raspberry, unwilling to be seen talking to or standing alongside her. It had not helped that the affair had motivated someone to post on the Cemetery Hill SafeHaven-Network – the local community's cross-platform network which interconnected most of the street's residents into a 'Safe, Healthy and Trusty Community' (but not Mary Raspberry, who had no interest in such things) – that 'The racist disgrace from number 49' had form, summoning up a four-year-old incident which had seen her accuse her part-time 'person of colour' housekeeper of stealing £20 from her purse and then have the police come to remove them from her property when they had refuted the allegation and refused to leave until paid compensation for unfair dismissal without notice. Likewise, the young lady at the solicitor's turned hostile, or at the least unhelpful: "Perhaps, if you'd called us rather than confront your neighbour on learning what happened to your cat we may have been able to help you, Mrs Raspberry. It's a very awkward situation now. There's little we can do, really. If you want my opinion, you could do worse than going to apologize to your neighbour for your incautious words."

But Mary Raspberry never apologized, the police soon dropped their investigation – citing her advanced age – and in the end, the recipient of much unpleasant mail and now acquainted with the marvel of the online digital world and the firestorm of venal comments directed against her on social media platforms, embittered, she had felt it necessary not to renew the leases of her upstairs flats' tenants; they too had changed, eyed and addressed her in ways she hardly appreciated. After their departure, she opted to keep the flats unoccupied, and save for the defiant 'devil note' she sent Audrey Pomeroy, from here on out resolved to keep her thoughts and company to herself.

The community made her into an outcast and something snapped inside her head. She could have upped and left, but like her neighbours rightly suspected her mind was set on being a nuisance, making certain Audrey Pomeroy couldn't forget her; not as long as the woman remained on Cemetery Hill. She still kept herself occupied with 'Measure for Measure', but now had taken to reading Shakespeare's other works; "When mercy seasons justice," she often whispered between her cracked lips for no discernible reason, a line from 'The Merchant of Venice'. "When mercy seasons justice." Alone, she listened to the empty old house creaking. Pester was still much loved, but she missed its virility; the once truant tom was now a cute house pet content to doze for hours who rolled on its back at feeding time and meowed sweetly, only venturing out now and again to return with a mouse or bird it would drop by its food bowl but never ate. It did growl warningly whenever anyone pushed the front gate to come to the house though.

There were times when Mary Raspberry did still wonder what her neighbours and the digital crowds would have made of her divulging having given birth to a couple of 'coloured' babies many long years ago, before the sorcery of easy contraception. This, if nothing else, made her 'of colour' by impregnation and, as the mother of two 'half-coloured' children, many times more 'of colour' than 'a sixteenth woman of colour' Audrey Pomeroy. Then again, as she'd already done with yet another product of her womb who admittedly could never be painted as 'of colour', just as soon as she had brought them into the world she had also abandoned them and their fathers; such choices had determined her life. So it likely wouldn't have helped. And besides, no one had much listened when she protested that for all she cared Audrey Pomeroy could have been purple, green or orange on the day she confronted her. That she was seeing red. That she'd spoken to the woman as an equal; a foolish and most nasty equal but an equal all the same. That when it came even to fools she'd always been colour blind. That no one ever taught her to discriminate or address others pursuant to their skin colour; make pitiful, condescending, nervous allowances for it. But this too was hardly likely to have helped. After all, no one could deny it, grey Audrey Pomeroy and her children weren't 'persons of colour', not to the eye, be it a sixteenth or a *thirty twoth*. "Perception," the police insisted; "It's not just about what you said, or about whom you thought you were speaking to, but how Mrs Pomeroy and her children perceived your words, Mrs Raspberry. It's the law."

Such was the time at which this tale took place. They who once enslaved people to promote their own homestead, who felled forests, slaughtered wild beasts and built empires and cities and burnt books and people they feared or disliked, now

15

made lists of good and bad words, of perceived rights and perceived wrongs, and – inasmuch as they could be detected or unmasked by judicious scrutiny of a person's conversation, demeanour or industry – lists of illicit thoughts, notions and longings. The celebration of justice, diversity and accountability, some were adamant, warranted blunt instruments, brutal but necessary measures.

For two years now, come 7 p.m., Mrs Raspberry would get up from her high-back leopard-skin armchair to pace her way to the kitchen at the back of the house. Pester would sit up as soon as she clambered to her feet, watch her go a few paces to give her a head start and then leap from its crimson-cushioned vanity stool to dart past her to the kitchen to roll on its back against the rug by the sink. "Poor Pester," she would say once there, before putting some soup to warm up on the stove for her supper, feeding the cat and sitting down at the table to eat. Today was no different. She was slow, a grey-haired shuffling silk robe with deadwood hands and feet. "Poor Pester," she said, and a little later, after sipping her soup, she stood up to head for the window overlooking the large back garden.

Under the sunset sky, summer was coming to an end and dead oak and cherry leaves gently swirled down towards the lush lawn. She remembered how she used to own the summers, when she could feel the warm air caress her inner thighs and was still called Amérique. She remembered when she became Amy, and later still when Amy became Frédérique, and then Madam Eimi, and then Amy again and Amy became Mary. Tomorrow was Thursday. Unless it rained, like every other week Jack would turn up mid-morning to do the garden. He would rake the dead leaves, set them alight on the bonfire by the shed against the far wall and mow the lawn. He was a tall handsome lad with winsome brown eyes. She would open the window, savour the smell of burning leaves and remember campfires and unhurried Spanish rivers; make it last as long as she could. Only then would she offer Jack a cup of tea and biscuits before Janice would arrive to do the cleaning and

16

shopping. Standing at the window sill Jack would grin, showing his big teeth, ask if she was well.

He had no idea. There was a time when she had it all.

"Small mercies," she whispered; "The spirit never dies."

And here for now we shall leave Mrs Raspberry and Pester, not to return until the time comes to catch up with them again.

TWO

Raped, killed, left for the crows.

Big wheels keep on rolling. The 5:10 from Exeter to London was running on time, traversing the dawn-mist-wrapped West Country steady on its eastern course to greet the rising September sun. Among the harried multitudes who set forth from the provinces every weekday morning to face the challenges and opportunities London has to offer, each measures up to their own arrangements; a young man in shirtsleeves with his eyes rapt on his phone may be dreaming of adventures; a girl in a pinafore dress pounding away on a device could be toiling for better things to come; providing it to be true that a glad face is a sign of a glad heart, a woman with a winsome puppy on her lap could well have the gladdest of hearts; a frail scruffy man in possession of a patched-up crutch is likely in need of assistance; and a child and mother's bond is being taxed as they wrestle with their angels.

"Mum? Does God protect you when you're on a train?"

"Yes. Of course, darling."

"And in a plane?"

"What—Yes. In a plane too."

"And in a spaceship and a car?"

"Of course, darling. In spaceships and cars too. God is everywhere; God protects everyone everywhere. All right?"

"Then why do people die in train and car and plane and spaceship crashes, Mum? Is it because they are sinners?"

"Oh—Well, I—I suppose so, darling. I guess it must be because they are sinners. Now be good and read your book."

At one time, Xavier Lombard favoured the sort of casual or

18

functional dress worn by most train passengers, but it was a while now since he was last seen out in anything other than a two-piece suit, preferably dark, a white shirt with the top button unfastened and crisp leather shoes. Of good proportion and manners, he carried this conservative outfit well enough to cut a fine figure, which was just as well, the reason for such presentation being that it was an advantageous way of coming across as quiet but capable, and confident enough to deter casual curiosity or quarrelsome contempt. Hence, although naturally concerned with his appearance, only a healthy modicum of vanity accounted for his disposition to promote such an image of himself. Still, a two-piece suit, even one of good cut and cloth on good shoulders, could only go so far in guarding a man from unwanted attention or familiarity. Admittedly, on a crowded morning commuter train, a suit was indistinguishable from the one next to it, providing little advantage to its wearer. So, along with the old wedding band ever-present on his left-hand finger, he wore cufflinks, which he varied according to whichever of the dozen or so watches he owned was showing on his wrist on any particular day. In this matter, where matching one with the other was very much self-indulgent coquetry, the same hardly applied to the cufflinks in their own right. Affectation played little part in his adoption of these ornaments, which, if anything, from a fashion perspective, belonged to bygone times. Merely, here were convenient contrivances, a proclamation that he was in want of nothing, sought nothing, subsisted beyond the mundane. While such jewels could be regarded as well-to-do society's gaudy status symbols, so far as he saw it their value lay elsewhere, investing their wearer with an intangible insulating shield. A man in cufflinks could be envied, resented, hated even, but is hardly ever going to suffer disrespect or come across as a failure. Not in European capitals. This notion's credibility was unprovable by evidence or argument, of course, still, Lombard believed it to be a self-evident truth and trusted intuition, swayed on the matter by the childhood memory of a well-cufflinked uncle he'd met only once; the man was introduced to him as his mother's brother, stayed for dinner then was gone. He'd long forgotten his name, nonetheless his silver cufflinks had made a great and lasting impression.

In any event, if challenged, as on occasions when suits, looks, wedding band or cufflinks proved wanting, Lombard could always call on his easy grin, which, contingent on the nature of the challenge and the party answerable for it, he could flash either to unnerve or to charm, and keep control of most situations. He had years of experience to show for it, years of vigilance, which had left him mindful of his effects on others. He reckoned he presented a healthy somewhat intimidating man with clean hands, of laconic disposition and possessing the right amount of allure to get his way. Which was all quite satisfactory; he was in want of nothing except to keep things this way.

All of which called into question his presence on an early Monday morning commuter train from Exeter, where he hardly seemed to belong. Well, the explanation was straightforward enough: the occasion was the outcome of poor choices, and – or so he would come to think in the coming weeks – possibly the plan of Providence.

Ordinarily, morning found him at home, whiling away the hours in his cobbled-lane fronted mews cottage off the Marylebone High Street, adequately safe from unsolicited attention. Sunday was home day, the day to attend to tidying up chores and sorting the laundry for the dry-cleaners. This Sunday, however, had him take a day trip to Devon to view an 'idyllic' two-bedroom detached cottage close to the coastal town of Dawlish which had caught his eye while browsing through a property magazine while waiting for his monthly trim at the barbers. The property, set in eight acres of paddock and woodlands, with a large pond and private access track, unusually had taken his fancy. Undecided as to whether this sudden interest in a countryside property was a mere whim or a sign of his readiness to leave London for quieter surroundings, he had made arrangements to view it, and, in light of the 450-mile round trip, had on this rare occasion opted against driving and travelled by train instead.

It turned out the estate agents knew their business well, for while every aspect of the property was true to the advert's depiction, they left out that the 'idyllic' cottage and attached land were hemmed in by barbed wire fences and flat country lanes lined with caravans and holiday parks. Soon enough, Lombard was in a taxi on his way back to Exeter station to catch a return train when he asked the driver to make a detour to the coast – he'd come this far for little reward, had time on his hands and had last seen the sea over a year earlier. Yet, this coastal jaunt had led to his getting stranded on a country lane due to an overturned lorry, his taxi stuck between the grounded vehicle ahead and the rescue services behind, whereby he would reach Exeter station too late for the last evening train to London's Waterloo. He'd booked into a hotel, ordered a light supper, lay the night awake enveloped in the peculiar silence of the provinces and made for the station in good time to catch the first service to London.

Such were the events which had led to his embarking on the 5:10 from Exeter and taking a window seat opposite a frail scruffy man with a patched-up wooden crutch sitting next to a young man in shirtsleeves. The girl in the pinafore dress was seated beside him, across the aisle from the woman with the glad face and winsome puppy, and in the seats right behind him, unseen, were the mother and child.

Early on, Lombard had considered moving seats. The nearby puppy attracted far too much attention as a great many passengers seemed compelled to fuss and babble over it whilst chatting with its blissful owner or anyone else who cared to join in. It came to a point when the girl by his side kindly offered to move to allow him to pat the puppy if he so wished. She'd just had a go herself, had shared gushing words with others about the 'adorable' animal. He guessed she was mindful of his being excluded from the general intimacy on her account and responded with a warm but brief grin that caused her to turn away with a nervous smile. Then there were the mother and inquisitive child sitting behind him, all the potential this carried. But in the end the excitement around the puppy had abated as the train picked up speed on leaving Exeter, and likewise, the child sitting behind him went quiet, possibly to focus on reading his book as directed. In any case, the train was packed, reducing the chance of finding a better situation.

So Lombard settled down where he sat, gazing out the window at the passing landscape as the day crept in over the dawn. The night had brought rain, allowing the rising sun still captive within the partial cover of clouds to paint glowing shafts of pink honey-flushed sparks across the open countryside and small towns that lined the way. Here it beamed to highlight the bountifulness of Southern England's farmlands, there it invested the otherwise unremarkable with form and lustre. Lombard hardly found any of it distracting though. Other more tedious matters occupied him. He'd neglected to shave following the night spent on his hotel bed awake and fully dressed, and mulled over whether his stubble, creased clothes and the shoes on his feet soiled from the previous day's rural jaunt in some way accounted for his fellow passengers' assumption that he may like to be invited to trouble himself over the puppy. As a rule, he was spared other people's whims and visions; most seemed to know better than to visit their good intentions onto him. And so, on account of such questions, he casually remonstrated with himself for his foolishness in travelling to view a property without first checking its location, for taking the train to get there and then, more perturbingly, having entertained the idea of leaving London. The situation in his Mews could be wanting at times, but certainly for now this hapless round-trip to Devon had made him eager to get back home, get out of his dirty clothes, shower, shave and take a late morning nap.

And here things may well have remained had the scruffy man opposite not produced a newspaper from a battered rucksack which – due to poor eyesight, no doubt – he proceeded to read held upright near to his nose, in such a manner that, as he turned the front page to peer inside, Lombard found himself looking at the mirror image of the front page reflected in the window in front of his eyes, and by such chance picked up the day's headlines: a poll suggested the forthcoming general election was too close to call; Trade Unions were gearing up for an autumn of strikes; an oil tanker forced off course by environmentalists had run aground off the Spanish coast; and, under a postcard-size blurry photograph of a youth, a heading beckoned 'This Is Our Reporter's Murderer. Do You Know Him?'.

With little else for distraction, peering at the paper's reflection in his window, Lombard found himself examining the photograph of the murderer until, from the void, it dawned on him that he was looking at a face with somewhat familiar features. The picture was blurry enough, yet he was confident he knew the 'Reporter's Murderer', beneath whose portrait a caption invited readers to find out more on the inside pages. He felt a lump in his throat. A watchful traveller may have caught him wincing while he swallowed hard, the only sign of his inner stirrings. Still, they would have been at pains to make much of it as he remained all quiet stillness, and perhaps, at such a moment, it may have occurred to them that a life adequately spent should bear its natural share of exultations, setbacks and surprises, and in this respect the life of the suited man in cufflinks had been adequately spent, enough to have schooled him in the virtues of self-control; all things have their place and a public display of agitation should have none.

It is indeed possible to come across such perceptive souls while on the move. As the scruffy man went on reading his paper, Lombard, now after an involuntary glance at the nearby puppy, merely turned back to his window. He could have looked at the news on his phone, but London and access to the morning press were less than two hours away, when there would be time to find out more about the murderer. Before long though, the sight of the paper being folded away got the better of his curiosity, so that he broke his silence to ask the man if he would be good enough to let him borrow it. The man, revealing some missing teeth as he spoke, was happy to hand his paper over but, sensing an opportunity, had a favour to ask in return. "Here. It's pure drivel, but be my guest. But since you ask, my good man, I wonder if I could trouble you with a request of my own. My phone's dead, I'm afraid. So if you happen to have one I could borrow to make a quick call, I'd be much obliged." For all his frail body and scruffy cardigan, the man was alert enough to realize Lombard was less than thrilled at the idea of handing him his phone. So he went on: "It's my wife. She's expecting and unwell and I had to leave her by herself to attend to my deceased sister's affairs near Exeter. Turns out the utility companies had disconnected the electrics from her bungalow so I tried charging my phone from a car battery but think I buggered its insides instead—And had no time to use the public phones at the station. She must be worried not to have heard from me. It would take a weight off my mind if I could reassure her that I'm on my way home."

Lombard was poised to return the man's paper, yet opted instead to hand him his phone. The other dialled, whispered a few short sentences into it covering his mouth behind his bony hand and handed the phone back with a grateful grin: "Went down a treat. Much obliged. You're a good man, Sir."

It took no time for Lombard to determine that he was right about the face in the blurry photograph. Inside, the newspaper had dedicated an entire page to the story accompanying the killing of their reporter – which had occurred two nights previously – and provided another photograph of its killer which, although just as blurry as the one from the front page, confirmed his suspicion; he knew the murderer.

The brisk, hot sweeping draught loaded with the smell of the previous night's rain which welcomed the travellers disembarking into the din of Waterloo Station hit him like a new day. Over a coffee near to the crowds in the main concourse, he browsed half a dozen newspapers; all covered the reporter's murder, albeit nowhere as comprehensively as the victim's own paper, so that he learnt little he didn't already know, except that, insomuch as it drew wide press coverage, the story had traction, hardly surprising given the nature of the murdered party's profession. Lombard finished his coffee and sighed. It was not nine o'clock yet. Under the departure and arrival boards, a heaving sea of upturned faces and bent heads immersed in phones and other devices reminded him of a rookery of penguins. In all likelihood, most had at least glanced at the news enough to be aware of the 'reporter's murderer', but his was just one more story among all the sound and fury. Still, the matter was of significance to Lombard, required making a call he'd rather not have to make, a call the outcome of which – he knew – was predictable. It was early enough in the day to possibly delay until afternoon, but the person he needed to speak to – whom he had no doubt would not have failed to contact him had they known already – was an early riser.

It is never pleasant to be the bearer of unwelcome news.

"How are you, Edward?" he said as soon as someone picked up at the other end.

"Xavier! Good morning to you. How am I? Well, bloody bushed should best sum it up. Meetings all day yesterday— Theatre in the evening—Conference calls through the night. No peace for the weary, I guess. Still, free at last: I'm on my way to the airport, off to taste some of the hard toil's wages. Anyway, to what do I owe this ante meridiem pleasure. I never figured you for an early bird."

"You're going away?"

"Yep! A few days of diving and other gaieties at my Sardinian hideaway to breathe new life into flesh and blood. You must find time to come one day."

Lombard grinned: "I will, Edward. Can you talk right now?"

"Fire away."

"I don't suppose you read today's Paragon?"

"The paper?"

"Uh-huh."

"Xavier, even if I could find the time, The Paragon is not a paper I would ever elect to read."

"Well, maybe you could make an exception today. Check this morning's copy. You'll find Alan Winston made the news—Frontpage."

"What? Our Alan Winston?"

"Uh-huh. Looks like he killed a man; a Paragon reporter no less."

"He killed—Are you sure about this? You're positive you got the right Alan Winston?"

"I am. It turns out he was laying low in the East End. From what I can make out, a couple of days ago the reporter turned up at his Mile End bedsit on some business regarding one of his housemates—Some old man who died the previous night while out walking his dog. Alan refused to let the reporter in, they argued and he killed him in the house's hallway in full view of a couple of witnesses."

"My word! And you're sure it's him?"

"The pictures they have are a little blurry—Surveillance camera enlargements—But it's him, alright."

"Jesus! But why did he—How did he kill the guy?"

"Why is anybody's guess; the dog walker who'd died the previous night was nothing to him. How: he shattered the reporter's Adam's apple, then, or so the witnesses claim, stood over him watching him slowly choke to death."

"I—This is mad, Xavier. Alan Winston? It makes no sense."

"My guess is the reporter was out looking for a story and Alan reckoned he ought not to be poking around his hideout; it went on from there," Lombard said; "The thing is, he got away. He's on the run now. They have his picture but no name. Not yet. The bedsit folks in Mile End knew him under an alias. That's why the picture in the papers. They're hoping someone will put a name to the face. I only just found out about it myself and thought you ought to know—In case you want anything done about it."

"Fuck! Done about it! What are you—What do you mean, 'done about it', Xavier? Do you know where he is?"

"No—I meant whether you think the police ought to be told who it is they're looking for."

"Oh. I—I don't know. This is crazy. I—What do you think?"

Lombard scowled: "It's not my call, Edward. But I'd say the choice is simple: out him to the police or let events follow their course."

"Right. Well, yes. Now—" The rest took a moment to come: "The diseased little punk! I never thought things would come to this, but now that they have, I thank God no one was home when he broke into Antonia's. He'd have bloody killed them, wouldn't he? Fucking little rat!"

Lombard stayed silent.

"Hell! I don't know, Xavier. I don't know what the right thing to do is. I so wish I'd not found out about this now— This morning of all mornings. What would you say are the odds against his being identified from the paper's pictures?"

"Against? Next to nil."

"Right—Right. I tell you what, in this case, I think it's probably best to do nothing for now. If you're right and it's only a matter of time before they make him out, I'd sooner stay out of it. I'll check The Paragon on my way to Heathrow and get back to you—Will call tomorrow if you don't hear from me later today. Meanwhile, keep me posted by text about any development. This is mad—Completely mad! Ah! I'll get back to you, Xavier. Thanks for letting me know."

"You're welcome, Edward," Lombard grimaced.

A little while later he got to his feet to leave the station when, in the shafts of morning sunlight filtering through the windows of the teeming concourse, he came face to face with the scruffy man from the Exeter train. In his threadbare cardigan, the man was lumbering towards the main exit on his one crutch under the weight of his rucksack and the drag of a large wheeled suitcase, plainly struggling through the packed crowds. Had their eyes not met, Lombard would have gone on his way, but on catching sight of him the other gave him such a sad pained smile of recognition it put paid to that. "Hello there," the man paused, clearly relieved to take a breather. "Still here?" Lombard replied with a grin. "Tell me about it," sighed the man; "Had to find a public phone to call the wife and, as you can see, I'm not about to break any speed record lurching about like an overloaded donkey with a bust hip to boot—Am scheduled for surgery in a couple of months unless they postpone non-urgent procedures again. Until then, it's all grin and bear it." "Where are you heading?" asked Lombard. "Oh. The bus stop across the bridge. The north side of Waterloo Bridge—To catch the Number 6 to Willesden. It stops within fifty yards of my front door at the other end." "Across the bridge?" "Yes. It's probably a ten-minute walk away, but I suspect it will take me a good twenty or more." "Right," concurred Lombard.

He was unsure whether his motivation came from a selfish need for distraction from his thoughts or pity for the misfortune of the other, but to venture a helping hand seemed risk-free enough. "As a matter of fact, I too am heading across the bridge. My car's in the car park. Let me give you a lift to your bus stop. It will save you some time." "Really? That would be such a—" "You're welcome." And Lombard grabbed the man's wheeled suitcase and started towards the car park. "Well, sir," said the man, following; "Thank you. It is now twice in one morning that I find myself feeling obliged to you. My name is Rex Mantle, by the way; Rex Mantle," he repeated. "Xavier Lombard," said Lombard.

By the time they pulled out into the London streets to catch the morning traffic, Mr Rex Mantle was beaming with gratitude and delight at being seated in Lombard's thirty-year-old Saab. It was a very long time since he'd seen one of these old cars, he explained. Especially in London, where most old petrol cars had vanished from the streets when the city's Mayor had made them subject to a hefty daily emissions charge. Was Lombard's car exempt, he enquired; had it been converted to gas or been given a new engine? It wasn't and hadn't, Lombard disclosed, but the way he saw things "I like my car; reckon the emission taxes add up to less than the cost of a new car; and figure the production of one new vehicle and spare parts and accessories far out-pollutes my old car staying on the road for another 100,000 miles." The man agreed, adding that he also believed that no car produced today would still be roadworthy thirty years from then – "Inbuilt electronic obsolescence" –

and, as they reached the north side of Waterloo Bridge, advised they stop to let him off in a side street rather than at his bus stop. "Anywhere near Southampton Street or Charing Cross station will do. What with the time it will take me to get out of the car and get my bags, what you don't want is to stop at a bus stop or anywhere near a bus lane. A couple of months back a friend of my wife did just that to offer her a lift after spotting her big and pregnant waiting for the bus and got a £100 ticket through the post four days later. They got cameras everywhere. No good deed goes unpunished anymore."

Lombard nodded, thought quickly: "You're going to Willesden, you said?"

"Yes."

"Then I guess it's both our lucky day," he went on; "You're going to get a ride all the way home and I won't be getting a ticket."

"Wow," he heard the other gasp.

The drive across Central and North-West London was uneventful. Mr Rex Mantle, pleased and gracious for being given a ride home, for the most part seemed satisfied peering out the windscreen at the bustling streets. Still, seated in a stranger's car, he couldn't help seeking the comfort of conversation, if not for his own sake, possibly to entertain his rescuer.

"Xavier Lombard. Is that French?" he asked.

"Uh-huh."

"My wife and I spent a few summers in Brittany a few years back; camping near the beach during the holidays. Near a town called Carnac. Beautiful place. We loved it."

"I have never been to Brittany."

"Right. Where are you from then?"

"Paris."

"Oh. And you live here now."

"Uh-huh."

"Where is that? Here in London or Devon? The Exeter train this morning?"

Lombard grinned: "In London. I went to take a look at a property for sale over there, but thought better of it."

"Ah—Yes. I'm with you there—Not that I have anything against the countryside, but like Samuel Johnson said: 'No, sir, when a man is tired of London, he is tired of life; for there is in London all that life can afford.'"

Lombard frowned: "Is that why your sister lived in Devon then? She was tired of life?"

"My sister," said the man, suddenly sombre; "I so wish."

He remained silent for a moment, his tired eyes fixed on the sun-drenched shifting scenery out the windscreen, and Lombard immediately regretted mentioning the other's sister. Then:

"Raped, killed, left for the crows," the man declared.

"I'm sorry?"

"My sister," the man clarified; "Do you know crows peck out the eyes of human cadavers? They found her half-naked at the bottom of her garden; on her compost heap. Teenage kids broke into her cottage to rob her. They tortured her for her bank card pin numbers, raped her and dragged her unconscious into the garden to leave her there to die while they partied the night away inside her place. Boys and girls. They caught them. They had their phones turned on the whole time—Rode to and from her home on their bikes."

Lombard sighed: "Huh—Bikes."

"Her name was Agnese."

"Right."

"Yes. My wife's expecting a baby girl. It would be nice if we could call her Agnese. But she—"

"It's a fine name," said Lombard.

"A fine name indeed," the man echoed; "But I'm sorry. Please accept my apologies. I shouldn't—There you are, doing a stranger a favour and—"

"It's okay."

When at last they reached Willesden, the man seemed to win back his spirit as he directed them to a leaden housing estate wedged against the North Circular's six busy lanes of traffic and into a street at the bottom of a square block of flats. The bleakness of the place was somewhat eased by the brilliant red of an old post box.

"There she is," the man said, standing on his crutch with a smile while waving and peering up the tower block as soon as they got out of the car. The sun's glare bouncing off the building's windows made it impossible to distinguish anyone in the third-storey window that held his attention. "There. She's good now I'm here. And much earlier than anticipated thanks to you, sir." Lombard handed him the bags he retrieved from the boot, grinned and held out his hand.

"Good luck to you, Mr Mantle."

"Thank you again," the other declared. And he shook Lombard's hand:

"You're a good man, sir," he said, as he had done earlier in the morning train from Exeter.

Lombard settled back at the wheel of his car to watch the man with his patched-up crutch dawdle away dragging his wheeled suitcase towards the block's grey metal security door. Mr Rex Mantle was going home.

THREE

Pugnacious, undaunted, kind and diligent little Jane.

Time takes on a reassuring permanence of its own among the dead. In the thick of London's steadfast pandemonium, the dead's resting places eclipse even the finest city parks as havens of peace, affording quiet shelter from the hazards of the industrious streets. Hampstead Cemetery, situated on Fortune Green Road in West Hampstead and also known as 'The Friends of Hampstead Cemetery', was just such a space. Spread across many acres, bounded to one side by a school sports ground, and a mere stone's throw from the brutal faces of the Finchley Road and Hendon Way, it was broad enough to be crossed by a public footpath and include a wildlife area planted with shrubs, wild flowers and trees. Over time, Lombard had grown fond of the cemetery the way one grows fond of a favourite café or walk. He would head past the grand entrance lodge and along the main avenue with barely a glance for the symmetry of the ordered rows of fine headstones, the Gothic style mortuary chapels, Celtic crosses or other eccentric memorials – such as a large stylized sculpture of a winged female angel raising her hands to heaven, a listed Art Deco statue he learnt was a husband's tribute to his wife who had died in childbirth – to make for the wilder meadow-like far end of the grounds where mature ash trees, yews, sycamores, silver birches, cherry-plums and willows shadowed humbler gravestones. He visited the spot often enough through the years to mark the passing of the seasons from the aspects of the trees, weather permitting lingered the necessary time to observe the unknown birds which always inevitably drifted silently across the far sky, or, nearer, the robins and long-tailed tits perching on a particular mausoleum's broken cast iron fence shrouded in ivy.

In one regard at least, he likely had something in common with the man answerable for the winged heaven-summoning monument in the grander section of the cemetery; he had first been drawn to the place on account of a woman, and not, as a bystander may well have imagined, the need for peace or some morbid attraction to the dead. Nearly a decade past, before the Council had turned the cemetery into a historic park by declaring it full, he had arranged for a friend with whom he shared a troubled relationship to be buried there. The matter was one of necessity; she'd made plain her wish not to be cremated, there was no one else to carry out the funeral duty and, not without reason, he felt partly at fault for her untimely death; she wasn't yet 30. This being the case, he never suspected he'd return to Fortune Green in the wake of her burial, for he had provided for fresh lilies to be placed monthly at her headstone for a one-year period. But one day – a good two years later – winding up in the neighbourhood on some other business with time on his hands, he had returned. It was spring, blooms coloured the trees and scented the breeze in the meadow-like corner where her grave lay, and the quiet and wild charm of the spot had seduced him enough to entice him back again, bearing lilies this time, because, as he saw it, a man bearing flowers looks inconspicuous among the dead. In time though, he had become a sporadic but reliable visitor, always bringing lilies, always settling on the same south-facing bench in the semi-shadow of a red cherry tree a few steps from her grave.

Today, his coming to Fortune Green was fortuitous, wholly attributable to his having given Mr Rex Mantle a ride home. His drive back from Willesden to central London and Maryle-bone had brought him to West Hampstead by way of the Finchley Road. The vicinity of the cemetery coupled with the clear September sky and the fact that he had yet to eat since the previous evening had led to his change of heart about heading home. He'd left his car in a two-hour parking bay, picked up a sandwich and coffee at a take-away, called at the local florist and made his way across the cemetery to his usual meadow-like place. Nathalie's familiar headstone stood at attention, an odd rigid marker of what once was a drifting whimsical soul. 'Here lies Nathalie. Born, now Dead', read its only inscription – Lombard never knew her age, nor for that matter whether Nathalie was her real name; he suspected not. He smiled on reading a fading graffiti scrawled with a marker pen above the inscription – 'Were you formed of libidinal gorges and pearly passes of lace, dear Nathalie' – suspecting it to be the work of teenagers; as often before, the nearby lawn was scattered with sweet wrappers, cigarette butts and empty drink cans. He laid down his lilies, walked the short distance to his bench, got out of his suit jacket, undid his cufflinks, rolled up his shirt sleeves and, facing the sun, turned his attention to his food and drink. He wanted to enjoy the soft sun and the warm caressing breeze, instead ended up mulling over the call he'd made earlier to Edward Duncan.

Edward Duncan had yet to get back to him; and he suspected he wouldn't. Not today, anyhow. He'd likely had a look at The Paragon, found no cause to question his inclination to let events follow their course. It made sense. What would make no sense would be to become embroiled in a national newspaper reporter's murder, the more so as it could only be a matter of days if not hours before Alan Winston would be named and likely captured. Besides, the Mile End murder did not concern Edward Duncan, nor could it – howsoever indirectly – prejudice his good name; Alan Winston was completely unaware even of his existence. All the same, Lombard was somewhat disappointed in Edward Duncan. The man's life was the sort most other men envy: all advantage and success, his pick of vices and virtues. That he was afforded the shelter of a privileged upbringing on no account provided that he should be equipped to meet high expectations – the contrary might actually be truer – yet Lombard knew him well enough to be satisfied that he'd not merely inherited but earned numerous of his achievements. Still, while his rise to the position of Executive Vice President of EcoWatt – a French multinational energy company that among other operations supplied gas and electricity to large swathes of Europe and Britain – was no mere accident of birth, it could never be said that his success was the fruit of charm and hard work alone. If it called for it, he could prove as merciless as any man. "Find out who's done this, Xavier! I want them to curse the day they stole that puppy! I want them to live the rest of their miserable life in penance for that puppy! I want them hounded like the dog they are until they can't even think of crawling to a dead body for a bone!" Fury such as this tends never to last long, fades with reflection as time stretches, but this was Edward Duncan's, and, in light of the circumstances was not uncalled for.

Unwittingly, a nobody who reckoned they were onto a good thing snatching puppies to order had broken into the home of a wealthy man's lover and stolen the wrong puppy. The Labrador cub they snatched was a special gift from Edward Duncan to his lover's sickly seven-year-old daughter. Tracking down the culprit hardly proved taxing. The stolen puppy was long replaced and forgotten by the time Lombard caught up with him, but Edward Duncan's resolve to have him suffer never waned. There were to be few if any allowances for the thief's youth – he was nineteen years old – or his indifferent circumstances – he earned a living as a cook prior to trying his hand at puppy-snatching. It was decided to put the frighteners on him, effectively persecute him without resorting to violence while keeping him in the dark about the identity of his tormentors. "Put the fear of God into the little shit! Make him afraid of his own shadow," as Edward Duncan put it.

Alan Winston was no seasoned criminal, did not belong to a criminal gang nor aroused much of anything really. He may have been bold and reckless enough to break into properties or snatch puppies in public parks, but he hardly shone even at that, content in the role of an underling stealing to order for a fee rather than involving himself in the more lucrative reselling and ransoming side of the trade. He lived by himself, the only son of an arthritic mother who was all but housebound looking after his bedridden father in their Camberwell Housing Estate maisonette. To knock him off course from his subsistence existence and drive him to take flight and, it turned out, go into hiding in a Mile End bedsit, proved a straightforward enough exercise. Now, though, he was front-page news for what appeared to have been a random unplanned killing. Lombard, while confident of the futility of pondering what-ifs – or of playing God by trying to ascertain unknowns, such as whether a killer was predetermined to become a killer before their crime – naturally wondered how much of what had occurred in Mile End could be attributed to what had become Alan Winston's hopeless almost feral situation. And he knew that likewise a similar question had at once perturbed Edward Duncan. His "This is mad" and "I never thought things would come to this" after hearing the news, told the story. And here lay the source of Lombard's disappointment. There was never a need for such remarks. It stood to reason that no one could have anticipated – or wished for – the event which had occurred in Mile End. In point of fact, only a short while ago, while discussing the swiftness of Alan Winston's utter downfall, Edward Duncan had begun to make reluctant noises about the possibility of letting the matter rest, to allow the youth command of his life again. On this account, fair was fair. Wanton cruelty found no favour in Edward Duncan's mind. Lombard's brooding on the matter focused on other issues. He thought reasonably well of Edward Duncan, sufficiently to be underwhelmed by the man's unseemly rush to defend himself from invisible accusations in the wake of being caught off-guard with unwelcome news. The truth of the matter was that in being so defensive Edward Duncan was guilty of little more than exhibiting a natural and healthy self-preservation instinct, yet by doing so in the manner he had, he had managed to fall short of Lombard's expectations, ensuring that, not for the first time today, Lombard found himself questioning his own judgement.

To his surprise, he felt disappointment; perhaps it would have been better if he'd never felt fondness for Edward Duncan.

He only became aware he had closed his eyes when his thoughts were cut short by a loud call with a soft Irish lilt:

"I tell you what now, Xavier—You look just like a castaway who spent the night gambling his life away. Surely, things could not be that bad?"

He recognized Jane McGinnis's broad face at once. In a loose blouse and skirt, awkwardly perched on a pair of cowboy boots, she stood beneath the midday sun beyond a row of headstones a short distance in front of his bench. Her fingers, fat and pink, were clasping the handles of a double-pram weighed down with two polka-dot-dressed dark-eyed small girls with chubby faces and long black eyelashes. She looked happy, an ebullient grin trumpeting her delight to see him. Time had turned the coy rosy-cheeked freckled girl with fragile fair hair that he remembered into a confident buttery woman with bleached highlights and round jowly cheeks. Even as he realized it was a good eight or so years since their last meeting, it dawned on him how she had known to look for him in the Fortune Green cemetery. Back in the days when she was a trainee accountant fresh from Ireland on her first adventure away from home and renting the flat directly above his, he'd made good of her youthful crush to now and again avail himself of her ready offers to help with secretarial chores and the like. Now he recalled how he'd tasked her with looking after Nathalie's burial arrangements, from the paperwork to picking the plot and sorting out the monthly lily deliveries. She'd acquitted herself well of her duties.

"I'm only kidding you! Hello there, Xavier. Remember me?" she said, nervously now, as he had yet to speak.

"How are you, Jane?" he said; although he bore her no ill will, he was displeased to see her there, annoyed she had come to violate his space, and had yet to decide whether to let her know it. He noted her heaving breast and forehead flushed with small pearls of sweat; she had hurried to come.

"How did you know to find me here this morning?" he asked.

"Oh. Well, the florist. I came here two or so months ago

after looking everywhere for you. I remembered her," she indicated with a glance towards Nathalie's grave; "I saw the fresh lilies and guessed they had to be from you and had a chat with the florist. She said you—Well, I guessed it was you; she calls you 'The Lilies Man'—Come here every now and again. So I left her my number and she called this morning to let me know you were back."

"I see. And you hurried here," Lombard grunted, running his eyes across the chubby dark-eyed girls in the double-pram; one was busy stuffing a biscuit into her mouth, the other cooing while playing with her naked toes.

"My twins," declared Jane, proud; "Anoosheh and Zoe. They're nearly two. I've got two other girls, but they're with my mother. And one more in the oven, as they say." And she shuffled from behind the pram to display her cone-shaped swollen belly inside her blouse.

She was pregnant. He grinned, eyeing the twins again. There could be no doubt that his old neighbour believed she had a good reason to have ambushed him. That whatever it was, as she'd just revealed, it had been good for at least two months prior to today. He ought to have asked her what she wanted, but had no desire to.

"Well, this is awkward," she finally let out as he stayed silent; "I'm sorry, Xavier. To be honest with you, I guessed you wouldn't be too happy to have me turn up here like this. I did. But everywhere I looked I could find no sign of you. The internet, old phone directories, social media; I even called detective agencies in case they'd heard of you and went by the old place in Islington. So when I came here and saw the lilies and realized you were still around and not gone back to France I thought this was my chance. I—I've just come all the way from Walthamstow, you know. Jumped in a cab and—I'd have called if I had a number."

"I'm sure you would, Jane," he said. She smiled still, but her fingers were tensely squeezing her pram now, and he couldn't think of anything he wished to say to her, wondered whether she was going to explain her reason for trespassing back into his life or think the better of it and leave.

He could have grinned, asked her to go – considered his options. However, among the memories of her flooding back into his mind was the time she'd nursed him through a particularly bad bout of the flu. Even though her motivation was questionable, her kindness and attentiveness could never be faulted, and, in that of such things songs are made, Lombard found the thought of causing her offence disagreeable.

"I recall a clever and sensible girl, Jane," he said; "Someone who on finding they couldn't find me would have realized this may be because I wished not to be found. Whatever it is you need, Jane, I'm afraid I can't help. I'm a ghost."

Although she seemed unsure how to respond, his speaking provided her some relief: "Oh, I did, Xavier. It did occur to me that you may wish not to be found. But—Forgive me for asking: what is it exactly you mean by you're a 'ghost'? You look well to me, you do."

"Is that a fact," he let out, then, adding despite himself – silence is always preferable to giving explanation: "My business is my own nowadays, Jane."

She took a good look at him, taking in what he said across the distance separating them: "Oh. Your own as in 'like a recluse', you mean? Or as in you don't do investigative work anymore?"

He grinned: "You look good too, Jane," he said; "Being pregnant suits you. It's nice to see you a happy mother after all these years."

"Oh. I—"

She understood he had no intention to speak of himself or of anything much else with her. She tried to conceal her disappointment behind a nervous smile and, not quite ready to leave it at that, sounded frustrated but determined when she spoke again:

"Well, never mind. It's like I said: I guessed you wouldn't be happy to have me turn up here like this dead set on telling you all about my dear husband Joseph—God bless him—And how I would not ask you for any favours but expect to pay full fees for your services. Well now, I don't suppose you remember my Joseph, do you?"

39

Lombard frowned.

"Of course you don't. Why should you?" she went on; "It's been eight years, right? But I introduced you two in the stairwell of the old house in Islington just before I moved out. The thing is he's with his maker now. They say he committed suicide—And they even have a recording of him throwing himself in front of a tube train to prove it, they do—But I say he absolutely didn't simply kill himself. Five months ago, this was. Left for work one morning and what do you know. No note, nothing. He surely threw himself under a train, but may God strike me dead if he simply killed himself. So here we are. I thought I'd ask you to look into it. The police are unhelpful and I don't wish to lay my life bare for a stranger to see. I so hoped you'd be in a position to help."

"I'm sorry for your loss," Lombard said, to say something.

"Thank you. That is very kind of you, Xavier. But there's no need for anyone to concern themselves with my state of mind. I'm over it. Four little ones to love and feed and another one on the go doesn't leave you much time to feel sorry for yourself. It's what their memory of their father will be when they're old enough that I'm bothered about."

He sighed. Her phone rang, she briskly reached for it inside a large handbag hanging from her pram, checked the caller's identity and switched it off.

"Anyhow," she went on; "Each to his and her own, eh? I better not keep you any longer. It's a shame this turned out how I feared and I'm genuinely sorry I ruined such a gorgeous morning for you. It's nice to see you again, Xavier. Good to see time's been kind to you. Take care now."

"It's good to know you're well too, Jane," he said; "Mind how you go."

Briefly, Jane's face took the look of a storm cloud – quite possibly, she'd hoped he would keep her from leaving, call on her to share more of her sad story now that he'd been made aware of it. She bit her bottom lip, then managed a frayed smile that tugged the corner of her mouth.

"You must really have loved her, eh?" she blurted out, snapping a blushing glance sideways at Nathalie's headstone.

"Bye now. Sorry again." And in a moment, she tugged and thrust her pram and marched away in the sunlight, her skirt lashing about her thick legs and her cowboy boots crunching against the gravel; soon she vanished beyond the mid-distance rows of headstones to return to the exertions that awaited her outside the cemetery gates.

Pugnacious, undaunted, kind and diligent little Jane was older but none the wiser, thought Lombard. After all this time, she still thought she could test or impress him. He was lighter for being alone again, somewhat glad she kept from mentioning – she was unlikely to have forgotten it – the wedding invitation she sent and he ignored. Now, he vaguely recollected the man she'd introduced him to all those years ago; he was tall and slim and dark, bore long eyelashes similar to those of the girls in her pram. By all accounts, the man was dead now, much the same as Mr Rex Mantle's sister and Alan Winston's reporter. It was a strange morning. In just about three hours he had been visited upon by three strangers' deaths, he reflected, surveying the headstones around him. And learnt of four living children and two more yet to be born. All by virtue of his failure to reach Exeter station in time the previous afternoon to end up on a morning commuter train to London.

He delayed a while to give Jane enough of a head start, got to his feet, unrolled his shirt sleeves, put his suit jacket back on and left Nathalie to her lilies, later to pause at the florist outside the cemetery gates.

"Did you take her money?" he asked.

"Sorry?"

"Did she pay you?"

The florist, an ageless woman in a straw beach hat, with a leopard-skin patterned shirt over her tights, knew exactly what he was alluding to, must have hoped he wouldn't stop by after seeing Jane walk out past her stall a few minutes earlier. In all likelihood, the two had exchanged a few words.

"Well, I guess whether you divested her of some of her money is none of my business," he said; "One thing though:

41

next time, if there is a next time, do it right. Propose to notify the sought-after party that they are being sought, rather than tip off their seeker. You can never tell who's looking for who or why, even in a cemetery. And besides, this is a place for introversion and reflection. Have a good day now."

Few people ever get to marvel at the short old cul-de-sacs otherwise known as mews that here and there run off the streets of London's West End or its adjacent affluent neighbourhoods; visitors to London hardly have reason to wander there and Londoners, inasmuch as they know them to be exclusive residential havens for the wealthy, just move past them. Generally cobble-stoned and lined with quaint terraced houses that tell of their utilitarian past as back alleys to the opulent nearby streets, well-kept, peaceful and oftentimes picturesque, they evoke heritage, privilege and good fortune. Lombard was pleasantly surprised when Edward Duncan had presented him with the keys and deeds to Cottage 12 Kiln House Mews, a recompense for services rendered. Four years on, having opted to make it his domicile, he still prized the peace it afforded while being a mere two minutes from the cafés, boutiques and bustling of the Marylebone High Street. Much like other Mews, his consisted of fewer than half-a-dozen lived-in dwellings among vacant pieds-à-terre belonging to seldom seen proprietors. Save for the old Kiln House building – which accommodated a digital imaging studio – the cobblestone alley was home to small two-storey terraced houses, and that they were described as "cottages" stemmed from the fact that they owned side passages and back yards long converted into garages, gardens or extensions.

Lombard seldom entertained or received guests, but on the occasions he did his visitors never failed to express admiration for the charm, quiet and advantageous situation of the property. And on most days he would agree with them; only an ingrate mind, or possibly a person in need of more commotion and company than that provisioned by the secluded situation, could have faulted the Kiln House Mews. For the most part, the circumstances suited Lombard, particularly during summer when the hot nights called for the breeze from open windows. Today, though, spotting the gleaming yellow Ferrari sitting in front of his neighbour's cottage, he wondered whether he was about to experience a second sleepless night in a row. All the same, it was good to be back.

FOUR

Monkey see, monkey do.

To one side, his neighbours were a middle-aged couple who spent at most two or three nights a week at the Mews. Of these two, Lombard knew as much as he wished to know: Irene and Sacha Gublitz-Stone commuted from Surrey, had two sons at university, worked in the medical field – he as a private clinical consultant in nearby Harley Street, she as a statistician for the National Health Service – were in bed before midnight, went out jogging in the early hours of the morning and were keen travellers. And on the other side, every once in a while – that is about once every fortnight – the owner of the yellow Ferrari swung by, a tempest come to blow away the calm. This one was young, fit, Dutch, played football for a Manchester club and by all accounts was very good at it. A year previously he'd become the owner of Cottage 10, a place for him to stay when visiting London, typically spending one or two nights attended by a posse of girls and rowdy hangers-on. Of this one, Lombard knew much more than he wished to; his Dutch neighbour, he'd come to think, was the outcome of too much money given too soon to fugacious youth.

For now, in the usual fashion, the man had returned in the dead of night to gather – it being late summer – with his noisy party in the narrow courtyard almost directly beneath Lombard's open windows, and wake him up. As ever, drinks and drugs were at hand down there, but Lombard had long ago observed that the Dutch sportsman – who was called Yann and clearly committed to fitness – refrained from both. Women, fast cars and narcissism aside, he possessed a predilection for making himself the centre of attention, which he thought to achieve by hosting well-stocked parties and entertaining his guests with outlandish tales of questionable taste and veracity.

Now, all head-against-pillow in the heated darkness of his bedroom, Lombard listened to the man re-telling a mugging story which of late had become his party tale of choice. He'd heard it enough times he could anticipate every word.

"So here I am, right—Two in the morning waiting for the automatic gates to open when I hear a tap-tap near my ear. And there she is, leaning against my window—A braless apparition in an open fur coat; all tits, eyes and lips, drumming long fingernails against the glass. So I wind the window down—Right—All the fucking way down. 'Excuse me, baby, you have the time?' she purrs in some Russian-like accent. 'I'm sorry, precious. I don't wear a watch,' I say. 'Oh,' she says, 'What about in the dashboard?' 'Sweetie pie, you're looking at a customized Maserati,' I say, 'Not the sort of vehicle driven by some loser who needs to fret about the fucking time.' And, fuck-me-if-I-lie, I never saw her move but I'm looking at the end of a silencer pointed right at my dick. 'And there I was thinking slick cars like this are for people in a rush, uh,' she says, grinning into my eyes, 'But that's okay, honey. If no watch, I guess your wallet will do, unless of course you want me to give you a customized dick too.' Hoo-hah awoogah! Thought I was gonna shit myself. Fact! But what do you know? Hello! I get a fucking hard-on! Fucking Mont Blanc grows in my pants while I'm looking into her eyes too fucking stunned to speak. 'Your wallet, baby?' she says. 'I got no wallet,' I say. And the fucking thing is, I'm telling the fucking truth—I don't have no wallet. But she doesn't buy it. 'No wallet, no dick. You choose, okay?' 'No,' I protest, 'For real. I never carry a wallet when I go out partying without a jacket. It spoils the line of my trousers, you see. Look!' So, her eyes turn to my trousers where I'm pointing to my flat empty pockets, and as I'm watching her finger on the trigger of her gun wondering should I fucking scream or what else, she sees the bulge in my pants and sneers: 'What kind of sick puppy it is who gets hard cock from being mugged, uh? Okay—Enough foreplay now, yes: you have five seconds to step out of your nice customized car. One, two…'"

This time, Lombard missed the punchline about how the braless apparition drove away at the wheel of his Maserati closely followed by an accomplice's car which had – "obviously" – tailed him back to his Chester residence.

As it happened, the night was playing tricks on him. He had ceased hearing the noise coming from beneath his open window. His mind had veered off course, lured by its own sirens who senselessly whispered of Alan Winston. In actual fact, the name itself was never uttered, not at first. Rather, it was only relayed, conjured up until the whispered murmurs changed into his own voice and grew pressing and precise enough to pervade his being and the darkness with the puppy snatcher's atmosphere, a buffeting invidious and muggy affair which led to his forcing his attention back to his neighbour's business. "Angel lust, isn't it?" a voice said. "Angel lust?" queried a woman. "Post-mortem hard-on. Happens when blokes meet a swift and violent death. Check it out." "You're shitting me!" "Huh-uh. On my life! Same for the sisters. Pussy flaps and clit fucking swell up. No one ever zombied back from the surprise to tell if this means they died happy, though." This too was familiar. Discourse on this topic invariably followed the carjacking story, which suggested it was exactly what the football player was busy paving the way for from the outset. In all likelihood, the familiarity of the ongoing conversation explained why it failed to hold Lombard's attention, why his mind drifted again, hijacked once more by the seemingly senseless winds of Alan Winston. This time, though, Jane McGinnis wafted into the draughts, rosy cheeks blustering about Alan Winston's innocence of her murder, insisting she'd committed suicide to show the world how desperately she needed assistance and that the object of her harrying the cook-become-puppy snatcher to make him kill her was to turn her death into a piece of theatre as a means to be counted; 'To be deemed statistically significant by you, Xavier'.

When Lombard opened his eyes to see the very first light of sunrise dulling the starlight in the sky above the dark roofs outside his bedroom window, he realized he had dozed off. Save for the mutter of distant conversation, now only quietness reached his bedroom from below. He felt hot and raw and parched, wished his neighbour bad things for having perverted the night into wearisome and unwelcome vagaries – for he knew that the part of the night which had afforded him dreams amounted only to a small portion of the whole. He got up, swigged down a couple of glasses of water chased with a shot of Calvados, returned to bed to lie down on his sheet hoping to find sleep again. Instead, he watched night turn into day as the sun rose high enough to strike the morning dew on the leaves of the plane tree outside his window, and he rose again to appraise the scene in the next-door courtyard one storey below. There, in the semi-shadow of the plane tree, empty glasses and spirit and Champagne bottles discarded on a wrought-iron table reflected some of the sun's glare, like pieces of a broken mirror. To one side, under a large striped parasol, a couple lay entwined on a chaise longue. They seemed asleep, all dressed and sun-glassed, their lean, locked bodies unmoving, he blonde, tanned, ear-ringed and tattooed, she all saffron hair and olive skin in a tight black skirt, a diamante stiletto shoe hanging heavy from her limp painted toes. They may as well have been petrified idols, reflected Lombard, before, recollecting the night's disturbance, wishing they were just that; some people are so beautiful it's hard to wish them well.

He stepped around his exercise treadmill, and, a moment later, in a T-shirt, his suit trousers and slippers, heading out for the street to get a coffee, croissants and a copy of The Paragon curious to see if there were any development on the Alan Winston story, he came face to face with his Dutch neighbour standing on the cobbles. The man, wearing only a pair of shorts and looking even taller and fitter close-up than he did from the window, was assisting a young woman in a short dress much the worse for wear, carefully steering her into a waiting black cab. "Hello there," he called genially on seeing Lombard; "I—" He never finished his sentence on account of his charge springing out of his hold. "Hello there," she aped her companion, leering at Lombard; "I'm Jennifer. How are you today? Do you live here?" she went on. "Forgive her— She's had a bit too much. Please. Come on, Jen," said the other grabbing hold of her shoulders again; "The cab's waiting and you're—"

She would have none of it: "No, no, I'm totally fine. Well-well-well, what have we here now; not a poor specimen at all," she stated, eyeballing Lombard, then leaning against his arm before standing upright again; "Still, I hope you mind not my saying that there's little evidence of my looking at a VIP or celebrity here. Say, is there even a price on your head, mister? And, please, I want you to know that I'm sorry and didn't mean to say it like this," she went on slurring while unfastening a tiny handbag to gaze into it gormlessly; "Damn and much obliged! I forgot—We don't do business cards no more! Oh well—Never mind," she said, looking up at Lombard again; "Our good lad Yann here's got my vitals, so do not even think of not calling me when you decide to vacate this dump, you hear me, mister? I'll make you a most excellent seven-figure cash offer. And tuppence and a good turn to seal and steal the deal."

By now, the football player had a firm grip on her shoulders and gently but forcibly eased her into the cab which drove away the moment he shut the door after her. "Wow! Hardcore," he let out with a sigh of relief, raising his brows in mock disbelief; "Please pay no notice to her," he added; "She is in the hospitality business; like always working even when having fun."

Lombard grinned, which his neighbour misinterpreted: "Oh! I got you! No, not that sort of hospitality business. For real: sorting out lodgings, transportation, receptions for VIPs—these sorts of things. She's always looking out for places to house celebrities and media folks. She got me this place, you know. Isn't that great? Anyway, I'm Yann. I believe we're neighbours. You're the man with the cool old car, right?"

Now, Lombard nearly shook the man's hand and excused himself so they could both get on with their own business. Yet, his bad night and the bad things he'd wished his neighbour were too raw in his mind. Appraising the tall fit young body in front of him – a particularly fair specimen of a man indeed – he saw an opportunity which seemed just too good to pass up; monkey see, monkey do.

"Well, speaking of cars and ladies: I take it this one didn't need to stick a gun at your dick and get a load of Mont Blanc before you sent her on her way, right?" he said dryly.

Predictably, Yann was confused: "Excuse me?"

"Look, Yann, I don't mind the noise and revelry. You're young and hardly ever here. The carjacking tale and ensuing conversation, though—Now I must have heard it two dozen times these past three months alone. It's getting sore. Any chance you could vary things a little?"

The man stared back with clenched teeth and a perplexed frown, clutching his fists.

"Say, I know a story about a ladies' panties thief I happen to be well-disposed towards," Lombard went on; "I'd be glad to share it with you if it would help. It opens all sorts of foreplay possibilities. What do you think?"

"I could knock you out with just one punch, mister," came the reply.

"And so you could," acquiesced Lombard; "So you could. But since you're good enough to bring this to my attention, let me trouble you with a short story of my own, Yann; nothing to do with panties. How old are you? Twenty-one? Twenty-two, maybe? Well, let's settle on twenty-one. That would make you roughly two-thirds as old as my cool old car—Or, in other words, two-thirds as seasoned. So here it goes: all those nice songs about 'killing is just another way to die' which I should think you're familiar with—Well, it isn't necessarily so. Killing is easy, Yann. For the most part needs no muscle or courage and makes no major difference in the great earthly game we're all caught in. Now keep that thought for an hour or two if you can, and think of me the next time you entertain the ladies."

And he walked away and out of the Mews, leaving the man

standing. He let out a deep sigh, quite confident that last night was likely the last time he would ever hear the carjacking story.

Disquiet thinks up many futile quests, seeks solutions, desires, explanations, and, oftentimes, by such wiles sets those it grips up for a fall. By afternoon, Lombard had called the Fortune Green florist to have her pass on the message to Jane McGinnis that, should she still wish to see him, he would be at the Regent's Park Central Circle café terrace between two and three that same day. Such an invitation had all to do with his reckoning that he ought to have been gentler with her the previous day, and he likely would have been had she not surprised him unawares after so long in, of all places, Fortune Green cemetery. She was a good soul, had always been kind and attentive, even after her initial crush on him had abated; now widowed with four children and pregnant, she had no claim to the harsh treatment he had meted out to her because of his being upset at her tracking him down. Still, he had no intention to indulge her about her dead husband – hers seemed the predictable tale of the grieving widow who won't accept that her husband was so unhappy he favoured death over living his natural life with his wife and children. In her case, bearing in mind that the husband's self-inflicted demise was captured on film, it was also likely that she'd come across trivial information that in her eyes concealed promises of some commendable rationale for his taking his own life. Such are the ways disquiet does its work. No, were they to meet again, he planned on being kind while warning her against the folly of reaching out to private investigators and likely being fleeced by the same, a distinct possibility now that he had turned her away.

Such were his intentions, and he smiled and felt gratified by the sight of her sunlit ebullient grin as he approached the park's Central Circle café terrace. It was ten to two. He was early, yet she was already settled in front of a half-eaten salad plate and ready to get to her feet in order to welcome him.

Unlike the day before, she appeared to be by herself, and – perhaps because today she had had time to – she'd taken some care with her appearance. Her hair was neatly arranged, her face made up, her lips vibrant red, and, amidst the café patrons' light and casual dress, she was turned out in a dark wide-lapelled skirt suit the like of which he recalled she favoured in her trainee accountant days. Never beautiful or even pretty – a face as broad as hers could be quite unforgiving – she looked her best unspoiled by make-up when her ruddy complexion, freckles and keen clear eyes naturally redressed the abundance of her features, a particularity she evidently had yet to determine. Still, as was her wont, she radiated with the glow that comes from feeling at ease and pregnant. He declined her offer to get him a coffee and settled across the table from her, noting a large shopping bag and a small handbag on the chair by her side.

"How are you, Jane? I suggested we meet here as it would be convenient for your girls. But no pram today, I see."

"No buggy—No nappies—No Mummy! I'm free! I left the girls with my mother. She's over from Ireland for a while—Helping me start sorting things out around the house. I'm about to put it on the market. It's a small terrace we bought a few years ago. It seemed a good idea at the time, what with Joseph's steady income? But listen to me blabbering on—How are you, Xavier? And don't worry, please—This is a fantastic place! I don't think I've been here for years. I just walked from Baker Street station, across the bridge over the lake with the swans and along the path by the bandstand and—Jesus, living so far out in Walthamstow you forget how great central London parks are. Gorgeous!"

She'd slipped back into the easy, congenial familiarity of old. For a moment, she went quiet, gazing around her as if giddy with delight, then repeated "Gorgeous."

"You're selling up," said Lombard helpfully, wondering whether this meeting had been needed after all.

"Planning to. Things are tricky now I'm by myself. I'm just hoping the house will sell for what I still owe on it. Then it's back home to Ireland for this country girl. There's family to help over there; it'll be safer and better for the girls and myself and the baby on the way. But—Xavier, this is so—" she beamed; "I was so glad when the florist called. I'm very sorry about yesterday. I know I shouldn't have come. I wasn't going to. I'd thought of giving the florist a message for you. But I was so worried she wouldn't bother, I—"

"I'm sorry too, Jane," he said; "I never meant to be rude to you. You're a good person. And, like I said yesterday, being pregnant suits you."

She blushed, turned to her salad to hide her trouble: "Oh. Thank you."

No words were said for a moment until: "Now how about you, Xavier? I've often wondered: any woman? Wife? Children?"

He grinned, sighed: "You just can't help it—Can you, Jane?"

"You're not going to tell me?"

He smiled this time: "Is the one you describe as being in the oven your husband's or—?"

"Oh. It is his. He—He died five months ago. This one is due in three months. Neither of us had any idea at the time—"

Lombard nodded, mindful she would be unimpressed by what was coming.

"Now, I don't know why you think I invited you here, Jane. I did want to see you, but I wouldn't want you to get the wrong idea. Like I said yesterday, I'm in no position to help you—I no longer do investigative work. But perhaps I can help in some other way if you let me. Now bear with me. Tell me, did you love your husband? Would I be right presuming you loved him and he loved you?"

Her smile was gone. She knit her brows, thrown by his question, then nodded, unsure.

"I'd figured as much," he said, an attempt at light-heartedness; "Was he a good man?" he asked.

"I'm sorry?"

"Was he a good man?" he repeated.

"He was."

"How long were the two of you married for?"

"Six years."

"And all your four children are his?"

"They are."

"So he kept you busy, I take it."

"To be sure, he did."

"Were either of you unfaithful?"

"Hell no—I mean, I have no reason to think so. I never—Why—"

"Good. Was he on medication? Antidepressants, antipsychotic drugs? Any history of mental illness?"

"Never."

"Had he recently been diagnosed with a fatal or degenerative illness?"

She shook her head.

"What about work? Money? Any trouble there?"

"Nothing out of the ordinary. Actually, he'd recently been promoted."

"Good. So no problems to speak of. He was a reasonably happy man, right?"

"I guess you could put it that way."

"Who threw himself under a train?"

She took a deep breath: "Indeed—Who threw himself under a train," she repeated.

"He didn't merely fall? Or—?"

"He jumped," she interjected; "Kilburn station. The platform surveillance camera recorded him jumping."

"And it was just another day. And he left no note—No form of explanation."

"It was and he didn't. That's right."

"Good. Now tell me: was he a man without sins, Jane?"

"Sins?" she queried.

"Uh-huh. Would you say your husband was a man without sins, Jane? I recall you being a good Catholic girl when we first met. I trust you know about sins."

She stared back at him, trying to guess where he was leading her:

"Now, did you ever meet a man without sins, Xavier?" she scoffed.

He grinned: "Indeed," he said, kindly; "So, what were his sins, Jane?"

Now she understood: "Oh. He had none which would lead him to throw himself under a train, Xavier; I can't assure you of that."

"If that is so, why would you want to change your generous opinion of his good character, Jane?"

She frowned above her freckles, confused and suspicious again.

"There's something to be said for thinking well of the dead, Jane," he said; "I don't doubt you married a good man. Just the same, folks who jump under trains generally don't commit to doing so on a whim. You'd think they'd have to have a good reason for it—Never mind good loving men with loving wives and beloved and lovely children. This being the case, the good wives of such good men may be well advised to foster their fond memories of their departed husbands. Much the same as no good thing leads a man to wish an end to his life, no good comes from digging up bones, Jane. I should think your husband would have left a word if he'd wanted you or his children to know what was weighing on his mind. Let sleeping dogs lie. And since you said that the police are unhelpful— And I should think you must have asked yourself why this is— I would positively steer clear of private investigators who may prove only too happy to part a grieving window from her money."

By the conclusion of his speech, Jane had regained her composure, her face exhibiting the patient, detached, disappointed air of someone who had already considered everything that is being said to them.

"As I told you yesterday, Xavier, I do not intend to lay my life bare for strangers to dissect. And like I said just a moment ago, I'm leaving London to return to Ireland soon. But for now, about 'letting sleeping dogs lie', when the day comes for my girls to ask about their father, I'd like to be able to tell them that he did not simply throw himself under some train one morning because he suddenly became tired of life. There's more to it than that. I know there is."

She was smiling, but he was aware she was all contained fury.

"Needs must, right, Jane?" he despaired; "Well, if nothing's going to dissuade you from visiting your grief upon your daughters, I guess you'll make it so."

"Make it so—" she exclaimed.

She glanced at the people eating and drinking at the surrounding tables, as if considering what to do, and seemed to settle on a plan which – he immediately recognized – rested on her well-founded presumption that he wouldn't just leave if she decided to threaten to make a nuisance of herself in full view and earshot of the café's patrons.

"I do like you, Xavier. But the truth is, you are a cynical man who sees mostly the bad in people," she said loud enough to draw the attention of the nearest tables; then, more quietly: "For your information, I'm not grief-stricken-mad and there couldn't have been a kinder, better, gentler person walking this earth than my Joseph—That's my husband's name, by the way: Joseph. If anything, he was good to a fault, so that on bad days—God forgive me—I could catch myself thinking of him as a little dull and a right pushover. But there was not an evil bone inside of him. And, yes, we were happy, and he was a devoted father. In fact, it was he who wished to have so many children. Now, I could tell you he was from Iran; that his parents were Christian refugees escaping the Islamic revolution who came to this country when he was two; that he was orphaned by the time he was eighteen; that we met at an office party when I still lived in the flat above yours; and that I fell for his gorgeous long eyelashes and he for this petite, plump, fair Irish lass who apparently reminded him of old Flemish paintings of angels. I could also tell you that he worked in various capacities at Waltham Forest Council Housing Department right up to the day he died, and that— To use your words—I was indeed very much minded to let sleeping dogs lie. But as it happens, I have cause to believe something odd may have been going on with him and I'm most definitely not frightened to find out what. I tried the police, but they sent me away with the good advice to 'move on' and seek counselling. That's when I thought of you, after I decided I had better move back to Ireland. You see, once I'll be gone, I'll be gone—And probably will never be able to afford to come back to London. And once away from the things and places I shared with Joseph, I should think I'll probably also begin to slowly forget him. The time I have left in Walthamstow is my last chance to find out the truth about what led him to end his life. And deep down, Xavier, it is very hard to suppress the need to know the truth. So very hard, you know. Especially when you have cause to think some odd things were going on. So please, I'm not an idiot or some grief-stricken mad widow."

Now she was staring at him icily, petulant, her heavy chest heaving within her tight suit and sweat showing on her forehead.

"I never said you were either, Jane," he said.

"Oh, but you did so, Mr Lombard," she lashed back, reaching for the plastic bag on the chair beside her to slam it on the table: "Here," she said, standing up and grabbing her handbag; "Clearly, it was presumptuous of me, but thinking the unthinkable, I took the liberty of bringing this to you. It's all in there—Including Joseph's bank statements and the footage of him jumping—On the tablet. Take a peek if you find the time and dare tell me I'm mad or stupid again! And if you can't be bothered, feel free to get rid of it. Goodbye now. I better go home and put my poor mother out of her misery."

"I wouldn't leave this here, Jane," he called after her, glaring at the bag she left on the table behind her.

"Oh, and two more things I could tell you," she announced loud enough for everyone else at the café terrace to hear while turning around to face him again: "Speaking of sins—No good devout Christian would ever contemplate the sin of suicide. You ought to know that. And speaking of suicide—A man about to take his life does not open his mail two hours before killing himself. Take a look, Xavier, and tell me I'm wrong if you dare!"

Lombard glared again. Several faces at the terrace were firing glances across the tables in his direction, mostly reproachful, as though he may have been guilty of having perpetrated some crime against the poor pregnant suited woman who was now clip-clopping away in ill-fitting heels. He grunted, turned his gaze back to the bag on the table and swallowed hard.

It would, without question, have been annoying to have to leave Regent's Park carting Jane McGinnis's plastic bag. Merely reaching for it had felt like staking a claim on contaminated property. By all means, she had acquitted herself with marked ability, put him to task for having disappointed her. She most certainly had not planned for it, but when the time came had known he'd refrain from making a fuss in public or, come to it, spitefully leave behind for anyone to find a bag containing particulars of her husband's suicide.

There was no way he'd let her get the better of him, though. He'd seriously thought of abandoning the bag on the table where she'd left it. But on peering inside and coming across a bundle of bank statements and a tablet device, he'd stepped into the café to hand it in at the bar explaining that his lady companion had gone and left it behind; it contained important personal documents and belongings, could they keep it safe until, on realising her blunder, she would return for them. They queried why he couldn't call her himself, either to let her know that she had left her bag behind or possibly to arrange to give it back to her, which he countered by stating that he hardly knew her and was going away that afternoon; "Please, make sure she gets it back; she's small, blond and pregnant. Her name's Jane McGinnis."

He had no idea whether she would return to collect the bag or opt instead to assume he would take it with him from a sense of obligation on finding out what was inside. It occurred to him that she may have been bluffing, was hiding nearby, ready to see what he would do, and would make her way back to retrieve it on seeing him step empty-handed from the café. Strolling back towards his Mews, he also wondered if she could be following him, but a couple of back glances failed to spot her. In the end, thoughts of Jane and her bag were put out of his mind even before he reached home; a couple of other matters took their place.

The first, while predictable, nonetheless also provided a source of surprise. Whereas the morning edition of The Paragon had found little newsworthy to report about their reporter's murderer, the afternoon edition of The Free Londoner piled up outside Baker Street tube station screamed 'Murderer Uncovered'. It was never really in question, but Alan Winston's fate now seemed sealed; not only was his identity confirmed, but the paper's front page also displayed a sharp, unmistakable photograph of him standing in Heathrow Airport waiting to board a flight. It transpired that he had absconded to Funchal in Madeira early the previous morning, using his own passport, making no attempt at concealing his identity and, by the look of him, quite carefree in a pair of Jeans, T-shirt and trainers, casually holding a dark holdall slung across his shoulders. Whilst more information would doubtless soon come to light, Lombard thought Madeira an odd destination for a fugitive wanted for murder. A small Portuguese island in the Atlantic Ocean with no beaches to speak of, best known as a holiday destination for pensioners, it made an unlikely hideaway for a nineteen-year-old. And, as far as he was aware, Alan Winston had no link to the place.

The other matter came as a much more welcome diversion, finding him, as all such pleasant intrusions heavy with promises invariably did, in the form of a text message:

'Florida concert cancelled due to fires. On flight back home w/Free week ahead. Will be in London this eve. How about I pick you up on way to Cumbria tonight? Let me know. Wild with Xpectation as always. Xxx'

FIVE

These people clearly have two problems. One is they
don't want to study history, and secondly, having lived
in this country for a very long time, probably all their
lives, they don't understand English irony either. So I
think they need two lessons, which we can perhaps
help them with.

It is said that strange, delightful creatures, not unlike exotic
places, owe their undying appeal to their mysterious nature,
for rare are those men or women whose lure survives too close
scrutiny or familiarity. All the same, it was a while now since
Lombard had formed the opinion that Kathryn Alibella
Turnwell – or Ali, as she preferred to be known – did not have
it in her to become a disappointment, and that, although the
opposite is commonly true, once in a while a kinship of the
soul can be mistaken for lust, or, in the best of cases, closely
accompany it.

That Lombard was so disposed was just as well since, char-
acteristically, she to whom he was in this way disposed, hardly
gave him time to get ready. Her car pulled into his Mews as
the sun was setting, ready to leave at once for the long drive to
Cumbria. Some weeks had passed since their last time together,
and as they headed north along the M1 motorway in the fresh
evening breeze from the open windows, Lombard, breaking
the silence heavy with anticipation that typically marked their
reunions, asked her if she wished him to drive as she may be
jet-lagged.

She laughed: "No one's ever gonna take the wheel from this
girl."

He grinned, and she kept her greedy gaze on the road ahead, now and again raising one hand to brush her wind-whipped hair out of her eyes.

Ali had come into his life the same way spring slips into a hard winter: at first hardly discernible, then sensed and stirring, to become in the end exquisitely intoxicating. One rainy afternoon, she'd stepped through the door of *Monsieur Chose*, a restaurant tucked away in an alley off the Marylebone High Street which, owing to its out-of-the-way location, saw little passing trade and so was reliably quiet in the intervals between lunch and the evening service. Lombard, along with a handful of regulars, valued these peaceful hours, spent many afternoons there, sitting over a coffee or a Calvados catching up with the news from a television set which was turned on for the pleasure of the staff readying the place for the evening shift. It was into this sedate, informal setting that Ali had made her appearance one autumn afternoon to settle in a corner opposite his table. He paid her no more mind than a pleasant-looking stranger entering a quiet restaurant deserved, yet noted that she ordered tea and at once turned her attention to a tablet device, starting to draw or write on it with a fine silver stylus. He had left before she did. She'd returned the next day, discreet as on her first visit, and again the next, until, before long, a pattern was set: two days a week she would show up at around the same time, settle at the same table, invariably wrap her coat on the back of her chair, sit in a way that afforded Lombard a full side view of her figure, order tea and, keeping her handbag securely in her lap, focus on her tablet often moving her lips in silent whispers while engrossed in its display. Lombard had no idea how long she stayed as he always left before she did, except on one occasion when an elegant grey-haired woman turned up to collect her. Inevitably, because of where he was seated directly across from her – and perhaps because it is impossible for a man not to fall for an attractive woman he sees regularly – he had become steadily more attentive to her, soon filled with agitation on the days she was expected. She couldn't be more than thirty-five, of delicate build with a narrow waist and poised shoulders. But it was her hands that had first caught his attention; they were quite sensational, sinewy, with strong thumbs and long knobbly fingers, yet moved effortlessly, as if floating through the air, reminiscent of willow tree sprigs flowing in the breeze. Habitually presented with her profile, and given that she generally wore loose sleeveless tops with her hair pulled up in a ponytail, he soon came to prize the lines of her neck and shoulder, and the fine down on her nape which awoke heady fancies of a soft and warm and perfumed shelter.

Of course, the object of such interest could not remain unaware of her effect for long, whereby she soon let him know about it with a few fleeting smiles and sideways glances. On the occasions he was too slow to avert his gaze and their eyes threatened to meet, she quickly lowered her own, like himself – or so it seemed – uninterested in encouraging familiarity or intimacy. And so things had remained, strangers content to remain strangers whilst all the time, certainly on Lombard's side, captivated by the other, so that when he had eventually been called away for a couple of weeks he'd wound up pondering whether he'd see her again, accepting he would miss her if by chance the break in his routine should coincide with her ending her afternoon visits to *Monsieur Chose*. It hadn't. She stepped through the door on the first day following his return, but things were different; she'd looked straight at him even as she stood in the doorway with a rousing unsettling smile across her lips. Taken aback, Lombard had failed to return her smile and turned away, welcoming the sound of her heels heading towards her regular table rather than, as he momentarily feared, coming his way. Once seated though, she'd resumed her routine, ordered tea and turned to her tablet, as if nothing.

It just so happened that the television news on that day focused on the furore born from the release of some old footage showing a current government minister addressing a conference on 'The Return of Britishness'. In the course of his speech, he'd taken to refer to a couple of hecklers of Afro-Caribbean origin who'd berated the previous speaker, using the words 'These people clearly have two problems. One is they don't want to study history, and secondly, having lived in this country for a very long time, probably all their lives, they don't understand English irony either. So I think they need two lessons, which we can perhaps help them with.' In the space of twenty-four hours, this footage had commanded universal condemnation, charges of systemic racism and calls for the 'unrepentant' minister to be fired, the ensuing media and social network storm prompting the Prime Minister to 'reluctantly' demand the minister's resignation, so ending what she'd stated was 'an illustrious career with a promising future'. Now, television pundits and politicians debated whether the Prime Minister had been too slow in asking for the minister's resignation, whether this reflected 'moral laxity' and 'evidence of ingrained prejudice' among the governing party's members. Thus driven to distraction by the television noise, Lombard had failed to see Ali bridge the distance between them, so that by the time he noticed her she was already standing close to his table with her coat and bag over one arm, her teacup in one hand and promises of infinity in her eyes. "A penny for your thoughts," she said, smiling; "What's the verdict? Guilty or not guilty?"

His surprise did not get the better of him though, and he guessed her question referred to the news: "Who? The man or the Prime Minister?"

"Take your pick."

"I'm afraid it's beyond me," he grinned.

She smiled: "Oh! Slow to judge, I see. Does that make you a good learner, then?"

"Huh. I guess the jury is still out on that one," he replied.

"Well-well! Curiouser and curiouser," she laughed, glancing at the wedding band on his left hand. "You may well think me too forward, but one of us needs to stop humming and hawing, wouldn't you say? Soon I won't be passing this way again. My work here is almost done. Still, if it would be your pleasure, I would very much like to introduce myself and ask about the ring."

Lombard's pleasure was never in doubt. He saw in her eyes that she knew it too; and he yielded, abandoned prudence:

"The ring is unfinished business," he revealed; "As well as to keep up appearances and likewise deter against inquisitive ladies. And quite reliable it is too—Normally," he added, light-heartedly, sitting up; "Xavier Lombard."

"Quite," she returned, puzzled but satisfied, putting her tea down to hold out her hand; "Hi. Kathryn Turnwell. But friends call me 'Ali'—For Alibella, my middle name. From your name, accent, looks and general manner, you're French, right?"

"Uh-huh."

When their fingers touched, and he felt her warm skin, he also sensed the most disturbing agitation he'd known in a long time; at once he recognized – not without trepidation – that she who was clasping his hand was much more alluring than even her outward charms suggested.

Kathryn Alibella Turnwell was born and raised in Zambia, the only child of an African-English cattle farmer and a reformed American socialite and jazz singer. Had her parents been favoured, she likely would never have left the half a million-acre farm of wild grazing land which was hers to inherit and, in all probability, never become an acclaimed classical pianist and composer – she composed music on her tablet, not, as Lombard reckoned, nurtured a social network existence. The chances are she'd have remained in Zambia. Only, either by a twist of fate or by reason of her mother who had passed away when she was still too young to remember her, besides being born with a condition defined by an intolerance to sunlight – or Xeroderma pigmentosum, which meant that too much sun could cause irreparable damage to her skin, DNA or nervous system – she had also inherited a grand piano as well as a forever grieving and melancholy father, and by the sum of all three developed a strong sense of self-reliance and independence very early in life. Truth be told, Ali was one of the most undomesticated and yet most grounded creatures Lombard had ever come across, all the while admirably combining stoicism with an easy generosity of spirit. She was all her own, yet open and willing to share herself, but to a degree.

Because of the danger presented by the sun – she defied all of her father's repeated attempts to send her off to the more clement skies of England – she grew up spending the African daylight mostly indoors, making up for it with long rambling evening horse rides across the wilds of the family farm. By the time she was eleven, she knew all there was to know about the stars and had come across tens of thousands of heads of cattle but hardly any people: cheated of her mother, her father had taken to a life of semi-seclusion and full-drunkenness, banning all but the most essential help and farmhands from their remote property. In the matter of her education, she was taught to read and write by the farm's cook, and in light of the nearest town being a full day's drive away, as well as her father's animus against housing a live-in tutor and her resistance to being sent to boarding school, she'd sought her own instruction from books. In this way mistress of her destiny, aged thirteen, she'd made provision for her future upon reading one particular book. "There was this 'History of the California Gold Rush of the Eighteen Hundreds' in my father's study. It was a big, glossy thing full of old photographs and extracts of letters written by gold miners to their families back home. Their letters were amazing; they were so well-written, graceful, so wistful. These people endured terrible hardships and danger, had left everything behind to make it to California to find gold, but in most cases they ended up losing even more: the few possessions they still owned, their health, their minds and, pretty often, their lives. More than their stories, though, the thing that hit me about the gold rush was the fate of the merchants who hooked up with them—The hustlers and hucksters with cartloads of pickaxes and shovels for sale. No losing their minds or dying in the dirt for this lot—Most actually wound up richer than the folks who dug, scrapped, fought, speculated, stole or even killed for gold. I saw a lesson here, and I guess it got my attention. It got me thinking, led me straight to my mother's old grand piano which had stood idle in our drawing-room all my life. Later, I realized I could already smell trouble ahead. Things were getting awkward with father—The drink tearing through his body and mind—Yet I never imagined I'd ever have to leave the farm. The dust and the horses, the cattle and the grass—Even the eagles and stars and all that made the sky, even the dreaded sun—All of it was mine. For miles and infinity. I could not think not-being-there. That gold rush book, though—It got me scared of it all disappearing. So I made my mind up. I had better find a way to ensure I'd be okay if I were ever forced to leave the farm for the horrors over the horizon. And with the sun my enemy, it sort of seemed obvious that, if I could learn it, I should try to transform my mother's piano into my own pickaxes and shovels. In an unforgiving world, I'd be a musician. Music's a tool for the soul; helps the poor endure, indulges the rich. It idealizes hurt, fosters dreams and stirs the spirit. That's why folks can't resist it; why they're willing to pay for it. The way I looked at it, music was as necessary to the human condition as a shovel is to a gold digger, and would stand she who mastered it in good stead."

This story best summed up all that Lombard admired about Ali; fearing the unknown, she would, as if it was the most natural of things, simply set out to disarm it. For years, testing herself against a box-set of Beethoven's piano sonatas which had been her mother's, at first with her father's help and then by herself, she'd learnt to play – and tune – the piano, pounding the keys until her hands had become the way they were now, practising until she'd mastered the skill to perform as flawlessly as talent permitted. "I'd have made Jazz if mother had left behind a Thelonious Monk box-set," she conceded; "Or Easy listening if Liberace." Inevitably, her father's drinking had led to illness and his demise, and within days solicitors had turned up at the farm with the news that her home now belonged to a Chinese mining company. Over the years, her father had re-mortgaged the property enough to surrender the deeds to it. At the same time, an unknown aunt who introduced herself as her father's sister had shown up from England to take her away. "I'm a classical pianist. And I'm very good at it," she'd told the woman at once. "That's very good, dear," the other responded; "I'd feared I'd find a shy cowgirl. Now I believe there's a music college not too far from us in Dalton-in-Furness. Provided your piano playing skills prove equal to your conceit, I should think we shall have you enrolled there in no time at all."

Her skills proved just that. From Dalton-in-Furness, she'd secured entry to the Royal Academy of Music in London which – and in due time this would prove auspicious – happened to be located on the Marylebone Road a mere fifteen-minute walk from Lombard's Mews, and before many years would pass, with her fortune on the up, she would return to Zambia intent on buying back the family farm, find that its new owner had turned her old wilderness into one of Africa's largest open-pit copper mines, and return to England carrying a torch against all things Chinese.

For all Ali's charm, Lombard never could match her candour when it came to making revelations. This had become apparent during their first conversation when she approached him at *Monsieur Chose* and all he knew of her were the stirrings of physical attraction she elicited in him.

Lasting only half an hour, this first exchange proved to be a journey of exploration between attracted strangers, full of surprises and signs of things to come. At the outset, she persevered with the TV news controversy story about the disgraced minister and the slow-acting Prime Minister, arguing against the former but in defence of the latter. Then, without a pause, she revealed that coincidentally she too owed her afternoon visits to the restaurant to "the latest hysteria for moral purity and purging—Certain individuals want others to bleed, you know!" She had been invited to give a semester of lectures on composition at the nearby Royal Academy of Music where she'd once studied herself, she explained, a favour to her old Principal whom she now counted as a friend and at whose Hampstead property she was staying while in London, her own U.K. residence being in Cumbria. However, on learning of her unrepentant "colonial" past, within a week a group of students had called for a boycott of her classes and for her to be barred from the Academy grounds. "I was born and raised on a farm in Africa, you see; half-English, half-American. Now they'd have me publicly diss my parents and repent of their and my 'imperialist' past. They know nothing of our past—Or I'd wager of Africa. Actually, instead of hounding me, they ought to learn about Africa, see what the Chinese are up to over there—Plundering the wilderness for copper."

She could have stayed away on the couple of afternoons she was contracted to lecture, she went on to say; instead, come class time she'd come to *Monsieur Chose* to remain for the hours of her boycotted lectures: "I told the Academy to let the students know I'm nearby, ready to show up at any time to give the class if and when they elect to take a stand against their own prejudices. Fat chance in this crazy world, I know. But I owe this much to the Principal who is still very supportive and is keeping me on the payroll."

At this, Lombard took her to be an academic from Cumbria and smiled, acquiescing: "It can be a crazy world indeed."

"What about you? Do you live locally? You seem to have an indecent amount of spare time for a man in the prime of life. Or is moping around London's eateries what this Frenchman does for an occupation?" she teased.

Lombard, heeding to instinct, uncharacteristically opted to be truthful, but only insofar as he determined to lie by omission only; a precaution against being perceived as deceitful. To risk their potential relationship with pretences she appeared discerning enough to expose seemed folly.

"I guess what I do does afford me a lot of spare time," he said; "But let me add, I'm no cast-out lecturer, nor in trouble with anybody."

Her lips had cracked in a sunny smile: "Oh—No! Please, do not be deceived by this fragile cover. I'm no lecturer. The truth is—I trust you have heard of Ludwig van Beethoven? I'm sure you have. Well—I'm a sort of a she-him. A *pianiste et compositeur*. A *virtuoso*, it has even been alleged."

He was unsure, wondered whether she was having him on: "I once met a Royal Navy Lieutenant-Commander who turned out to be a security guard in a High Street shoe shop," he remarked, testingly; "Then, on further acquaintance, he turned out to be a cocktail waitress."

She giggled: "How weird is that! That sort of thing happens to me at least once a year!" And, in a graceful gesture she raised and revolved her hands above the table between them: "Anyway! Here! Corroborative exhibits 'A' and 'B'. Then again, anyone's free to check me out at any serious music outlet; 'T' for Turnwell, Kathryn; classical section."

Such a playful show of confidence made it difficult to doubt her further.

"You can go outside and check me out on your phone if you want; I'm only suggesting you step out because I believe this place is rigged up with reception blocking equipment of some sort—Which is why I like it. Together with the present company, of course."

"I think I can take your word for it—You being famous," he said; "After all, why would an obscure attractive woman feel the need to masquerade as a famous attractive woman. To come across as a foolish attractive woman?"

"Oh. Would you mind?" she laughed.

"I trust I need no device to check you out," he returned.

"Good. So, tell me: unique as we each may be, how much if anything in common do we share besides afternoons to kill? What is it you do?"

And Lombard admitted to being a "private investigator of sorts", which, as was to be expected, claimed her undivided attention. He was an ex-Paris police officer, he told her, working in London as a "researcher" for the 'Brand Reputation and Protection Department' of a French multinational utility company – "A specialist and, I guess, a necessary job in an era of social media weaponization and widespread hostility from all kinds of crowds with grievances and multi-platform access," he said.

"You mean like environmentalist activists!" she stated.

"Uh-huh. Among others. There are lots of bellicose types out there."

What he neglected to say was that he worked in that capacity, and otherwise, exclusively for Edward Duncan, operating as an agent extraordinaire, aided, when required, by an ex-dark web marketplace administrator who made the other half of EcoWatt's London 'Brand Reputation and Protection Department'.

"You rascal!" she exclaimed, fascinated to the point of awe; "So what kind of things do you do? Does this kind of work pay well?"

"Now and again I'm called upon to encourage people," he said; "And I have no reasons to complain."

"Encourage people?"

"Uh-huh. Now and again some require encouragement."

"As in must be deterred or impeded, is that what you mean?" she charged.

He grinned: "Confused minds have been known to call for boycotts—Spread hurtful rumours," he returned.

She nodded, peering into his eyes while working hard inside her own. He noticed one of her irises was a slightly darker green than the other.

"Uh! Tricky," she said; "Now—You can know me; but how can I know you?"

He understood. She was not merely curious. She was a renowned concert pianist, forward enough to accost a stranger in a restaurant but not reckless.

"Kathryn Turnwell? Piano player? Cumbria, right?" he said.

"Correct. Piano player," she chuckled self-deprecatingly.

"I recall you saying you won't be passing this way again. How can—?"

"Not quite yet. I'll be back the day after tomorrow. Usual time."

And, two afternoons on he'd presented her with an envelope containing a sheet of paper with information about her bank, mobile phone and credit card records. Being presented with the ready availability of their personal details could prove testing for many, bring on feelings of violation and vulnerability, often together with – he knew – anger and resentment towards the messenger. This had warranted his providing her with just enough evidence to convince her of the nature of his occupation without risking unsettling her too much. But he needn't have feared. Examining her records, she looked in turn perturbed, pensive and impressed. "Gosh," she whispered; "So it's true that no such thing as privacy still exists." Then: "I don't suppose there's any point in asking how you got hold of this stuff, right?"

They'd met again, over dinner in a restaurant. Then, with the end of her contract at the Academy, she had left for Cumbria to contact him again by text within a fortnight: 'I'll be in London next Tuesday/Wednesday eve. How about it? Miss U. A'. And soon, he'd learnt that he liked to watch her take off her dress and brush her hair, and that his lips approved the curves of her nape – which indeed was the heady soft and warm and sweetly scented shelter of promises.

"Precautions aren't necessary," she advised.

He took her word for it; without saying so, both knew not to ask uninvited questions.

Cumbria was warm, untamed and peaceful; a late summer sanctuary. Ali had done well by her mother's piano. A few students and activist collectives advocating against her past and family had done little to prejudice her career. Along with praise and awards for her performances and recordings from across the world, had come the means to own properties both in England and abroad. Insofar as Lombard knew, her favourite was an old farmhouse near the Eskdale valley in the Lake District. It came with a thousand acres of wilderness made of heather-scented moors, furloughed fields, grasslands and great forests as well as – of some interest to Lombard – a barn accommodating a rusty broken down Aston Martin DB5 and a Ferguson tractor. She kept a small stable of horses which were looked after by her cousin Alice – this one was the daughter of the aunt from Dalton-in-Furness who'd brought her over from Zambia – who, together with her husband managed the property and its few sheep and goats from a cottage on the estate. Lombard knew the place well by now, not least because as Ali's guest he hardly ever left the grounds once inside the gate. The moment they arrived, she would proceed as if the rest of the world had ceased to exist, a whim made all the more possible by the deliberate absence of telephone, radio, television or means of communication with the outside from practically anywhere on the property; the place was remote enough that mobile reception was limited to a small corner a mile or so from the main house. Of the surrounding area, Lombard knew the coarse beauty of the rugged landscape discernible from the approach road, echoed in the names of villages like Miterdale, Hardknott, Burnmoor, Scafell and Ravenglass; and it sufficed. Of Ali, though, there could never be enough.

They stayed all of ten days, had an uncomplicated time, the sort that satisfies the senses and makes for light-headedness; slow nights inside open windows, late breakfasts in bed, afternoon strolls across the moors, and easy evenings when he would head for the barn to tinker with the old Aston Martin while Ali, openly re-enacting her African childhood, would saddle-up and vanish on horse rides as soon as the sky grew dark to return much later, lips flushed and eyes ablaze, drunk with dusk's wanton suggestions. She called these outings "replenishments", never looked more alluring than on her return, so aroused and fulfilled that for a good while afterwards nothing seemed to touch her. It could be intimidating, but never enough to make him wish not to be there, or not remain fascinated by her strange hands, which by now he'd had occasion to watch while they cast their spell on the piano. In some ways, not unlike the Cumbrian landscape, she was rugged and untamed, and like himself, now and again in need of company and deleterious transgressions. What does a woman lying in bed for hours gazing out the window as if the whole world is there only to serve her truly think about, Lombard sometimes wondered watching her. Well, this woman, concluding such silent contemplation one day had asked: "Where do you find a one-legged dog?" And when Lombard admitted to not having a clue, had gone on: "Right where you left it."

Had Lombard been merely an observer in the story of Ali

and Xavier, he, while reserving judgement on Ali's sentiments, would have recognized the likelihood of the gentleman missing the lady upon their separation, for he was no stranger to the feeling. Such disquiet, from which he once considered himself immune – certainly prior to meeting her – had accompanied their last few partings, and not liking it a bit he was determined not to let it happen again. To that end, as it was all bright midday skies when they drove back into London, instead of having her take him home he got her to drop him off along a bustling section of the Edgware Road. They bid each other goodbye with a kiss through her open window and he watched her pull away towards her Pimlico flat on her way to the airport and the resumption of her interrupted U.S. concert tour.

A moment later he was settled at a café terrace with copies of several of the morning papers. Catching up with Alan Winston's news was meant to keep him from tasting the tediousness of being alone again, partway stranded at the edge of things. It appeared to work at first, for it turned out that against all odds nearly two weeks on from his killing the Paragon reporter, Alan Winston was still on the run, and the dead man's paper remained committed to having him caught, devoting nearly an entire page to his story.

Despite his having been identified and known to have flown to Madeira, Alan Winston's trail had seemingly reached a dead end. The Portuguese police had tracked down the taxi driver who picked him up on his landing at Funchal airport, and he in turn had led them to a secluded road running across a remote plateau in the wilds halfway up the island's hills, recounting how even though there was nothing there but dust, shrubs and trees, his fare had known exactly where he wished to be dropped, at all times calm and never attempting to conceal his appearance. After a few days, the police concluded their search of the surrounding wilderness to put out a statement to the effect that they believed Alan Winston had come to this remote spot after arranging for an accomplice to pick him up safely away from prying eyes. This accomplice, they surmised, had to be a local person he was acquainted with. There could be no other explanation for his flying to

72

Madeira, heading straight for the hills on landing, and disappearing from the middle of nowhere. Accordingly, flyers of the fugitive had been distributed across the Island in the hope of flushing him out, which nobody expected would take much time. Given this state of affairs, The Paragon sought to make the best of the situation, keeping the story alive with tributes to their murdered reporter while printing revelations about his killer which – or so readers were warned – were advisedly presented so as not to prejudice the case against him. In the event, selected acquaintances' recollections presented as evidence of the ex-cook-come-murderer's bad ways – for not one of their "recollections" did credit to his character – had found their way onto their pages, together with intimate family pictures; one of these showed him in a Cadet uniform proudly displaying his Duke of Edinburgh Award badge, in another a sulky ten-year-old stood next to his mother during a seaside holiday. In addition, information linking the fugitive to Madeira had also come to light. One such link concerned his parents who were living in a Camberwell Housing Estate. It turned out they had spent time on the island in their youth, his mother working as a hotel maid and his father, at the time fresh from the army, as a hotel cook. The couple had met in Madeira, but also left for England never to return long before their son was born, all but making this information seem somewhat irrelevant. The other link appeared hardly more promising. About a year earlier, Alan Winston had spent a week's holiday in Funchal with an ex-girlfriend. The girl, a Londoner Lombard had called on some weeks previously while he was still pursuing the puppy-snatcher, was quoted as saying 'We only ended up in Madeira on account of being a bit naïve, you know what I mean. We'd heard it called "The Pearl of The Atlantic" and booked a week break there never checking it out. With a name like that we thought it would be a cool place to chill; sandy beaches, warm water, great party scene; all the good stuff, you know. Well—A bloody beachless rain-soaked rocky stump crawling with grey heads, rent-a-cars is what we found. Pretty but dull.' They ended up hiring a car, she said, which 'I—Because Alan never got his test—

Drove round and round the island's mountain roads from dawn to dusk, drunk most of the time'. She had no clue why her ex-boyfriend – who she also claimed not to have seen for months – had flown there, stating 'We were both equally glad to be back in London by the end of that week; and no, we didn't meet anyone there; it was much too tame for us, if you know what I mean.'

Almost as surprising as his flying to Madeira and having so far avoided capture, was the fact that Alan Winston's puppy-snatching exploits had yet to come to light; then again, it could be that this particular information was being withheld by press and police. As reported, Alan Winston's recent history read thus: he had left his flat and his job as a cook in a Knightsbridge restaurant a year earlier without notice, moved to a seafront apartment in Brighton where no record of him working anywhere existed, then suddenly disappeared until his murderous re-emergence in the Mile End bedsit where, in the four weeks prior to his becoming a killer, he'd rented a room under an alias while working as a cook in a Covent Garden Bistro. The Paragon was unsure what to make of it all. By way of explanation – and none of this was thought to bear on their reporter's murder proper, which they deemed to be the chance result of a heated argument gone tragically wrong – they surmised that he had likely slipped into a life of crime at around the time he left for Brighton and had run into trouble and returned to London to go into hiding. Besides – and this was presented as this theory's supporting evidence – some of his acquaintances, such as the ex-girlfriend from his Madeira holiday, alleged they had recently been approached by a strange man they described as either French or Italian who'd called himself an insurance claims investigator while asking all kinds of questions about him. Oddly, the fact that Lombard had perpetrated the deception by passing them a contact card with a bogus name and number – rather than to gather information the true object of this exercise was to ensure Alan Winston would be aware he was being hounded by a person concealing their identity, the more mysterious the better – was nowhere mentioned.

Over a light lunch on the Edgware Road, Lombard read all of these facts and much more, most of which belonged to the predictable fodder which accompanies sensational murder stories. Still, one particular piece caught his attention. It came from a rival newspaper to The Paragon, concerned a lodger from the murder house depicted as 'John Bowdion, an unemployed thirty-three-year-old man who calls himself a writer.' This man claimed he was to blame for the argument between the Paragon reporter and Alan Winston and its unfortunate outcome. It was him, he explained, who had barred the reporter's way to the room of the man who had died in the street the previous night. 'What with the old Jew dying like he did right in front of the refugee house round the corner, the journalist was here sniffing for trouble; looking for an easy headline—You can bet on it! Alan turned up and only got involved on my account; to help me. He was completely fine at first. And polite—Just asking the journalist to leave; as was I. But then he flipped when the man called him a 'loser'. He just lost it.'

Lombard was still running all this through his mind as he neared home a little later, barely noting a taxi cab pulling out from his Mews and driving past him. He had just switched his phone back on – the first time since leaving for Cumbria with Ali – frowned on seeing that Edward Duncan had made several attempts at reaching him, and instinctively turned around when the taxi that had just gone past screeched to a stop to reverse and come to a halt beside him along the kerb.

"Mr Lombard? Are you Mr Lombard? The detective?" a breathless middle-aged woman with a strong Irish accent and bags of dark rings under her eyes called through the cab's open rear window. And she opened her door and stepped out while he was still considering what was happening and how to respond.

"By God! I knew it was you. I—Did you not find the note I put through your letterbox earlier this week?"

"Ahem, I've been away," he replied without thinking.

A terrible storm had descended over him. He could guess who the woman was. She made for a wretched vision with her grey ravaged eyes and black dress against which a silver crucifix caught the early afternoon sun; she was, unmistakably, a timeworn distressed rendition of her daughter: broad-faced, large-breasted, fair and suffering the heat. "That's what I thought when I didn't hear from you," she said; "So you don't know?" "Don't know what?" "I am Maude McGinnis—Jane's mother. I'm afraid my poor Jane is no longer with us, Mr Lombard. She was killed when—"

"How did you know where to find me, Mrs McGinnis?" he interrupted her.

SIX

Whyever Joseph Aratoon had concluded that the time had come to risk visiting eternal hell, the reason, for now, remained a matter only his merciful God could answer.

Maude McGinnis had found his address in Jane's phone, under 'L', together with a photograph of his front door. "Here—Look!" the woman said, holding out the phone for Lombard to see while explaining she was using her daughter's phone owing to hers being locked to an Irish network.

Lombard swallowed hard. He recalled considering the possibility of Jane following him home from Regent's Park on the afternoon they met there but had hardly thought she'd dare. She had, though; and more. She had come into his Mews to photograph his front door and the Mews sign. The truth was, Ali had completely pushed her out of his mind, and now she was dead, mowed down by a speeding car in a hit and run accident, or "murdered by some bad people" as Maude McGinnis put it. And that was not all. With her had died one of her twins and her unborn child. The car that took their lives had never slowed down before or after hitting her. Bizarrely, like her husband's, her last moments were captured on surveillance cameras. She was on a Zebra crossing well-lit by Belisha beacons while on her usual evening stroll with her dog and her twins. The impact of the car had flung her thirty yards along the road and hurled the pram into a parked van. She'd died instantly, as had one of the girls in the pram, while the other, crushed but alive, was left in a critical state with a broken neck. The dog was spared. The hit and run car was later found burnt out in woodland a few miles away; it had been stolen earlier that same day. And the police had already filed the incident as an accident, or involuntary manslaughter by joyriders, for the surveillance footage showed there were two figures in the killer car.

Maude McGinnis had other ideas. Speaking feverishly while holding back tears, she conveyed all this information right there on the kerb by her taxi cab before revealing what had brought her to Lombard's; he, meanwhile, put out of sorts but loath to make a scene in the street, found he had better let her speak. It transpired that on her return from meeting him in Regent's Park Jane had lied to her mother, claimed "her old detective friend" had agreed to "investigate" the apparent suicide of her husband. Then, "spurred on by this good news", she had resumed her own investigation into the matter, whereby she had made a great discovery. "She came across an invoice for a map Joseph bought five years ago, you see. A great discovery," Maude McGinnis repeated; "This is why I needed to see you. She was killed only three days afterwards, you see, and I don't think it is a coincidence— No matter what the police say about joyriders. It's hard to explain—If you would come to Walthamstow I could—"

Like her bereaved widowed daughter before her, it appeared that this bereaved mother's distress was also scheming futile quests.

Lombard, irate on the double account of this unwelcome visitation and the thought of Jane following him home, was minded to dismiss the woman as curtly as manners permitted. Instead, heedful of the fact that her presence was due to her daughter's deception, he settled on sending her on her way as gently as he could, announcing he had only just returned from a long trip, was busy but would call in the coming day or so. "Oh, thank you, Mr Lombard, I knew I could rely on you," the woman uttered with a big sigh and pained attempt at a smile, stepping forward to hug him; "Thank you. My Jane always spoke well of you. She never forgot how kind you were to her when she first came to London. God bless you, now. There are so few beacons of light to ward off the darkness, Mr Lombard. God Bless you, now. Thank you. And by the way, you'll find the address and phone number to contact me on the note I put through your letterbox. Look after yourself now," she said by way of goodbye.

As the woman climbed back in her taxi and left – thanking him again – he hoped he would never see her again.

A moment later, he found Maude McGinnis's note on the mat inside his front door, together with two identical small packages which had been sent to him by post. He ignored the note but opened the packages. They shared a common return address, to a Jane Aratoon in Walthamstow. Further inspection revealed they contained a flash drive, bank statements, various documents and a note stating 'Take a look and tell me I'm wrong if you dare!' It turned out Jane, whose surname was Aratoon owing to her Iranian born husband, had not merely followed him to his Mews, lied to her mother, but also retrieved the plastic bag he'd handed in at the Regent's Park café to post its content directly to his address, taking the precaution to divide it into two small packages she'd assessed would fit through his letterbox.

Now and again the compulsion to become involved in a situation by reason of not having dealt particularly well with another can appear as seductive as a prayer; a shortcut to redemption, or a path to salvation. That said, at this time Lombard had yet to figure out that something of the sort might be going on.

Showered and changed, he ignored Jane's packages which he had left in his hallway, and called Edward Duncan. They agreed to meet for lunch at *The Melchior* in Portland Street the following day and, with Ali's warm scented universe now already mere memory, he let himself think of her without mourning her absence, for a spell, over a glass of Calvados, savouring the perks of the time they just spent together, eyeing without thought the pile of newspapers he had brought home from the Edgware Road café. At some point, one of his neighbours – the National Health Service statistician he knew as Irene – brought his daydreaming to an end when she came by with an invitation for him to call for a drink next door. "Hi there, Xavier. Good to see you. Listen, we have no idea what you said to him, but my husband and I wonder whether you'd like to pop over for a drink later this evening—As a thank you." He scowled, having little idea what she was talking about. "How are you, Irene?" "Oh. You don't know, do you? Of course, you were away. Well—" the woman said, pointing to his Dutch neighbour's property; "He's gone. Allegedly, he said you were a 'total psycho', wouldn't stay here a day longer. The removal men who came to pack his belongings said he decamped to Chelsea. Dare I say, a much better setting for him, don't you agree? And vastly preferable from our perspective, right?" "Preferable?" he said, surprised by the news, which he deemed something of an unexpected development given the almost benign nature of the exchange he recalled occurred between himself and his football player neighbour. "Well, absolutely. Do you not agree?" "I guess I'll reserve judgement on that until I see the next occupant," he said. And he thanked the woman while declining her invitation. "Ok. But you must come for that drink soon though—It would be nice to have you over once. If nothing else to hear what happened between you two. I don't suppose—" "Some other time, Irene," he dismissed her, grinning.

In the end, late into the evening, softened by drink and unable to prevent Jane's news from occupying his mind, wrestling with the notion that the now dead ex-trainee accountant was a fool, he gave in to curiosity.

Jane was no fool. Nor had she lost her senses. She'd remained the methodical and studious girl he recalled her to be. Inside the packages she sent him were copies of her husband's bank statements – annotated with red ink – a flash drive with a video file showing the same's suicide, and further documents and letters together with a detailed summary of her findings and thoughts. He couldn't tell whether she had prepared this summary on his account, but it was beyond question that she had given it time and attention. Acquainting himself with the material, Lombard conceded that, while short on evidence, there was merit to her rationale about her husband's suicide possibly amounting to more than a mere act of desperation by an unhappy man. Here she'd written and underlined the statement: 'A man about to commit suicide does not open his mail an hour before killing himself.' And there: 'No good devout Christian would ever contemplate the sin of suicide!' And also: 'Nothing here is the fancy of a misguided widow's grief!'

One early April morning, Joseph Aratoon had left home at 8:30 a.m. like he did every single weekday, expected at work half an hour later after walking the short distance to the nearby Waltham Forest Housing Services office where he had recently been promoted 'Department Housing Manager'. That day, he failed to get there. Instead, some three hours later, he jumped under a train at Kilburn Station way out on the other side of London. His whereabouts between his leaving home and his suicide were unknown; but he was filmed stepping into Kilburn tube station at 11:43 a.m. and ended his days there 11 minutes later. To the consternation of all who knew him, he left no explanation and none could be found, and no one noted anything peculiar about his mood or behaviour in the time preceding his suicide. At first, Jane had tried to resign herself to the fact that he must have lost his mind that day. Yet, three weeks on from his funeral, a letter addressed to her husband had come through the post, and opening it she had happened upon a short note which read: 'Hi Joseph. Hope you're putting the money to good use. There's more, of course. Please call when you're ready. You're needed again'. The note was printed, unsigned and ended with a mobile phone contact number. Curious, she'd called the number, and when a man answered with the word 'Joseph?' and she'd asked who it was she was speaking to, they had hung up. She tried the number again, to no avail; it would never be answered again. Still, at that time she dismissed the episode as merely odd. Only, not long afterwards, going over her husband's bank statements in order to cancel his direct debits and standing orders, she'd happened upon half a dozen mysterious payments into his current account, some made in the weeks just prior to his death, others in its immediate aftermath. All in all, over a period of five weeks, £5000 had been deposited into his account. Believing these to be mistakes she'd contacted the bank to be told there was no mistake: all payments were made to the account in cash from various branches across London. 'For the avoidance of doubt', they'd even sent her a confirmation letter which contained the line 'and so you will understand that the provenance of the cash deposits cannot be established or further investigated'.

Naturally, Jane was intrigued. She speculated that whilst the payments could be attributed to someone crediting the wrong account – a blunder they'd eventually realize and have put right by informing the bank – it could also prove more sinister; given the nature of her husband's occupation as Housing Manager, these could be bribes from an aspiring or existing council tenant, for she knew, such things happened and London council flats were much sought after. But, after considering the possibility, Jane just as quickly dismissed it: 'Deposits into his bank account not bribes — Too transparent — Not feasible. Bribes would be paid in untraceable cash + Joseph too honest / timid to get himself involved in such wrongdoings!' she wrote, again underscoring her words. Still, by now convinced the unexplained bank deposits and the moneys mentioned in the odd note sent to her husband after his death were connected, she just as readily rejected the 'crediting the wrong account by blunder' hypothesis – and with reason. First, on being returned his belongings by the police after his suicide, she'd found that her husband had opened his mail the last morning he left the house; inside his briefcase was his last bank statement, together with the envelope it had arrived in, which listed two unexplained £800 deposits alongside his usual transactions. And then there was the odd note again, or, more particularly, its syntax; the 'of course' after 'there's more' and the words 'you're needed again' all suggested that whatever was going on wasn't happening for the first time. And so, now on this trail, Jane had trawled through years of her husband's bank statements, ultimately coming across another lot of mysterious deposits. Some four years earlier, over a period of five months in a pattern similar to the recent occurrences, he'd received over £15,000. Here Jane had written: 'Siroun recovering from hole in heart surgery at this time — Joseph came home one day loaded with presents & bought family holiday to Turkey & paid some of mortgage off — said money settlement for attack by council tenant's dog.' However, a call to the council now revealed that no record existed of either a dog attack or settlement in favour of her husband, at that or any other time, forcing her to accept that he had lied. Whatever the reason for his deceit, she came to believe, 'the note sent to him after he died suggests his jumping under the train and both the old and recent mysterious payments into his account are connected. They must be! It's no coincidence that he jumped to his death after reading his bank statement that morning. He must have got himself involved in some bad situation a few years ago,' she added, 'I don't know how or why, but seeing the resumption of payments into his account must have led him to panic.'

On the day Joseph Aratoon had favoured death over his wife's love and that of the children they'd brought together into the world, he left his widow a great burden to shoulder, Lombard conceded at the end of perusing the notes and documents Jane had sent.

He felt a mild discomfort of emptiness inside. It was unrelated to Jane though, or her findings. He could see the logic of her argument. Her husband could easily have engaged in and benefited from shady activities. But it made no sense that what he may have done on a previous occasion would lead him to want to kill himself now. Also, although not trivial, the money involved was small change. And besides, it seemed obvious that the author of the note sent after his death hardly knew him, unaware as they were of his having killed himself all of three weeks prior to their posting it. Like he had told Jane when they met, no man commits suicide on a whim;

especially not a good Christian and father of four. Whyever Joseph Aratoon had concluded that the time had come to risk visiting eternal hell, the reason, for now, remained a matter only his merciful God could answer. And likely belonged to the mundane.

No, the cause of Lombard's malaise lay elsewhere, was more specific, related to his insight into the man's financial situation. Unexplained payments aside, the Council Housing Manager's bank statements revealed a precarious life. Each month, the man's salary and overdraft limit were swallowed up by strings of recurring direct debits covering the couple's mortgage and domestic outgoings. On the face of it, as the household's sole breadwinner, Joseph Aratoon had kept his family afloat at the absolute limit his income afforded, with no room for manoeuvre, indulgence or mishap. This could hardly count as extraordinary, was many a people's lot, but somehow, perhaps because by his own circumstances Lombard had never known such an existence bridled by perpetual financial insecurity, the father-of-four's unenviable position afflicted him – the kind of affliction that makes a man dread tomorrow's unknowns. In this matter, his watching the footage showing Joseph Aratoon's last act on earth very late in the evening hardly helped.

In the event, the three-minute-long date-stamped footage put the manner of Joseph Aratoon's death in Kilburn tube station beyond question. It showed the man, a dark, lanky figure in a brown suit with a coat draped over one arm and a briefcase hanging from the other, standing motionless on the nearly empty station platform, as would any traveller, until, with the train approaching, he suddenly stepped forward towards the platform edge and threw himself on the line, still holding onto his briefcase and coat. The picture was captured from too great a distance to determine his expression, but insomuch as his movements told the story, he appeared a man composed, in command of his thoughts and emotions.

During his stay in Cumbria, Lombard had again failed to get

the old Aston Martin in Ali's barn to fire up. Over time, he'd spent a fair number of hours tinkering with it while Ali was off on her evening horse rides, liking to think he was mechanically competent to bring its 6-cylinder twin carburettor engine back to life. He long ago established it was complete, had carried out fixes here and there, so far all in vain. "It came with the property and two keys. Let her rip and she's all yours," Ali had said. "It could be worth a fair amount once restored," he let her know; "Maybe as much as you paid for the whole farm." "Is that so? Then remember the one about a gift horse, Xavier."

By themselves, the car's body, chassis, suspension, brakes, interior and most of anything else would have required a hefty investment and expertise to be brought back to roadworthy condition, but far from attempting to restore the car, the challenge Lombard set himself was simply to get its engine to fire up at minimal cost. In that his outlay so far had gone towards the purchase of a few basic tools, maintenance products and a new battery, all was well. Now, though, having eliminated all other causes he could think of, he reckoned the engine's reluctance to come to life had to be due to an electrical fault, which could only be diagnosed with a decent multimeter. So, when Edward Duncan called early the next morning to push back their lunch meeting by twenty-four hours, he decided he may as well use his time to source such a device as well as catch up with his mail, sort out his laundry and see to various other chores besides going out to collect the new front brake calliper he'd ordered for his Saab a couple of weeks earlier.

He was about a third of the way through all this when Maude McGinnis had turned up again to knock at his door. He was in a T-shirt and bare feet. Naturally, her second un-wanted intrusion in as many days caused him some agitation, and not the best sort. And on this occasion, standing on the cobbles outside his door clutching her handbag in the same black outfit with the same silver crucifix as on the previous day, if anything she looked even more ravaged and distraught, the bags under her eyes darker and heavier, and crucially – he noticed at once – she stood alone with no taxi or means of transportation in sight.

"Oh! I'm so pleased to find you home, Mr Lombard" she declared, disregarding his scowl with the proud pain of a woman hurt; "I would have called you if I had your number but I don't so—I have a terrible confession to make, Mr Lombard. I had to come back to tell you about it before taking any more of your time. I lied to you, Mr Lombard. I am so sorry."

For a moment, growing grimmer, Lombard wondered whether the woman was about to announce that Jane never died. But not quite: "Yesterday; I lied to you, Mr Lombard— And I shouldn't have. You see, after meeting you at the park, Jane never said that you had agreed to help her find out what happened to her Joseph. It was terribly wrong of me to tell you she had. The truth is that she was so furious she— And I—If we could please have a word, Mr Lombard. I could explain it all to you now. And I won't take much of your time. I just need to tell you what happened," she implored.

Lombard delayed. The woman had returned to appeal to his humanity, deeming, after their previous day's encounter, that he was worth her time and that, evidently, she was worth his, trusting herself enough to have sent her taxi away – presuming she'd made the journey by taxi again. He wasn't impressed. He glared, filled with spite, but only inasmuch as it is easy to despise hungry eyes watching you eat. She was a wretched sight to behold. Had he not acquainted himself with the contents of Jane's packages late into the previous night, he certainly would have sent her on her way. Still, he reluctantly let her in, inviting her to settle at his dining table where she was glad to take him up on his offer of a glass of water.

"Thank you, Mr Lombard. I—"

"No need for thank-yous, Mrs McGinnis," he stopped her; "It's not as if you are giving me much choice. I'm sure I needn't point out that you invited yourself here. Now, please say what you came to say and try to make it quick. So, you lied, you say—And feel terribly guilty about it, is that it?"

"I did indeed. I am truly sorry," she apologized again; "Lying is an abomination."

"Huh," he grinned; "An abomination? You don't say. And here I was thinking it was one of the seven deadly sins," he went on, wryly.

"Not at all," she corrected him; "The deadly sins are lust, gluttony, greed, sloth, wrath, envy and pride. Lying is an abomination."

"Abomination?" he gibed.

"For sure. Proverb 6:16. 'There are six things that the Lord hates, seven that are an abomination to him: haughty eyes, a lying tongue, hands that shed innocent blood, a heart that devises wicked plans, feet that make haste to run to evil, a false witness who breathes out lies, and one who sows discord among brothers.' And, Mr Lombard, please don't tease me. I never travelled far from home, you know."

He sighed, wishing he'd paid no heed to the word 'abomination', and let her speak.

Maude McGinnis's mind was consumed with that most dangerous of poisons: guilt; the kind that stems from uncertainty. In her mind, she had drawn a straight line between her son-in-law's, pregnant daughter's and granddaughter's deaths, and much worse, held herself to blame for the last two.

In the wake of meeting Lombard in Regent's Park, she now explained, Jane had returned home furious and dejected. "Now, I totally shared her misgivings about Joseph deciding to take his own life, you see. Had you met my son-in-law you would know he was incapable of contemplating such a drastic deed. A timid but caring soul he was—A God-fearing man and a good Catholic too. And he loved Jane so very much. He would never have left her without the devil getting a hold of him. When she told me about his bank account and all that money business and showed me that note he was sent—Did she tell you about it? I know she—" "I know about it," he cut her off. "Right. When she told me about it, 'I'm with you,' I told her—'I'm with you,' I said. Like it says in the book: 'And you will know the truth, and the truth will set you free'. Where could be the harm in seeking the truth, I thought. Only now, Mr Lombard, I wish I'd dissuaded her. I do now.

Instead, when she felt so disappointed you wouldn't help her, I tried consoling her. And while we talked things over, discussed what she should do next, I came up with a crazy thought—I did. I said to her that whoever it was who put the money in her Joseph's bank clearly knew his account number. Yet the person who wrote to him after he passed away claiming to be responsible for the money most certainly did not know him; they couldn't have. In these days of instant communications, nobody gets caught writing to someone they know well three weeks after they've passed away. 'So what are the chances of knowing the bank account details of someone you don't know unless they gave or sent you a cheque,' I pointed out. And now—God is my witness—I so wish I had never said those words, Mr Lombard."

And presently – producing a crumpled handkerchief to pat her eyes while holding back tears – she went on to describe how Jane had revisited her husband's bank statements, focussing on his outgoings in the months preceding the first series of mysterious deposits made into his account four years earlier. Soon, she'd honed in on a £500 cheque – an unusually high expenditure for the man – and, due to his not unlike herself also being a stickler for order and keeping receipts, just as quickly established it to be a payment for an antique map of London, the kind Joseph Aratoon was known to collect. And by and by, Maude McGinnis claimed, Jane had tracked down the author of the odd note, only to die herself days later in a hit and run incident which she feared was no accident at all but rather the result of Jane's "great discovery, which would never have happened but for my foolish advice and interference."

"I'm unsure I understand: she tracked down the person who wrote a belated note to your son-in-law a few months ago thanks to a map he purchased four years ago? Is that what you're saying?" Lombard asked.

"It's complicated," she said; "You'd have to—I could show you if you came to Jane's. She bookmarked the pages on her computer browser. There's also an internet radio broadcast, I think it's called. I could show you if you came over. I would of course pay you for your time."

He still wondered what she wanted from him – asked her.

"I think my Jane may have been murdered because she was close to finding out what led my son-in-law to decide to die the way he did, Mr Lombard. If this is so, I would have to take the blame for it, I'm afraid. A heavy burden, it is. I was hoping you'd help me."

"Help you? Huh. Not half an hour ago I recall you saying you came here to apologize for lying to me, Mrs McGinnis. What was it again? That thing that the good Lord hates? An abomination?"

"I did—I did Indeed. I did, Mr Lombard. But like my Jane before me, this woman could do with your helping hand. If not to ease my torments by proving me wrong, to possibly give me a chance to seek justice in the case of you confirming my suspicions—So that the person or persons who hurt my Jane, my unborn granddaughter, my granddaughter and possibly my son-in-law may be punished for their crimes. Such an outcome would of course place an even heavier burden upon my soul than it already carries, but was it to be so it would be God's plan for its redemption."

Lombard scoffed: "God? What about the police, Mrs McGinnis?"

"What could I tell them now? Sure as I'm sitting here they already wouldn't hear a word about my son-in-law's death. And now they've already made up their mind about my daughter's. As I said, it is complicated. I have no evidence, Mister Lombard. Only the kind you call 'circumstantial', I believe. What Jane found out."

Lombard took a deep breath, looked the women up and down: "The apple doesn't fall far from the tree," he mumbled.

"I'm sorry?" she sniffled.

"The apple and the tree, Mrs McGinnis. Now, tell me— And please try not to lie to me again: when she returned home so upset after seeing me, did your daughter fail to mention that I told her I no longer did investigative work?"

The woman raised her thin painted brows: "Oh, she did now, Mr Lombard. She certainly did."

"Right. So, what are you doing here?"

"I—I believe she didn't believe you."

He grinned. The woman was clearly in a stormy place and in need of shelter, a harbour of sorts. He considered advising her that she was foolish to blame herself for her daughter's misfortune. That even in the unlikely event of there being grounds for her suspicions, Jane's heart was likely long set; she'd have gone on probing her husband's death no matter what, with or without her mother's support or advice. But he trusted such counsel would fall on deaf ears, and, with respect to her story about Jane's "great discovery", to say nothing of her being murdered, he gave it no credence. Nothing he had heard or read – be it about Joseph Aratoon or Jane – implied murder or foul play. It belonged to the realm of trivial tragedies; nothing men, women and children are murdered over. The only certainties were that Joseph Aratoon had jumped under a train and Jane was dead on account of a hit and run incident. And although months apart and in different places, both their deaths had been caught on camera, like pretty much everything else that happened in London since the Mayor and the town's transport authorities had fitted the streets and public spaces with surveillance equipment in order to inflict pain and penalty on just about anybody who broke or thought of breaking any civic or traffic rule. Yet, just about anybody could conceal their face, steal a car, invite themselves on a joyride, run over people and disappear.

"Speaking of apples and trees, Mrs McGinnis," he remarked; "Not a fortnight back I recall advising your daughter to let sleeping dogs lie; she clearly paid no notice. A moment ago, you invoked the good book on 'knowing the truth and the truth will set you free'; yet clearly the truth you think you may have discovered hardly set you or your daughter free. Now, didn't all of humanity's misery come in the wake of Adam and Eve's eating the fruit from the tree of knowledge, Mrs McGinnis? The original sin? No matter what the truth is or isn't, Mrs McGinnis, none of it will alleviate your pain—Or fix your guilt. The truth is overrated, Mrs McGinnis. A God-fearing woman's salvation is better served by prayer and chapel. Now that's the truth."

She was undeterred:

"I'm a mother, Mr Lombard. Wonderful are the Lord's works. But none prevail to sweeten a parent's bitter guilt."

He swallowed hard. Understood.

The ring from a phone inside her handbag – the same as he'd heard from Jane's in Fortune Green – startled her. She apologized, composed herself and answered. For the next minute, she mumbled a few 'I-sees' and 'oh-dears', and although it ought to have seemed unimaginable given her all too woeful appearance, her already broad face swelled up and her shoulders stooped with the weight of what she was hearing, leaving her looking even more crushed, her free hand squeezing the crucifix against her black dress. "I'm on my way," she said, hanging up, already getting to her feet; "I'm afraid I need to go, Mr Lombard. The hospital—Jane's little one—The injured twin just took a turn for the worse, they tell me, and they think she might need emergency surgery later on today or tomorrow. I'm next of kin and they need me to sign the consent forms. Anyway, thank you for having me. Jane spoke so fondly of you that I'm sure it would have given her great pleasure to know we met, even at this terrible time. Would you be so kind as to call me a local taxi if possible? Or direct me to a nearby taxi rank?"

Only now he wondered how old she was. On a normal day, she likely could have come across as a credible fifty-year-old. For now, however, she hauled a thousand years across her shoulders.

He had an idea: "Where is the hospital?"

"In Walthamstow. Next to Jane's. We got the child moved near as—"

"Will you be long in there?"

"Oh. I shouldn't think so—"

"Give me a minute to change. I'll give you a lift and then, if that's okay with you, you'll show me all those 'complicated' things you say Jane discovered."

"Are you sure now?"

Although in different boroughs and separated by a few miles, Walthamstow and Mile End were both in East London, near enough to each other in the circumstances. Rather than to give Maude McGinnis a lift, his target was to make it to Mile End. Then again, it was difficult not to feel pity for the poor woman, just as it seemed unlikely that she would ever leave him alone were he to simply let her go. He might as well take a look at Jane's 'great discovery', which she was so keen to show him. Then, even if it proved impossible to put her out of her misery or dissuade her from pursuing the path she was on – which he suspected would be the case – he would be rid of her. He'd see to it that she understood there'd be nothing she could ask from him. You can't squeeze blood out of a stone. Such a message can be conveyed even to a grief-stricken mother and grandmother looking a dark vision of unredeemable suffering.

SEVEN

Wherever they bury her corpse, her fate will be the
same: to be dead and rot.

There was little prospect of Maude McGinnis remaining quiet
on the long drive to Walthamstow, Lombard had anticipated.
But she was. Pensive, exhausted, she slumped in the passenger
seat, taking advantage of the chance afforded her to have a
much-needed rest, at some point closing her eyes to take in
the warm September sun beaming into the car. She hardly
made a sound, other than, without warning, to let him know
that she'd rather he dropped her at the hospital and then drove
on to wait for her at Jane's where her husband – who incidentally
was also named Joseph, and whom she rang on the way –
would provide him with a visitor's parking permit for his car
and look after him until she returned.

"I'd also be obliged if you could keep the things we discussed
about Jane and Joseph to yourself. The truth is none of the
family are aware of any of this unpleasant business and it
would be helpful if it stayed this way for now, Mr Lombard. I
told my husband you were an old friend of Jane's coming to
pay your respects. Jane's body is there, you know, beside little
Anoosheh, the twin—Will be until later today."

"More abomination, Mrs McGinnis?" he baited her.

The woman, it seemed, was prepared to lay herself open to
the Lord's disapproval on account of more than one lie.

He left her outside Whipps Cross Hospital and drove on,
finding Jane's house in a narrow street five minutes away,
a modest two-storey terraced residence with a red-tiled

93

porch and walled front yard indistinguishable from the other properties in the street. Joseph McGinnis came to the door to greet him. A man with a thick, slick backcombed mane of fair hair, a weather-beaten complexion which spoke of the outdoors and the busy eyes and laconism of those well-practiced in quietly passing judgement, he appeared a rugged rock to his wife's anguished presentation. In corduroy trousers and rolled up shirt sleeves, he shook Lombard's hand with the firmness his rough hands and thick forearms advertised. "Hello there. You must be Xavier. I'm Joseph— Maude's husband and Sheenagh's father," he said in an Irish accent identical to his wife's, his breath smelling of whiskey; "Here. Maude said to give you this—Parking permit. It would appear you can't visit around these parts without one of these on your windscreen. This ought to sort you out for a couple of hours."

Lombard thanked him, retraced his steps to place the permit on his dashboard and, heading back to the house, found the man in conversation with a couple of women standing outside the open entrance of the next-door property. "I can hear everything. Seriously. I know that a lady who lived here recently tragically died—But your kitchen is like right by my bedroom on the other side of the wall," one of the women was saying as Lombard joined them. "That's too bad indeed," Joseph McGinnis retorted; "The thing is, Miss, I'm responsible for building neither of the houses, you see. And we're only passing through. Here for the week—Burying my dead daughter." "Oh. I'm sorry about that. Like I said, I was aware that—I didn't know her. We only moved here three weeks ago. But honestly, if you could try to keep the noise down. It's like we're in the same room. And I'm sorry for your loss. But it's the thin walls—I can really hear every sound." Joseph McGinnis scowled at the woman, turned to Lombard signalling him to step in: "Every ewe is only as good as her feeblest hoof," he grumbled, shutting the front door behind him.

And he led the way along a nearly pitch-dark corridor past shut doors and a stairwell to the upstairs from whence came the muffled sounds of young children playing, and then down a small flight of steps into a kitchen flooded with the light from an open French window which looked out onto a sunlit garden. The near total shadow within the house outside the kitchen was no accident. All the windows' curtains were drawn, and within the dark corridor a wall mounted mirror had been covered with fabric, an arrangement echoed in the kitchen where a small blanket was wrapped around what appeared to be a free-standing mirror. Once there, Joseph McGinnis stopped by a display of food and refreshments on a clothed table – a few sandwiches, some biscuits and various soft and alcoholic drinks – offered Lombard a drink while filling himself a large tumbler with whiskey, grunted approval on hearing "I'll have the same", muttered "Help yourself to the buffet if you want something to eat!", and led the way out into the bright garden to the shade from a parasol which belonged to a plastic outdoor furniture set.

Overlooked by the neighbouring properties, the brick walled garden consisted of a treeless parched lawn dotted with toys with, near to a shed at its far end, a tethered small black and white dog that leapt and yelped as they settled down under the parasol, at which time it lay quietly down with its chin down and its eyes and nose firmly pointed in their direction. To judge by a newspaper and reading glasses on the table, Joseph McGinnis had spent time there previously. For now though, holding on to his whiskey tumbler, he seemed inconvenienced in his role as a host expected to start small talk with a stranger; the matter seemed simple enough, but to all appearances, he looked incapable of coming up with a fitting way to open conversation with a man whose sole distinction was that – from what his wife had told him – he had apparently known his deceased daughter. No words came to him as he downed his whiskey to stare awkwardly at the dog at the end of the garden, putting Lombard in the peculiar position of being the one to initiate conversation.

"I'm sorry for your loss, Mr McGinnis," he said.

"Oh. I'm sure you are," the man replied, peering at the whiskey he now gently swirled in the tumbler between his fingers. Then: "You're French—Knew our Sheenagh, I understand."

This was the second time he'd heard this name, leading him to presume it referred to Jane.

"That's right."

"You knew her well?"

"We were neighbours once. Some years back. But had lost contact lately."

"Oh. So I take it Maude called you."

"I'm sorry?"

"If you lost contact—Maude's been ringing everyone Sheenagh's ever known with the news. No sense of dignity. I guess she called you."

"Oh. Right—She called me."

"Well, you needn't have come. The bloody woman's a bully. She'd have the whole of London come to pay their last respects if she had her way."

Lombard frowned:

"Did you travel from Ireland?" he asked.

"From Ireland? Indeed. From Ireland. Flew over with Sheenagh's sisters and Dairine and Maude. Sheenagh's brother is expected later this afternoon; Air Corps—he couldn't arrange leave before now. But he'll be here for the funeral tomorrow."

"Right."

"Right," echoed Joseph McGinnis. "Tell me, Xavier—Xavier, is that what you call yourself now?"

"Uh-huh."

"Good. Tell me, Xavier: how would you fancy a dog?" he asked with a nod towards the dog tethered at the end of the garden.

"A dog?"

"Sheenagh's," the man pronounced; "He was by her side when she was run over— Is in great need of a new home now, he is. It's that or be put to sleep. And that wouldn't be right now, would it? Let me tell you: it would be a damn shame when you reflect that he is the only thing to have escaped unharmed from the car that claimed Sheenagh. Maude would probably tell you that it was God's plan to have him live. All the same, he'll be put to sleep—Unless some good soul would have him. So let me ask you again: how would you fancy a dog?"

Lombard scowled, observed the dog for a moment:

"He looks like a good dog," he said; "But I'm not looking to adopt a dog just now."

Joseph McGinnis nodded and, after taking a swig of whiskey said: "Well, isn't it hot today?"

"It is."

"It most certainly is," the man echoed; "It is hot."

And these were the last words that passed between them. Both went on drinking their whiskey until the sound of voices from within the kitchen relieved the quiet. Maude McGinnis stepped into the garden, looking the same as when Lombard had left her at the nearby hospital; pain, pride, black mourning dress and silver crucifix gleaming in the sunshine. But she was no longer alone. On either side of her stood two younger women, also in mourning dresses, and with them two little girls. The girls were Jane's, shared the dark eyes and long eye-lashes he remembered from meeting her twins in Hampstead cemetery. The women were unmistakably Jane's sisters and their father's daughters: thick-haired and wiry, one ungainly and the other pretty but tight-chinned, hardship and the outdoors etched across their features. Tightly gathered together like crows in the sun, the three women looked conspiratorial and furtive, with much-concerned biting of lips and crossing of arms over black dresses, probably discussing the fate of the twin at the hospital. At once the two children left them to run to their knees among the toys in the grass while the dog was all leaps and yelps again, and Joseph McGinnis ignored everyone. Lombard was not displeased to see Maude McGinnis, rose up to greet her, keen to proceed with the business which had brought him there, for he was riled up. Back at his Mews, the woman had failed to mention so many of her family were at Jane's, alluded only to her husband and, at that, had only done so once they were on their way. It seemed that, not for the first time, Maude McGinnis had deceived him. Now, he looked forward to taking his leave. However, Maude McGinnis had other ideas. "Did my husband give you the parking permit for your car, Mr Lombard?" she called. He told her he did. "Good," she said before quickly introducing Jane's sisters – he failed to catch their names – and announcing to the company "I think I'll take our visitor to see Jane now. Please come, Mr Lombard."

For a moment, he hoped that the woman was merely coming up with an excuse to get him away in order to show him the 'complicated' things she'd talked about earlier. But her husband appeared to know different. "Why trouble the man with all that macabre business, woman——He barely knew her. Can't you leave your daughter's corpse alone!" Joseph McGinnis intervened. "Jesus, Joseph! You don't be so quick to speak for other people now. Why don't you keep to your whiskey and trouble your mind over things that concern you. For eight years, Xavier and Jane knew each other. He was kind to her when she first arrived in London. And besides, I'm sure I'm not wrong to suppose he can speak for himself; isn't that so, Xavier?"

In this fashion, Maude McGinnis dropped the formality of addressing him as "Mr Lombard", and a moment later, having every intention not to let him speak for himself and respectfully pass on the chance to view her daughter's corpse, she led him back inside the house through the corridor's shadow and, by and by, opened the door to a candle-lit room.

"My sister Dairine, who is supposed to be mounting vigil over the departed. Take all the time you need, Xavier," she said after crossing herself inside the door and moving aside to let him step in.

Dairine turned out to be a large woman asleep on a chair with headphones plugged into her ears from a device resting on her lap; she was clearly also Maude McGinnis's identical twin. Amidst flowers and condolence cards, the room's furniture had been piled to one side to accommodate two gleaming black coffins; one small and the other larger, placed side by side. The small one was shut, but the larger had its lid open. Inside, lying in state, resting over white satin, Jane's embalmed face was bleached and waxy, and the rest of her was clad in a light pink dress with a crucifix placed on her breast and rosary beads laced between her fingers. Someone had manicured her nails, and the bump under her dress led Lombard to wonder whether it was customary to bury heavily pregnant women with their dead unborn child still inside them.

He swallowed hard, delayed over her coffin for what seemed an appropriate time as it crossed his mind that Jane certainly was not someone he'd ever thought he would see dead one day, and that all things considered he never should have seen her dead, was never meant to be there. He turned back towards the door to find Maude McGinnis standing on the threshold softly reciting a prayer into a large white handkerchief.

"My heartfelt condolences, Mrs McGinnis," he said; "She's a great loss."

"Such a brave girl," the woman sobbed; "So young. So much to look forward to—You have no idea how much I hope this has nothing to do with that terrible business about her husband, Xavier. Look at her—Within weeks of bringing a new life into God's world and now—I could never forgive myself if—"

"I'm sure. Why don't we see to that now, Mrs McGinnis," he cut her off. And he gently grabbed her arm to force her round and they left Jane and her still sleeping vigil to their candlelit duskiness.

By the look of it, the basement had recently been extended, providing, for such a modest property, an unexpectedly large windowless neon-lit open plan space that housed banks of filing cabinets and rows of shelves stacked with documents and filing boxes, all neatly arranged. Most wall space was covered with street maps, most framed behind glass. "This was Joseph's office and you're looking at his map collection," Maude McGinnis explained, leading the way to a desk with a laptop and loose paperwork; "There must be tens of thousands of them filed in those cabinets. It was his hobby. Well, more of an obsession, I suppose."

Neither were in a mood to entertain Joseph Aratoon's map collection though, so while she remained standing, she invited Lombard to sit at the desk and by means of a few documents and the laptop divulged the "great discovery" her daughter had uncovered shortly before her death.

Here she showed him one of Joseph Aratoon's old bank statements; it indicated that about three months before the first series of unexplained payments had made their way into his account four years earlier, the man had drawn a cheque for £500, a rare occurrence as, direct debit and standing order aside, he hardly ever used his personal account. Next, while trawling through the man's emails, Jane had determined this amount to be payment for a seventeenth-century map of London he'd purchased on an online auction site: "Look here, Xavier: Jane found this invoice. It says well done for winning the map, and there is the seller's name, address and phone number. The map's the one over there," Maude McGinnis said, pointing to a large map taking pride of place on a nearby wall. "Jane guessed he paid for it using his personal account rather than their joint account because he didn't want her to know how much he spent on it." And having established this much, in keeping with her mother's premise that the party culpable for depositing money into her husband's account was unlikely to have known him and had learnt of his account particulars by way of his having written them a cheque, Jane had called the number on the invoice and at once recognized the voice of the person who answered as that of the man who'd also answered the number from the note sent to her husband a few weeks after his death. "'It's the same man, Mum!' she kept saying, 'It's the same man! What does it mean?'"

"How could she be so sure? Did they talk much? Isn't it the case that the person who'd picked up when she called the number on the note had said just one word before hanging up: 'Joseph?'" Lombard asked. "Oh, they never spoke, Xavier. Jane said that this time around the man also only said one word: 'Hallo?'—Then, like when she'd called the note's number, he hung up on hearing her, and she never got through again. But she couldn't have been more certain he was the same man. Anyway—Let me show you. Here—"

Now, equipped with a name and address from the invoice, Jane had quickly tracked the man online, which proved easy since, to her and mother's astonishment, he turned out to be a widely known and respected film producer and director. "Look," said Mrs McGinnis, breathlessly showing him book-marked browser pages on the laptop, all of a sudden so excited as to appear to be released from her grief; "Avery Weyland. That's him. He isn't just anybody. And Jane came across this too, to make sure. That's him here with the deep voice."

Standing next to Lombard leaning forward towards the laptop, her breast weighing on his shoulder, she clicked here and there, for a while kept him listening to a BBC Radio Four podcast of a panel answering questions on 'The Role of Film-Makers As Culture-Makers', interjecting "That's him now!" whenever a distinctly deep and educated male voice spoke out of the laptop speakers. "It's quite some voice he's got on him, wouldn't you say? Jane would never have got it wrong. She had a good ear, you know." Lombard agreed the man's voice was particularly deep, most certainly deep enough as to be distinctive. A summary biography revealed that alongside being a film producer-director, the thirty-seven-year-old Avery Weyland was the son of an acclaimed novelist, had an actor for a brother, was currently married to a television comedienne and previously divorced from a serving Member of Parliament's daughter. In addition, he was the father of two boys. Neither his nor any other names connected to him were familiar to Lombard, but by the look of it, in the words of Maude McGinnis, Avery Weyland could not indeed be described as just anybody.

Therein lay Jane's "great discovery": four years earlier her husband had purchased online a map from a well-connected film producer-director, and before her untimely death she'd come to think, by reason of the latter's voice – although she never heard him pronounce more than two words on the phone – that he was the person responsible for the note about money sent to her deceased husband, and on this account was implicated in his decision to commit suicide. And this discovery, or so believed Maude McGinnis, had provided cause enough to warrant her murder.

"So what do you think, Xavier?" Maude McGinnis wished to know.

"I'm not sure what to think, Mrs McGinnis," Lombard replied without haste, eyeing a photograph of Avery Weyland on the laptop screen; somehow, the man's exterior made a good impression of what he imagined a film producer-director ought to look like: mid-thirties to forties, lean, casual smart, poised with an easy smile and confident gaze, sophisticated and engaging.

"Jane was adamant it was him."

"A deep voice is not that uncommon."

"A deep voice like his is. I certainly never heard the likes of it in all my born days."

"She never spoke to him, you say. How would he have known who she was when she last called?"

"She used the landline. He would have been able to check the calling number and, you see, if he knows Joseph's address and bank account details, it wouldn't be all that far-fetched if he also knew his home phone number?"

"Huh. It does seem odd; I give you that," Lombard let out, swallowing hard; "But murder?"

"What if he feared Jane was onto him?"

"Onto him for what, Mrs McGinnis?"

"The money. The money in Joseph's account—Whatever it means."

"A few thousand pounds, Mrs McGinnis. I trust I said it before, but let me put it to you another way: do you really believe a good Christian, father and husband would kill himself over a few thousand pounds? And then someone murder your daughter over the same amount?"

"I know it sounds contrary to common sense and to God's decency, but—This is why I came to see you. I—"

Lombard, realising she still leant beside him weighing on his shoulder, got to his feet and made for the framed map on the wall that had cost Joseph Aratoon £500. He found it to be a large, rather primitive drawing which depicted London as a rough circle made of tightly packed narrow streets nestling around the Thames; it was dated 1659.

"Expensive," he remarked.

"I guess it's an antique," Maude McGinnis ventured.

"May I ask, if anything, what exactly Jane was planning on doing about this Mister Weyland after her last call?" he said, turning back towards her. Standing by the desk beyond the crucifix against her black dress she was all grief and dark rings again.

"I had to watch the film of my daughter and granddaughter being hit by the car that killed them," the woman said; "I'm not saying the police are wrong about it being an accident. I don't know. But Jane was in no doubt this man was somehow involved with her Joseph. And—"

"Did she find out anything else about him, Mrs McGinnis?"

"About whom?"

"Avery Weyland. I don't suppose your son-in-law and he knew each other."

"Oh. I shouldn't think so. Oddly enough, reading about him Jane did find out that they were pupils at the same primary school somewhere in North London—I can't recall the name now. But they couldn't have been in the same class as there were two years between them."

Lombard grinned and headed back towards the desk where he contemplated the address on the map receipt still on the desk – 'The Orchard, Downshire Hill, London NW3'.

"And that's it? There's nothing linking them besides the online map transaction?" he asked.

"Well, there's the note and—"

"I know about the note, Mrs McGinnis," he interjected; "Now," he went on; "Everything has its place, wouldn't you agree?"

"Everything has its place in God's good creation," she replied.

He grunted: "Indeed, Mrs McGinnis; in all of God's good creation. But the problem here is that nothing seems to have its place—Jane, your son-in-law, this Mr Weyland, the bank money, the note, the suicide, death. Nothing appears to belong together, yet, oddly, it all seems connected somehow. I grant you that. But still, I do think you needn't torment yourself about the circumstances of your daughter's death, Mrs

McGinnis. In any event, as a favour to Jane, I'll see what I can do to help shed light on the disorder—Put things in their proper place. Okay? But I'm not making any promises. And again, at this particularly trying time for you and your family, I don't think you should cause yourself unnecessary distress by imagining the worst. I can't think of a better time for you to have faith; you understand, Mrs McGinnis?"

The woman understood, would have embraced him if he'd not taken a step back, instead thanked him profusely and led the way back upstairs, shedding tears of relief. He expected they would head for the front door and the freedom of the street outside but, as they reached the dark corridor on top of the stairs they were met by one of Jane's sisters who evidently had been waiting for them. She pulled her mother aside, quickly whispered in her ear, and, after nodding, Maude McGinnis turned back to him with a penitent air. By now, he knew her well enough to guess this meant he was about to be asked yet another favour. As he feared, he was right: "I'm afraid I have something else to ask you, Xavier. I'm very sorry. But Jane and Anoosheh are due to be buried tomorrow and—" she began.

Any time in the next hour or so, she disclosed, while standing in the darkness next to her grave-faced daughter, Jane's body was due to be taken to the local Catholic Church; there she would spend her last night. A hearse was on its way to collect her, but, as it was provided with just two men, she wondered if Lombard would be good enough to stay until their arrival to act as a pallbearer and help carry the coffin from the house to the hearse. Together with her husband and the two hearse-men, Jane's brother had been expected to make the fourth man required for the task, but he'd just called to say he was being delayed and so the family wondered whether Lombard would be good enough to remain until either the son or the hearse arrived, whichever came first. "I'm so sorry to visit this request upon you, Xavier. You won't be needed to carry little Anoosheh's coffin, though."

There are things which are next to impossible to say no to;

he ended up spending the next half-hour in the garden over tea and whiskey in the company of the McGinnises. In the sunshine and shade around the parasol, sombre circumstances made for a sombre mood. Jane's two playing daughters provided some background lightness, but conversely, the sight and sound of the recently orphaned children acting without a care in the world seemed to prey heavy on the adults' minds.

Still, everybody was obliged to him for staying, a kind act they repaid with conversation, or, at any rate, more conversation than he wished for, so that by the time he took his place alongside Jane's coffin to help carry it out to the waiting hearse, it was fair to say he'd become fairly-well acquainted with her family.

The McGinnises came from Knockavally, a locality in County Galway on the West coast of Ireland where, as century-old hill sheep farmers, the family kept over two hundred acres of land, Joseph McGinnis all but single-handedly looking after a herd of about four hundred and fifty purebred native hill ewes. The sleeping woman by the name of Dairine who kept vigil over Jane's body was indeed Maude McGinnis's twin; she never married and ran a laundry and dry-cleaning business the sisters had inherited. Jane's two elder sisters, one of whom was a veterinarian, the other a farmer, were both married, each with their own families, and Jane's brother – a fact he already knew – was in the Irish Air Force. By way of explanation for Lombard's presence, Maude McGinnis let it be known – again – that he had come by to pay his respects after being informed of Jane's passing away. This met with all round thank-yous, and he learnt that many visitors – mostly neighbours – had kindly come by the house to offer their condolences, although unlike he, who had turned up in a befitting dark suit – a much-appreciated gesture – few had made the effort to dress for the occasion, turning up instead in casual wear. "Says something about London, I guess," reflected one of the sisters. "It does indeed. Now what would they make of that in your holy scriptures, Maude? A great babel built on the land of Sodom, Gomorrah and Nineveh? Ah! Why the heck did Sheenagh leave home for a place like this!" commented Joseph

McGinnis, by then plainly speaking through the whiskey. "Leave it alone, Dad," cut in the other sister, then to Lombard: "You must forgive my father. He thinks the world lost its way the day men stopped wearing hats and showing deference to their social superiors." "Indeed I do. This place is the pits! The last true Englishman was Francis Drake. And he was a no-good scoundrel of a pirate, he was. But he was true and, to his sorrow I'm sure, an Englishman," Joseph McGinnis declared. "And you would know a no-good scoundrel if you met one, wouldn't you now, Joseph?" interjected Maude McGinnis. "No two scoundrels are alike, woman," Joseph McGinnis retorted; "You tell me—You should know: I know I'm not the only one to have eaten chips from your knickers." "Joseph!" "Father!" "Huh! Quiet I shall be. After all, this is no place for a man. This is London!" "This is London indeed, father," intervened one of the sisters again; "Where your Irish daughter married an Iranian and had French friends." "Now, I thought I told you all not to ever mention that one in front of me again, woman," Joseph McGinnis thundered; "Terrible—It's a terrible thing the man did to my lass, destroying himself and leaving his family like that—Most reprehensible. Don't mention his name again, you hear now!" "I didn't mention his name," the woman protested; "'An Iranian' is what I said." "Really? And what Iranian may you be referring to then, may I ask?"

This exchange aside, most of the time was solemnity and preoccupation. "It would have been good to bring Jane back home, have a proper wake and funeral and lay her to rest in our local cemetery, but the paperwork and cost make it difficult. This way at least she'll be near her Joseph," Maude McGinnis whispered away from her husband's ear; "He didn't have anyone, you know. No family to speak of after his mother passed away when he was a teenager. Jane was his whole life. So it's probably a good thing they'll be near one another now. And it will look better, someone with the same name nearby. He isn't in consecrated ground since he forfeited his right to that, of course. But these sorts of things didn't matter to Jane." Joseph McGinnis may have been drunk, but his ears still heard: "Of course these things didn't matter to her, woman. Your daughter was no fool. Wherever they bury her corpse, her fate will be the same: to be dead and rot."

And then, there were Jane's girls, and their injured sister in hospital, and the house and its contents. Soon, the family – including Jane's delayed brother – would head back to Ireland, but Maude McGinnis would remain in Walthamstow for a while, at least until her granddaughter was well enough to be discharged from hospital and the probate process was completed, so that the house and its contents could be put up for sale. Perhaps because it bore less emotional significance than most other questions, a soft option amid adversity, everybody joined in a discussion about what to do with the tethered dog after Joseph McGinnis asked Lombard again if he "would fancy having him".

"Bless you, Xavier," Maude McGinnis said when the time came to let him go; "I knew I could rely on you. About payment for your services—"

He told her not to worry about money, promised to be in touch, asked her not to come to his place again and, back at his car found a £100 penalty Charge Notice under the windscreen wiper; he'd overstayed the visitor's parking permit Joseph McGinnis had provided him by 28 minutes.

He grunted, leant back against his car and rang a former colleague. He could still call in favours, although he preferred not to; a favour received translates into an obligation of return. Nothing that had come to light in the past couple of hours suggested the police had not exercised due diligence in their investigation into Jane's death. Yet, before starting to look into it, it seemed sensible to verify they hadn't chosen to shrug off the incident as a random hit-and-run on account of the reckless nature of the crime and Jane's ordinariness. It was known to happen. Indeed, for all Maude McGinnis's fears and her daughter's "great discovery", he himself remained of the opinion that Jane's death was the result of a grotesque act of mindless violence, even if some out of place things quite possibly called for attention.

Detective chief inspector Mark Badal answered his call and readily consented to find out what his Walthamstow colleagues knew of the hit-and-run incident that had cost Jane her life. "It's a personal matter. She was an acquaintance," Lombard disclosed; "Her mother just needs reassurance that things were done properly to find the car's occupants. It would mean a great deal to me if I could reassure her on the matter."

EIGHT

What if they like it?

Lombard had reservations about engaging in matters relating to Alan Winston. By all accounts, the puppy snatcher was Edward Duncan's concern, not his. Given the media and police interest, he really ought to have consulted with the latter before heading to Mile End, which is what would have happened had the man not pushed back their lunch by a day and, in all likelihood, had Maude McGinnis not shown up at his Mews in want of a lift to East London. Still, this was only meant as a trip to satisfy curiosity, so it hardly seemed inappropriate, and besides, matters worthy of reporting may well come from it, although, truth be told, this was a matter of indifference to Lombard.

This being so, he left Walthamstow to head South towards Mile End as the late afternoon sun engulfed the rush hour traffic with firelight. Barely a fortnight had passed since Alan Winston's murder of the Paragon reporter, but whilst it made national news it ostensibly had failed to make much of an impression on the streets of Mile End. It took some time enquiring here and there to locate the murder venue, which, at the conclusion of a lengthy search for a paying parking bay with a free space, he found to be a three-storey high townhouse with a glass and wrought iron front door flanked by a few nameless doorbells at the back of a dead-end which had seen better days. Trying a couple of bells brought a balding man eating toast to the door who, catching sight of Lombard's suit, at once began to explain why he couldn't talk to him on account of the police having advised the occupants of the house against speaking to the media or anyone else, adding that in any case he knew nothing of the murder which had occurred in the hallway he now stood in as he was at work at the time. Lombard assured him he needn't fear, that he was not from the media or much concerned with a murder, having come only on a private matter necessitating his speaking with a Mister John Bowdion. "Oh. Johnny. He just stepped out. He took the old man's old mutt for a walk in the green around the corner. He should be back soon," the bald man volunteered with much relief; "You should have said so at once. Anyway, if you can't wait, just head to the end of the street, take a right, then a right again, and you should come across him on the green there." "Right. And how may I recognize him?" "Easy. Look for a fat pony-tailed bloke in a dirty red T-shirt with a grey cocker spaniel."

This proved reliable information. On stepping into the nearby green brimming with people picnicking or sipping wine on the lawns or otherwise enjoying the early evening sunset, he found just who he was looking for, although it would have been more accurate to describe John Bowdion as heavy-built rather than fat. Blond, pony-tailed and scruffily dressed, seated on a bench and connected by a retractable leash to an old grey cocker spaniel that stood six or so feet away from him gloomily staring at the ground, he looked older than the thirty-three years reported in the papers, possibly on account of the fact that he was thumbing away on his mobile phone with the ingrate` air of a man cross with the world. Perhaps this also explained why he had a whole bench to himself in the otherwise crowded green. Lombard observed him for a moment, realigned his suit sleeves and pulled them up to expose his cufflinks – today they were smooth gold set with a single small blood-red ruby star in the corners, matching his leather strapped gold watch – and stepped forward:

"John Bowdion?" he enquired with a placating grin.

"Who wants to know?" the man replied, looking up in hostile surprise.

"I do, Mr Bowdion. Laurent Lagarde," Lombard announced, holding out his hand in greeting; "A pleasure to meet you. A bald man at your residence was good enough to let me know I'd find you here; he mentioned you had a dog, so I put two and two together. Do you mind if I sit down? My feet are killing me." And without waiting he settled on the bench next to the man, took a deep breath and let out a loud sigh of relief. John Bowdion had ignored his offer to shake hands, instead holding onto his phone insisting on looking suspicious. Now, he ran his eyes up and down Lombard sitting beside him, paused on the cufflink he could see.

"Please, do not mind me," Lombard went on; "Do go on with what you were doing, Mr Bowdion. I apologize for the intrusion."

"Huh! Apologize for the intrusion? Well, you're right—I am John Bowdion. What is it you want?" the other commanded, ever more hostile; now the phone between his fingers began to beep shrilly.

"A mere minute of your time, if that's alright with you," Lombard grinned; "But please, in your own good time. I'm in no hurry and this is such a lovely spot to take advantage of such a lovely evening."

"Who did you say you were again?"

"Laurent Lagarde—Private investigator. Let me clear up one thing at once though: my being here is unconnected with the murder that occurred at your address recently—A terrible event I understand you witnessed and which I'm aware you are not at liberty to discuss until the police finish their investigation."

John Bowdion scowled then glared at the phone still beeping between his fingers. He switched it off to silence it: "What do you mean 'private investigator'?" he asked.

"Like a detective, you know. I'm here in London working on behalf of a Paris detective agency. But maybe you already read about me in the papers," Lombard suggested; "I'm the mystery man they reported has been asking questions about Alan Winston these last few months. And, to be clear, I am French—Not Italian."

John Bowdion frowned back at him, unsure what to say. Still grinning, Lombard gave him space.

"What is it you want from me?" the other said at last.

"A moment of your time, Mr Bowdion; a mere moment of your time, if that's all right. I'd appreciate it if you could help me with a couple of questions about Alan Winston. Such as— For instance—Did he ever mention anything to you about being harried or running scared?"

"Harried?"

"Indeed—As in running scared from a stranger—Such as myself perhaps."

John Bowdion sneered under his furrowed brows. Then:

"I couldn't say. I hardly knew him. Since you read the papers and claim to be a private investigator, I'd have thought you'd know he was only here for a few weeks and used a false name. Were you what he was running from?"

Lombard grinned, satisfied: "I shouldn't think so. It's just— You see, I read what you said about him only getting involved in that business with the Paragon reporter to assist you. So, naturally, I wondered if the two of you had got along—Got close. Men sharing a house, you know."

"There are eight bedsits in the house, mister. Ports for passing ships, mostly. What if we had got along, though? What would you want from me?"

"Well, I guess I'd ask you whether he ever mentioned a French girl who goes by the name of Justine. I guess that's what I would be asking if the two of you had got along."

Now he had John Bowdion's full attention: "Justine?" he chortled.

"Uh-huh. Justine," echoed Lombard.

"Right—Justine. What about Justine?" John Bowdion queried.

Lombard ignored him, so the other asked again: "What about Justine? Was she a girlfriend?"

Lombard grinned, running his eyes across the crowds lounging around the green. This was an easy game.

"Well, whatever she was," he said; "I don't suppose it matters anymore. What with him being a fugitive on the run now, it's likely just a matter of time before they catch him and my employer gets a sample of his DNA."

"You speak in riddles, Mister," John Bowdion brooded, clearly frustrated while attempting to put the particulars he'd just heard into some kind of meaningful shape; "I haven't got the slightest what you're on about regarding Alan and that Justine. Whatever it is, I never heard the name before and couldn't care less. So—"

It seemed a good time to put him out of his misery:

"Oh. My apologies if I gave the impression something sinister is going on, Mr Bowdion. It's quite the contrary, really. My understanding is that Alan Winston had a merry time with our young Justine. I'm told they met in Brighton before he came here to Mile End. She's seventeen, has a drug history, is expecting and believes he is the father. Little to write home about there, I guess. But she also happens to be the heiress to a rather large fortune and her concerned guardians want to know what's what. Given the event you know about, I should think they're praying he isn't going to be the daddy— Supposing they weren't already. A very messy business indeed— And I shouldn't really be talking about it."

"Huh! You don't say," John Bowdion exclaimed, putting his phone away to start rolling a cigarette between his nicotine-stained fingers. He nodded to himself with a sneer, as if amused, suddenly less taut and bristly.

"Damn it," the man let out now, heavy again.

There seemed little reason for Lombard to delay now; he'd got what he came for. But then a thought occurred to him:

"What about the old man?" he asked.

"The old man?"

"The man who died in the street the night before the morning of the reporter's murder. Did Alan get close to him during his stay at the house? Could that have been why he joined in your attempt to stop the reporter going into his room that morning?"

"Huh! Not a chance," John Bowdion dismissed the idea at once; "As I said, eight bedsits—Mostly revolving doors. The old man was ninety-one and very much minded his own business. Spoke to no one except his dog and me. We were the longest and only sitting tenants; four years to my account, six to his. Regardless though, Alan was barely here; either at work or out partying. His dead-end bedsit room was somewhere for him to crash, not socialize."

"I see."

"Talking of which, could I talk you into adopting an old dog?" John Bowdion now asked, jerking his stubbly chin towards the grey cocker spaniel at the end of its leash that had yet to stop staring sadly at the ground; "She isn't much to look at, but she's no trouble either. She was the old man's. I can't keep her. I put an ad out—'Free dog to good home'—But no bites so far."

Lombard frowned: "Well now—What do you know? This is the second time this afternoon I'm offered the opportunity to adopt a dog. And I'm afraid I'll give you the same answer I gave before: No thank you."

"Maybe you know someone who wants her—"

"I don't. If things are that bad for you, though, what about the dead old man's family? Won't they have her?"

John Bowdion scoffed between his teeth, as if something immensely stupid had just been said: "He had no family. Do you think a ninety-year-old man would choose to end up in some lousy Mile End bedsit by himself if he had family to call on?"

"It was just a thought."

"A dumb thought," came the reply at once; "Samuel Newman had no family, Mister. He was an old Jew—Polish born—An old Auschwitz survivor no one wished to know or cared much about; unless you count the local brats who hurled abuse at him on account of his Star of David medallion whenever he ventured out; or that slimeball Paragon shit-stirrer who hurried here to defame his character after his death."

"I'm not sure I follow," Lombard said, curious; "Why would a reporter be interested in the character of a man no one wished to know or cared about, Mr Bowdion?"

"On account of his being a Jew who croaked in the fucking street while remonstrating with a bunch of folks who were busy celebrating the news that a drone attack had just slaughtered a busload of Israeli commuters in Jerusalem. That's why,"

114

declared John Bowdion with a wry smile; "Old Newman was the good guy here. But when he heard of the circumstances of his death, the Paragon hack—A local man—Must have thought it would be a good thing if he could turn him into a villain. Likely had his headline ready already: 'Old Zionist Dies Hurling Abuse at Refugees'; or 'Israel's Policies Infect London's East End Streets.' Jack-the-fucking-ripper, right! The old man's not dead a night and this over-educated piece of work turns up here with the landlord's agent in tow wanting to get into his room to dig up dirt. I guess I ought to keep this to myself, but had Alan not turned up and taken exception to being insulted, the no-good fucking bastard would probably have got away with it too. I shouldn't be telling you this but—"

No matter what he shouldn't be telling, John Bowdion now told it all. He angrily lit his cigarette and spoke like a man possessed for the next couple of minutes. Lombard's casual question about the dead old man's family – or lack of it, as it turned out – had clearly touched a raw nerve, brought up all manner of dark thoughts inside John Bowdion's mind. A demon unleashed, speaking mostly to himself through a barrage of expletives, the man described how in the wake of the old man's death he had come face to face with the Paragon reporter and his landlord's agent in the hallway while coming downstairs from his bedsit to check on the old man's marooned howling dog; how he'd warned them that their trying to enter the dead man's room to look through his personal belongings was illegal and immoral; how he'd let them know his thoughts about The Paragon being an antisemitic rag which peddled prejudices and pandered to Jew-haters under the cover of politics; and how, as he'd already stated to the papers and the police, on arriving home to find him blocking the way to the old man's room, Alan Winston had opted to take a stand by his side and only resorted to striking the reporter after the latter had derisively called him a 'loser', and then had remained there to watch the stricken man choke to death before heading upstairs to gather his few belonging and flee. "So you see, it could be said that the drone that killed dozens of Israeli commuters produced two more deaths in London and made a murderer of another; all because a ninety-one-year-old holocaust survivor with no place to go and no one to love him just couldn't keep his mouth shut when some folks decided to celebrate the slaughter of Jews. Samuel Newman was a good guy."

By the time he fell quiet again, John Bowdion had begun to rock back and forth, perched on the edge of the bench and hugging his chest, his face a dark grimace and a rolled-up cigarette burning between his tense fingers. It made it difficult to decide whether he was in great pain, great trouble or both; at best, he looked like someone who had suffered a great wrong, a helpless indignant and seething soul in need of pity or kindness.

"Well—You say the old man had no one to care for him. By the sound of it, though, he had you, Mr Bowdion," Lombard remarked helpfully.

These words – expressed more out of pity than empathy – had a most astonishing effect. At once, John Bowdion stopped his rocking and turned to gaze his way. As Lombard was actually looking away, he could only see him from the corner of his eye, yet he could tell the man was scrutinising him, considering his profile, his suit, even his shoes, somewhat as he had earlier when Lombard had settled on the bench. Only this time, it was done with no hostility; just curiosity.

It hardly felt right:

"You cared, did you not?" Lombard said to break the moment, keeping his eyes away from him.

"Huh? Yes—Yes, I did," John Bowdion replied in a wavering voice, and Lombard grunted and swallowed hard; the man had fallen prey to emotion, by the sound of it likely even had tears welling up his eyes, as if overcome by Lombard's pitiful consideration.

It seemed wise not to foster this mood further and remain silent until it passed, which is what he did, seeking distraction in his surroundings. The green he was in was the size of a very large garden, in the middle of a pleasant square of well-to-do terraced houses. The early evening sun's rays lit up some areas with golden spears. One such sun-stabbed stretch, a far corner dominated by a large chestnut tree, caught his eye. There, two separate groups were lounging on picnic blankets set among loose conkers that littered the grass. One group consisted of two couples sipping wine and sharing food from disposable tableware, and the other comprised three hijabbed women with an infant chatting together. Lombard let his gaze rest on the scene for a while, more admiring the light than the people, then swallowed hard as his eyes fixed on the conkers scattered about the grass. He was never fond of conkers. They heralded autumn, were strange fruits that stole what little time remained of summer, by this seemed to cancel the present. For all that, much to his dismay and without warning – as if scythed by John Bowdion's mood – there and then a terrible sense of dread got hold of him, so that each of his breaths felt like a hiss nearer to death. Fallen in this barren furrow, his mind sought the comfort of Ali, nearly grabbed hold of her only for Maude McGinnis to grab hold of him; the woman with her crucifix and dark ringed eyes was a million years old and giving birth to an embalmed waxy pregnant Jane under her black skirt. 'Perhaps everything is just a test for something else,' he heard his own voice propose over these thoughts and visions, now recalling that the man he sat next to was some sort of writer while at the same time deciding he had better leave. He remembered he'd left his car in a paying parking bay. He trusted his passing malaise had failed to come to John Bowdion's attention, which seemed confirmed when he glanced sideways to find him staring pensively into the distance. The man still looked unwell, had resumed his rocking gently back and forth cradling his chest in his arms while taking quick breaths, but otherwise seemed calm and in control of himself again.

"The papers said you are a writer," Lombard said; "Is that right?"

John Bowdion slowly broke into a rueful grin, but stayed composed, speaking softly now, as if detached:

"You're being too kind. The way I recall it, what they wrote in the paper is that I 'call myself a writer'. An important and telling distinction, wouldn't you think? And yes, the slight was felt and resented."

"So, you are a writer?"

"I have a Master's degree in English Literature, a PhD in Creative Writing, worked as a script editor on a couple of produced pictures, sold one original screenplay, wrote a dozen more which remain unproduced and to date completed two unpublished novels no one ever read. Does that make me a writer or merely someone who calls himself a writer? You tell me."

Lombard frowned and rose to his feet: "I wouldn't know, Mr Bowdion," he said; "But since you worked in the movies and know about writing, perhaps you could tell me if you ever heard of someone by the name of Avery Weyland? I believe he is a film director."

John Bowdion looked up at him, frowned as if pulled into a new universe, no longer rocking, an odd expectancy rallying in his eyes:

"I've heard of him—Yes. He's also a producer. I'm more familiar with his father's work, though. Clive Weyland. He was a successful science-fiction writer. Dead now. Why are you asking?"

"Oh. It's in relation to another thing I'm working on."

"Oh."

"Time to go."

John Bowdion let out a sigh, frowning, looking as if he didn't want to be left alone now:

"Right. You know what you said about old Samuel—How I cared about him. Well, I did—I did care. He and I talked. He told me things about his life. He travelled the world after Auschwitz—After losing his entire family in the Holocaust. He did a lot of things afterwards. Not all legal. He spent some years in prison for it. I wanted to help him. Tried talking him into writing his life story. And you know what he said? 'What if they like it?' That's what he said. He looked horrified at the thought. Huh! 'What if they like it?'"

Lombard grinned: "Well, maybe he was concerned enough about this wonderful world not to wish to contribute his share of bad things into it—Like another bad and sad story."

The comment unnerved John Bowdion. He scowled, unsure: "Right," he said; "I guess it's one way to look at it." Then: "I'm sorry about all the rocking and being so highly strung, by the way. I wasn't—I'm not always like this. I have this chest condition where I find it hard to breathe when I exercise or get nervous—"

"Not to worry," Lombard cut in; "Illness can be a cruel intruder. It calls on the body and the next you know it ends up burning your mind; or calls on the mind and winds up burning your body. Mind how you go now, Mr Bowdion. Thank you for your time. And best of luck finding a home for the old man's dog."

"Yes. You too. Th—Thank you, Mr—"

"Lagarde."

"Yes—Thank you, Mr Lagarde."

And with one last look towards the old cocker spaniel that had yet to move at the end of its leash, he hurried out of the green without another glance towards the lounging parties in the sunny far corner.

Good intentions. Later on, John Bowdion's words about having wanted to help the old man revisited him, whereby, unsure why – although it could well be linked to Jane's husband's online map purchase – he recalled a story relating to helping others. It had fared badly. A man he once knew for a time had lived with his wife and young daughter in a remote cottage up in the hills of the Massif Central, at the end of a long narrow dirt track at the top of a steep country lane about a thirty-minute drive from the nearest train station. One day he'd advertised online an old valve radio he had no use for, and, in consideration of his location, had proposed to send it by post to prospective buyers. It sold, and the buyer promptly enquired by email as to when would be a convenient time to collect the radio the next day. Trusting that anyone minded to come in person to his remote location was local to the area and would drive there, the man had emailed back directions together with a map and advice about where best to park nearby in the event they found the track to the cottage too rough or narrow for their vehicle. A time of between one and two in the afternoon the next day was agreed. This occurred near the end of March, during the first week of spring, when the weather was changeable, so that the next morning a particularly heavy overnight snowfall had rendered the track to the cottage impassable. Up before 7 a.m. and snowbound, the man had promptly emailed the radio's buyer to warn them against coming, suggesting they call to make arrangements for another day. As the buyer wasn't due until 1 p.m. that afternoon, all of six hours later, it seemed reasonable to assume they wouldn't already be on their way, nor mind the delay. Still, they had phoned, turned out to be a young woman who revealed she was already on her way aboard a train from Toulouse – a town nearly one hundred miles away – and so, rather than turn around, would come all the same, set on hiring a taxi at the nearby train station when she got there. He tried to dissuade her, to impress upon her that if the snow made it impossible for him to get out, no taxi would make it up the hill or the track to the cottage. But she wouldn't be discouraged; in addition to advising him that the landscape her train was travelling through was snow-free, she pointed out the inconvenience involved in ending her journey to return home only to come back another day; besides, she really was looking forward to collecting the radio. Much exasperated but helpless to stop her, the man then decided it would be preferable to meet the woman at the station rather than have her try to come to him, and soon attempted to leave his cottage after fitting snow-chains to his car. But to no avail; the snow on the track was too deep and too soft. He'd called the woman again, robustly conveyed the seriousness of the situation, and to his relief she had heeded his advice, agreeing to return home and have him post her the radio at his own expense. And this was supposed to be the end of it, so that when the spring sunshine poured through the breaking clouds later that afternoon to thaw the snow, his mind was focussed on other matters, with early evening finding him starting supper to welcome his wife and daughter who – wise to the news about the improved weather – were on their way home from a short stay at his mother-in-law's. However, before this could happen, a young woman with buck teeth, a purse tied to a string attached to her wrist and a clipboard with the map he'd sent her, had come knocking at his door. She wished to pick up her radio, she announced, had changed her mind about cutting short her trip and decided on coming after all, observing that the snow he warned her about was nowhere to be seen. Despite the map with the directions to the cottage clearly visible in her hands, she explained that a taxi driver who was now waiting for her on the road at the far end of the track had spent over two hours exploring the nearby hills in search of his address, which accounted for her tardy arrival. Now, hauling the old valve radio, she planned on trying to catch the last train out of the local station and make it back to Toulouse, where, if successful, she would arrive home by two the next morning. It was readily evident why she had thought nothing of travelling so far at considerable expense to collect an old radio, or seemed unable to appreciate the situation about the snow, or why the taxi driver had opted to take her on a wanton costly trail around the area; she was simple, that is to say, afflicted by a condition which made her seem simple-minded. The circumstances called for both concern and annoyance – in equal measure – with concern prevailing in the end; the idea of the woman travelling by herself late into the night loaded with a radio proved too much to contemplate. In this manner, after remonstrating with the taxi driver who had only agreed to leave once made richer by his full fare, the man had resolved to drive the woman and her radio back home himself, leaving a note for his wife. The round trip took over four hours, and by 1 a.m., when he arrived back home to a dark cottage, he expected to find his wife and daughter asleep. Instead, he found them dead, their throats slit. As it happened, their killer had already been apprehended, the result of a collision with another car while fleeing the area, and would readily confess to the murders before the night was out. He was a drug addict who fed his habit through burglary. Driving through the area, by chance he'd spotted the man's wife travelling alone with their daughter and followed their car to the secluded cottage. Giving the woman a few minutes to settle in, he'd showed up at the door with some story about being lost. Short of breaking into empty properties, this was his tried and tested method of operation: he followed women back home where, satisfied they were alone, he would make his way inside to rob them. He found her alone, and set on overpowering her. That evening though, owing to his intoxication and the location being secluded, he'd also resolved to rape his victim, proved unsuccessful in this undertaking and, frustrated, opted to kill her and her daughter to ensure they would never be able to identify him. He'd likely have got away had he not later collided with an oncoming Land Rover and had the rescue services not come across stolen items from the cottage along with the woman's bank and credit cards inside his car. In any event, not very many months later the vengeful husband and father had sought out both the radio's buyer and local taxi driver and killed them, reckoning his wife and child would still be alive had he not found cause to leave home by virtue of the one's simplicity, the other's venality, and his own generosity.

No one who had ever known him prior to these events ever saw him again afterwards. Having dispensed retribution, he simply vanished.

NINE

Evidently, in some quarters, to consent to set free
thousands of your enemies in order to free one of your
own demonstrated an obscene mindset.

Lombard and Edward Duncan hailed from different environments, were headed towards opposite horizons, yet on crossing
paths had settled on trekking part of their journeys together as
if it was the most natural of things. In some regards, they
could be said to be darkness and light, contrasting colours of
a sunset skyline, or, as one happened to be the go-to-man for
the other's awkward situations, an advantageous union of
divergences. By all accounts, too much separated them for
easy friendship to flourish unhindered, but they shared that
rarest of things which now and again draws men together –
they trusted each other. Both would have been at pains to
articulate why this was. The essence of their trust seemed to
relate as much to the physical as the intellectual. Each understood
the other without a clear reason. Accordingly, neither man
was much troubled by reservations each may have had about
the other, or the particulars each knew of the other, or the
nefarious potential of such intelligence.

The truth be told, Lombard hardly minded leaving himself
open to the charge of liking Edward Duncan's company. But
in this, he was very much the norm. As already mentioned,
Edward Duncan was the sort of man other men envy. His fine
figure, seasoned manners, tangible good health and the easy
winsome confidence that came from being born favoured
made for an advantageous blend, worthy enough of admiration
to make it easy for most to make light of his lapses of character.

At times, it seemed as if those in his presence forgot their own inadequacies, as though his attendance somehow embellished their existence, cancelled out their failings. At others, by contrast, such abundance of good fortune could just as easily induce pardonable rancour.

Rather uniquely for someone of his claims, he was not merely punctual but habitually made meetings well before time. Lombard found him already settled at an outdoor terrace table when he arrived at *The Melchior* in Duke Street five minutes early. It was lunchtime, the place was bustling, yet the head waiter they both knew as Caesar was happy to pay heed to no others, standing by his table bantering as if this was the most natural thing to do midway through his busy shift. "Ah! There you are, Xavier," Edward Duncan greeted him. "How are you, Edward?" "The better for seeing you, Xavier. Now, Caesar here was just telling me he only just returned from his honeymoon—Second nuptials. And this time he reckons she's it; the one and only until the great crossover." "Congratulations, Caesar," Lombard grinned; "How are you?" "Thank you, *mon ami*—I'm as good as a pig's snout in a truffle trough," the head waiter returned. They all laughed, he took their order and left them to their business.

Edward Duncan seemed in a good mood. He wore a crisp pale blue silk shirt that complimented the tan he'd caught on his recent trip to Sardinia. Briskly, he sat forward, smiled, reached across the table to give Lombard a friendly punch on the shoulder and leant back in his seat. "It's good to see you, Xavier," he said before apologising for cancelling the previous day's meeting due to his being called on an errand to Wiltshire. "One of our companies' sponsors; some annual Newspaper award function," he explained; "Marketing exercise, you know—Big show, celebrities, press proprietors and isn't everything just wonderful and prizes all round and our company name gets great exposure—Well, for a couple of days at any rate. Anyway, Mother decided to bring Grandma. She thought it'd do her good—The old girl's still President of the Strand Royal Theatre and sits on the National Theatre Board of Trustees but scarcely goes out nowadays. Long story

124

short, she collapsed midway through the do and was taken to hospital by ambulance. That was the day before last. She's all good now; had a bad turn, as they used to say. They were ready to discharge her yesterday morning and Mother asked me to go pick her up and take her home. Poor Grandma— Her withering world shall shrink even more now. She was my hero when I was a kid, you know. A real daredevil—She piloted her own plane. She learnt to fly during the Second World War; delivered Spitfires and Lancaster bombers from the factories to the front-line squadrons. You'd never think so looking at her now though. Bless her soul. Be that as it may, Xavier, I got something for you."

While in Sardinia, Edward Duncan had bought him a pair of cufflinks at a local market. They were gold plated with swivel fittings, had a disc of black leather engraved with the letter 'X' mounted on the round face and came in a matching gold and black leather case. They were handmade, clearly inexpensive, but Lombard was touched. "Saw the 'X' and thought of you; 'X' for Xavier agent *X-traordinaire*," Edward Duncan teased; "Just couldn't resist. Who knows—Perhaps you'll find some use for them." "That's very kind of you, Edward. Thank you," grinned Lombard awkwardly; "Was Sardinia good?" "Oh—Heavenly! The kids love it. You absolutely must come to see the place for yourself one day, Xavier. Mind you, even paradise is vulnerable to prospective clouds. Some reality TV celebrity purchased the next property along the coast from us. I gather he's some TV chef who is also busy renovating a chateau in the Limousin for another TV show. He sure likes his speedboat and helicopter." "Huh," Lombard grunted, recalling his football player neighbour but thinking better of remarking on how taxing it can be to live among the wealthy and their lifestyles. "Can't help wondering about all these reality TV celebrities," Edward Duncan went on; "Moving to places where they ought not to go. Like a bad smell, they draw fans and the media—Flies to manure. Fare thee well, peace and gentle breeze." And they went on chatting casually through lunch, beyond matters such as media celebrities, moving on to gold, mining, cryptocurrencies and the impending eradication of cash, topics which, while close to Edward Duncan's heart, made for enlightening conversation from Lombard's point of view. In the way unpleasant business is often pushed back until it can no longer be avoided, not a word was said about what had brought them there until after they'd ordered coffee. "Now, I suppose we better get down to the ghastly business at hand," Edward Duncan announced; "And try not to let it ruin what has been a very pleasant lunch."

Lombard remained silent while Edward Duncan peered pensively at his empty wine glass. "I mentioned my grandmother and Wiltshire earlier," the man said at long last, somewhat sombrely; "Well, there were those two boys in a Cornish village once—Teenagers. One was poor, the other rich. They weren't close—The rich boy only visited in the summer holidays—But they'd known each other most of their lives, on occasions played together. The poor boy's mother was widowed. One day she fell ill enough to have to remain confined to their cottage, so that they soon started making do without. When winter came, aware of their predicament, folks some way away offered them a load of surplus logs from a felled ash tree, providing they could arrange to collect it. The task was beyond both boy and woman, but a neighbour with a van volunteered their help. However, driving back with their cargo, they'd broken down, required rescue and towing away, were forced to unload the firewood where they'd come to grief, which happened to be along the green fronting the local primary school. It took the woman a couple of days to find someone with a trailer to collect it. Only, when she and the boy turned up to retrieve it, they found it gone; it turned out the school janitor had deemed the pile of firewood an obstruction and risk hazard to pupils and parents, and invited people to help themselves to it. The boy had returned home, his mother passed away a few weeks later and he was dispatched to an uncle. No suggestion was ever made that the woman had died of cold—She hadn't—But this had not stopped a teenager with a confident imagination from thinking it; this was the rich boy. The thing was, his mother was the owner of the school, and on hearing what had occurred when next he came, he'd fallen easy prey to shame and anger. The opportunity to quench both came at a village fête. He publicly berated and slapped the school janitor who was there with his wife and daughters. And nobody dared do much of anything in return. After all, he was the son of the woman who owned the village school and employed its janitor.

And Edward fell silent and glanced at Lombard, raising his brows self-deprecatingly.

Had he known less about the man, Lombard would probably have wondered what to make of this tale. But as things were he was satisfied he knew how to read him, guessed this was Edward Duncan's way of letting him know he thought he'd been too harsh for too long on Alan Winston who, after all, at nineteen, was still very much a teenager prone to mistakes. "What about the rich boy's mother?" Lombard asked, helpfully; "Did she not reprimand him?"

"This she did—When she found out. But the harm was done by then."

"Well," Lombard grinned, welcoming this new situation as a refreshing development from the 'I never thought things would come to this' statement the other had made two weeks earlier; "Well," he said; "No one needs to beat themselves up about what happened to Alan Winston, Edward. He was no helpless child; had already set out on the road he was on before he crossed your path. I trust you're up-to-date with his news?"

"I trust I am—And still trying to figure out what someone on the run for murder would go to Madeira for. What is the sense of it? He cannot seriously expect to remain free for long on an island half the size of London. Most extraordinary."

"I've given this some thought," Lombard acquiesced; "What if remaining free was not his concern? Looking at it, he made no attempt to conceal his flight there—Used his own passport—And had to be aware he'd be caught on surveillance cameras once inside the airport."

"What are you saying?"

"I'm not sure, Edward. His killing the reporter, it's like I said: the result of chance. But flying to Madeira making no attempt to cover his tracks, who knows?"

"Could he be mad? I mean, killing a man without much cause or reason hardly qualifies as the action of a sound mind, does it?" Edward Duncan declared.

"I should think he had no idea how things would end. In any event, Edward, I drove to Mile End yesterday. Thought I'd see if our boy had said anything to his new housemates about being on the run from strangers on account of stealing a puppy. By the sound of it, he kept his predicament to himself. I'd have waited until we'd met before going but an opportunity presented itself."

Edward Duncan looked back at him, barely showing surprise, nodded ascent:

"Good. No link back to me or you through that door then."

"No. But unless he's dead and buried or somehow got off Madeira already, it's safe to say it's just a matter of time before he gets caught. Of course, if and when that happens, he may fix to keep his puppy snatching exploits to himself. You must have noticed the press and police appear to have no wind of it so far."

"I have. And you're right, Xavier," Edward Duncan replied; "Unless he's dead, they'll get him. So far though, everybody's doing a very bad job of finding him. Or perhaps he should be given credit for staying one step ahead of the chase. Either way, I too have been thinking, Xavier—I'd like you to go to Madeira. I reckon you'll do a better job than the local cops."

Perhaps, following on the heels of the man's poor-boy rich-boy story, this request hardly ought to have struck Lombard as a surprise. Still, he took a deep breath, unsure what was being proposed or asked of him.

"I wouldn't hurt him, Edward," he said.

"And I wouldn't ask you to, Xavier."

"Then why? To give him away to the police? You said it yourself, there's no way they won't eventually find him if he is at all findable."

"I'm sure."

"Then why?"

"Of that, I'm not sure."

128

"Then I must advise against it, Edward. There's nothing to be gained by further involving yourself in Alan Winston's fate."

"Are you saying you'd rather pass up the opportunity to go to Madeira, Xavier?"

Lombard swallowed hard:

"I'm surprised. Is it the reporter?"

"Oh—No–no–no. Not the reporter."

"Not the reporter?" echoed Lombard.

"That's right. It's more complicated."

"Things are never that complicated, Edward; People only make them seem so—Most of the time to better like or delude themselves."

"I'm not one to argue with you, you know that, Xavier. But, whatever you think, I'd appreciate it if you could try to find out what happened to him."

"Right. So, let's think forward to a time—Not unlike the present—When Alan Winston is gone—Into the void: where would be the good in bringing him back?"

"Put like that, there'd be no good to it."

"So—If your motivation isn't to cause him harm—Why would you want me to find him, Edward? What if I do find him?"

Edward Duncan puckered his lips, raised his shoulders helplessly and gently shook his head:

"I guess I'll cross that bridge when I get there."

"Huh. That's how far your thinking took you?"

"I must confess, yes."

"Well—It's a bad idea."

"I hear you."

"I'd sooner you changed your mind."

"I heard you and am asking again: will you go, Xavier?"

In frustration, Lombard decided not to say anymore.

"Road to perdition," Edward Duncan went on; "The boy was on a road to perdition well before he crossed my path. Isn't that what you said?"

Lombard frowned.

"Precisely," the man carried on; "No one needs to beat

themselves up about what happened to Alan Winston," he now repeated Lombard's earlier words; "I just want him found. And if he cannot be found because he is dust into the void never to be heard of again, all the better. But that remains to be determined. Will you go, Xavier?"

Lombard remained silent, clenched his teeth when he realized that without further need to think or speak, he'd already acceded to Edward Duncan's request; his mind had preceded him there; for it was recalling a time, long ago, spent within the walls of a cheap Funchal hotel room.

"Splendid," he heard Edward Duncan's voice; "Thank you, Xavier." He still had not spoken, yet the man had evidently read his mind.

Upon this, they remained quietly finishing their coffees, silent amid the noisy tables around them. Nothing more needed to be said. Yet, they delayed, neither wishing to part in the shadow of their exchange about Alan Winston. Edward Duncan, who could usually be depended upon in this regard, soon lit up the atmosphere hitting the right note when they caught each other's eyes appraising a couple of statuesque lipsticked men in identical tight tank tops bearing the slogan 'Believe All Womxn'.

"*What's in a name. That which we call a rose, by any other name would smell as sweet*," he remarked dreamily.

Later that afternoon, Lombard settled at his usual table at *Monsieur Chose*, ordered an espresso and turned his attention to the day's edition of The Paragon. The Alan Winston news remained unchanged; he continued to evade justice and was thought to be in Madeira. However, there was news about his victim. At the end of a lengthy delay the coroner had finally released the reporter's body – his funeral was to take place the next day; the man left a wife, a brother, two parents and 'a promising and very much unfinished career of limitless possibilities', concluded his obituary. The only other story in the paper that caught Lombard's attention – in the wake of his visit to Mile End purely on account of John Bowdion's assertion about The Paragon's uncharitable attitude towards Jewish people – was an article focused on the Middle-East. In point of fact, one of the paper's headlines concerned a hostage-prisoner swap between the Israeli authorities and a Palestinian faction which had occurred the previous afternoon. On the face of it, what had passed was this: for five years a Palestinian group had held an Israeli soldier captive, demanding the release of ten thousand Palestinian prisoners held in Israel in exchange for her return, and after lengthy negotiations the Israelis had agreed to release half that number, thereby closing a deal in which their one soldier was returned for their freeing five thousand prisoners. Still, in the main article relating to the event, the writer alleged this exchange to be 'yet more evidence of the Jewish State's obscene idea that Israeli lives are more important than Palestinian lives'. Lombard went over the piece twice to satisfy himself that he understood the facts of the story, and reckoned there could well be substance to John Bowdion's claim about The Paragon. The proposition advocated by the paper certainly lent the possibility credence. As a notion, it seemed to belong to the absurd, the fruit of tendentious partisanship, or the product of entirely prejudiced views. Evidently, in some quarters, to consent to set free thousands of your enemies in order to free one of your own demonstrated an obscene mindset. Or so the paper advised its readers. This singular position begged the question: what if the Jewish state had readily agreed to the original demand – not freed five but as many as ten thousand for their one soldier? Would this have been held to be a manifestation of their mindset being twice more obscene? Still, for all he knew, the premise of this debatable moral denunciation was untainted by prejudice; perhaps given the opportunity, The Paragon would – possibly already had – adopt an identical stance in the event of the likes of Italy or India or Peru resorting to freeing five thousand prisoners in return for one of their citizens.

In addition to causing him to call into question the ungenerous impression he had formed of John Bowdion during their meeting in the Mile End green, the thoughts born of such reflections served only to make the present bleak, driving him to summon the comparative safety of more pressing and concrete considerations, such as his having agreed to travel to Madeira; allowing Edward Duncan to talk him into it was one thing, what was to be done about it another entirely.

Beyond his parents having met on the Atlantic Island as itinerant hotel workers prior to his coming into the world – a fact which hardly seemed relevant – Alan Winston's only known link to Madeira was a year-old week's holiday he spent there together with a now ex-girlfriend. "Boring", was how the girl had described their time there in the papers. Yet, on the day he had turned into a killer fugitive from the law, the nineteen-year-old had thought of nowhere else to go; with no more than one week's wage for his fortune, he fled straight there. Of all places in the world, Madeira had called when his life floundered. It stood to reason that something – or someone – had enticed him there in his hour of need. And the only person who could possibly shed light on who or what this may be was a girl who maintained they'd kept strictly to themselves and were never apart the whole week they spent there. Lombard was acquainted with her. Her name was Letitia Balthazar. He'd approached her while still hounding Alan Winston prior to the Mile End murder. She was fair and comely, in her early twenties but aged beyond her years and hardly congenial for being honest, harbouring little fondness for her ex-boyfriend. She claimed they went their separate ways after Madeira, and that she'd never missed him a day since. In the course of their short meeting, she'd also broadcast her poor opinion of men, a development in her young life for which Alan Winston was reportedly answerable, and declared her mission to better herself by returning to study, due to start a Media Studies course at Bristol University in September. Against all this, Lombard wasn't prepared to swear she wouldn't keep information about their trip to Madeira to herself. But one thing was beyond question: she alone knew about Alan Winston and Madeira, which made it worth the trouble of paying her a second visit.

He recalled she was employed as an apprentice at a magazine dubbed 'Gazelle', an online publication marketed towards women with offices in Camden Town, not far from the Round House. This was where they'd met, in the reception area of a vast open office dominated by a pink banner shouting 'Gazelle'. It was roughly a thirty-minute walk across Regent's Park and down Parkway from Marylebone High Street, but it was nearing five o'clock and, besides, whether she still worked there was far from certain. It was September, for all he knew she'd upped and moved to pursue her studies by now. He would go to Camden first thing in the morning, and failing to find her, if necessary head on West to Bristol.

Sleep didn't come gently that night. By and by, the ticking hours left him stranded in the same dreary place he had visited earlier upon reading the Paragon piece about the prisoner exchange deal – into vacuous absurdity, but with the addition of night and its coercing tricks and games. If the true measure of gloom is contingent upon a heavy brew of disquiet laced with agitation, then for some time that night he may well have become gloom's very personification. All manner of deaths – all unknown a mere two weeks earlier –wheezed and whispered across his mind, stopping just short of causing nausea. There was Rex Mantle's raped sister from Exeter, eyeless grub to black crows. The Paragon reporter, left to die in the void when none could be found who would be exchanged for his life. Alan Winston, invisible on account of being obscured by clouds and busy dying. Joseph Aratoon, who jumped gingerly into *Gehenna*'s embrace clutching a handful of pound notes. Jane, mowed down by an express train at a zebra crossing which sliced her in two. Her twin daughters: one falling down a waterfall, the other coaxing her sister into the dark waters below. Maude McGinnis, guilty and nailed to her gleaming crucifix. And Edward Duncan, slapping his arms and sides to stay warm under a frozen dead ash tree. And then there was him, tasked with the roles of hunter, messenger and purveyor of answers.

Sleep didn't come that night. Not even after a few Calvados and a brisk walk along the dark West End streets, past high windows, wide doorways, fire-breathing clubbers, homeless wrecks, shaded restaurants and all-night cafés' lighthouses. Back in the Mews at sunrise, he listened to the world wake up outside his open windows, showered, shaved, put on a clean suit, briefly considered trying on his new leather cufflinks, settled on a pair of plain silver ones to go with a silver watch, and left on foot for Camden Town; anything seemed better than home, even calling at Letitia Balthazar's workplace.

Informed at reception that Ms Balthazar was indeed still working at the magazine, Lombard had waited a good hour on a banquette under the great pink 'Gazelle' banner before the girl showed up, her face all dimples, chestnut eyes and lean red lips. She was covered in sweat with a backpack and cycling helmet in her hand, all poise, her mousy hair pulled back in a band and her body squeezed into tight cycling shorts and a narrow sleeveless top which left her tattooed shoulders exposed. He stood up with a grin and she stopped in mid-step with an icy frown. "How are you, Ms Balthazar?" She remembered him: "You!"

"What are you—I don't know who you are or what you want, Mister. But I'm calling the cops if you don't leave at once. They told me everything on the card you left me last time was phoney, right. So you better leave. Now!"

"I understand, Ms Balthazar?" he said, still grinning; "But I'm unsure what good calling the police might do—Or why you should think the prospect might fill me with dread. Then again, I'd sooner you didn't. If you'd hear me out though: there are good reasons for my misrepresenting myself—In my line of work, discretion, circumspection and subterfuge are everything, Ms Balthazar. Now, I hope you can bring yourself to accept my sincere apologies for having been less than honest during our previous encounter. If you would just give me a couple of minutes of your time I could explain. You see, I'm working on a delicate matter I was not at liberty to divulge last time we met. However, in light of recent events, I guess there's

134

now little harm in letting you know the reason for my making enquiries about your ex-boyfriend. I'm a private investigator working for a French solicitor's firm tasked with tracking down Alan on behalf of the guardians of a French heiress who claims to be carrying your ex-boyfriend's baby, Ms Balthazar. The parties involved very much wished to keep things quiet but, unfortunately, what with the terrible incident which occurred recently in Mile End, such discretion is no longer a priority."

Letitia Balthazar had yet to move. He could see the cogs working inside her eyes while she glared at him, processing the information as he imparted it to her.

"I cannot say a word more," he went on before her mind settled; "But, in view of Alan's current misadventures, and the police's failure to catch him, the matter has become somewhat pressing. I'm sure you can understand, Ms Balthazar."

For a while longer, only she knew what threads were being weaved within her mind from all the lies he'd just told her. At last, her lean lips curled, twitched and puckered, betraying her thoughts:

"Alan got a fucking French fucking heiress pregnant?" she declared; "And she wants to keep the baby? Wow—Poor girl. But what does any of that have to do with me, Mister—?"

"Lagarde. Laurent Lagarde. Nothing whatsoever, I assure you."

"Well—Thank you for that. Then I hope you don't mind leaving. And if you ever see her, please tell the expectant heiress that she has all the sympathy of at least one of Alan's ex-pitstops."

"Now—You're being very ungenerous, Ms Balthazar," he said; "Not only towards the mother-to-be but to yourself too. After all, unless I have this wrong, didn't you and Alan once care enough for each other to remain lovers for the best part of six months?"

She hardly took a moment to breathe:

"Well, like they say in the movies: everyone can be a sucker once."

"Is that a fact?"

"I believe so."

"On that basis, what do the movies have to say about being a sucker twice, I wonder."

"What are you on about?"

At this moment another girl, equally young and athletic, stepped into the reception area with a cup of coffee and, with an openly antagonistic glance towards Lombard, asked: "Morning, Lottie. Is everything alright or—"

"Hi, Bea. It's okay. I'm good—Be with you in a minute," Letitia Balthazar replied, encouraging the other to leave.

"What are you on about?" she repeated once they were alone again.

"Fool me once, shame on you; fool me twice, shame on me," Lombard declared; "Twice a sucker, Ms Balthazar."

"What are you saying, Mister?" she scowled; "If—"

"Your boy Alan is a killer, Ms Balthazar. His being last seen in Madeira doesn't mean he hasn't made his way back to London—Or won't. He sure has proved resourceful up to now, staying one step ahead of the authorities. Now, were he to head back home, at whose door do you think he may come knocking, Ms Balthazar? A man with no place to go; no dreams to dream; no one to turn to; nothing to lose? He was rather fond of you, wasn't he? I noted you hardly had a good word to say about him to the press though. Now, a killer with little left to lose, who can tell what may next go through his mind? What I'm saying, Ms Balthazar, is that his facing justice rather than being out there roaming the world would serve you well—Then again, perhaps the movies provide ready-made pearls of wisdom about being twice a sucker."

She sneered: "Oh. I get it. You think I should worry he might turn up on my doorstep—Is that it? Well, if he made up his mind to do so, I fail to see how I could stop him."

"Possibly by helping track him down beforehand, Ms Balthazar."

"And how would I do that?"

"By being good enough to answer a couple of questions I have. About the time you two spent together in Madeira."

"I already told everyone all I had to say about it. Check

136

the papers."

"I know—I have. I only wish to seek clarification on some minor points, so to speak. Anything that might help determine what sirens other than yourself may have lured him back there, Ms Balthazar. One minute of your time. If you could— For instance, did Alan ever mention his parents met in Madeira?"

She sighed: "No."

"Right. You told the papers that you did all the driving while there because Alan never passed his test—Does this mean he doesn't know how to drive or—"

"He doesn't know how to drive."

"Good. No car for him, then. What about—Would you still stand by your statement that you two were never apart all the time you spent there?"

"Absolutely. Joined at the hip; no escape."

"And all you did the whole week is drive around touring the island?"

"And drink. Every day more bleary and wasted than the next. Groundhog Day up and down through the clouds and across pine forests in our little hired car."

"And nothing memorable happened?"

"Memorable? I recall the clouds, our little car and the pine forests."

"Did you seek to buy drugs at any time maybe?"

"I wish."

"Stop at restaurants and cafés? Shops?"

"We had to eat and drink."

"Strike up conversation with staff anywhere?"

"Well—Some restaurant tried double-charging us and we complained."

"Can you recall if anything at all drew Alan's interest?"

"Not really."

"You mean nothing you did or saw anywhere was noteworthy or remarkable in any way?"

"I didn't say that."

"What didn't you say?"

"Some things were okay: the cheap booze; picnics; swims. Actually, Alan was quite taken by our picnics and swims—

You know: eating in the wild and taking dips in fishing harbours or the sea. Fucking freezing it was too."

"And that's it."

"Unless you want to talk about sex. We made out quite a bit. But who needs to fly to a fucking rock full of grey heads in the middle of the Atlantic for that? Our pet names for each other were Bunny Rabbit and Stud Mobile, if you want to know."

"I see. So he wasn't all that bad after all."

"Well, let's just say men can be dicks in more ways than one. Now, I'd say your minute's up, wouldn't you?"

Still all petulance, she no longer seemed so hostile, possibly owing to the fact that she knew she was about to be rid of him.

"You're right. One more thing," he said; "Did you not contact him after I first came to see you a couple of months back?"

He knew she would lie even before she spoke; possibly even before she knew she would lie. Her lips and nostrils quivered as she opened her mouth to say "No, I didn't". She was a bad liar, which was no bad thing as it meant that everything else she had said so far could likely be trusted, regardless of how unhelpful it turned out to be.

"He told me you did, Ms Balthazar. And that you two also met, together with your new girlfriend," Lombard said; "He and I never met, but we did have a few phone conversations, you see." He was telling the truth.

The news threw her somewhat. Again, her mind was working hard inside her eyes. He guessed she'd failed to mention the occasion when speaking to the police.

"You're right. I had forgotten," she let out.

"I'm sure."

"Before you go on your way looking for Alan," she said now, as if trading his silence on this; "You might want to know the cops asked me if I could tell them anything about that road in the middle of nowhere he got himself driven to after making it back to Madeira. I tried telling them they might as well ask me about the M-25. They had me watch

138

films of the place, in case it would jog my memory—Like some people are so bloody vapid they can tell one fucking hillside or pine fucking forest from another. They even suggested flying me back there."

"Did you go back?" said Lombard.

She stared, bemused: "Do I look to you like I would."

"I wouldn't know, Ms Balthazar."

And he thanked her for her time, bid her a good day and left her to her demons. She wasn't finished though, had something else she wanted him to know which she shouted behind him: "You're wrong if you think Alan would ever want to hurt me, Mister. Not a chance. You wouldn't know. Killer or not, he wouldn't hurt me. And I hope never to see you again."

TEN

Abraham was spared the pain of having to sacrifice his son.

Rain was falling on London, the first in a long while, and heading home from his meeting with Letitia Balthazar through Regent's Park, Lombard stopped for breakfast at the Broad Walk Café between the trees and lawns. The still relatively early morning hour was doing nothing to brighten his mood, which he noted was oddly attuned to the heavy sky hanging grimly low over the horizon.

A man needs a reason to ride his time, whether it be love, family, work, greed, vanity, ambition or hubris; it is less hard for a man to die if he knows at least why he is alive. Lombard had owned some of these reasons as his own at some point or other – a long time ago. Nowadays, he made do without, himself counting as his sole advisor and solitary concern. All things told he did fine by it, steered his own path, dwelled beyond the world of grievances or the need to visit his woes upon deities or humanity. He required no noise, direction or company to endure or find purpose. The dawn was purpose enough, provided adequate sustainment, except that of late – as was happening today – he had inexplicably begun to experience peculiar moments of dreariness and dread. Although aggrieved by the agitation they caused him, he thought little of them, considered the unfamiliar environment they created more vexing than unpleasant. So far though, these visitations – which some might have described as angst – never had lasted long; today's, in contrast, had taken hold the previous afternoon, seized his night and, halfway through the morning had yet to release him.

On this account, seeking distraction over a croissant and coffee in the nearly deserted café, he found himself observing a young woman sitting by herself at a table with her back against a large window across the room from him. She was dark, with delicate features, coming across as rather fragile, an impression helped in great measure by her anxious stare, hunched shoulders and single-minded nail biting. There was no drink or food in front of her, yet her handbag sat on the floor at the foot of her chair as if she wished not to spoil her table with it. She was hardly alone for long as a tall dark man of about her age soon walked in and settled tensely directly across from her, so that Lombard saw only his wide-shouldered back. At once, the two began talking across the table, she defensively and he forcefully, emphasising his words with his hands. This went on for a while until two older couples turned up to join them with much screeching of chairs. These four newcomers also looked taut and strained. No one ordered food or refreshments. Instead, all spoke, to one another but mostly to the young woman, firmly, with all the urgency of admonishment, so that before long the recipient of their invectives yielded, fell silent, overpowered, rigidly listening to all that was being said with defeated eyes, all the time continuing to chew her nails. In due course, with the odd word now and again reaching his ears from across the room, Lombard figured out what was going on: the five were busy warning the young woman against divorcing the man across the table from her. The older people were the couple's respective parents; their words rang with "folly", "unicorns"; their sentences chimed forebodingly: "No idea what you're doing", "What will happen to you once you're on your own?"

For all its distractions, this scene failed to engage his thoughts or lift his mood. Rather the opposite. In its stead, Madeira stole him back. This time though, it was a Madeira free from Alan Winston whereby on account of his current dark disposition his train of thought led him beyond the now to yet more death.

The first man he ever killed had grey curly hair, a sallow furrowed face and odd lustrous bright eyes, which, after two years in the Foreign Legion and months patrolling the Guianese jungle, he knew was as likely a sign of malnutrition as an indicator of drug or alcohol abuse. The man was a *garimpeiro*, an illegal Brazilian miner who, like thousands of his kind had done before, had crossed the Oyapock river into French Guiana in search of gold. Lombard was nineteen and hardly cared for the feelings the taking of a man's life had roused inside of him. In any event, it was an uncomplicated killing, akin to shooting down a hostile wild creature. While on the whole the *garimpeiros* were hapless wiry men who owned little more than the clothes on their backs, they were also a great nuisance and an ecological disaster. Protected by the dense rainforest, they came across the hundreds-of-miles-long waterway which made the border with Brazil to pan the French side for gold using light portable petrol engines to hose down the earth with water before dumping vast amounts of mercury to separate the gold from the resulting mud. This process barely provided them with enough precious metal to scrape a living, but did a wonderful job of ruining and poisoning huge stretches of wilderness and riverways.

Whereas the little gold they wrested from the land hardly warranted expending men or money to stop them, the environmental harm they caused and the necessity to be seen to protect the integrity of French territory dictated they be deterred. So, seeing as the forest was too vast for the local gendarmerie to police, small detachments of the Foreign Infantry Regiment guarding the Guiana Space Centre were regularly assigned to patrol the Brazilian border. He had gone on dozens of these expeditions; a handful of men would be dropped from a helicopter into a remote area, spend the day searching the forest, on coming across *garimpeiros* seize their guns and gold and burn their huts and equipment before handing them a little money and food and sending them back across the river to Brazil. It was more show than anything else. All sides were aware the *garimpeiros* would re-arm and re-supply to come back into French Guiana to resume their mining when the patrol was gone. Had there been room in the helicopters — and there wasn't — the alternative would have been to transport them to jail and keep them there, which was both impractical and costly. The man he killed was one of a band of five they had captured and sent back across in the usual manner, except that on that day, these five had re-armed and returned at once from the Brazilian side of the water set on ambushing his detachment. Normally, the gold seized from such a band of men came to little more than one or two hundred grams; on this occasion though, they'd confiscated as much as eight hundred grams of the precious metal, a fortune to five *garimpeiros*, and they wanted it back and were ready to fight for it. The way it had gone down for Lombard within the sultry high-contrast world beneath the canopy of trees slashed by the overhead equatorial sun, he'd returned fire and hit his attacker. And that was it. All there had been to it. And later on that month he'd found himself on a ship bound to Lebanon which had called at Funchal for a three-day stopover.

The island had been his first stop on his first open sea trip, when unremitting gales had made for a most disagreeable Atlantic crossing that tested his poor sea legs. Green Madeira and its soaring peaks gradually emerging over the horizon had made for a soothing sight, and the brightly coloured town of Funchal winding down the mountains to a glittering harbour teeming with pleasure boats, hotels and restaurants looked a picture of desire, in that, crucially, it represented land. He never explored the Island, content to see out his stay within the confines of a cheap hotel near the harbour where he ate, slept and felt grateful to the world for staying put beneath his feet. When the day came to return to sea, he'd left with a wanting but favourable impression of his port of call: he knew Madeira had pleasurably balmy nights and days, even in February, a place of open windows and gentle breezes loaded with the sweet scent of blossoms; that its people spoke Portuguese; and that in one of its hotels a big smiling American girl by the name of Becky waitressed hard by day and lay all warm and clean and creamy by night, ready to melt to the sound of French being whispered into her buttery ear. He never heard from her again. She was not the first, gentlest, prettiest, sweetest or even most sensual girl he'd known. But, for reasons that escaped him – reasons so wondrous the world ought never to be allowed to explain these things – he'd never forgotten her.

These thoughts, visiting him as they did at the time they did and not altogether unwelcome, failed to lighten his spirit. Yet, because his reminiscing had sapped the last of his energy – or could it be a case of his long sleepless night catching up with him – on leaving the Broad Walk café to step out into the rain he welcomed the fact that he no longer felt at one with the heavy sky that hung low over London. He grinned: he was in the right place again; rain fell on the trees, pitter-patter against the leaves, lightly kissed his face for being blown by a gentle breeze, and he was going home. He wished he'd thought of bringing his coat when he left earlier; his suit would be drenched by the time he got back. He sighed: the sun had shone when he stepped into the dawn earlier, as it had for the best part of the summer; how was he to have guessed it would rain?

By the time he reached his Mews he'd settled on booking a return flight to Madeira for the next day. Whatever would come of this trip, he also determined to stay on the Island for at least three days, suspecting the ocean air and change of scene would provide a welcome rest. For all that, Alan Winston and Madeira simply left his mind when he caught sight of Maude McGinnis sheltering from the rain against his front door. Like the last time, she wore black, with her silver crucifix hanging from her neck and her handbag from her hand. Today though, she'd added a thin open woollen coat as black as her dress to her mourning attire, and stood with her neck bent, looking down at the ground as he approached, unaware of his presence, never mind his glaring frown.

His voice startled her: "What are you doing here, Mrs McGinnis? I told you not to come back. Don't you know how to use the phone! Or are you simply intent on coming here whenever the fancy takes you?"

"Oh. Xavier! Hello. I knew you would be upset and I can only apologize for turning up like this. but I thought—Jane's little one, the last of the twins, little Zoe, you know—Well," she passed away last night and—"

"She has—That's too bad," he returned; "But as far as I know it has nothing to do with me, Mrs McGinnis?"

"Of course. No-Nothing. It's me, I—" she exclaimed, fixing her baggy eyes imploringly into his, then frowned upon taking a breath and saying "Jesus. What happened to you, Xavier? You look like you saw the devil himself."

"The devil," he let out; "Well, maybe you're right, Mrs McGinnis—Maybe it's the devil who keeps knocking at my door. What do you think?"

For a moment there, anyone present would have been hard-pressed to tell which of the two looked the most disturbed – she for what she saw in his eyes, or he for what he saw that she saw in his eyes. He heard himself apologize while she spoke. She was holding back tears, and it took a while before he collected himself enough to make sense of what she was saying, so upset was he for having alarmed her. "—Don't know anybody else in London. I am so sorry, Xavier."

On catching sight of her standing against his door, he'd assumed she'd returned to press him about Jane; the truth was he'd hardly given Jane a thought since they'd last met. Now he realized she was not there to nudge him, but seeking shelter.

"I'm sorry about your granddaughter, Mrs McGinnis. And please forgive my loss of temper again," he said, doing his best to sound amenable.

"Oh—No need to trouble yourself now, Xavier; I'm sure you meant no harm by it. Like they say, the best thing to do when it's raining is to let it rain. The poor child—The poor child, you know—She was so terribly injured she might be best with God and her mother and father and sister. She might," she stated numbly.

He awkwardly patted her shoulder, gently pulled her away from his doorway to unlock the door and let her in, and what occurred next was most curious, unsolicited, and yet uniquely

– and most unexpectedly – gladly received.

"You look soaked through—You better get into dry clothes and let me make us a drink. Where's your kitchen?" Maude McGinnis commanded, getting out of her coat. And, owing to her being right about his being soaked through, unable to come up with a better course of action, he led her to the kitchen, asked her to ignore the mess, warned her he only had coffee, no tea, and left to head off to change and towel his hair dry.

On his return, now in shirtsleeves, he found her at the sink doing the washing up, noting she must have gone around to gather the empty water and Calvados glasses he was in the habit of leaving lying around. "You need somebody to look after you, Xavier," she declared with her back to him as he stepped into the kitchen; "All men I ever met are the same: happen upon their kitchen and there is the mouldy bread. Mouldy rhymes with lonely, my mother used to say. You need looking after, Xavier. Jane told me you had a lady friend once; but you never lived together and she passed away. And the ring on your finger is in consideration of somebody else entirely; somebody who may also be dead and belongs to a time you keep jealously to yourself like a man possessed by ghosts. You're not a bad man, Xavier—It shouldn't be difficult for you to find company and make someone happy. Jane always liked you, you know. Very fond of you, she was. Still, I made some coffee with your machine. I'm not too familiar with these sorts of things, but it's in a cup in the oven staying warm for you."

He swallowed hard: "Ahem. Thank you, Mrs McGinnis. My neighbours' cleaner stops by once every fortnight. She's due any day now, I believe. Not that she is really needed," he defended himself; "And about that mouldy bread, it's not the norm—I've been busy. And I'd sooner you didn't trouble yourself with the washing up, Mrs McGinnis."

"It's alright. I'll finish in a moment. And I will not suffer you to thank me indeed! But please, will you call me Maude now? All that 'Mrs McGinnis's makes me feel like a giddy headmistress. Fetch your coffee, Xavier. I don't know how you like it so didn't put any sugar or milk in it."

He recalled her saying 'the best thing to do when it's raining is to let it rain' while still outside the door. Under the circumstances, it seemed the wisest course of action. Having retrieved the coffee she'd made him, he settled at the kitchen table, where she joined him after finishing tidying up the sink to her satisfaction.

"Now there, thank you for having me. I won't keep you long. I know it's early, but I'm not one for coffee and wonder whether you would mind indulging this weary woman with a generous shot of that enticing Calvados of yours, Xavier. I promise I won't tell anyone if you don't," she added, retrieving a pen and pink post-it pad from her handbag to scribble a few words down on the paper; "Washing up liquid and scourer," she cleared up.

And a moment later he found himself frowning awkwardly across the table from her. She, on the other hand, looked uncannily mellow – as when she was in his car the day they drove to Walthamstow. The casual exuberance she'd exhibited while fussing at the sink had deserted her. She quietly sipped her Calvados, playing with the pink pad between her big fingers. At rest, she looked crushed, graceless, a weary worn-out creature indeed. The only other woman who'd ever sat in this kitchen with him was Ali. The few things he thought of saying somehow felt inadequate. Yet, strangely, the silence wasn't all that disagreeable. Still, he finally came up with something appropriate: "I guess Jane's funeral went well?"

"Sometimes God is testing us, Xavier," she declared without looking back at him; "The Lord seeks proof of our faith to gauge whether our souls deserve salvation. I know you're not a religious man—But I should think you understand."

He grinned:

"Not all demons need religion, Mrs Mc—Maude; or salvation."

"Do you believe yourself to be a demon, Xavier?"

"Only insomuch as I am a man, Mrs—Maude."

"But God created man in his own image. We are all God's creation."

"The lambs and all the things that crawl and slither and feed on each other's flesh. Indeed. And the men and women who shear, subjugate and own them all. Such invention."

"Do you not need forgiveness?"

He sighed: "For my money, they who speak of forgiveness in God's name are way too quick to judge the rest of us."

"They judge but God forgives—All is forgiveness."

"Well, Mrs Mc—Maude; if I may: can you forgive God for what has been taken from you? And would you be visiting my house right now if my calling was to serve God?"

She said nothing, pensive, then:

"Abraham was spared the pain of having to sacrifice his son," she said: "I was never given the option to sacrifice my daughter or granddaughters. Had I been, I'd never have consented to it. For sure. Could this be why they have been taken away from me? Isaac was spared only after Abraham consented to sacrifice him. And the Good Lord consented to sacrifice his own son Jesus for our sins. But I would never have consented."

And Maude McGinnis took a deep breath, keeping her eyes down, and he understood that she wished not to talk. She had come knocking at his door seeking shelter from the unhappy house in Walthamstow, from London's rowdy streets, and, for now, from her church's judgement. She had travelled into a foreign land, a stranger in London, the lost sheep of her own gospel who had come to the only 'other' place she knew. Lombard wondered whether the McGinnis family would now hold vigil for Jane's newly deceased child.

At last, when she was ready to speak, she seemed found again, reunited with her God enough not to allude directly to either her daughter or her now two deceased granddaughters. Instead, she spoke of their husband and father, with much melancholy: "Jane's Joseph was a strange one, you know. Never known such kindness in a man. He sure was no demon— Wouldn't hurt a fly. But Jane would say he needed to man up. 'Man up', she said. And a good soul he was too. If the things he shared with Jane were true, his parents were quite comfortable when they came to London from Iran. His father was a specialist surgeon of some sort, but he passed away, and his mother was much too proud to work. She never learnt English. When he was seventeen, she too passed away, and he was all that was left—No kin to turn to for help or comfort. Besides loving my Jane and giving her four children and a fifth on the way, his job at the council was all he'd ever done. He used to break Jane's heart—Day-in day-out, all by himself, assigned to deal with grievances and complaints. Often, his work would have him return home late and worn out. Some tenants set dogs on him, threw things—All sorts of things: dirty needles, food. She said he even had a TV set thrown at him once, you know. But he never complained. Jane thought his bosses took advantage of his good nature and singled him out to visit and deliver eviction notices to problem tenants. Poor Joseph. Still, he got them out of their small council flat in Holloway and into that nice house in Walthamstow. He did. Such a gracious man he was. A heart of gold. A Godly soul."

Lombard resisted the temptation to draw attention to God again, listening instead in silence. In time, but not before downing a second glass of Calvados, she readied to leave. "I let the police know about little Zoe," she announced wearily getting into her coat; "They offered their condolences, of course. Now Jane's been laid to rest—Bless her soul—The family flew back to Ireland earlier this morning. Only my eldest is delaying her return to help me with Jane's two remaining girls and all the things that need seeing to. Now there's no longer any need to stay here waiting for Jane's baby to recover, I can't be sure how long it will be before I'll be leaving with the other girls for home. I should think two or three weeks at most—I don't think I could leave Joseph alone at the farm much longer than that. I'll let you know if I don't hear from you before then. Thank you for having me, Xavier. You take good care of yourself now. And whether you like it or not may the good Lord be with you."

"I haven't yet had time to look into that Mr Weyland we—"

"Oh—It's alright. You needn't worry now, Xavier. I hardly see how you could have had time for anything by now. Do let me know when you do though. Please do."

Back out in the rain, she stepped into a black cab waiting outside – a black figure climbing into black – and watching the taxi drive away under the grey sky he guessed nothing had prepared her for her current trials. There was a time, he knew, when he may have admired her poignant fortitude.

Unless Maude McGinnis's suspicions about her daughter's demise being the result of targeted action were ever to prove well-founded, insomuch as Lombard was already set on looking into the matter of Joseph Aratoon and any association the latter may have had with the film producer-director Avery Weyland, the news of Jane's second twin dying was of little significance. The reality was, for all his former good opinion of Jane and his current qualified regard for her mother, he found the whole affair tedious to excess. Humble lives going about living and making babies; paltry amounts of money in personal bank accounts; a suicide captured on one camera; a lethal hit-and-run caught on another; a guilt-ridden mother enslaved to religion; a feted film producer who hailed from a world so far removed from all their quiet desolation he might barely know them from the grime. Jane was no fool – she had presented a good case. But it demonstrated only that her timid and model husband had likely broken one of the Command-ments. Given his occupation as a council Housing officer on a limited income, he probably had succumbed to greed, collected a few backhanders. By way of speculation, it tallied with the wording of the note sent after his suicide alluding to money and his being needed again. Were Jane to be proved right about Avery Weyland and his deep voice, given the nature of the man's occupation – film-making – it was hardly a leap to imagine the two could have come to a mutually beneficial arrangement where money passed hands, such as to facilitate access to certain locations perhaps. Still and all, as sensible Jane herself had already pointed out in her notes about another would-be scenario involving bribes, even her timid husband would not have been foolish enough to launder ill-gotten gains through his bank account.

Like he told Maude McGinnis, everything has its place. Yet in this affair, all was messy, whether or not one looked past the proposition that Avery Weyland, a successful film producer-director with pedigree and political connections, was implicated in the running over of a young widowed mother, her twin daughters and unborn baby.

When detective chief inspector Mark Badal's call came later that afternoon, it hardly helped shed light on the situation. In the event, the police had indeed exercised due diligence in investigating the incident that had cost Jane her life. Lombard had wondered about this for, if Maude McGinnis were to be believed, the offending hit-and-run car had been abandoned and set alight not far from the scene. Ever since the Mayor and Transport for London had rigged the streets of the capital with surveillance equipment to fine vehicles driven in contravention of the latest emissions regulations, it had become near impossible to drive anywhere within the North Circular without being captured on camera. Add to this the array of private and business surveillance devices directed at the streets, and it became unthinkable to go anywhere or do anything without being watched. Lombard reckoned that, even though the car's occupants could not be identified through the windscreen, they ought to have been caught on camera at or near the location where they set the car alight, and their next steps and escape captured, whether that be to a private residence, public place or to some other means of transport. The way it happened, the two figures in the car appeared to have known what they were doing. The vehicle had been stolen that same day, ten or so miles outside London's surveilled Emission Zone, near Cheshunt just outside the capital's orbital motorway. It had travelled down the A1055, across the North Circular and into Walthamstow's heavily monitored streets without stopping anywhere on the way, eventually to park within eyeshot of the Aratoon's residence. There, it had remained for an hour or so, until suddenly taking off fast to run Jane over prior to being driven back across the North Circular to a deserted lane in Chingford where it was set ablaze safe from prying eyes. A police search through the local surveillance camera footage had failed to capture the culprits. For lack of any other credible explanation, and partly on account of a witness who recalled hearing loud 'freak' music coming from their parked car in Jane's street, it was decided the killers were likely to be joyriders high on drugs, so impaired that they never spotted Jane crossing the road in the light from the Belisha beacon against the twilight sky. "Nasty story. And with it having just turned into a triple manslaughter incident, I guess the news won't be of much comfort to your acquaintance's mother," detective chief inspector Mark Badal ended; "But unless someone somewhere tips us off, that's probably as far as we're ever gonna get. Mind you, it happens. But I don't suppose I need to tell you that."

Within an hour of Maude McGinnis's departure, Lombard booked an open return flight to Madeira leaving the day after next and contacted the other half of EcoWatt's 'Brand Reputation and Protection Department'. Years ago, Edward Duncan had handed him a mobile phone he described as a "protected secure gateway" dedicated exclusively to communicating via an email application with a party he named "Monroe". Lombard had never met Monroe, had no idea of their gender, if they were one or many, only that – in Edward Duncan's words – they were ex-dark web experts for him to team up with. Whereas Lombard's preserve was the tangible world, Monroe's was the digital. Edward Duncan knew what he was doing; seeing that Lombard was most ignorant of much to do with computers or information technology, Monroe made a worthwhile addition to his one-man team, proving to be a true master at their trade. If the information existed as digital data, there seemed to be no limit to what Monroe could unearth. The provision of a name, number plate or phone number, if requested, would return reams of intelligence via a dedicated old fax machine Lombard had been provided with for just that purpose. Monroe defined the findings they provided as 'digital shadow'. Every person's, business's or property's digital shadow was up for grabs. Not merely financial, medical or other personal information such as browsing or shopping habits, but since the introduction of live wireless utility meters, they could also supply minute by minute records of when and how much water, electricity or gas was being used within a property, provide evidence of when and how many times a toilet was flushed, or a kettle filled or boiled, or a household headed for bed, or whether they had guests or turned on an extra heater. Lombard had cared nothing for revealing to Edward Duncan that Monroe scared him. And Edward Duncan had paid no mind to his words. Monroe was a ghost stealing mortals' digital shadows to procure and empower other mortals; a digital omnipresence. In some respects, Monroe was God; an almighty new God who, unlike the old, neither required nor provided redemptive confessions, or casts of characters such as Moses, Bathsheba, Jesus, Mary Magdalene or Muhammad to captivate the world. Just smart meters and raw digital data, invitations into all souls and all houses. For all that though, as Edward Duncan put it, "In today's world this God is a necessary evil."

For now, Lombard called Maude McGinnis; he wanted to know the phone numbers on the note and map receipt that Jane had linked. He also asked whether Joseph Aratoon had his own mobile number before he died. He had, and Maude McGinnis helpfully procured all three numbers, which he faxed on to Monroe together with Jane's landline number, adding:

> 'Any information/data about these numbers much appreciated, including, if possible, any traffic between them going five years back. Thanks. X.'

Edward Duncan never specified whether Monroe was his to use for non-EcoWatt business, but he'd done just that on a couple of occasions in the past and, in any case, if pressed, could say the query related to a tip about Alan Winston's whereabouts. Now, after enjoying an early dinner at a local restaurant, the remainder of a day that had begun with a sleepless night and a dawn visit to Letitia Balthazar was to end with his performing his own rudimentary online research about Avery Weyland. His efforts helped him flesh out the man somewhat, but did little to quell his scepticism about the venture he was embarking on.

A few years short of forty, Avery Weyland was the elder of three sons born into a wealthy artistic family. Among his direct relations, he counted a British novelist father; a New Zealander condiment heiress turned celebrity photographer mother; two siblings, both in the music industry, one an executive, the other a guitarist; a television comedienne formerly wedded to a book publisher for wife; and two teenage sons from a previous marriage to the daughter of a sitting member of Parliament. He also owned a celebrated painter and architect among his ancestors, had graduated from Art school, started a film production company in his mid-twenties, was a founding member of an artistic group which called itself 'The Aesthetic Establishment', and more recently had turned his energy to film direction, his ventures meeting with success enough to afford him press and media attention, regularly appearing on radio, television and in magazines depicting him at events such as the Oscars, Baftas or the Cannes or Venice film festivals – which he'd only just returned from attending.

On the face of it, the man seemed at ease with good fortune's trappings, such as a Grade II listed Georgian house on Hampstead's exclusive Downshire Hill and a cottage in the New Forest. Still, as if to confirm the often-cited truism that there is no such thing as a perfect family, or one that knows no tragedy, a couple of noteworthy adverse matters did blemish an otherwise much-favoured existence: his guitarist brother was currently serving time in a Turkish prison on drug-smuggling related charges and, some four years earlier, his father had perished in a house fire thought to have started during a botched burglary; no one was ever prosecuted for it.

All this was a great nuisance to Lombard. For if indeed it was to turn out that Avery Weyland – a man with much to his name and an equal amount to lose – had involved himself with Joseph Aratoon in an enterprise nefarious enough to invite hurting the likes of Jane, merely calling on him to discuss the matter would be pointless. Even in the event he would agree to meet, he was hardly likely to confess to having done bad things. By all means, there were other options, less civilized, more expeditious options. A gun pointed at his head might be one of them, might even prove effective. Only, he knew, there was no reckoning how a likely innocent man might react in such a situation; whether he'd faint, fight, cry, which false confessions or lies he may be willing to tell, or friends – if allowed to live – he might call on later; because for now nothing Lombard could make sense of called for Avery Weyland to be harmed or demeaned. For here was another consideration: his internet search showed that Avery Weyland was far from Walthamstow on the evening of Jane's hit-and-run, being entertained in Italy at the Venice Film Festival.

In this manner the day ended with a question: how to get close enough to someone of Avery Weyland's pedigree and status to determine whether he had cause to hurt Jane?

After all this, exhausted, he remembered to check Letitia Balthazar's social media pages, found she had deleted much of anything relating to Alan Winston or Madeira, and he surrendered to slumber.

ELEVEN

Films got to entertain—The same as whores.

Overnight, a great storm descended over southern England, the like of which had never been seen in the British Isles in late summer. Lasting a good five hours, it earned itself the epithet 'tropical' for laying waste much of the land in its path, uprooting trees, tearing up roofs, causing floods and much injury, taking a dozen or so lives before its winds and rains abated. Across London, the public transport system came to a standstill. For the first few hours of the early morning, the Tube was deemed too dangerous to operate; the drainage infrastructure and never-before-used tunnel floodgates had proved unequal to the prodigious amount of rainwater that made its way into its underground system. Come mid-morning, it was estimated that nearly an eighth of an average year's rainfall had come down in all of five hours, with pundits and government officials preferring to speak of global warming and impending doom rather than a natural disaster, all reckoning the damage to property and the economy surpassed that of the Great October Storm of 1987. Yet, throughout it all, the Post Office had carried on collecting and delivering the mail and Lombard – so exhausted had he been – never stopped sleeping. By the time he got up before lunch, the sun was up, reassuringly bright against the returned blue sky, and a couple of hours later, while heading Mile End's way, he would never have known of the night's upheaval but for the sight of the odd fallen or fractured tree along the way, and in some measure, the gormless expression of the crowds strolling the streets; the travel disruption prevented many from going to work, while others had merely seized the moment to play truant.

Lombard's return to Mile End was attributable to a vague idea he had formed in that untroubled time which occurs between first arousing and the mind being revisited by all the commotion sleep forsakes as it takes command. Night is a great advisor, and an absurd newspaper piece about a prisoner exchange suggested John Bowdion needn't necessarily be defined by his present circumstances, and thereby may prove of use if properly handled.

Lombard found a space in the same paying parking bay he'd used previously and, partly to take some air and stretch his legs, wandered to the nearby green on the off-chance John Bowdion might be out again walking his dead neighbour's dog. The green was cordoned off, a crew of men with chain-saws were clearing a couple of uprooted trees, one of which – the chestnut tree in the far corner which had presided over late picnickers two days earlier – had come down on the perimeter fence and a few cars along the kerb. He paused to observe the scene, recalling the odd sense of dread that had got hold of him last time he looked at that spot; he swallowed hard, and headed for the murder house at the end of the dead end.

Today, trying the unlabelled bells brought to the door a dumpy grey-haired woman in bare feet who apologized for not knowing whether John Bowdion was there, letting on she only moved into the house the previous evening and had yet to meet the other residents. She was about to go for help when the bald man who'd greeted him on his previous visit turned up. He recognized Lombard, seemed pleased to see him, explained that "Johnny's bell isn't working but I think he is in", and let him in with the instruction to climb to the top of the stairs and knock at the door on the left once on the landing. The stage of Alan Winston's murder turned out to be a surprisingly large grand hallway with black and white floor tiles and tall old-fashioned cast-iron radiators. Still, Lombard barely paused as he left the man and woman in the doorway to introduce themselves to each other.

What went on in John Bowdion's mind when he found Lombard standing on the landing outside his door may be best described as a mix of curiosity and anxious awe. Yet, as is the tendency of the lonely and lost, the man was set on appearing peeved at being disturbed, which insofar as he stood with his arms wrapped around his chest only served to make him look pitiable. "For fuck's sake, Martin!" he shouted towards the voices down the stairwell; "How many times need I fucking say it! Don't fucking let anyone in without checking with me first, you bald-headed cretin!" To appease him, Lombard apologized for turning up uninvited, assured him he'd have called if he'd had his number and indicated he had not returned on account of Alan Winston but, rather, to discuss a separate and delicate matter which required him to get hold of a film script as a means to approach and win the confidence of a film producer. He also presently added, before the other could respond, that he knew little about the film industry, was – "needless to say" – prepared to be denied his curious request, but hoped the contrary as it was important he got hold of at least one film script he could rely was unread by film industry folks; "I thought I'd mention this in case you rightly suggest that there are hundreds of film scripts free to download out there. I recalled you telling me you had a dozen or so unproduced works the other afternoon, is that right?"

This sort of approach invariably sets the stage for one of two things to happen: the target either sends him on his way at once, or bites. In that he appeared to be considering his options, John Bowdion had already bitten. For all his effort to appear as if he wished to set about dismissing the entire world, the same expectant glimmer that had glazed his eyes at the mention of Avery Weyland the last time they met had returned, as if the mention of film matters stirred up overpowering yearnings deep inside of him. Not yet middle-aged and the picture of raw disillusionment, John Bowdion bore his adversity the way of a threadbare winter coat. Yet, to exist free from desire or curiosity seemed beyond him – however many hours of anguish it quite plausibly cost him to feel his heart beating in hope within his painful breast. For now, he scowled, as yet unsure how best to respond, prompting Lombard to keep on talking, letting on he could also do with advice regarding dealing with film industry people, announcing there would be "financial recompense for your help, of course." But this too failed to stir a reaction, rousing the possibility that the man's misgivings might relate to a reluctance to let Lombard into his bedsit, whereupon Lombard apologized again for intruding and suggested he could take his leave to wait for him on the green outside. This, at last, shook John Bowdion from his trance. He mumbled a few words about the green being closed on account of the night's storm, then "Well, it's your time and your dime. I'm not sure I can help you, but why don't you come in," and, as Lombard stepped out of the dark landing into an unexpectedly bright and large room packed with labelled cardboard boxes stacked up to the ceiling against the length of an entire wall, asked "What's your name, again?". "Laurent Lagarde. But Laurent will do." "Is that Lagarde as in *La garde se meurt et ne se rend pas?*" Lombard grinned: "Is it okay if I call you John?" "Sure. I—You got me intrigued now. That film producer you're on about, wouldn't be that Avery Weyland by any chance, would it?" "Oh—I'd hoped to keep that to myself but I see you remember my mentioning him before." "Right. Huh—What do you know? Anyway—Ignore the mess—I didn't expect any visitors. Can I offer you something to drink?"

The bedsit consisted of a large studio room basking in the light from two streetside south-facing windows and a couple of large skylights set in the low sloping ceiling. A small modern kitchenette filled one corner, a partitioned shower room another, and the rest, not counting the wall lined with stacks of cardboard boxes, was taken by an unmade antique double bed and a huge table with matching chairs covered with papers, books, medicines, a laptop, a desktop, plates of leftovers and empty beer cans. While John Bowdion busied about making coffee, filling the silence with small talk about the storm which had kept him up on account of the rain and wind battering the skylights and rattling the slates above his head, Lombard settled in the dazzling brightness of the table, admiring the south view across rooftops towards the Thames in the mid-distance. He guessed the antique bed, table and chairs in the room had known grander surroundings, noted that the cardboard boxes lining the wall were labelled with removal company stickers, peered at an outsized framed black and white photograph of Marylin Monroe and a bespectacled man standing hemmed in by a pack of photographers. "Marylin Monroe and Arthur Miller," John Bowdion commented; "The aphrodisiacal actress and Pulitzer Prize-winning playwright. You can look but won't find one camera lens or face among the heaving humanity circling them aimed at the playwright. Speaks volumes for what we are." "She was a beautiful woman," Lombard said. John Bowdion scoffed: "I tried hanging it on my office wall during a doomed stint as a creative writing lecturer. Some colleagues and students objected, peered at an outsized framed black a sick celebration of women's objectification!' they fucking said. Really. You got to ask yourself, don't you?"

Lombard queried as to the whereabouts of the dead old man's dog, was told the landlord had had it taken away with all of the old man's belongings just the previous day; they'd also cleared up the few things Alan Winston had left behind to ready the room for a new tenant. "I've not met her yet. Anyway, old Samuel's belongings filled a small truck. No one knows where it's been taken to. On the other hand, Alan's fitted into a large shoe box. His mother was meant to come to collect it but never turned up. I think they decided to post it to her. I can't decide which is the more pathetic: the life taken in a small truck or the one posted in a shoebox?"

All of this time, notifications rang from multiple devices among the general mess on the table. "Sorry about that. I can't say it makes me proud but I'm quite the keyboard warrior nowadays. I don't know about you but cyberspace sure turned out to be manna from heaven for all that lurks in the human swampland." Lombard grinned again, reached for the coffee offered to him, watched John Bowdion switch off several devices on the table and, in the ensuing welcome silence, the man settled down in front of a laptop where at once he started rolling a cigarette with a wry smile: "Well, Laurent—Like I said, you have me intrigued. I'm not sure I'm the person to help you, but please do tell me more. Avery Weyland! Huh! Now there's an inside player. Mediocrity—impediment-not— In tandem with nepotism. Are you going to tell me what he did; how much trouble he might be in?" Lombard sighed: "I'd sooner you hadn't recalled my mentioning his name, John. I didn't think we'd meet again when I did." "Hush-hush, eh!" "I guess so. And whatever happens here I trust I can count on you to keep it that way, right?" John Bowdion paused for thought, his eyes all impish agitation. "Yeah. It figures—I get it. But can you at least tell me this: supposing you get what you're after, would it mean trouble for him personally? I mean—Serious trouble?" Lombard advised that, for all he knew, Avery Weyland had nothing to worry about. "Nothing to worry about, eh. Right—Right. Hush-hush. So, in how much of a hurry are you then?" "Hurry about what?" "This film business." "A fair bit of a hurry, I reckon." John Bowdion found this amusing. He snorted, lit his cigarette with a silver lighter and proceeded to explain that while he welcomed the opportunity to help land the likes of Avery Weyland in trouble, he had to be honest and admit he thought Lombard stood no chance of getting anywhere near the man by using a screenplay for lure. "No matter what screenplay. Mine or most anybody else's. You clearly haven't got a clue how things work in the film industry or the sort of folks you're dealing with," he sneered, going on to say that players of Avery Weyland's ilk never read or accept unsolicited screenplays from just anyone; that they only consider material sent by agents or lawyers, and even then, delegate the reading to their staff in a process which takes months and, whatever the outcome, is unlikely to result in his being wined and dined by the man himself. "To put it another way, Laurent, you'd stand a hell of a better chance buddying up to Weyland by posing as a friendly postman than an ingénue scriptwriter. By the way—And sorry for asking but what with you being French and all—I don't suppose you'd seriously be thinking of passing the work off as your own now, would you?" Lombard let him know this was not the case. He was looking for an unknown screenplay – "In digital format but ready to be printed," he specified – that met film industry standards. Its writer or subject matter were of no concern. In point of fact, John Bowdion could leave his name on it if he so wished. "Oh. God no—You wouldn't so much as get past his secretary with my name on the title page. You really don't know much, do you, friend? I don't get it. You got your arse all the way over here, yet you have no idea what you're doing. Or is this a shot in the dark kind of thing? Like a prayer?"

Lombard had come across John Bowdions before; shipwrecks, broken men carrying one cross or another which proved too broad or heavy for their narrow shoulders; they failed to adapt to their environment and hid their failure, like a bent spine, behind sarcasm, in empty defiance did their utmost to look as if they played for keeps. By all accounts, he himself could make such an impression; and would own that he did feel like such men at times. So long as everyone knew their place though, he never judged; everyone has a bone to pick. All the same, John Bowdion's display of familiarity had begun to irritate him. He did what he could to contain his sentiments.

"I appreciate you seeing me, John. Bearing this in mind let me be candid: I didn't come here to insult your intelligence. That said, nor am I here auditioning to be your friend, John. I'm here because I need help, for which I can pay, and because a line I came across in The Paragon inclined me to trust that there's more to you than meets the eye—That, maybe, you can be trusted to know your business. Now, you're absolutely right about my not knowing much about this script thing. Nor have I made my mind up yet. That's because I intended to weigh what I could glean from this visit first. And—" he paused to retrieve an envelope from his jacket's inside pocket which he placed in a clear space on the table in front of him; "Here. However this ends, a thousand pounds for your trouble. I hope it's okay. I've also been authorized to pay a further three thousand pounds were you to be good enough to provide me with a film script I may use for the purpose I explained."

John Bowdion took a deep drag of his cigarette, upset but

peering at the envelope without saying a word, and exhaled in a slow, deliberate manner.

"Why don't you educate me about the film world, John? Anything you think may be of use. Tell me: how different is it from the rest of civilisation, eh?"

"Oh! It's hardly different from it; the same fuck-you cesspit, that's all," the other scowled; "What's that you're were saying about a line you came across in The Paragon?"

"It's of no importance."

"Right. And this money you just put down stays here even if this conversation ends now."

"It does," returned Lombard with a sigh, getting to his feet as if to leave; "Thank you for your time."

"No. I mean good. Where are you going? I mean—If you want to know about the film world, don't go."

"Thank you, John," said Lombard, sitting down again; "I'm glad."

John Bowdion eyed him up and down, delayed on his cufflinks and smiled smugly; he knew things Lombard and his suit didn't:

"Well—Well now, you wish to know about the film world; the film industry. How to put it? Well, in this great country, at any rate, it's all about a select clique riding the gravy train. A gilded choo-choo of bells and whistles in which a favoured few mostly well-to-do politically or fashionably correct lottery winners joyride a golden loop, dipping their exquisitely manicured claws in free gravy. Now and again some bystander might be given the nod to jump on board the blessed train, allowed a whiff of the gravy, so to speak, but even then, only newbies who can demonstrate their unprincipled ways are ever let anywhere near the buffet car or locomotive. You got to worm your way to the gold and the inexhaustible public purse."

Lombard frowned: "I'm afraid you've lost me, John."

"Have I now? Well, come to think of it, it's not all that much of a surprise. But you asked. I tell you what, maybe we should talk about desire. They say you French folks get the 'desire' thing."

As he had on the park bench two days earlier, John Bowdion had begun to rock gently back and forth, holding his chest tight in his arms again. Lombard recalled his mentioning having a medical condition, but by the look of it, his speaking about the film industry was cause enough for his nerves to have become frayed.

"Have you ever coveted somebody, Laurent?" he went on; "I mean really coveted them—Yearned for their touch, their skin, their lips, their hair. So badly that the mere thought of their body being next to yours, the imagined warmth of their touch, kindles your limbs and fills your heart with sweetness. Well, if you know of such feelings, that's what movies were once: coveted forbidden fruit. Now, picture this. A whore in a brothel. If you've ever been to one, make it a German brothel; as in clean, safe and legal, with pre-vetted whores, sterilized rooms and medical kits on hand. Pick a room—Say, one hundred and thirty-one—And make the whore between its four walls beautiful as a Morning Dew Rose. Well, that's what the movies have become. Now, to each their own, I know, but which one is more desirable: the deliciously desired wild forbidden fruit or the safe, state-sponsored pension-funded fuck known as Rose in room one hundred and thirty-one?"

"I much appreciate the allegory, if that's what it is—But I'm still lost, John," Lombard confessed truthfully. And John Bowdion, shaking his head ruefully, in an attempt at being understood, now took it upon himself to embark on a lecture about "the moral turpitude of the British film industry", which he attributed to a recent former Prime Minister's cynical decision to provide it with yearly brides and tax breaks worth tens of millions of pounds through the office of the National Lottery and what he called The Film Commission. In doing so, John Bowdion held, at one stroke the government had made itself the industry's largest investor, and turned it into the most heavily subsidized industry relative to its size. Such generosity had met with British filmmakers' universal approval, of course, and the consequences, although predictable, proved catastrophic. At once, easy subsidy money had brought about the death of hard graft and visionary ideas. From then on, the new state-funded Film Commission had become the first and last port of call for anyone thinking of producing a film; "A shortcut to ready-to-wear money. No more hustling for pennies, striving to come up with 'The Great Idea' worth fighting for or sinking your life savings in, the kind that takes vision, belief, ambition, sacrifice and may well turn out to be a masterpiece and make your name, and, if all goes well, shed loads of money, or if not, be your absolute ruin. Fuck all that. At one stroke, raising development and production funds became a simple matter of yielding to greed by way of pandering to The Film Commission; filling up their forms and ticking their boxes. Pure Machiavellian genius."

In the end what Lombard made of it all – because the man went on at great length – was that John Bowdion held the opinion that state-money was toxic to the arts, a potent source of corruption, and provided for the creation of an environment fit for mediocrities, fortune-hunters and "freeloaders", favouring as it did political animals at the expense of genuine artists. Accordingly – he assuredly predicted – not a single British film masterpiece would ever see the light of day again until this bleak state of affairs was remedied. "Vacuous navel-gazing and revised history wrapped in topical mellifluous proclivities is as good as it gets. They declaim Shakespeare—For now anyhow, until he too shall be deemed to bleed the wrong blood. Anyone seeking to go it alone with a nonconformist screenplay hits a funding desert—Is deemed a misfit. It's not rocket science; I mean, if you were going to invest in a film, would you pick one that comes graced by Film Commission money, or back a maverick vision—Eat from the forbidden fruit? So, if you're in films, you see, nowadays the only game in town is Is-You-In-Or-Is-You-Out. Are you a swaggering swinger or a jilted lover? Welcome on board and come meet the stars! We aren't many but are special—We groom and guzzle and suck lollies and ain't half having fun! And don't worry pissing it all away—We got loads more coming from where it all comes from and bazillions more jam-packed hampers. And nobody gives a monkey's—Not a duck not a flying fuck! Films are that pre-vetted whore by the name of

Morning Dew Rose in room one hundred and thirty-one I was talking about. Cash put up and punters serviced—Your dick gets done and disinfected and the way out takes you past the other Johns waiting for their turn; and like you were before them, the whole queue's aware they won't be raptured out of their mortal coil when they come, but at least they feel well-safe no one's going to put their dicks in a vice."

Lombard watched him for a moment. For the whole time he'd spoken, John Bowdion never ceased his gentle rocking, or released his chest from his arms' grip. Now, still rocking, he was gazing at the clear sky outside the window in front of him, his half-consumed roll up cigarette extinguished between his fingers. Whether he was aware of it or even cared, the man exuded pain and self-loathing, looked so damaged he made it easy to think he might be contagious or deliver bad luck. Yet, as Lombard had thought earlier, the stacks of neatly piled cardboard boxes with their removal company stickers, the elegant antique table and chairs and bed and other items around the room suggested he'd seen better times, likely not too long ago.

"You make it sound like everybody in the film industry is a whore," Lombard said.

"Huh! Films got to entertain—The same as whores. Now, very sorry not to be more positive," he went on; "But you asked. And maybe now you understand why I don't think much of your idea of using a screenplay to bait Avery Weyland."

"I do, John. This is very informative. I'm glad I came—And think I should be able to put some of the things I've just learnt to good use."

"You do?" John Bowdion uttered in disbelief, glancing at him with suspicion.

"If the film industry is merely another place where money rules and makes for bad things, I may do just fine."

"Not with a screenplay, you won't," the man insisted; "Never mind one of mine."

"You must raise your sights, John."

"Raise my—Huh! Not one of mine, Mister. Damn straight."

"If that's so, I hope you don't mind my asking, why would this be, John? What happened between you and the film industry? Did something bad happen to you, John?"

It turned out John Bowdion very much did mind being asked, which ought to have been somewhat predictable given his demeanour so far: "Did something bad happen to me! What do you think?" came the retort, quick as a whip.

"I'm sorry—"

"Huh!" the man exclaimed, all of a sudden ceasing his rocking to glare at Lombard: "All that sound and fury signifying nothing! It would all be sweet purring if I wasn't so hurt and out of luck, right," he snarled, turning away towards the sky again to resume his back-and-forth rocking. "You don't say! It's a fucking wonder animal welfare organisations are so fond of using the word 'humane' and its derivatives—You got to ask what the animals rescued from humanity's depravity would make of the term 'humane' implying 'compassion'. You remind me of those idiot cops who were here asking questions about what happened in the hallway the other day. 'Why were you so set on stopping the reporter from entering Mr Newman's room. Mr Bowdion?' 'Because he came here to try to pin dirt on the dead old Jew,' I say. 'Right. Would it be fair to assume you are Jewish then, Mr Bowdion?' 'What's it to you?' I say. 'Well, you did allege that the reporter worked for an antisemitic organisation, did you not?' Fucking morons! All of five feet and four inches of her—Fucking moron! 'Let me ask you a question,' I say, 'Would you fucking ask me if I happened to be a dwarf inside if I'd stood tall for a little person, you moron!' Huh! Well, they cautioned me for using offensive language to an officer of the law. Can you fucking believe it!"

Lombard took this outburst – which was regrettable in that unlike most of the rest of his performance his last question had been somewhat sincere – as a signal to leave. "I have to go now," he announced, checking his watch while rising to his feet; "My parking meter is about to run out. In any event, I apologize if I offended you. But I'd like to think that you misjudged my question, John. There was no malice to it. The thing is, I've long since learnt that a good story's worth more than all the great lectures in the world. But I'm sure I'm not telling a writer anything he doesn't already know."

He left his card with the envelope of money on the table, told John Bowdion to call him – the sooner the better – once he had had time to think about what they'd discussed, and thanked him for sharing some of his knowledge. Stepping again through the hallway downstairs, he did pause to take in the scene of Alan Winston's murder, thought little of it and left.

Not unlike the time before, Lombard fell prey to uneasy agitation on leaving John Bowdion. Still, on this occasion it hardly counted as a nuisance. His mind was on other matters. Being near to Walthamstow he considered calling at Jane's house to ask Maude McGinnis whether she knew where to find the mobile she told him on the phone Joseph Aratoon had owned. It could prove useful in that Monroe may be able to assess if it was ever used to communicate with Avery Weyland. Instead, recalling the dark house where Maude McGinnis was now mourning the death of three of her descendants, he opted to call her on his return from Madeira. Insomuch as he was prepared never to hear from John Bowdion again, he also wound up mulling over ways to source the film script he needed, for nothing he just heard persuaded him against the plan he'd already formed. If anything, the opposite was true; greed is potent but exploitable.

Unsurprisingly, Monroe had come good. Lombard found a roll of paper unspooled from the fax machine on his return home. However, what Monroe had sent was mostly raw data for him to wade through, which he did, thereupon determining that Jane had correctly identified Avery Weyland's voice. The number on the map receipt she'd called from her landline was registered to the film producer of Downshire Hill in Hampstead NW3. The number on the note to her husband was tied to a store-bought pay-as-you-go Sim card used in an unregistered phone that had remained active for less than two weeks, and was used just the once to answer a call. This call came from Jane's number, had lasted less than five seconds, at which point the phone was switched off never to come to life again. Of further interest, when Jane's call was answered, the receiving phone's signal placed it in the West End Soho area where Avery Weyland's Dean Street film production office was also located. Coming to Joseph Aratoon's old phone, Monroe had only been able to provide two months' worth of records, the rest having been deleted. What there was showed no traffic with Avery Weyland's number, and his phone had suddenly stopped sending signals on April 3rd at 11:54 a.m. Another look at the date-stamped footage of Joseph Aratoon's suicide in Kilburn station revealed this to be the exact time the man had thrown himself under a train, suggesting his phone had died with him, leaving only its digital shadow.

Jane had been right, and while none of these findings remotely suggested Avery Weyland was involved in her death, they were incriminating enough to warrant not ruling it out as a possibility. This was unwelcome news. Lombard had hoped to find cause to dismiss Maude McGinnis's suspicions. Instead, it had just become even more pressing to find some way to reach Avery Weyland.

As if by providence, he was brooding over such concerns when John Bowdion called just as he was about to start packing for his trip to Madeira. The man had thought things over, and let it be known that he was willing to loan Lombard one of his screenplays. Its title was 'Masters of Beasts'. The work was a few years old, had only ever been sent to one producer who'd returned it unread. It was a dystopian science-fiction tale set in Britain in the near future, he advised; "Are you familiar with the parable of the escaped Jews in the cellar? In America they make it about fugitive slaves or runaway slaves." "I'm afraid not." "Well, it's inspired by it. A hundred folks hide in a cellar. The people hunting them are searching the house above their heads. What are they to do when a baby among their number starts crying: Door 'A'—Smother it to save 99;

Door 'B'—Volunteer the lot of them for execution? In my script, a media-led mawkish hysteria pushes humanity through Door 'B' when a deadly virus visitation leads to the potential death of less than half a per cent of the population. It's about inverted morality—Championing collective martyrdom for the sake and profit of a few under the cover of 'virtue'." "Right. And you say it hasn't been read." "Correct." "I've got to ask: is it presentable?" "Huh!—I wouldn't have spent six months writing it on spec if I didn't believe it was. But if you think—" "No, John—It sounds just fine. Great. Thank you for your trust. Let me say that I'll do a good job of presenting your work, and look after it too." "Well, as you mentioned its authorship is irrelevant, I thought I'd use my mother's maiden name on the title page: John Jones; to spare it from my toxic name and keep it my property without the need for an affirmation of ownership. It's in digital format, all set to be printed—As you requested—And ready on a flash drive for you to come to collect at any time."

Lombard would have thought that both of their time would be better spent with the file sent as an email attachment, but as John Bowdion refrained from offering to do this – and the option must have crossed his mind – it had to be assumed that he anticipated receipt of the rest of the moneys promised before parting with his work. Given the news about Jane having been right about Avery Weyland, Lombard feared that delaying or making unsolicited suggestions might cost him the man's goodwill. Thus, with the first shadows of evening cooling London's streets under the sunset sky, he headed for Mile End for the second time in one day, on this occasion parking right in front of the murder house at the end of the dead end. As visits went, this one was meant to be brief, last the time it took to hand over the money and pick up the promised flash drive. Only, he never accounted for the whims and fancies of desperation and loneliness.

It so happened that in the time it took Lombard to reach Mile End, John Bowdion had done more thinking; to have his assistance sought, it turned out, also afforded him a rare opportunity to have influence, so that he now acted as if he had a vested interest in Lombard's venture. Without so much as an idea about the intended use of his screenplay, and only a suspicion about its intended recipient, he'd decided to look at the sort of material favoured by Avery Weyland, and concluded that his first-choice script was possibly ill-advised in that it was "Too intellectual and too sci-fi. Sci-fi's not good, I think. His father was a popular sci-fi writer; I understand he and his mother sold the film rights to all his books to the U.S. Purney Production company after he died." Accordingly, he'd readied another screenplay, one he termed 'a mainstream thriller'. "They Bite at Night, it's called—It's got sex, drugs, heaps of expletives and sentimental slush; right-on-wake-up-rebellion-conquers-all-to-make-a-better-world-for-the-children type of thing. It's set between the Somerset countryside and New York's slums, ostensibly telling the story of two half-brothers divided by race, religion and the ocean, but in reality is an allegory about 'found innocence'. Note: not 'lost' but 'found' innocence. It's the last script I ever wrote—I was still desperate enough to think I might be allowed in the door if I sold out like that. Anyway, I never found out in the end—Could never bring myself to send it out."

Lombard, he insisted, had better take a look at both works once back home, and pick which would best serve his purpose.

This was readily agreed, yet Lombard was not to be allowed to escape so easily; it transpired John Bowdion had been thinking about more than screenplays.

"You asked what happened to me earlier on, Laurent," he said: "Well—You're right—What you said when you left— You're absolutely right: stories are way more telling than angry sermons. I get it. And yes, I guess you could say that something did happen to me—Me and the film lot! I was a better man once—Much better than what there is to see today. So, if you would spare the time, I'd—I could offer you a beer and tell you about it. I see you parked in the residents' bay in front of the house, which is fine at this hour; they're only operational until 6:30 p.m."

Such tortured desperation, naked solicitation, did nothing to seduce Lombard. The man, standing in his baggy T-shirt against the setting sun flooding the roofscape outside his bedsit windows, stared at the floor, crushed, waiting, a quietly feverish pasty-faced six foot tall slightly chubby spectre who, it now emerged, had offered his help as a means to secure a small recompense, the companionship of a listening ear. It ought to have been a simple matter to leave him to his demons. He'd already handed out the flash drive, taken his money, had little left to offer that anybody could want. Least of all Lombard.

"That's great, John—Thank you," Lombard said, checking his watch – it was seven thirty; "I'm due to meet someone at nine but I'd love to hear your story, indeed. And have that beer."

TWELVE

*Where she set out to beguile the world, he'd behaved
beastly as nature, proved equal to it, in grace and
wickedness.*

In and of itself, John Bowdion's tale was a mirror of his
woeful appearance, the way some people physically become
what befalls them. In his case, it was bad luck compounded by
notions of integrity, and – as they who fail all experience in
good time – rejection. The last of the sun would be gone and
the first stars shine faintly in the sky before Lombard would
return to the freedom of the streets again. But he couldn't
begrudge the man, and left him lighter and better for having
lent him his ear. By then, it had also become evident that
John Bowdion's determination to share his story was no mere
attention-seeking exercise, nor a simple whim or want for a
sympathetic listener, but rather, a performance motivated by a
mission to make a positive impression for fear of being badly
thought of or condemned for crimes of which he was innocent.
Pitifully, the poor man cared about Lombard's opinion of
him.

"I wasn't always this pathetic, you know," he began; "The
way it goes is people without influence who get hurt simply
disappear or end up like me, don't they? Wasting silently away.
The bastards depend on that."

John Bowdion was raised in a small town in rural Wales.
His love affair with cinema dated back to a time when, still a
boy, he'd dreamed of becoming a film director until what he
called his "poor people skills" had woken him to the fact that

he was unlikely to succeed at a career that required leadership qualities. Still, there would be no denying him the entirety of his ambition. He liked words, and so elected to become a screenplay writer. He completed his English Master's, earned a Ph.D. in Creative Writing. While yet to have held a single industry job or sold a single original line, but "Having done all they tell you to do", he was signed by a prestigious London agency by his twenty-fifth birthday. "As happy as Larry staring at the stars, I was. And the stars were within reach—Welsh country boy making it big in London! Ripe and ready as morning glory. It's hard to believe what miracles a good word from a good agent can perform for a compliant and eager nobody. Script editing gigs; a steady job on a TV mini-series; before I knew it I'd bagged a deal for my very first original screenplay on the strength of my being great and a one-sentence pitch. Happy as Larry was now a dog with a bone, to go with a gorgeous up-and-coming actor trophy- girlfriend with whom he purchased a totally new-build flat overlooking the Thames. But to those who have, right! I was halfway through my own commissioned screenplay's second draft when, one day, my terrific agent called with a script editor gig. It was meant to be a quick hatchet job for a top producer-director team; in-out and a prodigiously obscene cheque. They had a 150-page script they needed to cut to size in a real hurry to secure the last tranche of development money. It was a Monday—'Bring it down to 120 pages by Friday and the cheque's yours,' they said. It was an original spec script by a first-time writer who'd been fired from the project a year earlier for refusing to do the necessary cuts, is the tale they told. Some other writer—Much higher up the food chain than myself—Had just left them in the lurch after doing seven unusable drafts. Now they came knocking at my door! Well, cutting and slashing away over four days and nights, I merrily but conscientiously shed 30 pages, pocketed my cheque, conveyed my appreciation to my excellent agent for having got me the gig, and returned to work on my own baby, which really was all I cared about—To see my own vision translated to the screen, big and bright and beautiful, was truly all I fucking wished for. But then they came calling again. Thanks to my fantastic work, they said, the film's 10 million pound budget was now secured and a date set for first day of photography; how would I like to head to California with the crew, be part of the team, writer in residence, the man on call to do rewrites and tweak the script during shooting, on salary with expenses? Well, how would I! They didn't need to ask twice. For a while it sure was fun: there's little to complain about being on the road with a film crew, trying hotel beds and schmoozing with bonafide movie stars—Never mind in California, USA. Better still, I hardly had to work for it— Mostly just hung around sets and locations playing 'hot-young-new-writer'. But that's just it. First, I noticed that my name now figured where the original writer's used to be; not just on the screenplay's title page, but on the film's promotional material and press releases. Then, before long, I'd also be introduced everywhere as 'the writer', and called on to speak as 'him' too. Now, no one had ever said anything to me about my being credited as the author of the work; I'd done a hack job on the thing, not written it. This was some serious mix-up. Everyone was aware that—What with the second writer's seven drafts having been discarded—the final script was very much all or nearly all the original writer's creation: same narrative arc, characters etc.; just shorter and tighter, a couple of characters poorer and plot developments dropped to help get it down to 120 pages. Still, it looked like the team had tacitly decided to make me its writer—THE writer. Now, I may have been a little green and impressionable and just as full of it as the next up and coming superstar, but I didn't need a billboard to figure out that the guy whose work it was was being painted out of the picture, so to speak—And once I got that clear it didn't take me long to want to find out what the hell was going on. It turned out the writer of the work was a cook. A fucking cook! He'd come up with the script in his spare time. One way or another his work had landed in the director's lap—Who'd liked it and taken it to his agent— Who'd liked it and sent it to the producers—Who'd liked it and talked him into entrusting them with his work. So dumb

I was, I couldn't figure out why so many folks who'd liked his work and had secured millions on its back should be so keen to shaft the poor bastard. But they did. In fact, they'd got rid of him at the first contractual opportunity, claiming—Even though they never invited him to discuss his work with the production team after he'd signed away his rights to the material—Claiming he refused to edit his work. It's only when I realized that the director, one of the producers, the second writer, one principal actor as well as—What-do-you-know—Yours truly, all shared the same agent that the penny dropped—Jobs for the boys and girls! Gravy! Fire fodder! They'd come across some poor sod's freelance work and realized its 'marketability' made it worthy of exploitation. Easy money, which—Who'd have thought it—Shed light on why no one had seemed much concerned about my editing expertise. This made me their errand boy; a mugger's accomplice; a useful idiot to be paraded around like a monkey. The original writer was a mere inconvenience, an impediment standing in the way of the millions allotted to all those working on his creation. Actually, this would only be made official much later on, when no less distinguished a body than the Writers' Guild of Great Britain would demote the guy's role in his own creation to that of 'a contributor'. But I digress. I guess this was when, unlike my newfound friends, I found myself demurring. The truth is I was never much bothered about the writer; the idiot had clearly signed a bum deal and had it coming—Tough! No, my concern was myself—Only myself. I had no desire to be a cheat—A fraud. I was better than that, you know? I didn't want it against my name that I'd stolen another man's credit. I did not need to. The future was mine. But nor did I want to rock the boat. And so, since no one actually ever spoke to me about the situation, I thought—If not to clear my conscience—I'd cover my good name. And do it smartly. All I had to do was get it on record that I did not consider the work to be mine, but do so without alleging wrongdoing or even appearing to raise the matter. Well, the opportunity came at a promotional junket set up by the producers some time after we all got back to London from the States. The film team and media were doing what they do best—Enjoying their perks, sharing anecdotes, a lot of posing, posturing and loving. It was going splendidly, everyone making all the right noises when some anodyne query about the script caused, as was the norm by then, all eyes to turn on me. 'Well,' I said, 'That's a very interesting question. First, though, just to clarify one thing, I would like to state that although I have worked very hard on this fantastic project I am not actually the script's original writer'."

And with that out of the way, John Bowdion had happily gone on to address the journalist's question. And for some days afterwards, unaware that much of anything had changed, he'd gone on "feeling no pain". It would take a while before it dawned on him that nothing was the same, that whatever he'd ever say about films or whatever screenplays he'd ever come up with after uttering these last words would hardly matter. "Eight bloody words: 'I am not actually the script's original author'. And there was no going back. No forgiving. Everything concertinaed. Less than a week later I was 'let go' by text message: 'John, at this stage of the production it is the team's feeling that a fresh pair of eyes might better serve the project. Thank you for your contribution.' My agent dumped me the very next week, citing 'an overcrowded list of marvellous new clients to look after'. In a twist of irony—Or so some might think—I was also fired from my own screenplay and had my original screen credit shared out with two other writers." But this really was only the beginning of his trouble. He'd soon found himself ostracized by his former industry friends and colleagues, come up against closed doors. In time, resigned, he'd given up writing screenplays and tried his luck as a novelist, but found the literary agents' and publishers' doors just as inaccessible. "I was locked out." For a while, he settled on making a living as a creative writing lecturer at a London university, but this too ended badly when he'd crossed words with a "roused *Pasionaria*". This situation had eventually taken its toll, cost him his nerves, health, few remaining friends and girlfriend, but, most of all, judging by the unrest in his voice when he came to mention it, his mother's affection and respect; "Your friends turning into ghosts once they see you're no longer on the winning team is one thing. Your loving girlfriend ditching you with the words 'You blew it, boy, and I didn't sign up for this' is a little harder to take; then again, I have no problem wishing her bad things. But your mother taking to calling you 'a disappointment', at which point she also disinherits you entirely in favour of your more successful younger brother—All because of eight bloody words—Well, that's cause for pause."

Late that evening, after making a few calls, Lombard wrote the following email to an old acquaintance in French Polynesia:

Ma chère Gisèle,
C'est bien réconfortant d'avoir entendu votre voix et de savoir que vous allez bien. Je sais que je n'écris pas souvent, mais je ne vous ai certainement pas oubliée et j'ose espérer que ce petit mot sera aussi bien reçu que vous l'êtes dans mes pensées. Bien sûr le fait que je vous écris pour vous demander un service ne plaide pas en ma faveur, mais croyez-moi quand je dis qu'il m'est impossible de penser à vous sans sourire aux souvenirs du temps passé.
Toute mon affection,
Sam

À propos de ce dont je vous ai parlé:

Please find attached the file with the two screenplays to be printed, bound in standard screenplay format and sent by express courier to: Avery Weyland, Monty Productions, London W11CC.
As discussed, enclose an envelope with 4000 Euros in 200 Euro notes (I shall transfer money to your account in the next hour) together with a handwritten copy of the letter below, to be signed 'Xavier Lagarde'. I have no memory of your handwriting but, if it happens to be somewhat feminine, it would be good, if you can, to get a male acquaintance to pen it. Do let me know as soon as it is done. Merci encore.

Letter to copy by hand:

Xavier Lagarde
Pape'ete
Mahina Tahiti

Dear Mr Weyland,
Please find enclosed a couple of screenplays, one of which I most earnestly hope you will find worthy of attention.

It would take too much of your time as well as be inappropriate to try to expound my reasons for sending you this material along with this covering letter, but perhaps you might find it helpful to know that, were you to consider either of these works suitable for production, I would be prepared to underwrite half the production cost subject to a four million Euros ceiling.

I shall be in Britain within a week where, bar unforeseen circumstances, I will remain for three days before heading home to Guyane.

I would be in your debt if, having acquainted yourself with the enclosed material, you could contact me at the following number at your earliest convenience so that we might discuss the matter further (07773____).

If I haven't heard from you before then, I shall call your office before my leaving Britain.

I very much look forward to hearing from you.

Sincèrement vôtre,

Xavier Lagarde

PS: I hope you will forgive my sending the enclosed money, which is only meant in consideration of the time and trouble related to going over the enclosed material.

The thrust of this approach was to do away with most if not all of the obstacles a stranger would naturally meet while attempting to introduce themselves to an established film producer and director who also happened to be a member of the establishment. The proposal was meant to appear outlandish and intriguing in equal parts, as well as – as most deceptions must – appeal to greed. In such regards, Lombard was satisfied his plan was well-served. Likewise, the inclusion of money with no return address was designed to make it awkward for the recipient of the package to dismiss the letter's solicitation, and the unreasonable proposal to meet within a week to discuss the works – in effect affording next to no time for their reading or consideration – was calculated to underscore its sender's unfamiliarity with the ways of the film industry. This left the matter of the selected locations, French Polynesia and Guiana. Neither were chosen merely on account of their exotic sound or colour, but rather for the advantage of providing cover, all the better for their cover being French; well-heeled movie insiders could be relied upon to be well-travelled, something to keep in mind for a man set on masquerading as a 'provincial' fool with money to spare. Laying claim to far off places well off the beaten track about which little information is available, in the circumstances, seemed a rational thing to do. Were it all to go according to plan, Avery Weyland or someone from his office should be moved to call within a week or two, which, coincidentally, would afford Lombard the time to acquire a suntan worthy of a man inhabiting the equatorial latitudes.

That night, while awaiting sleep to envelop him from the darkness, memories of the time he hunted ragged gold miners in the Guianese jungle visited him again while his mind was being distracted with thoughts of Ali, so that soon he was taken by the realisation that the two of them shared something in common. It had never occurred to him before, but while still teenagers, both of them had been touched by humanity's lust for gold. Ali's reading of California's Gold Rush had warned her of the potential hardship that lurked beyond the bounds of childhood and the safety and freedom of her father's farm, whereupon she'd sought only advantage from her fear, strived for excellence as a means to salvation from potential trials and future wretchedness. He, on the other hand, never showed such predilection or fortitude. Nature and its laws had overpowered his spirit long before he'd killed the grey-haired *garimpeiro*; he never mused over whether the man sent touching letters back home or, for that matter, whether he'd had a home or even someone to send letters to. The truth be told, the sight of the miner's lifeless form lying in the dirt, the ease with which he'd robbed him of not just his life but his entire future, only served to feed his pragmatism; as it was, by that time he had already come across enough whims, foul smells, cravenness and viciousness to feel little more than pragmatic. He'd seen the ways of his elders and dreaded the future, wise to the fact that at nineteen he was in his prime, had peaked, was as free and fit as any breathing creature had ever been, that the way forward would spell only his growing weaker and uglier and, by and by, bondage to the tyranny of necessity, conceit or, were he so disposed, the pursuit of power or riches or all such futilities. There was nothing to withstand except bestial nature herself. This made him woeful, some might have said made him most mean too, given that for a while, setting about to defy the inexorability of decline, he'd pursued as ferocious and mindless a path as his senses could stand, provoking and tasting death again, oftentimes. That he'd come through, weakened and mellowed out, made him nothing like Ali though. Where she set out to beguile the world, he'd behaved beastly as nature, proved equal to it, in grace and wickedness.

Such considerations were meant to dull his mind and lull him to slumber that night. However, the sudden thought that John Bowdion may have included an address on his scripts' title pages led him to reach for his laptop. Not an hour had passed since he sent the files to Gisèle, not time enough for her to have done much if anything with them. Despite John Bowdion's advice, he'd felt no need to look at either screenplay, opting instead to send both, which could only serve his design better. Now, he did look at them, found no address on either, and then, allowed his eyes to casually glance at the first page of the one titled 'Masters of Beasts'.

'FADE IN:
Pure black screen. The haunting SOUND of a hot
breeze blowing across the Savannah grasses rises and
remains as the following pre-title text starts to roll:

As far as is known, what here follows
Not so much took place in the Garden of Eden,
Beneath some rock or amongst the stars
— Or even as an event over the horizon.
But it did happen. At some time.
Possibly at a place not unlike your own,
Where come high tide the best of swimmers
Can get caught drifting too far from the shore.
For those who told the tale owned its truth,
And imparted it to those who told it after them,
Not necessarily the uppermost form of authentica-
tion,
But enough of one so that for now,
It has never been shown a lie — Or some fancy or
deception.'

Lombard went on reading, the way the eyes gaze at a passing
landscape, paying no more attention than necessary – he
hardly ever read – and soon found sleep.

INTERLUDE

Masters of Beasts

As far as is known, what here follows
Not so much took place in the Garden of Eden,
Beneath some rock or amongst the stars
— Or even as an event over the horizon.
But it did happen. At some time.
Possibly at a place not unlike your own,
Where come high tide the best of swimmers
Can get caught drifting too far from the shore.
For those who told the tale owned its truth,
And imparted it to those who told it after them,
Not necessarily the uppermost form of authentication,
But enough of one so that for now,
It has never been shown a lie — Or some fancy or deception.

This was a place where summer wilted into autumn
And winter bloomed to spring.
A place of rivers and meadows
And wilderness bedraggled with wastelands.
Where trees rustled in the rain
And lips in equal proportion served love and venom:
A kiss — A sermon.
And where youth's instruction
Provided they washed behind their ears,
And the elders wrote down the Judgement Laws
And sheltered from the cold.
A place where notions of immortality
Were deemed best left the domain of the Gods.

The tale goes that in such winsome yet unsuspecting location
One day emerged a bear.
Out of the cold it sprung
— Blown in with the winter Far Eastern breeze.
And it was a bear like no bear seen before
— A peculiar bear of sorts but still a bear.
For one thing it spoke. And for another like no other
It could show up at once everywhere.
Be in all places and forthwith be gone
— By no means be anywhere and forthwith be there.
And it was a clever bear — It knew its left from its right.
And was neither he nor she
—Yet it was truly mean and beastly.

"Out of every 200 people who breathe,
One shall be mine to devour in time," it said;
"Old, young, fat, lean—I'm not fussy!
All which I catch shall please my appetite.
Now my hunger may be finite but let me be clear
—My visitation shall be great.
So, I repeat: the great, the good, the weak, the ugly
—One out of every 200 shall my treat be."
This the bear proclaimed, and no sooner had it done so
Than it carried out its threat.
This it did: 199 People it visited
And one more it slayed to please its appetite
—All out in the open.
And then again, again and again
— In all open air places it visited at once one in 200 passed on.

The People never had seen anything like it
— Never at any rate in the form of this bear of sorts.
At first they paid it limited heed,
Trusting it to be bragging forest fury with next to no teeth.
But it soon enough set them straight
— A bear of sorts it may have been,
But by all means this bear was no mere beast
To be denied, deterred, declawed or derided.
A thousand dead focused the People's mind
— Ten thousand more set their prospects back.

For the bear showed up here and everywhere at once.
And it was a clever bear.
It knew its left from its right. And was neither he nor she
— And was truly mean and beastly.

Now a great consternation took hold of the People
— A great panic; dire rhetoric.
Such that dread and sombre predilections weighted all heads.
The bear was on all sides, scores died
And nothing known to the world could prevail upon it.
Only one path remained: poor wretches seeking direction
The People turned to their Leaders:
"What's to be done?
Woe betide any soul who meets the bear's wanton business!
So many of us are deadly done for we'll soon be digging up bones."
And without further ado
Their Leaders did what Leaders do.

They issued forth onto the stage with their Savants in tow
Pledging all kinds of cures.
After all — so much for being the betters of the pack
— They were called upon to lead.
In keeping up with the particular of the predicament
They soon settled on just the solution.
They passed a 3-way threefold Decree:
'Stay Indoors—Save Lives—Protect our Defenders'.
"We're at war," they declared;
"And the enemy is the God-damn bear—Cursed be it!"
Orders followed and all locked themselves up.
"We must all do it to get through it," they said.
And indoors and safe from the bear the People stayed
— "We're all in this together."

The idea — as broadcast by the Town Criers
— Was to save lives and starve the bear.
The sooner to have it die of hunger or — failing this
— Have it depart for richer hunting grounds.
Or yet —failing that
— To buy time to come up with a means to harm and kill it.
But it was a clever bear. And patient it was too.

It was never going to go nowhere.
Or fret about the rate of rotation of its dinner arrangements.
One out of 200 was its requirement.
It never said anything about having a hurried disposition.
And for all all knew may even have known
That slow eating agrees with the digestion.

Well, the case was that while confined within their houses
The People too needed eating.
Along with all manners of supplies and worldly protection
— From both the bear and one another.
Some had grown forlorn; some quite mad
— Even praying and funerals were restricted;
Some sour and pasty
—Too much being alone;
Parted kindred ordained to remain parted.
Be that as it may,
Ways and byways could never be fully barren of Humanity.
Enforcers, Providers and Town Criers now in the Leaders' pay
Had to be permitted to circulate,
Whereby the bear could never be denied,
The whole time picking its set part of their numbers.

The reality of this extremity now took the form of a great lamentation.
More grew forlorn — Sourer and pastier
— More lost their minds and some grew merry.
Few rebelled and far between a dozen more protested:
"This is folly," they said;
"By no means is self-imprisonment akin to 'Going to War'", said they;
"Quite the contrary.
It is surrender," they insisted;
"The same as soldiers yielding their country to the enemy
By virtue of their commander-in-chief's zero-casualty battle policy."
Those questioning the sense of living sequestered
As a means of survival were shortly corrected.

Dawns followed dusks
And a great resignation followed the great lamentation.
Rains followed summers
And each day the Leaders followed the deadly bear's numbers.

"Numbers don't lie," they said.
Now they let the People out for a breather and up they went.
Back inside everybody was sent and down they fell
— One for every 200 of those in the open air.
Tears followed cries and the Savants,
Regardless of the Town Criers' much touted assertions,
Failed to dream up a bear-defeating remedy
— 'All in and Protect our Defenders' continued to be.
Stranded on the path they furrowed earlier,
The Leaders could follow only their own footsteps.

By and by — in the course of a hot summer evening
— At the end of a very long day,
While no People were still free
— All around now being sheer resigned melancholy,
Perchance a herd of wildebeest on their yearly migratory way
— Two million heads in all, they said;
Past a copse of waterpear trees
Perchance a great wildebeest migration erred Humanity's way.
On their travel, finding peace where ordinarily all was People's industry,
They'd drifted some way from their trail,
Stumbled to the edge of a blockaded village,
And on noting their error at once set out to withdraw
— But they were too slow.

The front of the herd was seen,
For the village had a posse out on watch for the bear.
Beneath a banner bearing a brutish dragon
A small band of Defenders-at-arms manned a barricade,
Each head concealed in a barrel-shaped wooden cask
With prized out slats for the eyes.
"Who goes there!" bemoaned a voice;
"Halt at once or be done. Are you with the bear?"
At the outset the wildebeest were unsure of the situation.
They'd seen much before,
Known of People for generations,
Could even recall seeing them learn to walk on their own two feet.
But as of yet never had met one who bore a wooden cask for a head
— Or seemed so defeated.

"Please accept our sincerest apologies for wandering this way,"
The head wildebeest said,
For the smart ones amongst them could talk too;
"The land is so tranquil we strayed off course. We shall go at once."
From what the wildebeest knew of Humanity,
This ought to satisfy the posse.
"Oh—I see: you're wildebeest," a wooden cask said:
"Good—Stand at ease and away with you."
The wildebeest gave thanks and without further adieu
Made to leave, but a voice interjected:
"I trust from your surprise at our strange countenance
That you have not heard, have you?
We're being terrorized by a bear
—So much for the country's tranquillity—It's what it's come to."

To be sure, no wildebeest knew of the bear,
Nor wished to postpone departing on account of it.
But some among the village barricade had other ideas
— Clearly itched to tell their story.
How the bear had come
— Blown in with the winter Far Eastern breeze.
How it was a bear like no bear seen before
— A peculiar bear of sorts but still a bear
How it could show up at once everywhere.
Be in all places and forthwith be gone
— By no means be anywhere and forthwith be there.
And it was a clever bear
— It knew its left from its right. And was most mean and beastly.

This was a lot to take in for a wildebeest
But the People's business was not yet done.
The most effusive among the barricade let it known
That their name was Johanna.
And so much they wished to tell,
Not to be thwarted they threatened to unravel:
How the confined People prayed — Longed to gather out again
— Yearned for society.
How their Leaders sought to save them
— Mortgaging three fourth of the country to aid the needy.
How their Savants toiled round-the-clock

To fix an elixir to kill the bear — As yet to no avail.
How the Town Criers braved the morning of each day
To unveil the latest calamities.

Well, it is nature's good grace that all things must pass
— Even the most drawn out cry.
But by the time the one named Johanna had cast their spell,
The head wildebeest was overwhelmed.
"My—This all sounds grim," said he;
"But, if I may, what of the casks on your heads?"
"Oh—This' to hinder the bear," Johanna said;
"It aims to catch us with a grab of our skull in its paws.
Ingests us whole—The head, then the neck then the torso
—Scorning all from the waist to the toes,
The parts of which form ungodly heaps
For our treasured ambulance crews to see to.
Truth is the cask hardly helps— Is mere wood chips for the bear's paws
—But it makes us feel safer."

It was getting dark now but still, the head wildebeest delayed
And took a look around.
The sight of his fellow wildebeest
Poised behind and on either side of him
Cheered his heart.
"This is grim," he said,
Just as every village door beyond the barricade burst wide open.
Briefly, from every threshold cask-headed figures banged tambourines,
Chimed bells, clapped hands.
"Fear not, wildebeest—This is their daily show of worship
To we who defend them," Johanna said.
Then from one side
A spirited crowd dragged in a naked figure covered in tar
And hoisted it up a tree.
"Don't mind them. This stranger was caught heading this way
With the bear in tow," Johanna said.

But the greater disruption had yet to come.
Now a distant explosion rocked the ground itself.
"Be not alarmed. This is the sound of our youngsters
Toppling our old statues to erect their own." Johanna sighed

— And a yell and a song issued from two of the barricade's casked-heads:
"Down! Yes!" — "And the toppermost now will later be bottom
—For the bottomest now will later be top."
"Pay these no heed.
They only heckle and sing on account of being troubled,"
Johanna declared;
"Their ship steers wide rivers blind of wild mountain streams."
And in a dream all fell quiet again
— The wildebeest picked up where he'd let off — He had an idea.

"One for every 200 of you?
These are the numbers the bear slays?" he said.
Johanna: "To please its appetite."
"And you know not how to overcome it?"
Johanna: "Our Savants are on it—But like I said: it's a clever bear."
"Must be hard on your sons and daughters
—Don't your children need to play outside?"
Johanna: "It's hard for all of us
—We all need the open air. The praise of strangers.
The thrills and perils of getting together.
None here shall ever be satisfied by captivity."

The wildebeest had an idea, and not without trepidation
Now elected to hazard an opinion:
"If I may be so bold as to suggest:
Could you not take a leaf out of us wildebeest's playbook?
Make accommodation for the bear?
Look upon it as more of a storm and less of a curse?
You may know that each year on our 1000-mile trail
We wildebeest lose near two in every 100:
To the Lion, the Hyena, the Wild Dog,
The Cheetah, the Leopard, the Crocodile—And other hunters.
Yet it is near a million years now that we roam the plain
—Fit and unbound; proud and hearty.
For long ago we agreed that life and freedom commonly exact a levy."

Well, it was plain — Where at first the wildebeest had only erred
He now had spoken out of turn.
Ahead of him at the barricade the cask-headed People started tsk-tsking.
"Bloody Nora—Who does the wildebeest think he is!"

— Johanna no longer was too friendly.
"Such savage notions have been promoted before
—Though never as yet by a plain wildebeest.
None ever dared.
We are not immoral creatures without consciences, wildebeest
—We care.
To forgo their own may be to a lowly beast's betterment
—But we stand together—For one another.
Enact feats beyond your discernment
—You are speaking of things beyond your comprehension."

This being the state of affairs,
No reason remained for the wildebeest to stay there.
It was late and dark and it was hot,
And it had been a long day even before this parley.
"We better be off now," the wildebeest said;
"We crossed a river a little way from here.
Just beyond the waterpear trees
—Would you mind if we camped the night at the riverbank there?"
"Be our guest—And help yourself to the water too," Johanna said;
"It costs nothing.
You be safe now. And please feel free
To return for goodbyes before making off tomorrow."
"Indeed. And you be safe from the bear," the wildebeest said;
"Parting is such sweet sorrow."

That night under the stars by the riverside
The wildebeest smelled the water, the air from the plain.
He'd never felt better
Amongst his millions of slumbering brothers and sisters.
It was just as well as — for a while there
— Johanna's words had caused him vexation.
No wildebeest should get above their station:
Amid their towers the People still held to be Masters.
Masters of conscience, Masters of wars;
Masters of beasts and the 10 Commandments.
Masters of the Wheel and the Little and Great Bear,
The greater they held to be Masters of death.
So used they'd grown to be Masters of all
They now sought to rival their homespun undying Gods.

And here it is where this ends
— With the dew of dawn the wildebeest rejoined their trail.
They never visited the village again
— Steered well clear of beaten tracks and barricades.
What happened to them is not known;
Nor of what came to pass to the bear or its foes.
But rumour has it that the People became so mortgaged
To the meanest of their own,
The bear became the least of their woes
— Their children wound up bound to greedier predators.
But it's only rumour.
For their towers and barricades tumbled into dust
— Nothing in space remains.
And for all their kisses and sermons
Not a ghost of their spells haunts the Creation.

Only this tale — Not so much from the Garden of Eden.

THIRTEEN

A fresh concealed wild garden dappled with light,
water, colours and shade steeped in heady fragrances.

Funchal – whilst possibly taller, wider and wealthier, hogging more of the rocks, forests and seafront which contained it as it unfurled upwards into the hills – was equal to the impression it had made on his mind many years ago: the colour of springtime, the fragrance of blooms and rains, wild and fresh in the way of a teeming riverside. He never sought the guesthouse in which he'd known American Becky. Presuming it still stood someplace among the glittering new seafront hotels near the pleasure-boat rich marina, he wouldn't have known which way to look for it. Still, for a moment, he wished it had been there, waiting for him to step through its doors to a more wholesome and brutal point in time. In the event, he booked a room in an indifferent 4-star shimmering white hotel next to a gleaming shopping mall, enjoyed a late light lunch in a small restaurant overlooking the ocean and, a mere two hours after landing, headed for the nearest taxi rank.

It was beyond doubt that a great many things – not all salutary – went on in bustling Madeira which its crowds of fleeting visitors never got to know about. All the same, the local people came across as cordial but provincial, the sort for whom – unlike London's Mile Enders – news of a murderer hiding among the population warranted both excitement and conversation. All hands working at the taxi rank knew of Alan Winston, or '*O assassino inglês*', as he was known in this part of the world. To get hold of the driver who had ferried him up into the hills above the canopy of clouds two weeks earlier took little effort; his posing as a journalist, the lustre of crisp Euro notes and a rudimentary knowledge of Brazilian Portuguese ascribed to a stay in the Amazon Forest proved most helpful.

Leaving Funchal's built-up coastal area to drive up into the wild interior of emerald forests and steep mountains along winding roads and through an endless maze of tunnels boring through the rock, the taxi driver – who had a flyer showing Alan Winston's face with the caption 'Please Call The Police If You See This Man' in both English and Portuguese prominently displayed inside his cab – proved keen to share his opinion of *o assassino inglês*. He'd known at once there was something "*tricky*" about his fare, he explained in bad English. "I do this job too long to not see things, you see." Everything about Alan Winston had jarred. He was "not like the other English people coming to our island". He was "too young—By himself—Carried only a small sports bag for luggage." And he was curt, uninterested in conversation or the scenery, "chewed gum like an American" and had paid for his ride with a £20 note without much caring for the exchange rate or checking his change, even though, unlike Lombard in his dark suit and cufflinked white shirt, "he looked too poorly dressed not to worry about money". And of course, there was the location he asked to be taken to: the intersection between Route 211 and Route 109. The driver had made him confirm this, put it to him that it was up in the hills, a bleak remote spot, but there was nothing doing, he was told to mind his own business and drive. "Uh-huh. I knew all wasn't right with him, you know. You can always tell." By now, he shared the local police view that *o assassino inglês* had arranged to be picked up at the intersection; it was the only explanation for his vanishing into thin air after being dropped there, although he confessed to being niggled by one detail: "He was very calm, in no hurry. And there was nobody there when I left him at the intersection. And there is no place to hide there. A *fugitivo* in the open road in the middle of nothing with the possibility of police driving by is very strange, you don't think?" A loquacious and helpful character such as he, was guaranteed to feel thwarted when told to go on his way, not least as he clearly felt somewhat proprietorial towards his 'English Assassin', but Lombard asked him to do just that when they reached the spot where he'd dropped Alan Winston off, and the man left shaking his head after warning of an impending downpour and explaining that the nearest inhabited property was a hotel about three kilometres away.

Standing by the side of the road, Lombard waited for the taxi to disappear the way they had come until, alone in the breeze and enveloped in silence, he took in the scenery. The intersection between Routes 211 and 109, a dusty T-junction halfway across a bare featureless plateau of sandy-coloured grit and sparse low-lying bushes, made for a bleak setting indeed. A stark contrast to the colourful seashore or lush forests lining the mountain roads from Funchal, it was hard to imagine why anyone would wish to make it their destination; never mind a runaway from the law just landed on a foreign island. Whereas all had been balmy sunshine lower down by the coast, here leaden clouds hung low and brooding, hemming the near horizon on all sides and charging the air with moisture, denying any view beyond the plateau's pine-tree boundaries. Other than the T-junction with its meeting ribbons of tarmac and signpost displaying the road numbers and nearby localities, there was nothing here. The cab driver was right. This was no place to be and no place to come to. Yet, Alan Winston had flown all the way from London to ask to be taken nowhere else. And Letitia Balthazar, on being shown photographs of the intersection by the police had failed to identify it.

Lombard remained there for some time, seeking to make sense of the spot, observing six cars drive by, the occupants of which all eyeballed him, with good reason likely wondering what he was up to standing by himself in a suit in such a place. Then, with no warning, the storm the taxi driver had warned him about ruptured the low cover of clouds, unleashing a bone-chilling pounding deluge. Volleys of icy rains lashed across the plateau, and with no shelter in sight, there was little to do but get out of his suit jacket, roll it into a bundle around his wallet and phone and head for the relative cover of the nearest line of pine trees some two hundred yards away. He was just about to reach this refuge when, as suddenly as it started, the rain stopped, the sky lifted, the sun burst through the sodden air and the whole plateau and its surrounding forests and mountains and horizon came into view: on three sides tree-covered peaks soared into the blue sky, and on the other, the way he'd come, deep green valleys tumbled down towards the great silver ocean.

Out in the open, his soaked clothing starting to steam in the hot sun, Lombard wandered back to the intersection unwrapping his jacket to find that his wallet was dry but his phone would no longer switch on. He paused at the signpost again and started exploring the three lengths of road joining at the T-junction, walking along each one to the plateau's edge before retracing his steps, scrutinising the landscape and nearby rugged terrain. It hardly mattered what he was looking for amid the gritty soil and low-lying bushes, for he came across nothing worthy of attention while waving away a few motorists who slowed down to call through their open windows offering him a lift. The exercise took the best part of an hour until, at last, with the sun now fast coming down and his beginning to feel cold inside his damp clothing, he waved a passing car down and, explaining his phone was out of order, asked if he could be taken to the nearby hotel the taxi driver had told him about.

He would come across another 'wanted' flyer of Alan Winston at that location and get a taxi back to Funchal where, refreshed, dry and satisfied that the only thing the matter with his phone was a flat battery, he ended the day in the pleasant company of one of his hotel's receptionists; olive-skinned, brown-eyed and chubby-cheeked, Josefina was at reception when he returned damp and ragged from his afternoon outing. They struck up conversation after he asked her if the hotel had a tumble dryer to see to his wet shoes – he had brought only the one pair – and, after volunteering to see to it for him and bring the shoes up to his room once dry, she'd commiserated about his "very beautiful" but ruined leather cufflinks. "What is the 'X' for?" she asked impishly; "X-rated?"

Lombard grinned; she was forward. "X-*actly*," he joined in. She laughed; they were both forward, and she never let the ring around his finger bother her.

The following morning he woke late feeling rested, half-swayed by the notion that Alan Winston had made it to the barren plateau in the expectation of being picked up by some local he'd likely kept in contact with after his short stay on the island, and the same was now providing him shelter. Still, he was only half-swayed. Now, over breakfast, having opted not to shave, he studied on his phone a satellite view of the plateau and its surroundings, which served to confirm what he had observed; beyond the couple of roads making the T-junction, there was nothing there aside from half a dozen small streams which ostensibly ran across the roads he had surveyed. These had not come to his attention. The map identified them as *ribeiros*, which stood for brooks, or streams, suggesting they may be natural drainage ditches – or culverts – piped beneath the road. He had no recollection of water running in such channels during or after the storm, but then the downpour had lasted mere minutes, little enough time for an efficient drainage system to handle what the sky had thrown at it. Still, by midday, now at the wheel of a rented car, he headed back into the mountains to find the plateau basking in sunshine as he pulled at the T-junction. For a while, he coasted along the road following the pattern he'd walked the previous day, taking his exploration further afield in each direction. As he suspected, his eyes had missed only the *ribeiros* which, in the midday sunlight, it was now plain to see, showed as narrow shallow dry open ditches that hardly stood out amid the dusty scrubland terrain. They turned into concrete culverts as they crossed under the road. He counted six of them, a foot wide at most, recalling that the satellite view on his phone had revealed that as many as four of their number grew wider further along the plateau before they disappeared from view within the dense green valleys that sprawled down towards the distant ocean. Lombard left his car by the roadside, got out of his jacket, rolled up his sleeves and, by and by, following one *ribeiro* after another, always downstream and back again, discovered how each journeyed a similar dramatic transformation. Their unpromising ditch-like aspect proved deceptive, for they soon presented small puddles, turned into running rocky brooks, and then, on nearing the plateau's edge, flowed into deep green ravines where, under the cover of trees, some transformed into steep boulder-filled streams broken up by waterfalls. Without fail, their end then came abruptly, their waters pouring into isolated man-made dammed pools that fed complex irrigation channels; these, he'd also read earlier, were *levadas*, centuries-old moss-covered stone structures designed to carry the rich supply of water found on one side of the island to farmlands in other drier parts.

After nearly five hours of trudging the length and back of three of the *ribeiros*, tired, hungry – at least he could drink directly from the streams – suffering the heat and aching feet – his leather shoes appeared to have shrunk or stiffened somewhat from their spell in the tumble dryer, and besides weren't best suited for trekking across the rough rocky ground – he considered calling it a day. By now he held out little hope for discoveries, and was already brooding over the next step he would have to take in his hunt for Alan Winston. Tramping the length of the fourth *ribeiro* downstream to the inevitable dam and *levada* a fair distance away only to walk right back hardly seemed worth the trouble. Only, he'd gone through too much to back down now, and set on giving the expedition another hour before calling it quits, still some way from the plateau's edge, he suddenly lost sight of the *ribeiro* he was following, as if the dust and hard ground in the near distance ahead had swallowed it up. A rational explanation was always going to account for such an occurrence. Logic dictated the stream had run into an underground conduit, sparing him further pain. But this was not so. Instead, arriving at the rim of a narrow ravine with steep bracken and grass covered escarpments, he found himself standing above a sparkling pool nesting within a bank of mossy boulders and long grasses sowed with wild flowers – a fresh concealed wild garden dappled with

198

light, water, colours and shade steeped in heady fragrances.

To one side, the *ribeiro*'s clear water ran down the small cliff face just beneath his feet, forming a leisurely waterfall which splashed and rippled across the pool below; to the other, the pool's water flowed idly away along the ravine's bottom, twisting and glistening before disappearing into the dark shadow of a copse of laurel trees. It made for a captivating sight, but Lombard's attention was arrested by something else entirely; a few paces from where he stood on the plateau, a few yards from the ravine's edge, the remains of a small bonfire formed a dark stain against the grey ground. It couldn't have been there very long, otherwise rains such as the previous afternoon's would have washed away all traces of it. He approached it. Among the ashes and half burnt twigs, some scorched items were plainly identifiable: charred remnants of sports shoes; a seared bag handle; a twisted circuit board, likely from a mobile phone; burnt bits of denim; a belt buckle; a couple of door keys; what looked like a burnt-out wallet and various other singed effects, including what appeared to be the fragment of a black British passport's spine. Squatting over this, Lombard reckoned he'd got lucky. It appeared Alan Winston had fled London fixated on coming to this strange place, whereupon he'd destroyed all of his possessions. And by the look of it, he'd taken his time over it, made sure the flames consumed most of everything; yet, rather than heading down into the cover of the ravine, he'd lit his fire out in the open, well away from the road but not quite far enough to be safe from sharp-eyed motorists.

Lombard swallowed hard, picked up the blackened door keys, wiped them clean between his fingertips and pocketed them as he rose to his feet to turn back to the ravine and the bejewelled pool garden below. After a time, he took a picture of the scene with his phone and sent it to Letitia Balthazar with the question 'Familiar spot?' together with a word of apology for troubling her again. He wasn't so much anticipating a reply as expecting her to text him an expletive or two. But the minutes ticked away with nothing but the sun burning in the clear afternoon sky and the soothing sound of water splashing and lapping in the wild garden below, and presently he set out down the steep incline to the bottom of the ravine. He examined the pool – it was clear, a good breadth and waist deep – and its lush fragrant bank looked unspoilt, showed no evidence of disturbance. He delayed long enough to steal a handful of refreshing water and breath in the tonic from the air, and then proceeded along the ravine and into the shade of the laurel trees.

The round trip to the expected *levada* in the valley below took under ninety minutes, in the course of which he found no sign of Alan Winston anywhere in the stream or among the trees or boulders or rockpools or dips along its banks. Once back at the pool, faced with the climb up the sharp escarpment, he chose to rest, even though the sky above the ravine was fast closing with the same low brooding clouds that had caught him unawares the previous afternoon. He was exhausted, had eaten nothing since breakfast, was done with walking and, foreboding clouds aside, could think of no reason not to pause to sample the bracing water, heady colours and fragrances around him; for it had to be said, the place was enchanting. He took off his shirt, shoes and socks, and kneeled on a boulder to splash his face and nape. Now he rolled up the hems of his trousers and settled down on the boulder with his feet in the soothing water, letting out a sigh containing the particular and singular pleasure that only absolute relief provides. Just clear of the water falling from the plateau above, he thought he'd remain there for a short spell, listening to it splash and spatter long enough to clear his mind and indulge his tired limbs, but as his eyes became transfixed by a small patch of sparkling rustling white water catching the light from the sky above he ceased heeding to time ebbing away, at first in enjoyment of the moment, then distracted by the thought that it was a good thing he'd come out all sore but unscathed from the day's walking feat, and later, abruptly, numbed by an overwhelming sense of utter emptiness. And behold his mind discarded all that was bearable while a most terrible bitterness grabbed hold of him and the greatest desolation engulfed his soul. From deep inside him rose a devastating lament, replete with dread. In a heartbeat – a frightening moment of unnatural lucidity he would later attribute to hunger, exhaustion, intoxication from his luscious surroundings and too many hours spent in the sun – he perfectly observed and understood that the tiniest part of the sparkling water flowing past his eyes signified more than the absolute sum of all his experience. That there, within a particle of fresh water, lurked the only truth. He saw what can never be seen. He saw it absolutely. The sole purpose, the sole aspiration, the sole perfection was permanence. That which is immutable. And nothing that breathed or lived or half-lived was permanence. For permanence could only be the one thing – the void. Only the void was immutable. And at this time of bitterness, desolation and lamentation, he understood that all he had ever needed, had ever done and shall ever do was already inside of him. All of it and only inside of him. And none of it mattered. At all. He was everything, and the sum of his actions and thoughts and longings were delusions; dreamed by the immutable. At this point, some minds might have contrived sublime self-serving spells, or mused on the triumph of the rational over the animal, sought some much-needed noise even, but he was too daunted to be defiant or hatch escape plans.

In the end the gathering clouds came to his rescue, released him from himself. An icy downpour not unlike that of the previous day roused him from dread and contemplation, pried him free from the pool's hold and compelled him to climb out of the ravine. In the twilight and pouring rain, peering back down into the dark watery island from the safely of the plateau he failed to see the grey donkey that stood looking up at him from inside the dark cover of laurel trees.

But both would return.

FOURTEEN

So long, partner.

It went against Lombard's disposition to mull over what some may have regarded as an epiphany. His concern was the tangible, which fulfilled and occupied him adequately, as might perhaps be best illustrated by the following story.

Although an expert at warding off badgering strangers, even so seasoned a traveller as he, must now and again give way to particularly persistent fellow travellers. On this occasion, such a character assumed the form of a French professor of quantum mechanics on a flight from Lisbon to Paris. The man, returning from what he described as a ground-breaking experiment, was too excited to keep to his own company, and for reasons best known to himself had mistaken Lombard for a quantum physics enthusiast. He couldn't have been more wrong; Lombard neither cared for nor understood such diversions, but still, the man had launched into a long and fervent discourse extolling the wonders of entangled particles, quantum tunnelling and all such marvels, proclaiming that space-time physics was in the midst of being completely re-evaluated. What Lombard rightly or wrongly thought he understood was that the other was proposing that life and the whole of the universe truly existed only within the framework of some sort of other-worldly two-dimensional computer game, consigning the three-dimensional physical world to an illusion born from encoded information, not dissimilar to a hologram, in which space and time are mere false-perceptions. By coincidence, Lombard, normally not one for quotations, had noted near that time a singular remark concerning such preoccupations.

He could not recall its author but it had left some impression on his mind: '*Time exists in order that everything doesn't happen all at once—And space exists so that it doesn't all happen to you*'. "Well," he said to his talkative and rather enthusiastic French fellow traveller; "I can't be sure I fully understand—But between you and me, a happy cat is a sleeping cat." "How do you mean?" "I mean, both the cat and myself are very much aware snakes exist; yet neither of us goes around checking every rock looking for snakes. Not supposed to, you see. It would take all of our time and drive us crazy." "You must indulge me—I'm not following." "Never mind. Let's just put it this way then: while this space-time thing may well be riveting to those who make it their business—Like your good self—I for one earnestly hope you never crack it—As in 'be careful what you wish for'." And Lombard had grinned and the other had left him alone.

What he'd meant to say was that the occupation of living could at times ice up his blood, try his forbearance or set his senses ablaze, yet the last thing he needed was for a quantum mechanics professor set on overhauling Creation to tell him the human condition was a pointless comic strip illusion inside some holographic projection; whether it was so or not. All things – even futile and spiritual musings, or the tides – have their places and must pass. Time and space could well be the only things that stopped people from mindlessly butchering each other. What would come of the earth if all consciousnesses ceased hankering about tomorrow's instalment? Which reality did the good professor believe he'd contribute to if he were to be proved right someday? What would be the place of cats or snakes or rocks within a holographic universe? Lombard reckoned that as long as people felt sore on being short-changed or being called a bore, for as long as they sought the warmth of a fire when cold, the proper province of the mind should remain the tangible; and only the tangible, within space and time. The dull comfort of symmetry itself was preferable to the learnt absence of everything. Let the snake be! This is what he'd meant to say. Or then again, perhaps he'd just wished to put the professor in his place; for after all, speaking of illusion or perception, it was true that education or the repetition of a single occupation could indeed provide almost anyone with the appearance of intelligence. One late morning, Lombard had made mention of this encounter with the quantum mechanics professor to Ali, and, Ali being Ali, she'd produced a book of poems from her bedside table, declaring: "On the subject of 'be careful what you wish for', it may be that a little more eloquence and less combativeness would have helped you get the message through to your professor. Here—Listen:

'I came from the sunny valleys
And sought for the open sea,
For I thought in its grey expanses
My peace would come to me.

I came at last to the ocean
And found it wild and black,
And I cried to the windless valleys,
"Be kind and take me back!"

But the thirsty tide ran inland,
And the salt waves drank of me,
And I who was fresh as the rainfall
Am bitter as the sea.' "

They both knew Lombard could never have expressed himself with such elegance, and needless to say, he never committed the verses to memory or sought to recall their author's name – one Sarah Teasdale – but he wholeheartedly agreed with Ali and their sentiment, and would readily admit that in some way the simple grace of the words helped sharpen and brighten his own thoughts on the matter.

Hence it followed that once back from his waterly tribulations on the plateau up in the hills above Funchal, come evening at his hotel, refreshed and fed, Lombard got on his phone to visit The Paragon website, presently coming across the Heathrow Airport photograph they'd printed of Alan Winston waiting to board his flight to Madeira. As he recalled, it showed him in Jeans and trainers with a dark holdall slung across his shoulders, but the photograph was too grainy and taken from too far away to make out his belt buckle or whether any of it matched the burnt fragments he'd come across amidst the bonfire ash. He also called Letitia Balthazar. She had yet to answer his text with the picture of the pool in the ravine. Now, she picked up after just two rings. "So much for promising not to bother me again," she rebuked him. All the same, she granted that "It could be someplace we stopped at for a swim and picnic. Looks vaguely familiar. But like I said, we were drunk most of the time, so I wouldn't—"

That's as much as she had to say.

It was progress of a sort. Although the realm of speculation, Lombard was convinced the charred items by the pool's ravine were Alan Winston's. Yet, if true, this raised more questions than it answered, and all the potential scenarios the circumstances brought to mind seemed a stretch. For openers, it called for Alan Winston catching a plane from London with the sole intent of making it to a bleak Island plateau in the Atlantic Ocean for the purpose of incinerating his belongings and vanishing. If so, why here, a foreign land he barely knew, and by what trick had he contrived to disappear after destroying everything he owned? By all means, the plateau's seclusion could have afforded him the opportunity of being met and provided with a new set of clothing and identity papers; only, in such a premise, why delay longer than necessary by setting his belongings alight with the risk of the flames or smoke being spotted from the road, and then leave evidence of the fire behind? For another thing about this Madeira business had been begging for an answer from the outset: why had Alan Winston made no attempt to hide or conceal his appearance between travelling from London and being dropped off on the plateau? He'd have known about surveillance cameras – they were everywhere, long gone were the days when anyone went anywhere unaware of being monitored. And he'd have known the taxi driver who picked him up at Funchal airport would connect him to the plateau. It was as if he did not care, or was so confident he would get away he needn't take precautions. Of course, something else entirely could have occurred: another party could have burnt his belongings. In his hour of need, he may have been lured there by false promises, duped by a person or persons intent on divesting him of the little money he owned and much more. Malevolence and misadventure have ways to catch up with murderers on the run. Not least accidental murderers; helpless outlaws fast become helpless prey, meal tickets for hardened criminals. Whatever delusions some entertain about their place in the world – and Alan Winston was clearly nursing his own set of delusions – in actuality few are ever prepared for the wanton viciousness of those who make it their business to take in and feed off lost souls; from all kind of debauched procurers to master officials and self-appointed leaders. Yet, had such a fate befallen him, his predators could hardly have been expected to have hung around the plateau to burn his property and risk discovery. Besides, there was no sign of bones in the fire's ash or anywhere in the ravine or near or within the pool. Or of a body. Lombard had looked, not just on account of this last scenario, but, on coming across the bonfire, allowing for the possibility that the fugitive had made it there intent on ending his life.

If it is in the nature of things that there always exists a rationale for facts on the ground, in this instance Lombard reckoned he would likely be able to furnish it in time. For now though, all options remained open. Alan Winston could have long sailed or flown from the Island, be thousands of miles away, answering to a new name while learning a new country. Perhaps, subject to his disposition, part of his time was taken up trying to figure out whether to blank out, embrace or come to terms with what had become of him in the Mile End hallway. If he was no longer in Madeira, his trail would likely end now, his name never to be heard again. Whereas if he was still around, whether dead or alive, buried in the plateau's dirt or a corpse left for scavengers, a deranged soul wandering the wilderness naked, or a sound mind blending with the natives, unless wild dogs had consumed all portions of him in only two weeks, Lombard trusted he would find him.

But all such things – the void, permanence, the immutable and those matters that concerned cats, snakes and rocks – could not have been further from his mind as he lay on his bed near the end of the day. But he did think of water inside his closed eyelids; Alan Winston's body could have been taken away from the dirty plateau and thrown into the sparkling ocean. Then, the great anaesthetic ocean that is sleep carried him away into yet unknown fancies, leaving his stranded slumbering body behind.

In the darkness, he never heard the loud rings produced by the hotel phone on his bedside table, nor, later, as the first light of dawn roused the world outside his fifth-storey windows, the summoning knocks at his door. It was unlike him; he ought to have been alert, usually was even while asleep. But the previous day's fresh air, long trek and new developments had left him exhausted. Still, he did feel the hand stirring his shoulder, and heard a man's voice beckon:

"*Monsieur! Monsieur! S'il vous plaît, Monsieur! Réveillez-vous!*"

He opened his eyes and started so violently that he caught sight of a figure reeling away backwards from him, as if struck by a fist. It was a dark man in a light two-piece suit. He guessed this was the one who'd been shaking his shoulder, for he was now looking back at him wide-eyed trying a smile while explaining in passable French that he was the hotel manager and was very sorry for scaring him and waking him so early. Three other people were in the room with him, all further away, standing near the door; two were men he made out to be the local police on account of their dark blue hats and uniforms, the other a grey-suited woman with a lapel badge which he somehow managed to read: '*Segurança*'. All eyes were on him, as if confounded by the way he'd bolted awake. The hotel manager, keeping his distance, pointed at the police saying "*Comme vous le voir, le situation est très sérieux. Nous sachons pas—*"

Sitting up on the edge of his bed wearing only his under-pants, Lombard glared, sighed, swallowed hard and managed a grin to ask the manager to speak in English. "Oh," the man said, much relieved; "Very good, sir. Let me tell you—You have no idea what a load off our minds it is to find you sound and safe in your bed. We feared the worst when you failed to answer your phone or the door." "Really. What's this all about?" Lombard breathed, stirring from the blanket of sleep still enveloping him. "Your hired car, Mr Lombard. You— Please, did you by any chance lend it to someone yesterday?" "My car?" "Yes. I believe you are visiting here on your own but could you have met someone and lent them your hired car, maybe?" "Lent it? Not that I recall." "Good. Then, could you tell us where you parked it before returning to the hotel yesterday?"

After thinking about it for a moment, Lombard said he believed he'd left the car along the kerb not far from the hotel entrance. "Ah yes—So you didn't leave it in the hotel car park, is that right?" "I guess so." This seemed to provide some comfort to the hotel manager who quickly exchanged words in Portuguese with the other three. "Are you going to tell me what's going on or am I going to have to guess it all by myself?" Lombard chipped in. "Ahem—Of course. My apologies. Well—We have a situation, sir," the manager announced, showing the all-knowing bearing of those who are about to disclose some grave news as yet unknown to their interlocutor, holding a dramatic pause which, for as long as they can make it last, gives them a sense of mastery over their audience if not time itself. For now though, he requested that Lombard produce his hired car key fob, and when this proved impossible after a cursory search of his room and suit pockets – which only produced the keys he'd retrieved from the bonfire – the man made good, providing an account of the events which had led to his coming to wake Lombard up in the company of two police officers and a hotel security guard in the early hours of the morning.

An hour or so earlier Lombard's car had been found perched on its roof at the bottom of a small cliff in the wilderness on the other side of the island. How it got there was unknown, but it was evident that whoever was at the wheel at the time had veered off the road and tumbled fifty yards down into dense forest. Despite serious damage, the car headlights had remained on, so that it was spotted in the darkness, and on reaching it the rescue services found it empty but with the key fob still inside of it and, alarmingly, blood on and around the driver's seat. A call to the car hire company had returned Lombard's details and, on account of the blood, it was assumed that after the accident he had left the scene injured and confused and become lost in the wilderness – a stranger in a strange land stumbling in the darkness. Be that as it may, the way the hotel manager put it, "All the time, thank you God, you were sound and safe in bed!"

Now, given that the key fob was found inside the vehicle and he could not locate his own, the four in the room quickly agreed that he must have left it in the car which had then been stolen after he parked it in the street; in all probability a crime of opportunity. Lombard confessed to having been tired and otherwise engaged at the time he returned with the car. All this meant the injured person whose blood was in the wreck may still be near the scene of the accident in a life-threatening condition, and the party of four hurried away to convey the situation to others it concerned, bidding him goodbye with the recommendation that he contact the car hire company as soon as possible.

Alone, he sat back down on his bed. The sun was climbing fast up the clear sky outside his windows, casting beams of crystalline light into the room, warming his bare skin and infusing every object and texture with a gilded glow, so that everything looked unlike it ought to – or unlike it looked ordinarily. The light, rather than reflecting off things, suffused the surface of all it reached, thinning out everything, as if adding air and dust through all it touched. Had he taken the trouble to open a window to let in the sweet-scented breeze, he may well have enjoyed the moment, lost himself in Madeira's fragrant bracing morning display. Instead, he groaned, headed for the bathroom where, catching his reflection in the mirror, he paused on noting the slight sunburn on his face, a mark of the previous day spent outdoors. He considered shaving, but then, happening upon never-seen-before grey speckles scattered in the dark stubble along his jawline, for the second day running decided against it, curious to know what grizzly display time had made of his beard.

The hire company deemed him entirely responsible for the misadventure which had befallen his car. The result was predictable: he was charged the full deposit against damage he had paid on hiring the vehicle. The affair was resolved in a reasonable manner – no doubt helped by his gracious bearing of the blame – and, with a twice repeated light-hearted warning about needing to be better at remembering to lock the car and keep hold of the key fob, he was allowed to hire a new vehicle. Come mid-morning, after a full breakfast, shoed in a pair of new trainers and supplied with a steak sandwich, he headed off back up into the interior to the intersection between route 211 and 109.

This much was certain: anyone of sound mind and healthy body wandering along the bleak plateau far enough to chance upon the ravine's bejewelled watery garden would find it perverse not to scramble down the steep escarpment that led to it. Lombard had been tired the previous afternoon. Today, he realized the extent to which he'd failed to appreciate the overpowering enchantment of the place. There could be no other reason to be there but to head down into the heady smells, the dewed green grasses, the coloured flushes of buds and petals, and the fresh dappled luminous water, which existed as one world in three distinct parts: the waterfall, fine and diffuse – a living, rustling meshwork of freshness; the pool and its mossy boulders, beckoning and dazzling – at this midday hour it dazzled, mirroring the sun burning in the clear sky overhead; and the black and silver rocky stream flowing into the emerald canopy of laurel trees – which went on to stretch into the distance as a luscious ribbon of rich greens. The whole beckoned, stirred the senses. It would have been unthinkable for Alan Winston to reach the spot and not head down into such wonder.

For the time being, though, Lombard was not quite ready to climb down there. Turning back to the plateau he noticed that the previous evening's rains had dispersed the charred items and ashes near the ravine's edge. He wondered whether to collect what there was, but thought the keys he'd already picked up were enough for his purpose, and, aware the breeze had departed and he was beginning to sweat, decided he had better move on.

In his new trainers and shirtsleeves, under the full glare of the sun, with his sandwich and jacket left in his car parked at the roadside near the intersection with its signpost, for some time he trudged to and fro along the lines of an imaginary grid extending from the ravine's edge to the road, sweeping the plateau for signs of Alan Winston, or, as it may be, evidence of recent ground disturbance. In due course, finding nothing, he clambered down into the ravine and set out to explore the densely-forested banks on either side of the stream. This time, unlike the rudimentary search he conducted the previous day, having by now also concealed his jacket and sandwich in the long grass by the pool, his mission called for much stopping and probing. He scanned hollows and dips, probed every shadow within the tree canopy, surveyed the expanses of moss-covered boulders, combed through ferns and chest-high bracken, scoured the stream's deepest rockpools as well as its turbulent stretches of white water, all the way to the anticipated man-made dam where the wild water abruptly transformed into a narrow-walled canal hugging the hillside on its way to farmlands much lower down the island. In short, he looked in all the places an object the bulk of a man may lie unseen, immersed, buried or scavenged, until he was satisfied nothing answering this description had escaped his attention, and, by and by, as the daylight dimmed, the breeze returned and the shadows deepened in the first hint of evening, he scrambled back up along the stream. He reckoned Alan Winston's body was nowhere to be found in the ravine, and pondering what to make of this, soon discovered he'd been preceded to the pool.

In the course of adventures, Lombard had had the chance to acquaint himself with various creatures, in the process grown to develop a particular admiration for donkeys. In his opinion, they were incomparably more hardy, savvy, reliable and sensible than the best of horses – truly dependable and generous beasts of burden, loyal companions in all weathers and environments. It was a while since he had last seen one in the flesh, but he could tell that the one that now grazed contentedly among the grasses by the pool with its back to him was mindful of his approach. While it had yet to suspend its grazing or even stir to acknowledge his presence, one of its ears was back and twitching, alert, while the other was forward, suggesting the creature was little concerned at being disturbed. It only slowly turned as Lombard came to a stop a couple of paces from where it stood, to face him, but still went on grazing with its head down, indifferent. It was a jack, a stout, brownish-grey beast with a neat coat and a dark stripe running the length of its back. To determine its age would have required closer examination, but it stood healthily heavy, with a large straight back, proud legs and well-angled feet with neatly trimmed hooves, all reliable indicators that it was of good years and strong, both of fine service and, in return, well-looked after. This was clearly a domesticated animal, and one with a trusting disposition, comfortable with a stranger in close proximity. Seeing that it was unattended, Lombard presumed it had made its way there on its own, likely by way of the steep escarpment from the plateau above that he used himself, for he'd seen no sign of the animal along the stream corridor he'd just explored. He also knew that much as they could wander off on their own, donkeys preferred company to solitude. On that account he looked up to survey the rim of the ravine above their heads, half-expecting the silhouette of its keeper to either be standing there or to appear at any time against the sunset sky. But they were alone, and, at length, the creature raised its head to gaze desultorily straight back at him, so that for a while – or so a spectator might have construed – they locked gaze in a placid face-off, one steel-faced, the other quietly chewing, its eyes slightly widened, measuring one another.

Lombard eventually stretched out his arms and gently rubbed the grey coat just behind the animal's ears, and in turn the donkey slowly lowered its head and shut its eyes. "Hello partner," Lombard whispered, and, possibly, the two united in ecstasy, and the moment would have lasted had the ringing of his phone not stabbed the air and brought it to an end. Retrieving the device from his back pocket he failed to recognize the caller's number and, for some reason, answered presuming Letitia Balthazar would be at the other end wishing to share some detail about the pool which had just come back to her.

He was wrong.

"Hullo there! Ahem—Am I—Mister Xavier Lagarde?" a young honeyed female voice enquired eagerly at the other end.

Lombard swallowed hard; only one person with his number would know him by this name, but it was too soon for them to be calling; if at all, the package he'd arranged to have sent from Tahiti to Avery Weyland could only just have reached London.

"Speaking," he said.

"Ah! Good aft—Lagarde! This is—My name is Charlo—I'm Ave—sistant. We rece—"

The girl went on speaking, but her words were clipped, the connection too broken up to give her words sense. Reckoning he'd have to get out of the ravine for a better signal Lombard told her he was driving and would call back soon from a place with better reception. She appeared to understand him before they both hung up.

This was a surprise. His package could hardly have been with Avery Weyland for more than a couple of days at most – presuming Gisèle had expedited the matter the very day he contacted her – and already the film producer-director's assistant was calling. Certainly, it could be a matter of them seeking clarification or, then again, wishing to let it be known they were so unimpressed by his unorthodox daredevil approach that they sought an address to return his package and money at once. Still, his package had reached its destination and they'd called.

"*Eh bien, qui aurait cru ça,*" he said, pocketing his phone to lock eyes with the donkey again.

He gently patted the animal's head, turned away to retrieve his jacket and sandwich from the nearby grass and sat on the ground among the carpet of flowers beginning to close their petals for the night, consciously steering clear of the boulder by the pool he'd favoured the previous afternoon, and set about eating as the donkey resumed its grazing. Darkness was coming fast but he made time, rose at last to his feet only once the donkey decided to move and start along the stream towards the shadow of the copse of laurel trees, whereupon it disappeared. Now he knew which way it had come. "So long, partner," he breathed, and, like the animal, he left, grabbing his jacket to start up the escarpment and out of the ravine. There were stars already clearly visible in the dark blue sky above his head as he strolled back to his car free from any thought, his mind a blank canvas. But remarkably, it occurred to him that, if he could, he might well have wept, without a clue nor care as to why.

He waited to return Avery Weyland's assistant's call until back at his car parked at the plateau's intersection. Now they could hear each other fine. The girl introduced herself as Charlotte Lottway. Telling him to call her Lottie, in the same sentence she asked whether it was alright to address him as 'Xavier'. She had a genteel pleasant voice which evoked fair young English features, called to mind a comely rosy-hued complexion so becoming in the light of temperate skies, and breathed of ready good manners. She disclosed that she was the person in charge of screenplay development at Monty Productions, and that Avery Weyland had asked her to contact him to seek "a couple of clarifications and possibly set up a meeting. I must tell you, Xavier—Your parcel made quite an impression around the office, ha-ha-ha! Quite a storm, as a matter of fact."

"Well, I'm very sorry about that," he replied.

What they wished to know was: were they correct in

presuming by his letter that he would be prepared to commit up to four million Euros in the production of a film based on either of the scripts he had sent; who was John Jones, the author of the screenplays; was he, Xavier Lagarde, from French Guiana and connected in some capacity to the film industry; and why had he sent his proposal to Avery Weyland's company – was it on someone's recommendation perhaps?

He answered the first point in the positive; explained the second was a delicate matter he'd rather discuss *en tête à tête*; and made fun of the third and fourth: "Generally, I like to think of myself as a not too stupid man who can account for himself, Lottie. But when it comes to the movies, I'm afraid I may be just a fool with a fat wallet. No—I chose your production company at random from a list of London film production companies. As it happens, you are the very first folks I contacted."

Lottie understood. It was all good, she assured him with the kind of eager pliancy which, more than the keenness of youth, revealed an achiever's quick and enterprising ruthlessness. In a beat, she changed the conversation to the screenplays. She'd already gone over one of them – 'They Bite at Night' – had had a quick word with "Avery" about it. She said they thought it had potential: "Absolutely love the opening dialogue, by the way—When Sam says 'Nowhere in the good book does it say "Thou shalt not love", does it now?', and then the Barry character replies 'Maybe so. But neither does it—'" Lombard pointedly stopped her: "It's not much use talking to me about the screenplays, Lottie—You might as well talk Mandarin; I'm afraid I read neither of them." And again, after laughing and without missing a beat, she announced that Avery would like to meet him but that it may be difficult to arrange as they understood he wasn't due in London for another few days and would only be there for a short stay. "Have we got this right, Xavier?" The issue, she revealed, "Is that Avery is here in London for the next five days but then has commitments that will keep him away for several weeks. It would be absolutely brilliant if we could set up something, though. What about your end, Xavier. When do you think you might make it to London?"

Lombard said he had just arrived in Paris from Tahiti but could be in London the day after next if it helped. It did, and so they fixed a meeting for the day after next at 11:30 a.m. at the Monty Productions office. "Perfect. That's great. Both Avery and I are looking forward to meeting you, Xavier. *Au revoir.*"

Now the hasty response to his package made sense; it was all down to Avery Weyland's busy schedule. And now he wasn't surprised as much as impressed. His scheme had exceeded even his own expectations. All that was left was for him to assess whether the man had it in him to kill when they met. He trusted he'd know. Unless Mr Avery Weyland turned out to be a skilled psychopathic serial killer, something would give when tested by the right sort of predator. He was confident of this. The only requisite was to get close enough to the man.

Josefina welcomed the sight of him as much as he welcomed the sight of her when he stepped into his hotel reception. She teased him about his tan and trainers, taunted him about his car key fob, and revealed they had caught his car thief. He turned out to be a young waiter from a nearby restaurant. Returning drunk from a late night party he'd spotted the car with its fob and set out to drive himself home, undaunted, the way of an intoxicated mind who has neither driving licence nor driving experience. The police had arrested him at the hospital where he'd made his way to have his injuries seen to. His life was not in danger. Lombard asked Josefina if she had any plans after her shift ended, went up to his room, showered and waited for her.

That night, lying beside Josefina's warm body, he thought of the donkey that had walked away into the copse of laurel trees along the ravine's stream, wondered how he could have failed to spot it on its way to the pool. He guessed he was focussed on other matters at the time. What couldn't be in doubt though was that the creature had good shelter – that much was obvious; its neat coat spoke for it. Donkeys need cover from the rain, or more crucially, cover to recover from the rain. They were desert creatures. Their coats weren't water-proof, just as soon absorbed and trapped the rain, and so this one would be in poor health with bad skin infections if it lacked shelter to recover from Madeira's subtropical daily downpours. But instead, the animal's coat glowed brown and grey with only the richest dyes. Later still, he woke in the darkness to find Josefina's body gone. Alone, his mind mulled over what would come about from meeting Avery Weyland. The night was weaving its tricks, setting challenges from the darkness. Who was he to think he'd know how to read the impeccably credentialed producer-director? Another delusional fool? Indeed, the repetition of a single occupation could indeed provide almost anyone with the appearance of intelligence. What did he know? He'd do well to call on Monroe and have them set their devilry in motion. Monroe could command the man's phone and every other smart device he owned – remotely infect and tap them all. But that wasn't all. Thanks to some word analysis software they dubbed 'MonkeySpeaks' which monitored and recorded conversations, texts and emails, Monroe could also flag any word or words which, when captured in real time, would initiate a notification to be sent to Lombard's phone, allowing him either to eavesdrop live on an exchange or play or read a record of it in his own time. Lombard's one contribution to 'MonkeySpeaks' was his suggestion – by now soundly tested – to instruct the system to flag profanities rather than specific words; fear and anger are most dependable expletive-inducers. In the event that his scheme to meet Avery Weyland would prove to be a convoluted wasted exercise, he'd call the producer-director anonymously, profess to be a blackmailer with evidence of his association with Joseph Aratoon and his mischief towards Jane, and follow the 'MonkeySpeaks' trail the other would likely leave from there on, for whether guilty or innocent the man would have to be reactive to the allegation. Perhaps this is what he should have done to begin with; rely on Monroe. As Edward Duncan put it, "In today's world this God is a necessary evil." Indeed.

Lombard would call Monroe.

FIFTEEN

On the Jews.

These days, the nearest Lombard came to experiencing something resembling homesickness arose from the odd agitation that tickled his senses whenever he settled back into the intimacy of his car after time spent away from its steering wheel. To be reunited with the vehicle and to drive it was very much akin to a homecoming, or more precisely – for after all it was only a machine – much like what he imagined a homecoming to be, and the emotions thus stirred fostered a sense of homesickness, which proved comforting insomuch as longing for a rediscovered good thing far outweighs the hollowness of apathy.

A little before midnight, he headed for Mile End at the wheel of his Saab, beyond the West End's brash nightlife of turbulent crowds and lurking prowlers, across inky places where London took on the semblance of a tethered slumbering dragon, flashing traffic lights here and glowing windows there, hissing hot steam from underground stations' gangways, an un-slayed beast fettered into hushed nocturnal inertia, its resting limbs and veins to be coursed. Indeed, it was small things such as this that he feared missing the most in the event of one day leaving the city for the countryside. For now, seeing as the meeting at Monty Productions was not until 11:30 the next morning, there was time for him to check whether the keys he'd retrieved from the Madeiran plateau were Alan Winston's, and he soon pulled up at the kerb across the road from the dead end's murder house just as a fine rain began to mist his windscreen.

But for John Bowdion's lit-up third-floor windows, the house with its glass and wrought iron front door stood in darkness behind the pale halo of the lampposts. Lombard moved to climb out into the street but stopped short when a small car came screeching to a halt to double-park beside the van just in front of him, at once filling the dead end with the boom of a loud bass beat. The car's four doors swung open and in an instant over half-a-dozen hooded youths leapt out into the rain. Some held beer cans, some smoked, all swaggered as they scrambled into a loose rowdy pack, a couple of them opting to lean against the Saab's bonnet with their back to Lombard. Pitting their every word against the music throbbing from their open car, bragging about the "totally fucked up" time they'd just had and "how fucking mental" their next outing will be, none were aware of Lombard behind his dark windscreen. A few curtains twitched in the windows of the nearby buildings, but the youths were left untroubled until all but one piled back into the car which fast-reversed in a squeal to disappear the way it had come. With the patter of the rain once again the only sound, Lombard remained in his seat to observe the one youth left behind. Hunched inside his hood, he cut a lonely figure as he gingerly leant forward to pick up a couple of beer cans tossed on the tarmac by the departed pack. He seemed to mutter to himself and then hurriedly sidled along the pavement deeper into the dead end to a nearby house where he briefly stopped to toss the beer cans into a waste bin before disappearing through a side door.

As it happened, the commotion had alerted John Bowdion who, making out Lombard's Saab, had opened his window to peer down through the rain. Lombard only caught sight of him after he climbed out onto the street. He'd thought it safe to come at this late hour, had no wish to share the man's company again, and no desire to reveal what had brought him there, but short of stepping straight back into his car to drive away, there was no ignoring John Bowdion's urgent whispering calls:

"Laurent! I thought I recognized your car. What are you doing here? Wait! I'm coming down."

When the other opened the front door a moment later, standing out in the rain Lombard made out he was in the area and thought he might stop by on the odd chance John Bowdion was still up. Far be it from him to wish to disturb him though, or to plan on staying at this late hour; he sought only the answer to one question: could John Bowdion recall Alan Winston ever alluding to a Portuguese girl called Josefina? The man, naturally, responded in the negative, momentarily looking disappointed that his visitor's late call was unrelated to his screenplays. All the same, he barely let such concerns bother him. Rather, something was changed about him; he seemed animated by a sense of urgency. "I'm glad you stopped by, Laurent. Please, come in. I must show you something— Something truly fucking unbelievable just happened," he insisted, breathlessly, very much behaving like a man who would not be denied. "I see you've been away," he went on, noting Lombard's suntan while looking him over in the light from the hallway behind him; "Lucky you. Isn't it amazing how much can happen in just a few days sometimes! Come in, please."

Without question, the last few days had made a great difference to John Bowdion. His gaze was direct. He seemed healthier, sturdier, taller. No longer did he look merely a wretched creature – now he looked a wretched creature with newfound confidence, a newfound backbone, swaggering almost, as someone who has just received some longed-for good news may allow themselves to. It would have been simple enough to get out of being led up the stairs to his bedsit – ordinarily Lombard would have – but prudence dictated otherwise; a mere few hours away from meeting Avery Weyland, it seemed advisable to keep the screenwriter onside. The alternative was to risk giving him cause to alert the producer-director – the prospect being a reality since the other had guessed the intended recipient of his screenplays. "Right. But I can only stay a moment," Lombard said, grinning.

In the bedsit, all was much as he recalled except for a battered metal trunk sitting open on the floor and heaps of bundled envelopes and loose letters spread across the large antique table; the trunk was half-full of yet more bundles of envelopes. "Here. This is what I wanted you to see," John Bowdion whispered almost reverently, standing over the trunk. This display of deference made it clear that his whispering was the product of awe rather than, at this late hour, consideration for his neighbours. "Old Newman—Samuel—Sam—He left all these to me! I had no idea. He left all these to me," he said; "Can you believe it!"

In a low voice, he now set out to shed light on the cause of his excitement. It turned out that while packing away the belongings of the departed old man whose death out in the street had in effect precipitated the events that had led to Alan Winston's killing of the Paragon reporter, the landlord's agent had come across this metal trunk padlocked and furnished with an envelope taped to its lid which read: 'In the event of my death or disappearance, this trunk is to be given to John Bowdion in Flat 6 — Its contents are his properties. Please return the trunk to him.' For all that, it had been left behind in the dead man's room when they'd come to collect his belongings and furniture. It was not until three days later, when an electrician was let in there to inspect the old wiring, that the annotated trunk had been rediscovered and John Bowdion made aware of its existence. The trunk was never his, proving a complete surprise and mystery when presented to him. Still, he'd readily taken possession of it and hurried to saw off the padlock the minute he'd become acquainted with the note the old man had left inside the envelope on the lid:

'Dear John,
Nowadays you're the only person I know who takes an interest in 'words' and shows much interest in the vicissitudes of this old Jew's life. These are the reasons why I'm leaving my unsent correspondence to my long departed kin in your care. I have no wish for anything to be done with it. You're welcome to read it if you like – most is in Yiddish! – but you don't have to! All I ask/would appreciate is for you to hang on to it for a little while after I'm gone (which, since you're

reading this, I thank God I must be by now). It would be good if you could store it for a couple of months. The thought of all my 'schmaltzy' words being cast away on a tip at the same time I take my leave of this world somehow grieves this lone, done for, wary and weary old man. For reasons I care not to explore, the idea of disappearing 'a petit pas' rather than totally in one great leap seems less terrible – go and figure! I thank you in advance and am much indebted to you for our chats, which though short and few, were of more comfort than you possibly could imagine!
May you find your own peace and strength, John; you're not one of the bad ones!
Samuel Newman.'

Once open, the trunk had revealed dozens of bundles of sealed envelopes. Each bundle contained between twelve and thirty odd envelopes held together with an elastic band, and each envelope was handwritten with just a name and date, but no address or postmark. It turned out that each bundle covered a year – from 1946 to the present – and all the envelopes were addressed to one of just four names – Mame, Tate, Gitta and Joshua. In all, there were just over a thousand envelopes split into over seventy bundles enclosing the musings of Samuel Newman who, within a year of being liberated from the Auschwitz-Birkenau Extermination Camp, had taken to writing regularly to his dead mother, father, sister and brother, all lost to the holocaust, right up to a few days before he'd met his own death, all the time hoarding this correspondence the way others sometimes store away letters penned to imaginary friends or a forbidden beloved. Two days of elementary inspection of the whole – and the resource of an online Yiddish-English translation site – had taught John Bowdion that his old neighbour was even better travelled than he knew, and had worn many hats, from cigarette and gun smuggler in post-war Eastern Europe to Formula Three racing driver in France, gambler, bank robber, nightclub owner; he also turned out to have spent time in the USA, both as a free man and a prisoner. Once, he'd also got married – to a French-Israeli woman – and knew of two children he had fathered. He'd lost contact with one, but the other – a British born citizen who'd grown into a lonely man with a history of depression that had led to his taking his own life – was the reason he'd settled in London thirty years earlier at the age of sixty-six. He'd come to Britain to care for his depressive son, in vain it turned out, and soon afterwards, old and with little means, had found himself stuck in London to end up in the Mile End bedsit.

This much John Bowdion had gleaned from reading a few randomly opened letters written in English, for most were in Yiddish, and others still in French or German. But already he'd had a few dozen of these translated, he announced not a little proud. "This is such a treasure trove—Unbelievable stuff!" The trunk and its contents gave him an exuberance of spirits of which there'd been little sign previously. "You got to read this," he breathed excitedly while handing four printed sheets of paper to Lombard; "It's the last letters he wrote— Last month's. I literally just got them translated from Yiddish so the language is a bit clunky. But it's dynamite. Fucking dynamite! All the things this crazy world's been bullied into burying. You must read it, Laurent; it won't take a minute. Can I offer you a drink?"

At times, unbound enthusiasm can be contagious – not only did Lombard take the printed sheets, but he did so in all manner of ways, wanting to and wanting not to, indifferent and curious, prejudiced and open-minded, scornful and keen. This was how it was.

"No. I'm good. Thank you," he said with a sigh, swallowing hard; "I can't stay long." And still standing on his feet he began to read.

'Dearest Gitta,
You will know how much I miss you if your antennas are out. Earlier today I couldn't help thinking of you as I returned home after being forced off a bus because of an argument with a silly woman.
Little Sister, I still remember how much we laughed at the story of Eve being a rib! How sorry we felt for poor Aunt Rachel, who was much too smart and pretty for

horrid Uncle Saul to possess. How you used to say that God had to be both male and cruel for having cursed women with the marks and hindrances of childbearing—Particularly the most spirited among women whose worldly lapses were laid so bare as to display them! How if you knew how to, you would make yourself a boy to be free to run as fast as you please! 'I'd as well run to Gehinnom as a man as wilt away as a slave and wife!' And you meant it too! Well, sweet Sister, today, in the part of the world I live in, you would not need to turn the brave gorgeous girl you are into a boy (although it would amuse you to know, some do exactly that now, thanks to science).

No, dear much beloved and much-missed Sister. Women now are their own masters! They needn't marry nor bear children to prosper and thrive if such is their desire. The equal of men they are in all things. Sit freely at café tables, are writers, journalists, scientists, entrepreneurs, judges and leaders! They even serve in the armed forces and play sports professionally. And insofar as bearing their lapses for all to see, this long ago was wrested from God's hands and placed into their own by means of pills and various other advancements. Were you to be here to warm up my world today, dearest Gitta, no ambition would be too high or not permissible to you or your heart! You and only you would be the limit of your reach and, I know, would be so happy, proud and fulfilled for it. And for sure, I too would be proud of you.

Purely on my own account though, I must admit to being unsure about this new situation. Every day that passes means my time away from you is mercifully getting shorter while I grow the more tired; too tired for this world which doesn't need me and goes on as it always has, providing scoundrels and imbeciles and good souls and geniuses in unequal amounts. The time was when I had needed to watch out only for about half of those scoundrels and imbeciles. Now, with Eve competing with Adam to drive motorcars, there are twice as many crazy and mean drivers on the streets to look out for! As if crossing the road wasn't already fraught with enough danger before, when I was young. One maniac has become two!

Now, dear Gitta, if you have not grown too bored yet, you may wonder what of this story about my being forced off a bus. Well, it's late now, and my memory of it seems to have faded with the light, I'm afraid, and my loyal canine friend Moses waits impatiently by the door for our evening walk.

So, for now only, I'll let you be with many tender thoughts, sweet-sweet Sister.

Your loving brother Sam.'

Having finished this letter, Lombard started the next, pulling a chair to sit down while ignoring John Bowdion who was standing watching him waiting for his reaction.

'Dear Father,

Here is news for you: it isn't easy to be a Jew.

'Tell me something I don't know,' I hear you say.

Well, let me try. The God of the Israelites must be a mean trickster to have saved me from perishing with you and Mother and my brother and sister to keep me alive so long that I should now witness the return of the Get-the-Jews fever of yesteryear.

'Here we go again,' I hear you now, 'The world gives three cheers to Jew-haters, and my son cries life's not fair. Tell me something new, son.'

Well, I'll try again. Dear Father, it has pleased God that I should number among the surviving Israelites of my generation. Yet, every so often, I must wonder what I owe the pleasure to: his infinite kindness or boundless malevolence?

Oh, I hear you here too: 'Has there yet been a Jew who never asked such a question? What's next: why did Esther save the Jewish nation?'

You're right, Father. I sound like an ingrate. Enough. Let me tell you how it is.

Years ago, when I lived in Spain, I used to like going to bullfights; the blood, the colour, the crowd, the dirt! Now, I ask myself whether we Jews are not the world's bulls, in that like the Spanish bulls they rear to kill, they keep some of us alive between antisemitic orgies for the express purpose of diverting themselves with our blood again come the next corrida. It wouldn't surprise me if they thought we were bored while waiting for their pleasure between persecutions and killings. I wonder: do they think we forgive them come night?

Well, Father, your son who is now so much older than you ever were, this Hebrew-born prince of vagabonds has grown angry and fearful. The people's post-Holocaust contrition and tolerance of the Hebrews has ended. You know of Israel. These days, more and more are openly challenging our right to have a nation or to defend our children with swords or words. A Hebrew's proper place, they'd have it, should again be that of a stateless vagrant at the mercy of the whims of his fickle hosts. Here in London, I now regularly must endure abuse when I venture out, which I do less and less. My local police and well-meaning neighbours' idea of support is to suggest I desist from displaying the Star of David I wear around my neck.

I'm left to ask what demons inhabit the human spirit? Despair, Father! Yesterday, out with Moses on our evening stroll, a group of teenagers harried me all the way home when I failed to poop-and-scoop. 'Have mercy for an old man,' I implored, 'Bending down isn't the breeze it used to be; my hips and joints are killing me.' Nothing doing! By the time I got back, I'd been spat at, taunted to 'clean the streets with a toothbrush like Yids used to', called a 'woman and child killer', and—Think of it!—A fake Israelite! 'We are the true Israelites,' they chanted on all sides of me, 'You're nothing but a dirty Yid impostor; we're the true Israelites!' Now, I can give as good as I get, but this! And these boys and girls weren't the usual suspects, Father. They were black! I suppose I must have written you a thousand times about the American soldier who grabbed hold of me as I lay taking what I thought was my last breath in Gunskirchen. How he was a black person. How I'd never seen a black person before. How I thought he was the Messiah; come to save us! I say, how things change, Father. Only bad things come from America now. Terrible things. Horrors of many hues. Like this notion among some black people that they should steal our account with God for their own promotion. Have we not withstood, been robbed, enough? By whites and by browns. Now a people who shares portions of our pains joins with them. Oh, like all devils before them, they make loud noises about ending hatred, but they are bringing terrible things, Father. Former slaves now sit at the table with former masters. Fake blushes of virtue conceal the white and brown man's bloodied claws while the taste of power sways the black woman's judgement. They make a perfect communion. The one reckons he has atoned, the other she's arrived. This advantageous coupling's one bargain with hatred: the Jews! He shall be free to go on hating us and she shall be free to join him in depravity, as if the true measure of power is to abuse the children of Israel; as if, sharing in the banquet, she developed an appetite for human flesh, a pound of it to be exact, and pricking the Jews that she casts as über whites. Pharoah and Jezebel, they are all dancing with Hitler, Father. They deserve each other and together deserve their misery. Rifts are now growing where none were before. Despair—Despair—Despair! I've done my share of bad things to survive, but never to feed depravity. Shall they ever let our people go, I cry! Our people be!

Your old son is much displeased with God for prolonging his time here so long that he should now occupy his mind with such raw notions as he just wrote, Father. I've been a dog, I've had my hour, my kicks; why turn me into a rumpled old man beset by ugliness and fear? A dog to be kicked? Enough of the meat grinder! To be released, to be released is what I yearn for. I can no longer look back, can no longer look ahead or watch the present and feel generous. I'm bewildered. Death.

Reunion with my kin surely will herald better and
sweeter things.
Other than this, I'm well.
Forgive my intemperance.
Your forever respectful son, Samuel.'

"So what do you think," John Bowdion queried as soon as
Lombard lifted his eyes to put the printed letters down on the
table; "Quite something, isn't it? Un-fucking-believable,
right?"

"Reads to me like the dark ramblings of a sad and tired old
man," Lombard said, rising to his feet to leave.

"You can say that again! Poor old Sam. I never knew really.
I thought I did but—As I said, this stuff is dynamite. You can't
say these things. They'll shred you to pieces if you try. It's like
he speaks a totally forbidden tongue. And from what I've been
able to see so far, the rest is just as edifying. I just can't—"
John Bowdion revealed he had already formulated a plan. He
would get every letter translated into English and compile
them into three volumes for publication; each volume would
include about twenty years of Samuel Newman's "unsent"
correspondence. Always whispering – as if conspiratorially
now – he could barely contain his enthusiasm: "I don't think
anything like this has ever seen the light of day. If no British
publisher dares touch it for fear of controversy, I'll take it
elsewhere; approach foreign publishers. Someone somewhere
will be the equal to it. One thousand and eighty-seven
letters—1946 to the present—Written to four deceased family
members who all perished in Europe's gas chambers. There's
never been anything like it. Someone will publish this. I can't
wait. I already—"

Lombard frowned: "Whatever happened to 'What if they
like it'?" he interjected.

"What?"

"What if they like it," he repeated; "Am I right in recalling
this was what the old man's response to your suggestion that
he should write his life's story: 'What if they like it?'"

John Bowdion looked back, gormless, but only for a moment;
his mind was clearly set on not letting the old man's wishes

hinder his plans. He furrowed his brows to let out a loud sigh of exasperation: "I know—I know. The thought occurred to me already. But think of all the good this could do. And then, he gave all this to me. He gave it to me! I mean, who's to say he didn't secretly want to tell his story—Maybe he was frightened of rejection. Look at his note—How he says that it grieves him to think of all his words being lost after his death. Maybe he changed his mind. People do."

Lombard grunted and swallowed hard: "Well, now he's dead, if turning the man's words to your advantage will not be your ruin, I guess not much harm can come of it."

"My thoughts exactly," John Bowdion approved: "I'm sure old Sam would be thrilled to know his amazing words were about to be published for all the world to read. It would be a credit to him—And honour his family, don't you think?"

Lombard grinned. In light of the man's near crusading zeal on matters of antisemitism and his admission that he was unfamiliar with Yiddish, he considered asking him whether he was Jewish, but, recalling his indignation over being asked the same by the police on a previous occasion, he thought it unwise and, later than planned, made his excuses, wishing the man "Best of luck with your project. I'll get back to you when I no longer need your screenplays; which should be soon." The truth be told, another consideration kept him from lengthening his stay – the company of John Bowdion, as had been the case on previous visits, seemed to spawn its very own inescapable sense of impending doom and dread.

To Lombard's satisfaction, no offer was made to accompany him back down the stairs, so that once back downstairs he was free to pause by the front door to try the keys from Madeira. As anticipated, one of the keys turned in the lock. This much was no longer in doubt: the items in the ashes on the plateau above the pool were Alan Winston's.

Had Lombard questioned John Bowdion as to his bloodline or faith, and had the latter been agreeable to answering – which on account of his newfound excitement he may well

229

have conceded to on that particular night – he would have learnt the following particulars. John Bowdion was a child of the Welsh hills and valleys, of Methodist stock through and through, with a measure of English blood from his mother's side and conceivably – the vagueness being due to the matter having never been openly discussed – a soupcon of the Romany from one or more of his great-grandparents. Granted, the places of worship of his childhood village went by the names of Ebenezer Chapel and Enon Baptist Church, and close by were localities labelled Carmel, Goshen, Bethel and Nazareth, with yet more sites of reverence such as Bethesda Apostolic Temple and Mount Zion Primitive Methodist Church, but these Hebrew sounding buildings and locations were in truth his only link to the nation of Israel, and come to that, he could only claim to have stepped into any chapel of any denomination on just a handful of occasions – funerals and weddings mostly – growing up, as it were, in a household indifferent to God; "What have we got to be grateful to God for nowadays?" his father would ask, never failing to answer himself: "Fuck all!" And on this question, John Bowdion was his father's son, in that this sentiment echoed precisely his personal spiritual outlook: he had no time for God. Still, in a curious case of convergence – or possibly a curious case of his own adversity identifying with the plight of the people of Israel – while a dedicated unbeliever, he had come to view the Jews as mankind's chosen people, making it his mission to champion their lot wherever appropriate, a state of affairs some may have regarded as evidence that he was as mad as ever a man in full possession of his senses can be. But madness – if madness indeed defined the particularly wretched condition of his mind – can provide some benefits to an imaginative mind. The situation here was this: a man who'd failed to get ahead in society, and lost most of the things he cared for into the bargain, his will to live had become contingent upon his angry despair not turning into indifferent resignation. As mentioned already in the course of this tale, a man needs a reason to ride his time. This man, angry and impotent in the face of his misfortune in much the same way as an innocent man put behind bars would be, had sought to find a rational explanation for his ruin where some may have sought solace in fatalism or notions of revenge. Yet, no matter how hard he tried, all thoughts on the matter inevitably led to the same unhelpful conclusion: essentially, he'd fallen short not on account of God or his own limitations but because he was born good in a bad place; cursed with a conscience in a world devoid of scruples. The trouble with such a proclamation was that it proved self-defeating, provided him with no comfort and contributed nothing to alleviating his torments. Rather the opposite: for to acknowledge such a proposition as true amounted to an affirmation of the worthlessness of his ways. If mankind's natural state could be defined as devoid of scruples, then what was the purpose of scruples – or the likes of him? Wouldn't championing the notion that scruples are mere meaningless impediments be akin to proclaiming morality and decency futile fancies, and so challenge the worth of those, who like himself foster such fancies in their minds and hearts, all the while vindicating they who wrong the world on a day-to-day basis? "He who brands mankind wicked has no fucking jurisdiction lamenting his unjust fate," John Bowdion would have proclaimed had he not kept this advice to himself. Thereby, he'd steered clear of the commonplace shelters of disappointment – fatalism, cynicism, the embrace of mediocrity, cruelty – unwilling to dismiss his suffering as pointless or to deny his own morality or aspirations; the world could not – could never – be just a wicked place, and his fortune had to have better success in reserve yet.

And by and by – the idea wasn't formed in a moment of inspiration, by serendipity, on a given day or over a couple of summers, but rather much the same way as a shoreline is born of and contoured by the ebbs and flows of the tides – John Bowdion had come to the opinion that the Jews were indeed very much 'chosen', but that God had absolutely nought do with it. Quite the opposite. Satisfied that across millennia of wars, plagues, self-harm and abuse, one of humanity's constants was and remained the relentless persecution of the people of Israel – as in "They never stop killing Jews, do they?" – he'd determined that their fate was evidence that God didn't exist. Were an otherworldly lifeform to witness mankind's antics, or so he reckoned, they'd only need a cursory glance at the wretched Jews to deem humanity Godless, for what else could be made of a species that revels in maligning and torturing one of its own, now demonising their character, now passing malevolent laws against their name, now slaughtering their people, now embezzling their book and plagiarising their precepts, now denying their children a haven or the right to self-defence. Surely, greatness and serenity would forever elude a world sullied by such mischief, and on that account he grew satisfied that anyone with a conscience or a longing for a better tomorrow had a duty to look out for the Jews, for mankind and people such as he would remain doomed and cursed as long as the persecution of the people of Israel continued. Goodness and better things could only come with the end of their ill-treatment.

In other words, merely to endure, John Bowdion had found himself a battle cry for a crusade. In his circumstances, sickly, with little means or influence, this involved exposing anti-Semitism wherever he saw it, such as in the pages of The Paragon, or the streets of Mile End.

On leaving John Bowdion that evening, Lombard too found himself distracted with thoughts of the Jews. The old man's letters, particularly the second of the two, had made their mark on him, but not the best kind. The odd sensation of dread provisioned by John Bowdion's company was now steeped in unease. He reckoned he'd come across his fair share of 'Jews' over the years, not least when nipping across to Tel Aviv while serving a short stint in the French contingent of the United Nations Interim Force which monitored the Blue Line between the Lebanon and Israel many years earlier. Insofar as he knew though, no Jew he ever crossed paths with had proved worthy of attention on account of their Jewishness. In point of fact, he'd have been hard pressed to venture much of an opinion about Jews, nor for that matter was he entirely clear about what made a Jew a Jew: their faith, their culture, their race? If Jews were special, none he'd ever met had stood out from the crowd. But then again, it was also true that their name had always haunted his world, indistinguishable from Lucifer's or other invisible trespassers and fiends. Growing up in Paris, their name suggested only bad things. Back then, the word 'Jew' performed a valuable service, provided an expedient insult fit for most if not all situations, a handy slight that applied to anyone despised, regardless of their offense; such that it was much favoured. What he understood of it by the time he reached eleven years of age was that those it referred to were Christ's killers – and that made them bad; and that they called themselves 'God's Chosen People' – and that made them proud and arrogant; that they'd been picked on forever – and that made them weaklings; that most grown-ups despised them – and everyone knew there could be no smoke without fire; that the Germans and others had tried to kill them all and they'd let them rather than fight – and that made them cowardly; that they were wealthy and controlled everything, especially the poor – and that made them mean and devious; that they'd built themselves a country on stolen land – and that made them thieves. In short, whoever the word 'Jew' was thrown at, the odds were it would fit their crime or failings. No better all-encompassing term of abuse was ever devised; one that covered all wickedness. In that fashion it had slipped through his lips freely, until by way of adventures, trials and his own wickedness he'd come to realize that no one people had a monopoly on mischief, and that were any faction truly in control of all things, they were unlikely to be a persecuted lot fated to seek shelter in Jerusalem and forever doomed to fight over a scant strip of land.

That night, for the first time, he queried the internet for a definition of the word 'Jew'. It returned so many contrary interpretations and such judicious hostility that he quickly called it quits, although not before taking the trouble to read the response of an author by the name of Mark Twain to an American Jewish lawyer who asked about Jew-hatred:

'Tell me, therefore, from your vantage-point of cold view, what in your mind is the cause? Can American

233

Jews do anything to correct it either in America or abroad? Will it ever come to an end? Will a Jew be permitted to live honestly, decently, and peaceably like the rest of mankind? What has become of the golden rule?'

Although it was late and his mind had already half-turned to the meeting he had lined up with Avery Weyland in the morning, he hardly failed to notice that Mark Twain's words dating from 1897 eerily echoed those written by the old Jew from Mile End to his long-deceased father; yet one spoke of immortality and the other of being done with living in a world where all hues of people kill Jews.

'On the Jews
If the statistics are right, the Jews constitute but one quarter of one percent of the human race. It suggests a nebulous puff of stardust lost in the blaze of the Milky Way. Properly, the Jew ought hardly to be heard of, but he is heard of, has always been heard of. He is as prominent on the planet as any other people, and his importance is extravagantly out of proportion to the smallness of his bulk.
His contributions to the world's list of great names in literature, science, art, music, finance, medicine and abstruse learning are also very out of proportion to the weakness of his numbers. He has made a marvellous fight in this world in all ages; and has done it with his hands tied behind him. He could be vain of himself and be excused for it. The Egyptians, the Babylonians and the Persians rose, filled the planet with sound and splendor, then faded to dream-stuff and passed away; the Greeks and Romans followed and made a vast noise, and they were gone; other people have sprung up and held their torch high for a time but it burned out, and they sit in twilight now, and have vanished. The Jew saw them all, survived them all, and is now what he always was, exhibiting no decadence, no infirmities of age, no weakening of his parts, no slowing of his energies, no dulling of his alert but

aggressive mind. All things are mortal but the Jews; all other forces pass, but he remains. What is the secret of his immortality?'

SIXTEEN

A ravishing supernova nursed by bright amber stars.

Sporting his new suntan and four days old stubble, Lombard turned up at the Monty Productions office in Dean Street purposefully late and fitted out in his idea of a provincial traveller's 'practical casual rich' uniform: light tweed jacket, loose linen shirt, corduroy trousers and Yves Saint Laurent suede monk-strap shoes. The mild day with wispy clouds veiling the sun lent itself to such an outfit, and the whole was put together to come across as well-fitting but ill-assorted, so as to broadcast means but a certain lack of refinement, as would befit a man of the world more accustomed to backwaters than to cosmopolitan sophistication. Of course, he had dispensed with his cufflinks, but retained his watch and wedding ring, which agreed with his character's role. These preparations proved satisfactory, for his meeting with Avery Weyland would be to his advantage, even if it hardly went as he had anticipated. At all events, his surprise was to his profit, under-scoring as it did his ignorance of the ways of the film industry, much to his host's comfort and diversion; for who, when it comes to it, does not delight in that special moment of getting the better of a fool?

Monty Productions' offices were located just outside Soho, extending across the four storeys of a townhouse wedged be-tween a Boutique Hotel and a sex shop. A few properties further along the street a blue plaque advised passers-by that one Karl Marx had once resided in the neighbourhood. Access was through an opulent black door bearing a burnished gold sign that led into a grand foyer in which an enormous desk of lustrous metal and glass stretched beneath bookshelves displaying leather-bound volumes of classic literature and oversized art books. Much of everything on display, from the sofas of buffeted ivory leather, the richly framed posters affirming the company's achievements and the lofty receptionist who sat perched behind the desk in a red silk décolleté shirt, seemed fashioned to fill visitors with a sense of importance, if not an instant yearning for riches and fame. Such theatre announced that more than another mere player or trader in cinematic commodities, the master of the establishment was a thriving arbiter of taste. Still, for all that, Lombard's eyes caught only one prize: Charlotte Lottway, or Lottie, as she wished to be known. Occasionally, among the many beautiful women in the world, there appear creatures beyond compare whose appeal is both compelling and inebriating, women who make men feel good simply for being there. Charlotte Lottway was such a creature. A winsome figure in her mid-twenties, she turned out to possess none of the fair English features or rosy-hued complexion her genteel voice and phone manners had suggested. Comely, on high heels in a tight sleeveless midnight-blue pencil dress, with lazy dark hair tumbling to her bare shoulders, a poised gaze, a dark warm sunset complexion and features that alluded to the far tropics, she captured the eyes and mind – albeit not merely on account of her favourable form or effortless grace. The true instrument of the fascination she aroused was borne by her lips: these, full as they were and along with a small patch of skin beneath her nose – about that part of the face known as the philtrum – whether by reason of a pigmentary disorder or an exploded birthmark, glowed from what could best be described as a rich copper-coloured nebula, or a nursery of small bright amber stars. The effect against her dark skin was extraordinary, lent her mouth the aspect of smouldering coals, which, together with a dozen or so moles of various sizes that fanned out from her left cheek down across her neck to her upper chest, combined into a dazzling display, endowing her with the ethereal splendour of a small constellation, so that when she smiled – as she did on catching sight of Lombard – her gleaming teeth could have been stars, or suns to cheer the world. "Xavier! So nice to meet you! I'm Lottie—Avery's assistant. We spoke on the phone."

She greeted him with the kind of delight typically reserved for a returning friend or lover, her hand clutching a gleaming phone while she squeezed what he took to be a couple of red bound screenplays across her breast with her bare forearm. He afforded her his most charming grin: "The pleasure's all mine, Lottie. My apologies for being late. I thought I'd walk from my hotel but completely underestimated the distance."

She laughed, let it be known that "Avery" was expecting him and led the way into a small glass elevator which slowly took them four storeys up, standing so close to him their arms and shoulders touched and he breathed only her perfume as she entertained him with queries. "When did you arrive in London?" "Last night." "Good. From France?" "Yes. Paris." "I hope you had a good trip." "I did; there's nothing to travelling these days really." "Absolutely! Where are you staying?" "The Beaumont on Portland Place." "Wonderful! Great choice. I know the place well." "Right—Are you yourself a visitor to London?" "Oh no. I live here. But I visited friends who stayed there." "Right." "Is this your first time in London?" "I've been a few times. Just passing through though. I'm planning on staying with an old friend in Devon for a few days—We haven't seen each other for years." "How lovely! Can I ask: are you from French Polynesia or Guiana? We noticed you wrote to us from Tahiti, but your letter advises that you will be going home to Guiana. All very intriguing, I must say! Ha-ha!" "My apologies. I was in Tahiti on business. Home is *Guyane*; Cayenne." "Cayenne! How exciting! I must confess, I had absolutely no idea where French Guiana was until I looked it up after reading your letter. But I do know of that wonderful old movie, you know: 'Papillon'? With the great Steve Mc-Queen. Does that awful penitentiary still exist?" "Ah now— It's the first thing everyone asks when they hear where I come from," he said genially; "And I always reply the same thing: No—They shut it down back in the 1950s. But *l'Ile du Diable* on which it stood is still there—A few kilometres from where

I live." "How interesting! By the way, I hope you don't mind my saying so, but you speak and write very good English for a Frenchman, Xavier." "Thank you, Lottie. And may I say, you aren't half-bad at it yourself—For a most exotic and becoming English rose." "Ha-ha. Thank you," she returned, striking his arm with her elbow flirtatiously; "Yes. Well, that's the one I'm always asked, Xavier. I am English—Although a diplomatic mongrel sort of English. My dad, who is Anglo-Indian, met my mum 25 years ago while posted as Deputy High Commissioner in New Dehli. She is Hawaiian-Mexican, was also a diplomat, and worked at the U.S. embassy in India. All that mixed-race 'Corps Diplomatique' assembled to beget little me, ha-ha. So, you might say I'm quite a mixed-breed but most definitely and quite happily English."

Thus acquainted, they stepped side by side, laughing, into Avery Weyland's office, which, in contrast to the flashy décor at reception, was plainly furnished, as if to state this was a no-nonsense honest place of work, that here things were real and counted.

Avery Weyland stood behind his desk with his hand out-stretched to greet Lombard, looking very much the man he'd come across online – lean, smart casual, poised with an easy smile and sincere eyes. He had a firm handshake, direct gaze, and rather big teeth inside his thin lips, which somehow seemed at odds with his deep gravitas-lending baritone voice. He made no attempt to conceal his sizing up of Lombard; on the contrary, he overtly ran his eyes over him as if to make a point of it, possibly an attempt at coming across as both spontaneous and upfront. And while he was so engaged, Lombard's eyes absorbed an unattributed quote inside a small plaque pinned to the wall behind the man's desk:

'One of the commonest weaknesses of human intelligence is the wish to reconcile opposing principles and to purchase harmony at the expense of logic.'

"Avery—Xavier. Xavier—Avery," Charlotte Lottway felt it necessary to introduce them.

"Xavier! A pleasure to meet you." "The pleasure is all mine,

239

Avery. Thank you for taking the time to see me. I'm very grateful. As I told Lottie, I must apologise for being late. I—" "Think nothing of it. As it happens, I was wondering: have you got any lunchtime plans? Are you free this next hour or so?" "Ahem—No, no plans." "Splendid! I hope you don't mind, but I took the liberty to book us a table at a nearby Italian restaurant; a more convivial environment to make acquaintance than a stuffy old office, don't you agree?" "*Dis-moi ce que tu manges, je te dirais qui tu es,*" Lombard grinned. "Ha-ha—Indeed," Avery Weyland laughed before asking Charlotte Lottway what time the table was booked for. "12:10. Twenty minutes from now," she replied without checking her watch. "Good," the man exclaimed; "That gives us just the time we need." And he sat down, invited Lombard and Charlotte Lottway to do the same across the desk from him, reached for an envelope and pushed it towards Lombard. "First things first: your money, Xavier," he said smiling; "I'd very much like to keep it, but I'm afraid that's not the way we do business. I understand from the chat you had with Lottie that you're unfamiliar with the ways of the movie industry, so no offence need to be taken by either side. How Amazing! She also tells me you chose our small production company randomly from a phone directory or the like. Is that so?" Lombard peered at the envelope on the desk in front of him without reaching for it, presuming it contained the 4000 Euros he'd asked Gisèle to send together with John Bowdion's screenplays: "I see," he said; "O ye of little faith—There was I, thinking it would take a sweetener to have you look at the material I sent." "Ha-ha. I should think a four million-Euro investment would be incentive enough," Avery Weyland let out; "But let me be candid: it was enough! Your letter—Truly one of a kind! I believe it took me three readings before I got my head around it. I had to ask Lottie to call you to make sure it wasn't a hoax. Then she tells me you're clueless about films or who we are and, to top it all, never read either of the scripts you sent us! Now that's some story, Xavier. How could I not want to meet you?" "I should hope that I owe this kind invitation to meet to more than a wish to satisfy curiosity, Avery," Lombard returned with a dry grin. "Oh! Of course, Xavier. Indeed. I understand you travelled to England sooner than you planned for this meeting. I hope it didn't prove too inconvenient. I'm afraid I'm due in China in a few days and, as we speak, we're in the middle of a shoot and our director has just taken ill; a very unfortunate contretemps—Well, a calamity, really, not to put too fine a point on it." "I'm sorry to hear that," Lombard remarked. "Oh, we'll live. Anyway, where was I?" "You were candidly telling Xavier that his letter was one of a kind and his four million-Euro commitment to invest in a film was enough of an incentive to read the scripts he sent you," Charlotte Lottway advised with a smile. "Right. Yes. I think I better explain how things are done here at Monty Productions. We make movies, which puts us on the glamorous side of the entertainment business. As I'm sure you know—Or can Imagine—The allure of the lights, the stars, the razzle-dazzle attracts all sorts, not all—How best to put it—Reputable citizens of the world. Dirty money has a way of seeking the path of least resistance, and, to say it as it is, we in the film industry have an insatiable appetite for funds to finance new ventures. However, to cut a tediously long story short, here at Monty's, only clean money will do, Xavier. Transparent accountancy is the way. In this country, independent producers like ourselves must rely on The Film Commission for development and production funds. And they expect no less. I hope you understand. Four million Euros is a fair bit of capital, certainly enough to start putting together a decent sized production. But it would be starter money."

Lombard grinned: "I like a man who lays his cards on the table from the outset, Avery. It makes for trust and team spirit and guards against protracted misunderstandings. I'm with you—And wouldn't have it any other way. I most certainly would never think of committing good money to an outfit mixed up in money laundering or shady deals. And no one need worry about the *transparency* of my capital. I assure you it is both legitimate and verifiable."

Avery Weyland nodded favourably, all smiles:

"I'm delighted to hear it."

Lombard smiled back.

"Good," he said; "I was born into fisheries and mining—Old family businesses. We boast a decent fleet of shrimp trawlers; harvest and process enough shrimps off the coast of *Guyane* to satisfy a fair share of global demand. The mining concerns are in *Nouvelle-Calédonie*: nickel for the most part. Not doing bad either."

"Fisheries and mining. Fascinating—You must tell us more about it!"

"I'm a geologist by trade, though. Mostly in the gold business," Lombard went on; "I'm the guy they call when they discover gold or other precious resources and they need mining feasibility studies done; that is, evaluations of whether proposed mining projects are economically viable from a conservation and profit viewpoint, or how they might impact the environment and local communities. Risk and profit assessment, in a nutshell. I don't know much about films, but I do know about mining."

This seemed to have the desired effect on his hosts; they exchanged smiles: "Damn! We sure could do with a guy like that in our business, couldn't we, Lottie?"

"You can say that again," Charlotte Lottway riposted.

"That sounds great, Xavier," Avery Weyland went on; "So I should think a man with your experience wouldn't be surprised to hear the entertainment business dictum that there's no such thing as a guaranteed safe-return investment in movies?"

"I guess he wouldn't, Avery," Lombard grinned; "Just the same, I may as well let you know: money is not my paramount concern in this venture."

"Just hold your horses!" the man exclaimed; "Four million Euros. Why would you—"

"My primary concern is for one of the screenplays I sent you to be made into a film—To be produced, as you might put it, To proceed, I require no more than a good faith pledge that you would undertake to oversee and complete the production of an industry-standard film based on either of the works. What happens afterwards, how it may turn out and perform at the box office, is immaterial. Like I think I told Lottie, I'm not into films. I've read neither of the scripts. It's about the writer."

Now, both Charlotte Lottway and Avery Weyland looked lost for words.

"The writer?" the film producer-director eventually said; "The writer?" he repeated; "Indeed—That is the other thing I wanted to ask: who is the mysterious screenwriter, John— Er—"

"Jones. John Jones," Charlotte Lottway rescued him.

"Yes—Thank you. Yes, who is John Jones? We looked around for a scriptwriter of this name, but got no joy."

Lombard nodded: "I'd love to tell you. But before I do, I need to know whether you consider either of his works worthy of production. In other words, now you've had a chance to look at the screenplays—Subject to audit etc. as I understand it—Are you actually contemplating taking my money?"

Avery Weyland laughed: "Well, Xavier, it would be fair to say that both Lottie and I agree that—"

Whatever he was about to say, Charlotte Lottway interrupted the conversation to let it be known it was noon, and unless they left at once or called to confirm they were on their way, the restaurant would turn their table over to other patrons. That was all Avery Weyland needed to hear, and the three of them rose to their feet to make their way to the elevator. "Should I bring along the scripts?" Charlotte Lottway asked Avery Weyland softly. "Of course—Of course," came the impatient reply.

Avery Weyland was as talkative as his voice was deep. For the next hour or so he, Charlotte Lottway and Lombard made for a loquacious table at *Ginetta's*, a bustling Italian eatery a couple of blocks away from the Monty Productions office. The moment they'd left his desk to make for the lift back down to reception, the conversation had shifted to general matters such as French Guiana. Avery Weyland disclosed he'd nearly lost his sight ten years earlier for contracting "onchocerciasis" – or river blindness – while in Brazil filming a documentary expedition in the Amazonian jungle "show-casing ecology and deforestation". Like Charlotte Lottway before him, he asked about the Cayenne prison, brought up 'Papillon' and Steve McQueen alongside Dustin Hoffman, and endorsed Lombard's choice of The Beaumont as "a great place to stay". He also spoke of the autobiography on which the screenplay of 'Papillon' was based, stating he had it from good authority that its author was an impostor and the events depicted in both book and film had happened "to others". By the time they strolled into the balmy heat of the eatery to settle at their table, Lombard was beginning to feel ill at ease in his casual uniform. To stay in character but for reasons which escaped him, he let it be known that he was a vegetarian who ate fish, which earned him mild teasing from Charlotte Lottway, who rebuked him that this made him a "pescatarian", as vegetarians are meant to avoid fish the same as meat. "What do you know? You learn something new every day," Lombard remarked light-heartedly before ordering a *salade niçoise*. Their table provided more than enough space for four to sit comfortably, yet Charlotte Lottway settled close enough to him that again he was caught in her perfume as their elbows and shoulders and even their knees nudged against each other. As had occurred at Monty Productions' office, they sat facing Avery Weyland who had half the table to himself. Except where no alternative arrangement existed, no woman Lombard had ever come across would accidentally elect to sit close enough to a male stranger so as to have their bodies touching, leaving him to wonder whether the girl was merely overtly flirtatious or had been put up to it, which seemed scarcely credible in the circumstances. True, four million Euros could buy many things, but his hosts hardly looked wanting, and there was the girl's looks and stock to consider, for it now also transpired that her father was the current British Ambassador to Mexico. Still, her sweet musky fragrance was heady, the brush of her lithe, stirring limbs not disagreeable, provided distraction from the growing discomfort of his clothes. While staff and patrons alike would stop by to greet or exchange a few words with his lunch companions, who appeared well-

244

liked, Avery Weyland soon enough launched into a promotion of Monty Productions. With the proud air of a parent devoted to his progeny, he embarked on what could only be described as a sales pitch, so that, again, Lombard wondered what was truly going on; was it possible that the man had no time for either of John Bowdion's screenplays but all the same was set on trying to convince him to invest in his company? "Monty's present success did not come easy," he affirmed. To turn a small Art House music video venture into what it had become – an award-winning independent operation overseeing the production of around three feature-length films a year along with a dozen or so music videos and the odd television documentary series – "took hard graft" and the best part of two decades. Now, they were about to expand into China after his decision to partner up with a medium-sized Beijing producer – "Tomorrow belongs to the Orient!" And there was more. He planned on relinquishing the day to day production side of things to devote himself to his long-held ambition of becoming a full-time director, which all being well would be soon after his overseeing the Chinese merger. "Much to my chagrin, I recently promoted my beloved Lottie to 'Head of Feature Development' of our London office. Lottie's graced our company with her delightful nous for some time now, knows the ropes, has a splendid work ethic, capable hands and many more assets it would take too long to mention. It pains me to say I shall miss her so terribly as my assistant and deputy. But there you are; comely wings must be allowed to fly."

At the close of this unexpected public relations exercise, without transition, the man embarked on a lecture about the film industry's fundraising mechanisms and protocols, going on at length about distribution deals, percentages and all such things as went above Lombard's head, before embarking on a short speech about the film trade. "More than any other trade perhaps, our industry is particularly exposed to the ebb and tide of human affairs, the success or failure of each venture hinging upon many imponderables. A film's fate is only truly controllable at the inception stage. Once the elements required to get it to 'first day of photography' are assembled—Finance, crew, cast etc.—It's as good as setting an unruly child loose, the start of wild speculation at the whim and fancy of all its players, investors and arbitrary outside forces. You may find I speak in hyperbole, but that's how things are from a producer and investor's perspective once the show hits the road. Anything can sink the ship. An actor's breaking-up relationship—A director's poor health—Death—Bad blood among the cast—Bad weather—Industrial action—A flu outbreak—A hostile review from a critic—Anything from a dog biting your bankable star's ankle to a change in social trends can spell disaster, delay production, break morale, blunt the sharpest project into the dullest of films. People have no idea how many 'great endeavours' fall through the cracks and into oblivion—Or get pulled by distributors for not being instant hits, regardless of merit. In short, the film trade is an unpredictable lover, Xavier. Give it the best or the worst, it hardly matters; mediocrity and excellence are equally likely to turn into box-office success or flop. A lot of it is about the imponderables. And luck."

"Right. This is all very instructive, I suppose. But would you mind my asking why you're telling me all this, Avery?" Lombard ventured, grinning past a growing sense of disappointment. By now, his observation of the writer-producer with the deep voice and easy manners had already given him cause for pause; the elaborate plan he'd put in motion to appraise the man's character already appeared an exercise in futility. This hardly seemed the place to seek answers that may give closure to Maude McGinnis. The matter was not so much that Avery Weyland was giving nothing away. The truth was much simpler: Lombard found it beyond him to read the man, to see beyond the good breeding and pleasant manners and display of ready bonhomie and patter. The likes of Avery Weyland owned the world, did not fear nor serve it; and this one was provided with confidence and the skills to ward off ordinary scrutiny.

"I wouldn't want you to think me rude, Avery," he went on; "But I'm unconvinced I need to know much if any of this. I thought I made clear already films aren't my thing, and that

246

I'm not here anticipating making a profit. You must forgive me, but all these words I'm hearing are beginning to sound to my ears like you may be about to propose I invest in your outfit outside of any commitment to produce either of the screenplays I sent you. Like I said: this is about the writer. If you aren't keen on his work, I would not wish to take more of your time than necessary by prolonging this most pleasant meeting further. Like my mother used to say, 'A fool and his money are soon parted,' but not at any price."

"Oh. Not at all, Xavier," protested Charlotte Lottway, worried.

"I'm afraid you're right, Xavier—I ought to make a better account of myself. Please, forgive me for giving you the wrong idea," Avery Weyland pleaded mockingly, holding his large hands up and open on either side of his shoulders in exaggerated contrition; "Far be it from me to give you that idea. There is a method to this madness though—I assure you. And you just got me where I was heading: the writer! We need to talk about the writer. So: who is he, Xavier? Who is John Jones—A name that sounds more British than French. A friend? A relative? A lover?"

"He is British," Lombard confirmed.

"And his material is original? He owns all related underlying rights?"

"I should think he does."

"Has he had any work produced?"

"I believe these are the only screenplays he's written."

"Right. Well—To cut to the chase, Xavier, we've had a look at his work, and both Lottie and I agree that at least one of his scripts is a no-no. Utterly ridiculous—"

"Ridiculous?" cut in Lombard.

"I'm afraid so. It belongs to the absurd. And that is to put it kindly. For one thing, I don't think I've ever come across a script starting with a narrative ballad in verse that takes over half an hour to read. Imagine."

"Actually, you got the wrong end of the stick there, Avery," Charlotte Lottway interjected; "The ballad is meant to be segmented throughout the film—Like chapter introductions, if you like. There's merit to it actually."

"Ah—I stand corrected. Just the same: preposterous. That one takes the proverbial biscuit; even by the standards of cheap contemporary dystopian sci-fi. Dark forces in the guise of the press and media and IT companies convince the people of the whole world to go into some open-ended voluntary self-confinement to save one in every two hundred from dying from some virus—So that many more end up dying of isolation and lack of care than from the virus itself. Really! And if it wasn't bad enough already, this near future it is set in is indistinguishable from the present."

"I don't know, Avery. I think you make it sound much worse than it is," Charlotte Lottway remarked; "It could happen when you think about it. It's not that far-fetched really. What with the web, social networks, free content and porn. You must admit it takes just one weather-warning from the Met Office for people to decide to stay home, does it not? Not that I think there's much wrong in being a responsible citizen by keeping the emergency services from being over-whelmed. I don't. I'm just saying, that's all."

Avery Weyland grinned, mildly irritated: "Stay in for a day or two, Lottie dear—Not months or years! But we digress," the man went on; "Yes, Xavier—As I was saying, Lottie and I agree one of the scripts is a no-no—Isn't that so, Lottie? We're still on the same team, I presume?"

She smiled her starlight smile: "Absolutely, Avery."

"Good—So that's one out of the way. But then, we also agree that the other has potential. With a lot of hard work and contingent upon your financial support etcetera, I believe it could be developed to form the basis of a great little film. By little I mean a film with a budget near the eight-to-ten-million -pound mark—Which would also secure at least one if not two bankable stars."

"It's the script I mentioned to you over the phone, Xavier," Charlotte Lottway intervened, her dusky skin aglow, her voice a well-practised soothing melody, showing no desire to hurry things along as she took it upon herself to take the floor in what Lombard perceived to be a well-rehearsed moment;

"The one called 'They Bite at Night.' We are very excited about the material. We feel the style and overall dramatic narrative are well-conceived and worth preserving and we're confident that, in the right hands, with some input and a little rewriting by a fresh pair of eyes, we could do justice to the many good things that are already there—Iron out the flaws in the original concept and transform the whole into a truly thrilling and exciting project. I am absolutely positive that it could be developed into a compelling and commercially successful feature film."

"Precisely," Avery Weyland concurred; "This meeting would not be happening if that weren't the case, Xavier. Yes, financial enticements are very welcome, but believe me, it would be folly for us to commit to something we didn't have faith in. We most definitely could work with this one though," the man went on, smiling at Charlotte Lottway; "Lottie will tell you about it in more detail at some other time. For now, what we need to address is, as my still gracious assistant so divinely imparted—'O glory of the Angels thou art!'—Is that the whole needs a fresh pair of eyes."

Lombard grinned, letting it be known that he didn't quite follow, which was true.

"Uh-huh," he went.

"O' innocence," the other implored.

"Is this important?"

"Important? Writers can prove rather prickly where their work is concerned, Xavier."

"Is a writer not just another vain man seeking attention, Avery? And when it comes down to it, a poor writer just another poor man seeking fortune?"

"Oh! Is the writer we are talking about poor?"

"Without two farthings to rub together, as I believe you say here in England."

"Ah! Without a sou!" Avery Weyland riposted; "Well—Ha-ha—Quite! Well—In this line of business it—How to put it? Well, as a rule, even the neediest of screenwriters quickly learns that you can get a long way with a bit of charm and good dinner conversation; glorified court jesters should know their place! Only, when the chips are down, cracks often appear and the great minds quickly split into two distinct species. To use your own words, some see themselves as 'just another man', mindful of the fact that making films is a costly collaborative creative process. Whether they seek validation or are mere careerists, they have it in them to be appreciative of the great opportunities and perks thrown their way. Then there's the other lot, the dreamers, who think themselves masters, artists, visionaries, are deluded or naive enough to think they can redress the world's wrongs or so conceited as to take their own words as Gospel, their heads so high up their own arses! This lot feels they ought to have absolute control over their creations, never mind who pays the bills and takes the risks. From personal experience, Xavier, I'd venture that your writer is the dreamer sort. It's there in his writing. Don't get me wrong, some of his work has merit, can be original in places, reads as the labour of a keen if not deft mind with pretensions to entertain the masses. But it's clear the man has yet to understand the film format's limitations. I'm not merely talking technical skill here, but self-indulgent arguments and tortured explorations that come across as amateurish and expositional. The man's not shy of peddling his viewpoint. For my money, this is as good an indicator of 'dreamer' as you'll find. Now I could be wrong, but I'd say his willingness to let others turn his 'visions' into commercially viable products is likely next to non-existent. While many writers merely yearn for fame and fortune, others, though just as vain and driven by lucre, are prickly creatures indeed. Am I right, Xavier?"

"You're the professional, Avery. If it's all the same, I shall defer to your judgement here."

"In that case, let me say it again: your writer's a dreamer, which could spell trouble ahead, Xavier. You see, no film company could embark on a project without acquiring the underlying rights needed to develop the work and so on and so forth. This is a sine qua non requirement—Especially if the rights-holder of the script has no industry track record. No financier or distributor could commit money, no actor or director commit time to a venture a screenwriter has exclusive rights to; the man of letters would be in a position to hold all to ransom at any time for any reason. The exploitation rights are essential to—Well, the long and the short of it is we would need these rights prior to investing time or, for that matter, your money in the project. And given the script's shortcomings and the need for fresh eyes we mentioned, we could not offer sole-screenwriter credit to Mr John Jones either, which I fear he'd probably demand. To put it another way, for us to work together, he'd have to let go of his ownership of the material. We would treat his work as 'source material' only. Tricky."

Lombard now understood where this was going, decided the moment had come at last to deliver, though not quite the way he'd planned, the tale prepared for the occasion.

"I think I'm with you now, Avery," he said: "I wouldn't worry about the rights or credit situation; provided we come to an arrangement, I can get you whatever you think you need. Perhaps, if it's okay with you and Lottie, I think I better say a few words about myself and John Jones."

"Please," Avery Weyland invited him.

Lombard sighed and pulled his chair slightly away from Charlotte Lottway's to be free of the heady distraction she caused: "Like I said, I was born in fisheries and mining—Fourth generation. I was never meant to run the family business; my elder brother was. And for a while, order prevailed: he did—Considerably expanded the family's operations in the years after our father died while I busied myself learning to be a geologist and sowing my wild oats. Then, eight years ago, he and his wife were murdered. Three burglars broke into their home, stole money, jewels, even my brother's gun, but as they were all shot dead within the hour by the police giving chase, nobody's quite sure why they murdered my brother and sister-in-law. Still, the family brand became mine to tend to with his passing, along with my 12-year-old orphaned niece. All in all, I tried to discharge my responsibilities conscientiously; by this, I mean in a way I'd like to think my brother and father would commend. I married, and perhaps because my wife and I have yet to conceive, I have come to look on Rachelle—My niece—As if she were our own. But little girls grow up.

Two years ago, after graduating in Art History at UCLA in California, Rachelle came to London to study Art Conservation at the Courtauld Institute. She's a good girl, never gave cause for concern, so my wife and I never considered not letting her do as she wished. Just the same, after settling in this country, she met and fell in love with this 40-year-old English deadbeat father-of-two who introduced her to life on welfare. Before we learnt even of his existence, she'd quit her studies to up and leave for some grim-sounding town in Wales to be by his side. It's bad. There's nothing we can say to her, and, come next month, she's set on marrying him. My wife says it's just a young girl's crush; it will pass, and she'll come back to her senses and raise her sights again. For myself, I say her middle-aged deadbeat lover ought to be put down before he has time to bring her to ruin. But I can't do that. So—Well, it turns out that before taking to luring young girls into a life on welfare, John Jones—Yes, it's him I'm talking about—John Jones briefly displayed ambitions. He did Media Studies, but, or so the story goes, got a girl pregnant with twins and became a house-father when the girl moved on. I have it from Rachelle that he wrote those screenplays I sent you—His attempt at turning his life around, she says—But he just as soon gave up on the notion after failing to secure much interest. Now, my niece has her mind made up. I can't legally stop her from becoming Mrs Jones. What she doesn't know, is that in five years from now she is to come by quite a bit of money—Most of it from my brother's estate. Since I can't save her from herself, and before her money gets into the wrong hands, I thought I'd try helping her by helping her husband-to-be instead; buy him a career, so to speak—If such a thing is doable. I got her to send me these screenplays by telling her I know people who may be able to get them into the right hands, and asked her to keep it from him. I lied, of course. I made a list of award-winning British film companies and sent them to you with a financial sweetener only because you were at the top of the list. Before you ask, I suppose you're wondering why the pantomime—Why, instead of this outlandish exercise, not simply hand a cheque over to the lovebirds? Well, it may be the sad act of a fretting uncle, but since my niece as her heart set on becoming Mrs Jones, I reckon it my duty—For my brother's sake—To at least try to impart some notion of self-respect to her Mr Jones. I take it he's never held a proper job or had any money. Given what I know of men, a free gift's unlikely to accomplish much aside from further setting him in his ways. At forty, he's too long in the tooth to change, but if he turns out to have any talent, even a modicum of it—As you seem to think he may—He just might be made to learn the value of work and reward. Desperate men and straws, I know, but in the circumstances, it's the best shot I have. Besides, for all I know, his mind is set on his bride-to-be's money; she has none today, but he knows of her family. Rachelle's young, needs to make her mistakes—*Il faut que jeunesse se passe*, as we say—But no harm can come of keeping an eye out for her. If there is any chance of making a half-decent man of her deadbeat lover by paying to bring his work to the screen, I'm happy to see to it. Unlike my wife, I'm not sitting easy waiting for Rachelle to come to her senses. She is—Was my charge. As you see, I'm a desperate man. So let me assure you, I'll get the man to sign anything which needs signing if it means you'll make something of his work. I'm sure a leech like him will sign just about anything to see his name in lights."

This tale had taken a fair amount of invention, but he reckoned it was fit for purpose. His invented brother's death – murdered by burglars – echoed what he'd read had been Avery Weyland's own father's fate; a commonality of tragedy was likely to kindle a sense of kinship in the producer, soften him up. Likewise, bearing in mind that self-made people can appear intimidating to those whose wealth is inherited, the same went for the part about the source of his declared fortune. In all its aspects, the whole was designed to cast him as an old-style brutish type of man, uptight, a small-town soul, provincial, uncomplicated, the kind modern Englishmen find easy to condescend to. The aim was to distract and entertain, not charm or challenge his prey. For all that, now Lombard had presented his story, there was no telling how it had gone down with his audience as they both remained silent while he soothed his parched mouth with cold white wine; whether exception was taken or responses were merely being weighed.

Neither spoke for what seemed a very long time. Avery Weyland grinned in that good-natured but forced way hostage listeners do when bored or engaged in their own thoughts, and within her scented dusky glowing flesh Charlotte Lottway smiled tight-lipped, if anything betraying bewilderment, which enhanced her natural splendour in that it lent her a pensive unpretentious air, an alluring but unfledged blackbird still innocent of the world.

"Mercy!" Lombard implored playfully, wincing for good measure while putting his empty glass down: "I'd sooner not ask, but did I say something wrong?"

"Oh. Not at all, Xavier. Not at all," Avery Weyland protested cheerfully: "It's—I simply—Most extraordinary! Ahem— True love knows no reason; not your habitual potential investors' table talk! Ha-ha!"

Lombard wasn't quite finished: "I was about six the first time my parents took my brother and me to Paris. It was October, I'd never been away from *Guyane*, or seen Autumn yet. When I asked my father why the leaves from the trees were brown and falling to the ground, he said it was in readiness for winter: 'It's nature's offering to the living. Come this time of year in this part of the world she covers the earth in gold to ask forgiveness for the dreariness to come', is how he put it. I hope you can forgive my dreary story."

"That is sweet," gushed Charlotte Lottway.

"I think I realised what he meant when winter set in soon afterwards," Lombard continued.

And Charlotte Lottway's copper-coloured nebula-ed lips burst into a smile, a ravishing supernova nursed by bright amber stars.

In a while, the reason for Avery Weyland's unashamed sales pitch would become clear. The man had little intention of taking the lead in producing John Jones' screenplay, rather would entrust the project's development entirely to Charlotte

Lottway as "her first jaunt in a producer's role". However, it would be done under the Monty Productions umbrella, with Avery Weyland acting as Executive Producer and mentor to "my protégé". Subject to "Xavier's generous investment receiving the go-ahead from the company's accountant and solicitors", Monty Productions would undertake to develop the project in an ideal position from which to secure, at once and at the very least, match-funding from the Film Commission. This would also mean that Lombard's money wouldn't be required until "First Day of Photography". In other words, to set Lombard's mind at rest, Avery Weyland proposed not to use his capital until the production was greenlit and a "racing certainty". Furthermore, in view of his contribution, Monty Productions would also offer him a percentage of the net profits in line with standard industry practice, in addition to an "Associate Producer" or "Executive Producer" credit, and, with regards to John Jones, a guaranteed "shared 'screenplay-by' screen credit".

Lombard needn't pay much attention to any of this, but came to appreciate the reason for Charlotte Lottway's obvious keenness in this affair. And since his lunch companions were in effect proposing to accept his money while feeling under no obligation to either recruit or heed to the aspirations of the author of the material he would be financing, he also came to realize that their behaviour very much echoed John Bowdion's pronouncements on the film industry, suggesting the two were merely involved in routine rather than in a concerted effort to dupe a naive investor.

SEVENTEEN

Marion Raspberry – A good man.

It was left that on receipt of Lombard's audited accounts Monty Productions' solicitors would draft a conditional contract to "start the ball rolling". For the time being, the project would retain its original 'They Bite at Night' name as its working title. Meanwhile, Lottie was to be the principal conduit between Lombard and Monty Productions with regard to financial, creative and legal matters, leaving Lombard to wonder when, if ever, Avery Weyland and he would meet again.

By all accounts, or insofar as he seemed to have got the better of his lunch companions, the meeting could be considered a success. Yet – whether by virtue of the producer-director's owning the world or his being too judicious to give himself away – Avery Weyland had most certainly remained beyond Lombard's scrutiny. An hour and more in his company had hardly helped shed light on his character. Lombard was none the wiser than when he'd first stepped into the man's office. Could Avery Weyland have it in him to kill or order the murder of the likes of Jane and their children? It remained a hard sell. Still, nothing can be said to be certain in the affairs of men. The only certainty, for now, was that the man's imminent departure for China came as no help, making their meeting again soon unlikely. The whole left Lombard in a troublesome situation, unsure as to what to do next, whether to venture further down the path he had just successfully ploughed or to move on, that is to head home, shave his four-day-old stubble and fall back on Monroe and 'MonkeySpeaks' to shadow

Avery Weyland and see what may come of that. Under the circumstances, the latter seemed the better option, for he reckoned that the only thing of note his elaborate subterfuge had exposed so far was that neither of his lunch companions should be underestimated. They turned out to be accomplished performers; professional hustlers; masters of their trade; a comely twosome deft in the art of enchanting and coercing their prey, be it for gain or recreation. They made a formidable team, to be worsted – presuming such a notion belonged to the feasible – only by predators even more accomplished or resourceful than they were.

This was how things were when the time came to part ways on the kerb outside the Italian eatery; Lombard was of a mind to wish Avery Weyland and Charlotte Lottway farewell, ready to cut his losses and never see them again. And, the truth be told, if not yet reconciled to it, he was hardly averse to the idea. But his hard work – or could it be providence, or his four million Euros perhaps? – was to afford him rewards. In the event, he'd done well, for Avery Weyland queried how long he planned on staying in London. "Two or three days. It depends," was his reply. "Then you must come to my mother's garden party tomorrow afternoon—I insist," the man said; "At the beginning of this beautiful friendship, it's a perfect opportunity for me to make it up to you for having made you come to London sooner than you planned. You'll love it—That or find it an education. Trust me! Lottie will pick you up at your hotel tomorrow at three and be your escort for the afternoon. How does that sound, Lottie?" "Perfect." "Splendid. So it's all agreed!"

In this manner, all was arranged before Lombard could even consider declining the invitation. And after Charlotte Lottway suggested calling him a cab, a gracious offer he resisted with the excuse of looking forward to a postprandial walk along Oxford Street to The Beaumont in Portland Place – where he had no intention to go or for that matter to rent a room – while bidding him goodbye, she leant forward to kiss him on both cheeks without hugging him while offering enough lips and flesh to stir his senses: "Until tomorrow at three then. What is your room number?" "Oh. I can't recall," he grinned; "You have my phone number though. Give me a call when on your way and I'll be there."

Lombard found himself walking home under a clutter of confused thoughts, unsure what to make of Avery Weyland's fortuitous invitation; as mentioned already, he was very much in two minds as to whether to pursue his masquerade, unconvinced of the merit of having further meetings with the producer-director. Adding to his woes, Charlotte Lottway called within minutes of their parting company. He'd never picked up the envelope full of cash Avery Weyland had returned to him. He and they – with other things on their minds – had left the man's office oblivious to it sitting on the desk, and now the girl insisted on bringing it to his hotel in person later that evening, stating she would be in the area at around 10:30 p.m. Again, this was visited upon him, leaving him in a position necessitating his either booking a room at The Beaumont or calling the whole game off before evening, all of which stirred yet more unrest in his mind. He took exception to being pushed into making rash decisions, was aware of the danger of getting caught within his own subter-fuge, so that, presently, he entertained the thought that it may not have been a bad thing if he'd remained in Madeira by the stream in the ravine to focus on Alan Winston instead of rushing back to London on what now appeared an utterly futile quest. Still, he would not allow doubt or emotion to prevail over necessity or common sense, so that before reaching home again he had come to accept that no rational purpose would be served by turning down another opportunity to meet with the producer-director; here, in view of developments to come, it may be important to point out that he was in no way swayed in this by his failure to find cause to quarrel with the idea of spending more time in Charlotte Lottway's company. In any event, his decision to attend Avery Weyland's mother's garden party did nothing to lift his mood. The net result of all this was that, once out of his 'casual-provincial' uniform, he booked a room at The Beaumont for the next couple of nights, retrieved his 'Xavier Lagarde' identity papers and, fittingly suited and cufflinked, drove to West Hampstead and Fortune Green Cemetery with the purpose of mitigating his contradictory spirit; for the moment anything seemed preferable to remaining between four walls or making alone for the cosseted environment of a hotel, even one as pleasant as The Beaumont, which he too knew well. He'd kept busy these past few days, had spoken to many strangers, woven many lies and listened to many tales, and for it – and now hostage to his own scheme – was in want of a reprieve from the living and all the noise.

The florist wore the same straw beach hat, leopard-skin patterned shirt and tight leggings he recalled she had on when he last called, and looked perplexed and not best pleased to see him when he stopped by to make his habitual purchase of white lilies. A mere couple or so weeks had elapsed since his last visit, nothing like the usual long-established month or year-long interval, and she made plain that she had yet to forget their last encounter when he'd confronted her for calling Jane about his being at the cemetery. He could have left her where he found her, but her quiet hostility nettled him, taunting his already irritable disposition.

"She's dead. And so are the twin girls she had with her," he let on while paying for his flowers.

"I'm sorry?"

"The pregnant woman you called last time I came; don't you remember? Well, she's dead. And so are her twins and her unborn child. They were killed. Have a pleasant day now."

In the afternoon sunshine, as was his ritual, he left behind the symmetry of the ordered rows of fine headstones near the cemetery entrance to stroll past the mortuary chapels, Celtic crosses and other memorials and make for the meadow-like far end of the grounds. Here, among the yews, birches, cherry-plums and willows which furnished humbler gravestones arranged like charred corpses against the end-of-summer scorched golden grass, sanctuary came into sight; beyond the mausoleum with its ivied broken fence teeming with robins and long-tailed tits, his south-facing bench awaited, unoccupied, a welcome permanence which, no matter the time of day or year, appeared forever to claim the semi-shadow of the red cherry tree sited a few steps from Nathalie's grave. He paid no mind to her headstone today, or its inscription, or the sweet wrappers or drink cans on the nearby grass, merely laid down his lilies and made for the bench where, allowing for the fine weather, he got out of his suit jacket, undid his cufflinks, rolled up his shirt sleeves and, facing the sun, closed his eyes to the soft breeze to lend his mind space. At first, he thought of nothing, expelled all noise, his skull a rigid shell weighed in silence, so that he opened his eyes to observe – as he had so often done over the years – the indistinct birds that drifted effortlessly across the far sky above the distant tree line. He was tired, wearied, seized with lassitude. Briefly, he sought lightness, summoned Ali to the fore of his mind, but failed to keep her there; she formed no part of all that was wrong, was exempt from it, existed pure from the affairs that cast him down. Had her ghost here and now consented to his summons and lingered for his pleasure, it would have been the ruin of him; the ruin of her; the ruin of them and their ruin. He was free, unencumbered by obligations or wants. He never was every man. He never was yielding. He was untamed, unfettered by chains. How was it that he could allow himself to become the partner of so much misfortune and such vagaries? There was Maude McGinnis and her guilt-twisted grief. The woman so desired to exist and so feared nothingness that she tortured her soul with the contemplation of another universe: God's Heavens – so as to lend the natural pain of living the heart of religious hope. He could call, tell her he had met Avery Weyland and vouch that the man was not involved in her daughter's and granddaughters' demise; she'd never know different, would endure the rest of her existence the easier for it. He ought to; but couldn't. And there was John Bowdion, a man neither very good nor very bad, but mediocre. There is no man so wretched as not to retain inside his skull a lofty idea of his own worth; such was this hapless man's fate. Sheltered within his tedium, he suffered each day for judging the world, yet when put to the test couldn't come up to scratch and respect the one wish of a dead old Jew he professed to admire. And then there was young Alan Winston, who tried and failed to learn how to be free; doomed. Not a bad sort but a coarse fool whose bloodstream was laced with the adversity and servitude of previous generations, which neither God nor lofty notions could cleanse nor save. He was his own naked involuntary movements, unequal to humanity's ingenious deceptions. And then came Edward Duncan, who, despite or because of his advantages, could just as soon hate as attempt to mimic virtue. He too suffered; like the others he too endured. Lombard could call him, tell him about the bonfire on the Madeiran plateau, vouch that Alan Winston was dead. He could. But he wasn't going to. For he too was prey to the scorn of his own tyranny. Why else would he be partner to so much misfortune? He wasn't supposed to go wrong. He was not one to err. He wanted for nothing, couldn't even flatter or console himself with notions of desire; not enough contempt ran through his veins to construct admiration as an antidote. He never was every man; he sought no alibi nor dream.

It is at this moment – very much claimed by lassitude – that his interest was sparked by the sight of a young man and his girl lying on the scorched grass among the gravestones a good sixty or so yards away in front of him; somewhere between the trees lining the horizon and his bench. If not for the man's pose – he was stretched out on his back with his legs akimbo and one arm crossed behind his head in the shade of a birch tree – he would not have paid them much attention. The girl had caught his eye when she'd run the short distance to a nearby gravestone to steal what looked like a red carnation which she now twirled in her hand as she lay beside the man with her head resting on his chest. Neither seemed to be speaking, if nothing else the man appeared asleep, but none of this mattered. Only the man's bearing on the scorched yellow grass did, for it stirred the long-forgotten memory of an image Lombard had once spent many hours observing: Bruegel's The Harvesters.

One day, before he reached his thirteenth birthday, his

mother had been taken to hospital expecting to give birth to 'his' sister, only complications had caused her to lose the baby and very nearly her life too. For some weeks she had remained convalescing at the hospital, so that for the first time ever Lombard had been home alone with his father. However, possibly on account of the strain of the situation, the latter had come down with a bad bout of flu, become bedridden and delirious, and, with telephone advice from his mother, it had fallen to Lombard to look after the sick man, shopping, cooking and feeding him, soothing his fever with cold flannels, even, on mother's recommendation, tying him down to the bed-frame to keep him from hurting himself during particularly wild bouts of feverish delirium. In this way, Lombard had learnt that the man he thought of as 'Papa' was not merely a pâtissier but had once served as a soldier who'd experienced life under fire and as a prisoner of war. This finding, coming at a time when he experienced a previously unknown intimacy with the man, made quite an impression on him, could well have been the reason why – together with a sense of dread, natural concern and fear of letting his parents down – he'd taken his nursing duty to heart and determined to spend as much time as possible at his sick father's bedside, a place from where he'd soon acquainted himself with the poster reproduction of the Bruegel painting which hung on the wall across from his parents' bed. Until then, his parents' bedroom had remained alien territory. Even on the few occasions he'd caught sight of its interior, nothing there had earned his interest. Now though, captive beneath the poster's commanding position, his eyes started poring over it the way a cat surveys an aviary, and by and by, he'd found himself marvelling at the realisation that he was developing a liking for it. Yet, at first, he'd found it unremarkable, if not somewhat funny. The peasants it depicted in a glowing golden field of wheat – not least those picnicking in the foreground – were gross, poorly drawn, and at least one among the lot seemed to be gazing out at him kind of dumbly, while another figure, a man stretched flat out on his back in complete abandon, had his private parts clearly outlined inside his trousers, and elsewhere a woman gathering wheat was the same shape as the haystacks surrounding her, even appearing to have her hat or hair made of wheat. Then, there was the painting's name, The Harvesters, yet it showed some people eating or at rest, as if the painter meant to suggest they were lazy. And while one man wearily carried a large pitcher back uphill through a corridor cut out of the tall wheat, another with a scythe looked like he was about to strike and likely smash a similar pitcher half-concealed within the wheat. Whether the work held artistic merit, it was never his place or inclination to wonder, but soon, without words to articulate his feelings, through his eyes alone, he'd come to know a pleasant physical sensation – akin to warm agitation and irrational anticipation – from the contemplation of the image, in addition to feeling puzzled that such excitement could be born from its observation. It was as if something strange, something potent but invisible, existed beyond or within the colours and lines that shaped the image, and stirred his senses. For instance, he soon realized that the whole scene was depicted under a strange greenish sunless sky, yet all glowed like gold. He spent a great deal of time scrutinizing the poster, until he knew it well, could call it to mind on request: the people resting and picnicking on sheaves of wheat, eating bread and pears and drinking bowls of milk in the shade of a pear tree in a partly harvested field; the people at work, gathering the wheat into bundles, busy mowing it with scythes, or picking apples falling from a tree shaken by a man hanging upside down from one of its branches; the steepled church beyond the trees; two strange birds flying low over the field; the women making their way across the gold with sheaves of wheat over their shoulders and backs; then, unfolding further, the rich green valley where more people thrived and played by a village stream, and yet another wheat field, and further still a bay with ships sailing across the sea, and finally, in the far haze, more land and hills stretching into the sky. In the end, Lombard had conceded that understanding what made the image stir his senses was beyond his faculties and comprehension of things. His young mind knew no words to construct concepts to explain such a phenomenon. It hardly mattered though, because thereafter, for quite some years, he would often call the image to mind in times of threatening anxiety, finding that the mere thought of it had a pleasant, calming effect, as if through it he was allowed through the doorway of some greater better purer place. Still, much later, by then having learnt to try to interpret the signs of the world, and more knowing of sensations in general, he would come to think of the warm agitation stirred by the painting as not all that dissimilar to that which precedes intimacy with desire, and form the opinion that the work's appeal lay in its unseen substance, which he determined to be permanence; the permanence of day-to-day life, of flesh, of death, of dreams. And order. Words to explain this still failed him, but he trusted instinct.

In time, his father had recovered, his mother returned home, but things were never to be the same again. Not long afterwards his mother had left and soon a new woman took her place in the parental bed in front of the Bruegel poster. Lombard too had soon run away, to take his turn at adventure and test a soldier's life. "*Ah oui! C'est beau, non? Le blé—Le blé et la moisson, mon fils,*" his father had said when he asked him why he kept the Bruegel painting in his bedroom; "*Il n'y a rien de plus beau au monde que de se réveiller chaque aurore devant un champs de blé prêt pour la moisson.*" The man was a pâtissier, and, evidently, had his own notion of the creation.

Lombard almost felt a debt of gratitude towards the man lying flat under the birch tree with his girl resting her head across his chest. The two were still not speaking, she gently twirling the flower she stole between her fingers, he seemingly asleep with one hand tucked behind his neck. The fortuitous recollection of the old painting was a welcome intrusion into an otherwise tedious afternoon, like the unexpected visit of a long-lost steadfast friend bearing trusted news. Now, again, he closed his eyes at the sun, and sighed, attempted to summon up more of the painting than he remembered; its intimate lines, shapes, planes, colours. It was no use. The impression still inhabited his mind, a ghost of the tonic of old just about agitated his senses, but what remained truly amounted to little more than memory, a likeness or shadow of the awkward pleasure which could once even bring a smile.

He swallowed hard. Later he would call Edward Duncan and let him know that he believed Alan Winston was alive and likely still hiding in Madeira, suggesting he should return to the island to find out for certain. His thoughts then moved to Charlotte Lottway. He couldn't recall meeting a more arresting being, wondered whether she was naturally flirtatious or merely mercenary towards 'Xavier Lagarde' whose money and desperation to save his niece was to provide her the opportunity to become a fully-fledged film producer. Seeing as he was set on playing Mr. Lagarde a little while longer, no doubt this would soon be cleared up; now she'd proposed to come to his hotel late in the evening ostensibly to deliver moneys which could have waited or been sent, he could only speculate as to how much of herself she was disposed to offer, and all other considerations aside, looked forward to finding out.

At one time it would not have been incautious to state – at the very least until the recent advancements brought about by men and women's ingenuity and laying aside notions of immaculate conception – that all tainted souls, no matter their gender or colour, were born of a woman's womb. How this reflects on the men and women accountable for what is no longer a self-evident proposition should, for now, be left open to conjecture. Still, in regard to such arrangements, Mary Raspberry would not be spared. Some years before, fate or accident had introduced her to a most amiable man while on a return train journey from Scotland to London. She was already in her sixties, the man in his thirties, and they had become close travel companions by virtue of their seating allocations. For reasons which had yet to become clear, the man had proved extremely thoughtful and generous and keen to engage in conversation and by such means somewhat charmed his way into Mary Raspberry's heart, possibly more so than an obsequious traveller ought to have been permitted. In any event, having secured his conquest, instead of merely going on his way when time came to bid goodbye at the end of their journey at London Euston station, the man had handed her a note with his contact details, suggesting they should remain in touch and possibly meet again. Mary Raspberry had done well to conceal her emotion, for on reading the note she at once recognized the name of one of her long-abandoned children, as well as realising why she had felt strangely beguiled by her young travel companion. Several options were open to her, from leaving things just as they were to confessing to the man her suspicion. Then again, a prey to natural caution but all the same curious, she had opted instead for prudence and soon hired a private investigator to find out more about the man; a decision she would regret. The man had indeed turned out to be her son. He'd lost his father when still an infant to be looked after by his paternal grandmother who, when her turn came to pass away, had left him her small estate and sent him into the care of an old aunt from whom he'd also ended up inheriting capital and property. Thereafter, although blessed with pleasant looks, a decent mind and appreciation for life, he seemed to have made it his mission to charm inheritances from old ladies as a means of making a living. It turned out that by the time he'd come to Mary Raspberry's attention, her thirty-four-year-old discarded progeny had succeeded in becoming the beneficiary of no less than five old women's legacies, while having never married or worked a day of his life. The realization that she'd been targeted by her own son as a potential victim left her sickened. "How can such a base lifeform have come from my womb—My flesh!" she told the detective who'd delivered the news; "Rotten fruit of my loins!"

Now, resting her aching feet and legs on a bench in Fortune Green Cemetery, her fading eyes caught sight of Lombard who had just got to his feet. In rolled up shirtsleeves with his suit jacket flung over his shoulder, she watched him turning towards the cemetery entrance, from where she had come some minutes earlier at considerable trouble to herself. He was near enough to hear her, she thought.

"Young man!" she called; "Would you be good enough to lend a helping hand to this old woman."

Lombard stopped and turned to see, twenty or so yards away under the sun, a small grey withered figure in a black coat, hat, shoes and sunglasses seated next to a cane on a bench with a bouquet of white daisies and a handbag on her lap. Her cracked lipsticked lips and rouged cheeks reminded him of someone but he couldn't recall who.

"If you aren't in too much of a hurry, could I ask for a moment of your time to help me back to my feet and out of here?"

Lombard hesitated before stepping towards her:

"Of course."

"Thank you. You're an angel," she said, slipping her handbag around her forearm and grabbing hold of her daisies before holding out her one free arm and cane for him to help her up onto her feet; "I'm afraid I only come here once a year nowadays but even that seems to be one time too many."

"You're welcome," Lombard said, gently grabbing hold of her elbow to pull her up.

There was very little of her, just a frail bony body with hands the colour of dead wood.

"If you would be so good," she said now, pointing towards a grave in the near distance; "I may as well do what I came to do."

And shuffling on her stiff feet and cane while leaning her body into his supporting arm she led them to the grave she indicated. Lombard swallowed hard on catching the words engraved above a carved image of an oak tree on the granite headstone:

'Marion Raspberry – A good man.'

"There," said Mary Raspberry, dropping her bouquet of daisies on the grave; "To a good man indeed. He was a tree surgeon, you know. Died on the job—Wouldn't have wanted it any other way."

Without letting go of her elbow, Lombard had already taken a small step away from her to scrutinize her face again:

"Mrs Raspberry? Mrs Mary Raspberry?"

She was still turned towards the grave: "How discerning of

you, young man," she let out, sneering; "Yes: Mrs Raspberry has come to pay her respects to her last husband, Mr Raspberry; he was also the last man to earn the distinction of being buried in this cemetery before they turned it into some sort of museum, I believe. Or so I was told."

Lombard frowned:

"The headstone says nothing about you being called Mary though, does it, Mrs Raspberry?" he returned.

She paused for thought:

"How—"

Now she turned to look up at him, took off her sunglasses and scrutinized his face with her cloudy dark eyes:

"Ahem—Do I know you?"

"Xavier Lombard. The private investigator you hired years ago; it was in regard to a son of yours, I recall."

She winced, looked unpleasantly surprised: "Ah! Dear me! Yes. How could I have forgotten you: the bearer of such bad news."

Lombard grinned: "How are you, Mrs Raspberry?"

"By the look of things, not half as well as you, Mr—?"

"Lombard," he grinned again.

"Indeed. That's right: Mr Lombard. I remember now. You must forgive my irascibility," she said through her stiff cracked lips, squeezing the cane in her bony fingers while putting her sunglasses back on; "And for failing to recognize you. It's been a long time and—But how about it? You haven't aged a day. What serendipity sent you to my succour in such grim surroundings? A dead wife?"

"The pursuit of peace and quiet," he said.

"Huh! Well now, you should be so lucky. Here you are—Ambushed among the dead by a living ghost. No place is safe, Mr Lombard—No place is safe. Now, if you are in no hurry, I'd be obliged if you could be so kind as to lend me your strong arm for the way back out of here, where I intend to catch a cab back home."

Lombard checked his watch: it was not 3 p.m. yet, he had time.

"At your pleasure, Mrs Raspberry."

"Well—Then I shall be in your debt, Mr Lombard."

And arm in arm, with her leaning her light frame into his body, they slowly made their way towards the cemetery entrance gates, exchanging few words as Mary Raspberry required all of her strength to shuffle forward. Still, by the time they reached the street, Lombard had ascertained that she still lived in Highbury and volunteered to give her a lift back, which she graciously accepted.

"Oh," she said on catching sight of his Saab; "I remember when these were new. I was already old by then."

At first, no words passed between them during the drive to Highbury. She could never be described as shy or demure, but an eternity had passed since Mary Raspberry had last allowed herself to be spontaneous with strangers, and besides, she only vaguely remembered Lombard, who although not a complete stranger and a man she remembered for his discretion and reliability, qualified at best as someone she'd met in his professional capacity on no more than two or three occasions. For his part, Lombard could think of little to talk about with an old woman who hardly seemed as if she sought conversation. The atmosphere within the car was not unpleasant, yet, since it is a general rule of nature that a certain tension should grow between people not intimate enough to sit side by side in an enclosed space in complete silence for a long time, he soon felt compelled to ask Mary Raspberry whether she still resided in the "beautiful" house he recalled visiting her in years earlier.

"I do," she said; "Alone too—Well, with my cat."

Lombard grinned: "Yes. I recall: a rough grey thing."

"Oh. No. Grey's long gone—This one's a tawny common sort. They castrated him."

"Huh!"

"A sixteenth coloured woman got him castrated."

"A sixteenth—I see."

Mary Raspberry sighed, then glanced sideways to evaluate Lombard. She liked what she saw, but her trust in others had long ago been tested:

"You aren't recording us with some kind of portable device,

are you?"

Lombard frowned.

"No—I suspect you aren't. Why would you? Well, that's how it is: a sixteenth coloured fully grown woman saw fit to get my Pester castrated and now the two of us live alone in my big house and I no longer rent the two upstairs flats."

Now it was Lombard's turn to get the measure of his passenger with a sideways glance; the old woman stared straight at the windscreen from behind her sunglasses, the sunshine that broke inside the moving car now and again making bright patterns across her red cracked lips and rouged cheeks. It would hardly have been surprising – or so it occurred to him – if her mind had begun to fail her since their last meeting years earlier.

"I should think this probably does make me a very bad person," she went on.

"How is that?"

"A decrepit old woman—Living alone with her cat— Keeping two flats empty above her. Surely, this is most reprehensible."

Lombard thought through her words, tried to give them sense, then decided to get the measure of her:

"Has some upstanding citizen been casting stones, Mrs Raspberry?"

She scoffed:

"Huh!"

"Huh?"

"Sticks and stones! Much worse: words! Once upon a time I—" she now started; "In the likes of people is the ruin of this woman, Mr Lombard; no one much wishes good things for old Mary nowadays."

"If the world ages perhaps it is for Mary to remain young at heart," Lombard replied, grinning.

"Oh—A gentleman. Well, Mary's heart is in its right place. It isn't for her to question her heart."

"Good."

"Indeed: it's like I said: in the likes of people is the ruin of this woman."

270

"That is a rather broad statement, Mrs Raspberry. A sixteenth coloured woman castrated your cat, you said—"

He heard her sneer, and then heard her sigh, and, on account of the woman's advanced years, once again wondered how much of her wits remained. Silence returned in the space between them for a while, then, sounding like someone who'd thought long about the words passing her lips, Mary Raspberry spoke.

"Mary's heart is in the right place. Only last night, I was listening on the wireless to talk of a wretched excuse of a movie. Agitprop tripe passed off as a frivolous murder mystery. Its postulation: fallible rich white people are unworthy degenerates. Its plot: an old wealthy white patriarch makes the cut as a hero for disinheriting his flawed kin and slitting his own throat to ensure his money goes to his young help, a poor refugee's daughter so pure she is incapable even of lying without breaking into a pustulant rash. Mary's heart is in the right place, Mr Lombard. To place a mark on people on account of pedigree or wealth is no virtue. To be flawed is no vice. As for purity, what will they think of next: all 'Marys' ought to be virgins? Dear me! Such poppycock is *the cunning livery of Hell.* The message should be feared. The knaving messengers cursed. The deception laid bare. The fools duped by it all pitied. For myself, I shall never slit my throat but leave all I have—Which is not insubstantial—To my cat and a few institutions concerned with the welfare of handsome young men. Mary's heart is in the right place!"

Mary Raspberry tittered, amused, and Lombard again wondered about the old woman's wits. While working on her case many years ago, he recalled finding out she'd had an eventful life, making it difficult to suppose that she could get all worked up about a voguish movie. Because, by chance, he thought he had a fairly good idea of the film behind her unease. While seeking information about Avery Weyland online, he'd come across mention of it. Its title escaped him, but together with Avery Weyland, its writer-director had put in an appearance at the recent Venice Film Festival, attending the prestigious event as its guest of honour. The film Mrs Raspberry had heard of on the radio had met with worldwide acclaim, broken box-office records and earned the writer-director the largest advance for sequel rights in cinema history; nearly a billion US dollars. All the same, the reception to the film had not been universally positive. 'The same old "no stone left unturned to make a buck", or in this case, richly-clad palefaces ridiculing other richly-clad palefaces to tickle the world pink, the trickery being accomplished by means of unashamed virtue-signalling with all the zeal of new missionaries of old imperialism running for the hills,' one critic had ventured to some controversy.

Lombard suspected this may well be the context in which the film had come to Mary Raspberry's attention on the radio.

"It's strange," he said, to say something: "I've been hearing a lot about the movies of late."

The old woman's reply was not immediate.

"Well, beauty has always pleased Mary, and films once afforded her leisure. But she never served a master—Never mind the heinous sort," she said.

"Good for you," Lombard remarked.

"Good for you! Do not presume to patronize this old woman, Mr Lombard," came the retort.

"Please, Mrs Raspberry," he now said, sincerely; "Without wishing to disabuse you, I was—"

"Nefarious feats such as this film are no laughing matter! They are sweeping the ground from under all of our feet. Think of it! Ask yourself: what would people twisted enough to conceive such a grotesque concoction come up with if they'd been masters of the Book and the Gospels—Imagine the tale."

Lombard frowned:

"That is some proposition, Mrs Raspberry."

"Is it? Well, ask yourself: what would they have God do once he realized his children were flawed? Once Adam and Eve had transgressed, succumbed to the serpent, eaten from the tree and bred Cain and Abel? Would they have him merely evict the lot of them from Eden? Not likely! They'd have God slit his own throat and turn Eden over to another litter—From another dimension. Possibly a sixteenth sort of a dimension, if such things as *sixteenths* lived, breathed and were identifiable at the Creation."

Lombard grinned:

"Now you sound just like someone I recently became acquainted with."

Mary Raspberry was not listening.

"At least Robin Hood stole from the rich to give to the poor," she carried on, clearly speaking to herself; "He did not disown his kin or commit hara-kiri to help the oppressed. Huh! I'll have you know. When mercy seasons justice—When mercy seasons justice," she now whispered between her cracked lips.

Lombard frowned. The frail old woman by his side was certainly petulant and possibly obsessive, but he was no longer in doubt about her mental faculties; he trusted she was all there.

"They wouldn't," he said.

"They wouldn't what?" she asked.

"They couldn't," he went on; "What tale would there be left to tell once they'd had God kill himself and his creation?"

"Well," she said; "Not just a gentleman but bright too. I trust, in another place, at another time, we—This would have been cause for celebration."

He nodded:

"I'm sure," he said.

A short while afterwards she let it be known that they were nearing her home. "We've arrived. It's just over there—Downhill around the bend: number 49. If you'd be a prince—Park as near to the front gate as you can and rev your nice old car engine a few times. Don't be shy—Make some noise! And after that, if you can indulge this cantankerous old woman a little longer, I would be delighted if you would walk me up my steps to my front door letting me hold onto your arm. I can manage, but would dearly love my neighbours to see a handsome man accompanying me home."

Lombard obliged her. And once she had got her wish, once alone back inside the refuge of her home, Mary Raspberry sat down to pet a purring Pester and say:

"Hello, Pester. Mary met the most gallant man today. And Mary thinks the gallant man didn't think too badly of Mary either. And Mary invited him to come by to see her anytime he wanted. He shan't, of course. But all the same it was good to hear him say he might."

Once upon a time, an Egyptian of antiquity – in place of a member of the Tribe of Israel – wrote The Book of the story of Pharaoh and the Jews. 'Let my people go,' begged Moses, the leader of the Jewish slaves. Pharaoh listened and thought. After a while, feasting his eyes on the wealth his armies and people had accumulated over time, saddened by the excesses and indulgences of his sons, daughters and the people of Egypt who knew no want, he came to the decision that he would do his own kind a great favour by disinheriting them all and granting the entirety of his Kingdom to his slaves, the people of Moses. When rumour of this reached his kin, they plotted to have Pharaoh killed in such a way that the blame be placed on Moses and his Jews, so as to have them once and for all be ruined and discredited. But Pharaoh became wise to their tricks; he foiled their plan and defeated their scheme by killing himself in such a manner as to save the Jews from blame. And soon afterwards, he who had previously begged Pharaoh to let his people go became the Jewish ruler of Greater Egypt and of all the wealth it contained. And thereafter the Tribe of Israel reigned supreme over the earth, never to be homeless or poor or persecuted or enslaved again, master of all it surveyed, without one of its sons or daughters ever having been known to break into a pustulant rash while telling a lie.

EIGHTEEN

Mind how you go, Lottie.

'They say the best things in life are free. Absolutely. But with the addendum that the person who first came up with these words never feasted their eyes upon an Aston Martin DB5.'

Here was a statement which, on most days, Lombard might well have seconded, for insofar as he was concerned no other manmade contrivance he knew of – never mind a motorcar – measured up to its lines and forms. His quiet tinkering with the old Aston Martin in Ali's barn was motivated by more than the challenge of simply getting it to fire up. Although the feat in itself would be remarkable enough to be cause for a moment of self-indulgent self-congratulation, Ali's casual pledge of "Let her rip and she's all yours" had never left his mind ever since it had crossed her lips. He'd done well not to look keen, but for all that suspected Ali knew; she teased him enough about the time he spent "fooling around with Aston" in the barn. Be that as it may, it was really owing to his appreciation of the said vehicle that the quote had piqued his curiosity while leafing through a newspaper at some prior time. The words were attributed to a man whose story he was as yet unaware was dominating large parts of the Western media, and this particular pronouncement of his had apparently been judiciously selected to indict his coarse character as well as broadcast his power and privilege. Naturally, it was no surprise that the man's story was of a salacious nature.

He was British born, a maverick self-made magnate who over three decades had built from the ground up a reputable international entertainment brand; from first operating an all-night café in East London, he'd opened a chain of nightclubs, branched out into live music and concert venues, then moved into music production, promotion and distribution, by and by coming to boast his own achievements through the creation of his own airline. He was also a man of his time. Every bit as accomplished a self-publicist as he was a shrewd entrepreneur, he'd turned himself into a celebrity, his own brand's be-all and end-all, much noted for never missing an opportunity to share the limelight with the powerful and famous or to promote his various charitable activities. However, three decades of hard work and great fortune all seemed to have come to an end when an ambitious reporter had penned allegations denouncing him as a serial rapist. The reporter claimed to have secured evidence to back his assertions after tracking down a handful of legally and otherwise 'silenced' female ex-employees and aspiring singers whom he had convinced to 'speak their truth', in some cases under the cover of anonymity. All allegations related to historical deeds and misdeeds for which only anecdotal evidence could be provided since none of the facts were reported or investigated at the time of the affirmed offences. In the event, where there was smoke there was fire. The man soon admitted to 'a voracious sexual appetite', acknowledged inviting aspiring female artists who sought to land a recording contract with his organisation to ride in his Aston Martin with a view to having his way with them, and likewise conceded that he was driven by ulterior motives when he asked females applying for cabin crew jobs at his airline to join him in hotel rooms for interview. He acknowledged being 'a sexual predator', acknowledged he'd abused his position of power to 'try to extract favours from those who sought things and dreams I had the means to offer or deny them'. All the same, he refuted all allegations of rape, or of forcing himself in a sexual manner on anyone, was adamant that all intimate sexual contacts which occurred between himself and his accusers were consensual, even – in an attempt to shore up his case – produced letters to demonstrate that he'd had a year-long 'affectionate affair' with one of his present-day accusers. All with little effect. By their very nature, his high profile and alleged crimes at a time of instant information consumerism, contributed to a situation in which neither the media nor the general public could get enough new 'incriminating' revelations to assuage their appetite. In this, they were not half helped by further allegations from yet more 'victims', whose number soon grew from a handful to over a dozen. He was duly arrested. A trial date was set. Men everywhere labelled him a monster. Groups of women offering slogans such as 'Believe all Women' collected across all sorts of platforms. All called for 'Justice' and the end of 'Old Machismo'. News anchors, pundits, solicitors, politicians competed for suggestions as how best to punish 'this evil man', proposed the seizure of his considerable assets to recompense his accusers. The reporter credited with exposing him was presented with a prestigious international award for his 'achievement in journalism'. Celebrated singers, actors and writers – some of whom were known to have once called the man 'a friend' – were outraged and moved to declare that, not unlike Christ before him perhaps, in the future the man's name may well end up being used to signify 'before' and 'after', as in 'before and after men could get away with abuse of power and rape'. And the Mayor of London, seizing the opportunity to further his credibility, jumped into the fray, declaring 'This monster poisoned our children's air with his petrol-guzzling car—He must never again be allowed to poison women with his dreadful male supremacist behaviour.' It hardly mattered that none knew what had truly happened in the man's Aston Martin or hotel rooms. Sexual activity had taken place, on this all parties agreed, but he said one thing and his accusers and their champions said another. There existed no evidence of his innocence or guilt; forensic, toxico-logic, digital, textual, audio, video or by way of anything else; no tangible proof to corroborate the claims of his accusers, which, as if commensurate with gravity, pulled in more and more supporters as their numbers grew, most markedly from among celebrities of all stripes. Still, aside from a misguided journalist and one well-known actor – one stated: 'This ought not to be a case of "Look at the ugly old witch walking with the Devil" or "The Jews poisoned the Well!"—This isn't the Middle Ages. For the sake of all and society, the law of "beyond any reasonable doubt" must be applied sensibly and permitted to prevail'; the other remarked: 'This monster, for all his monstrosity, is not *all* guilty men; should he be martyred and scapegoated for all of men's sins merely *pour encourager les autres?*' – still, beside these two erring voices, who it is said were 'sun-setted' – or let-go and barred from all social platforms and gatherings – few seemed much interested in matters of law, evidence or precedence. In places where the notion of justice based on evidence was cherished as a serious matter for the public good, the possibility of being branded a 'rape apologist' mattered much more, overpowered all considerations, even common sense. As anticipated, no one ventured to defend the accused's wrecked reputation once his trial got under way. Since one of the accusers had provided anatomical details of the man's genitals, the presiding judge thought it apt for the prosecutor to present a photograph of the man naked as evidence of his wrongdoings, and a jury of 12 men and women convicted him of some but not all of the charges levelled against him; he was forthwith sentenced to 30 years in prison, the sort of tariff commonly reserved for murderers and all such miscreants. Afterwards, given that it was estimated it would cost the British capital alone in excess of two hundred jobs, the Mayor of London was asked whether he thought the sale of the man's airline and other assets to compensate his victims should proceed. The good Mayor declined to air an opinion on the issue, but took the opportunity to remark: 'I think that I speak for all decent people when I say the jury have done us all in London and beyond a great service— Thank you.'

Up to this point, the affair had proceeded to the contentment of most; a monster had been caught by the toe, had hollered but was not let go. Private and public celebrations were held both on conviction and sentencing days. The only contention occurred later, when it was suggested by the supporters of the reporter who had started the whole denunciation rolling – now himself a leader of sorts with a sizeable social digital following – that some of the funds raised from the disposal of the convicted rapist's assets ought to be used to commission a statue of the offender, a life-size memento to keep on public display so that people would never forget the monster or how society dealt with his kind. It was a novel concept. The idea called for further new social arrangements of things, new deportment, new perception. Not everyone was fully signed up to the idea though. Some pointed out that statues were erected for communities to remember the brave and the great, although, as happened more and more, many had recently been toppled for offending new orthodoxies. The matter was considered, indeed the statue was commissioned, but in the end after much soul-searching it could not be agreed where to put it. As The Paragon asked in an editorial: 'Where in our fair new Xanadu should the statue of Evil be erected? A car-park? His birth town's main square? A prison? Its horrid presence would render any place too disagreeable to visit.'

Many aspects of living were being re-arranged. But the notion of erecting monuments of reviled lifeforms as memorials had yet – if it ever would – to take root. And despite the Mayor of London's comments, for many with taste and discernment the gas-guzzling Aston Martin DB5 remained a much-loved beast; a state of affairs which agreed with Lombard.

Charlotte Lottway thought of herself as Venice, which as it happened, she'd recently visited in the company of Avery Weyland: all wondrous radiance and uniquely imperfect. She was not known to stick her neck out for anyone, nor had much predilection for politics or militantism. Like most, she'd followed the spectacular public demise of the former music magnate from a distance; yet, unlike most, she'd actually met the man, some years previously in Ibiza when working for an independent producer in the music video industry. As a matter of course, he'd made eyes at her within hours of their encounter. Unless intimidated by her looks, most men – or so things stood prior to the above-mentioned affair which seemed to have rendered some of them a little timid – most men hardly failed to make a pass at her, or to provide her with amusement while coming to grief trying to conceal her effect on them. They couldn't help it, couldn't keep their eyes or thoughts from her form which she'd long ago learnt how to present to her advantage. More than this though, her impact was in no small part due to her disfigurement, the once much hated most visible blemish on her otherwise exquisite lips which, by its colour and together with the formation of moles on her cheek and neck, seemed to captivate most people; its blazing flush against her dark skin appeared to be particularly effective on men, mesmerized them, commanded their full attention, as if awakening a sense of wonder or possibly some odd and old protective instinct within them. She knew, because her younger sister who in most ways looked a mirror reflection of herself, but a flawless one, presenting a face and lips free from marks or imperfection, only ever made it as second best with the boys when they were together; a consolation prize.

Still and all, the music mogul never stood a chance. He was fat and short and middle-aged and she needed neither his money nor *laissez-passer*. He'd tried, understood what was and what was not available, and moved on, at no time afterwards giving her cause for concern. Then again, she was fortunate. She seemed to have been born under a lucky star. Always gave away just what she wished to give away, never more, and always got away with it, even if on occasion she could be given too much, or at other times, not quite enough. In any event, the lesson she took from the man's ruination was that too much love can kill, and that many men and women positively protest much too much. In matters of intimacy, she was both easy and broad-minded, reckoned 'each to their own' and '*vive la différence*'. "In the same way sex ought never to have been the jurisdiction of religious zealots calling out sins and hellfire, it should not be the domain of fanatics with lists of dos and don'ts—Dos and don'ts about flirtation; dos and don'ts about seduction; dos and don'ts about masturbation; dos and don'ts about passion. Making fucking rules and lists has nothing to do with sex. Everyone's watching too much porn."

This much she'd shared with her younger sister who'd raised

an eyebrow after she'd ventured that it would be well if the public censure of the disgraced 'rapist' could stop at least until he'd had his day in court; "We should give justice a chance before throwing stones —That is if justice can still be given a chance, what with all the baying for blood." And – for reasons which shall soon become clear – this is as much as she ever said about the matter to anyone other than her sister and a few men she slept with. In truth, self-interest more than notions of justice was her main consideration. Her sister, on the other hand, as was her wont, was mostly interested in getting the keys to all doors and feeling free to roam all the corridors safe in the knowledge that all roaming tigers were on a leash.

It would have been a foolish person who would trivialize Charlotte Lottway as a mere feast for the eyes. Ravishing, she was, but she was just as astute, and shrewd enough to know how to satisfy her desires and meet her ambition – and discerning enough to know her limitations. Had it been up to her, she'd have liked nothing better than to live the life of a gifted artistic Goddess of some kind or other, but her self-confidence never blinded her to the reality that she was without the talent or imagination necessary to summon the Muses. Still, she hardly minded, wise to the fact that her reward was to be blessed with good luck where talent was lacking. She was well aware that in another time, a young woman of colour wouldn't have fared as well as she expected to, even one with her looks and privileged background. And, making up for her youth and as yet limited experience, she was not merely well-read but perceptive enough to sense that anything wrestled from men and women can just as easily be lost to their next whims or fancies; as illustrated by the rapid and total downfall of the music promoter and airline owner. Fortune is fickle, and it was only right that she should make the most of hers.

For all that, for all her luck and looks, she was still some way from where she wished to be, and few – if anyone – could guess how hard she had grafted even to become Avery Weyland's assistant, the inconveniences, frustrations and boredom she had to put up with. She was fond of Avery

Weyland, whom she'd cajoled into rescuing her from the music video business when he expanded his production outfit with the revenue from the sale of the rights to his dead father's novels, but was not minded to play second fiddle to the man's interests for too long. The film business was café society, a great fantasy mill which a bright mind like hers could work and dominate. She was heedful of the nature of its particulars – it existed only as a suggested notion, tricks of perspective and presentation. Say 'Bee' and how much of the world whispers 'Honey' – or 'Sting'. Films were confections, magic tricks aimed at audiences willing their makers to fulfil their delusions. 'Bee' could be either sweetness or pain, as determined by the package. 'A + B = C'. All that mattered was to arrive at the predetermined 'C', and 'C' could waft with the breeze, drift with fashion, bend with trends, always yielding to its masters. Charlotte Lottway was a quick learner. She knew her business. And in no small part thanks to Avery Weyland, had become familiar with the mechanics of 'making films happen'. However, pitching, hyping, flattering and hustling money were all things she found inherently unrewarding. Or beneath her, perhaps – she was unsure. This was not to say that the film production business was without its perks and appeal, merely that it failed to satisfy her conception of her future. In short, she wanted to go places, envisaged realities beyond the grind of film production. Still, for now, wherever her future lay, she was happy enough to be adventuring with Avery Weyland, whose film company was affording her a convenient and pleasurable pathway to what she imagined were better things to come.

As it happened, insofar as they had potential, she quite liked the screenplays sent by the odd millionaire from French Guiana – although, in all fairness, nowhere near as much as she cared for the man himself – and was very much set on seizing the opportunity Avery Weyland afforded her to exploit one of them as a ticket to the future. And she knew exactly how to proceed with the one they'd selected. It was atmospheric, gritty, at its core a rather simple story about an ultimately doomed relationship between half-brothers – one from the US, a Jew; the other from the UK, who grew up a Muslim – who learn of each other's existence from their deceased Jewish New Yorker mother's last will and testament. They meet, grow fond of one another, each forced to come to terms with their own demons, but ultimately part company resigned to the fact that the things that separate them are too big a hurdle for the world they inhabit. For these two, the daily waters they navigate means brotherly rapprochement is an unattainable island. Charlotte Lottway saw the story as an allegory for the human condition, with at its centre the pivotal question: is it possible for an individual not to conform to his community's expectations without coming undone? As drafted, the answer was an unsentimental 'No'. Nurturing and interdependency between a person and their environment beats free will and freedom of action. The characters find they could only get along and become one if 'the others' around allow it, an unrealistic expectation given the disparity between their respective communities. She guessed it was either inspired by or a nod to Sartre's 'L'enfer c'est les autres'. A noteworthy proposition. All the same, a very outmoded one. She knew that for all its merits, this exploration of an age-old theme would today be better served by changing the message, and the project have a more bankable future with the two main characters turned into sisters and none of that Jewess mother from New York vieux jeu backstory.

This being so, she very much hoped Xavier Lagarde would not be visited by a change of heart about helping out his niece and would deliver promptly on his pledge to have her loverboy sign the required assignment of rights agreement. Meanwhile, she also wondered whether she may have been a little too forward with the man, too brazen perhaps. Avery Weyland had taken her to task for it after lunch, mentioned the word "promiscuous", only to pitifully apologize the moment the word had escaped his lips. "Come on, Avery. Where are the men I have deceived? I never give more than I advertise," she riposted, unperturbed; "I like him—I'm sure he likes me. What's wrong with liking?" "Is that a question or—" "Oh.

Please—" "Well, I'm sure you saw the ring on his finger, Lottie. On your head be it if you blow it."

It went without saying that she had seen the ring on his finger; as if a woman could fail to notice such a detail. Still, she'd also noted he hardly pulled himself away when their arms or knees touched, and barely seemed to mind huddling together in the office lift. She had the bit between her teeth.

Lombard could never be accused of having hungered for her, which gave her cause for vexation, but, if nothing else, also made the challenge she set herself more exciting. He spoke in a voice heavy with sleep when she called his room from The Beaumont reception on arriving at 10:30 as was agreed. She couldn't know it, but after dropping Mrs Raspberry in Cemetery Hill, Lombard had returned to his Mews to pick up a bag with a few clothes and his 'Xavier Lagarde' passport before walking the short distance to The Beaumont where, once in his seventh-floor room, cosseted from all noise and obligations, he'd lain on his bed in shirtsleeves but with his shoes on and fallen soundly asleep. This was unintentional. He'd planned on resting a little and getting a bite to eat before once again donning his 'casual-provincial' uniform to head down to the hotel bar at around the time Charlotte Lottway was expected. But weariness had got the better of him, he'd drifted into it, succumbed to its call, and now, groggy, in the same crumpled suit he wore earlier in Fortune Green, he found himself in his hotel room doorway looking at the splendour of stars that lit up Charlotte Lottway's smile. She stood in the hallway in front of him, dazzling.

"How are you, Lottie?" he said.

Groggy feeling aside, her presence stirred his senses, the way prey can't help but react to a lure. She wore a fetching high-waisted short black dress that hugged her hips, just tight enough to signal the top fullness of her mound of Venus. A nacre and gold band held her hair pulled back, and lush scarlet lipstick coated her incendiary lips, matching her nail polish. Most of all, her skin seemed to radiate warmth the way of a dark lustrous pearl, so that, had she been more modestly dressed and presented, she'd still have provoked agitation. For all that, she wore rather plain flat shoes, and like a fleeting breeze also managed an air of indifference, as if paying no mind to the impression she knew she made on the world.

"I apologize," he said; "I meant to wait for you down at the bar but fell asleep. Had the strangest of dreams too."

"Dreams!" she shot back; "How wonderful! Nice ones?"

"Oh—Egyptians, Jews and slit throats—Wouldn't think it counts as nice. I guess my mind's restless with too many things my ears picked up these last few days."

"Well now—'*The snake which cannot cast its skin has to die*'," she said.

The words made little sense to him, but he decided not to ask as she decided not to explain. Instead, she looked him up and down approvingly, resting her eyes on his black leather shoes: "I see you shed the Yves Saint Laurent suede monk-strap things," she remarked in fun; "I approve."

He grinned, tried and failed to come up with a reasonable explanation for his change of dress since their afternoon meeting. Instead, the sight of her, her manner and intoxicating scent combined to form a heady tonic which fully woke him up. For a moment, neither spoke, each measuring up the other.

"So, here we are," she laughed; "The Beaumont. I don't think I've ever been on the seventh floor. I love rooms with views. Do your windows look down over Regent's Park by any chance?"

"It's dark," he replied.

"Good. I like dark. Don't you like dark things, Xavier?"

He grinned.

"Please," she went on, teasing; "I brought your money. Now, call me odd, but handing out envelopes of cash to strange men in hotel corridors makes me feel weird. Are you going to let me in or—"

He hesitated, only momentarily, and moved sideways to invite her inside, then followed her as she pulled the envelope he saw earlier in Avery Weyland's office from her handbag and crossed the room to put it down on the desk opposite the bed.

"What do you know?" she laughed, turning back to face him; "Call me funny, but ostensibly handing out cash to strange men in hotel rooms makes me to feel just as weird as doing it in corridors. I guess it's a good thing it's your money— Otherwise it may feel like something illicit—Reckless even— was going on."

"Technically the money's not mine," he corrected her, playfully – they already both knew how this game was meant to end, but had to make sure; "It was gifted to Avery Weyland— And I don't recall accepting it back."

"Oh. In that case, I guess I ought to feel reckless. What do you think?" she teased.

"It's okay, Lottie," he returned; "There's no need for you to feel obligated to feel anything. All things being agreed, the screenplay and my money shall be yours as things stand."

She looked straight into his eyes, with all the allure of an enraptured bird of prey:

"I may be broad-minded, Xavier, but do not make the mistake of thinking me cheap. The bubbles fizz but the whole could just as easily go flat," she quipped.

Now he looked straight into her eyes, provoked and taunting:

"Well—Are you?"

"Am I what?"

"Feeling reckless?"

"Need you ask? Still, I wouldn't want to think badly of myself," she went on, glancing towards his ringed finger; "Good or bad, a healthy girl's appetite should crave only what is on the menu."

"What the eyes don't see—" Lombard said.

Briefly, she pulled her head back, chin up. He was unsure whether what he saw in her eyes resembled gratitude or the delight of anticipation. Still, she gave the room a quick glance, stepped towards him to kiss his lips – her lips turned out to be as warm and pleasant as their design – and made for the bed. He thought she was about to undress but, sitting down on the bedcover, she proceeded to pull her phone and a small metal pill box from her handbag, saying matter-of-factly with a mock sigh:

"How complicated having a good time has become. Have you got your phone handy?"

"My phone?"

"Uh-huh."

"Why?"

"Surely; you wouldn't want to worry I might lodge a complaint about you having taken advantage of me, would you, Xavier? Not after the Mr ------ pandemonium. Or has the infamous cause célèbre failed to make it to the far reaches of French Guiana and Polynesia?"

He recognized the name she mentioned as that of the disgraced music promoter.

"It hasn't. But I fail to see what my phone—"

"How refreshing," she interjected; "I take it you've yet to become acquainted with the new reality of insouciance. I'm afraid, ever since the ----- saga, prudence has become the watchword before a liaison—As in you can never be too careful. We video ourselves declaring 'consensual consensuality' and absolute sobriety and sound-mindedness in readiness. I'm informed there's some app that helps make the process quick and simple, but have yet to look into it. It's not like I do this sort of thing often."

Lombard frowned, sceptical, and she laughed.

"Ha-ha. Crazy, I know. It's okay. You needn't bother if it's all the same to you. I don't suppose you want me to film you on account of your ring, right?"

"My ring?" returned Lombard; he was still trying to grasp the implications of Charlotte Lottway's words as she panned her phone around the room, making a point of avoiding getting him in shot.

He still stood on the spot where she'd kissed him and now watched her filming herself stating in a few words that she was sober and sound of mind and about to have consensual sex "in The Beaumont's Room 713 with a Frenchman by the name of Xavier".

"There," she said, putting her phone away to reach for the

small box she'd retrieved from her bag earlier. She produced a couple of pills from it, put the box away, got to her feet and stepped towards him. This time, she wrapped her scent and limbs around him, the whole of her, and kissed him again, a long kiss, rich and moist, then breezed softly in his ear:

"Here—To make things better."

As she gently bit his ear, it took him a moment to realize she was holding a small blue pill near to his face. He winced, whispered in her ear:

"Thank you but no. The bubbles fizz just fine, Lottie."

"It's not for you—It's for me," she breathed, kissing him again.

"In that case don't let me stop you," he breathed back between kisses.

"It's nothing bad—Everyone does it."

"I'm not everyone."

"Huh. Why do some of you older men still want to be Vasco De Gama?"

"Maybe because nature's treasures are fine as they are, Lottie; or have you come down to earth from Heaven, Lottie?"

She laughed again, and they went on kissing and whispering and caressing and pressing up against one another, all the time standing in the middle of the room.

"I'm touched. But what if I make you breathless?" she said.

"Try me."

"I will. But who will rescue you when I do?"

"What if it is I who should make you breathless?"

"Well—If you do, I will not call for rescue. Do you think you can do magic, Xavier?"

"Huh—I should be okay as long as it's consensual, Lottie."

"The last man I gave myself to promised me the sun and the sky. He tried, I got bored. Are you absolutely sure you don't want me to send the statement I recorded to your phone?"

"I'm sure."

"How sure?"

"What's the problem, Lottie? Don't you trust yourself?"

"Oh, I do. I want to make sure that you feel safe, that's all.

I like my men to be in good working order. Worried men underperform—Drive with the brakes on, if you know what I mean."

"Really. Well, the only person here who sounds worried is you, Lottie."

"Suit yourself."

And she freed her body from his embrace, causally flicked one of her pills between her teeth and walked away from him undressing. A moment later, open and naked in the light from the bedside table, she was sitting on the sofa, immodest, bereft of all civilization, a Princess for a Prophet. He could never have not joined her, not got close enough to take her, and they got things under way, made their own arrangements, and then she provisioned herself.

A little later, in the shadow of night, Charlotte Lottway stood silently smoking a cigarette and fast fingering her phone in the open window overlooking the darkness of Regent's Park in the distance below. Behind her, stretched flat out on the bedsheet with his hands behind his head, Lombard watched her silken bare flesh, then let his eyes wander with the cigarette smoke gently wafting into the London night sky beyond her head, away from the light of her phone screen. With his own flesh still warm and suffused with her scent, he thought nothing. No word formed in his unstirring mind until she flicked her cigarette into the outside world, switched off her phone and turned to head for the bathroom declaring "Nice view." What finally came to him, for reasons he knew not, spelled 'the best things in life are free', and he grinned, recalling how much this venture had cost him already. And when Charlotte Lottway returned and lay down by his side on the bed, she rested her head on his chest unexpectedly tenderly. For a long while they remained thus, quiet, alive to the rhythm of their breathing and the punctuations of the night traffic through the open window. At one point the girl absent-mindedly started rolling the ring around his finger between her fingers, but quickly stopped.

"Will you still like me tomorrow, Monsieur Lagarde," she

said softly with a small snigger, invading the silence.

Lombard smiled: "I was just about to ask you exactly the same thing."

"I have no choice—I shall be your escort at Avery's mother's party. Have you forgotten?" she replied.

"Oh yes—Avery's mother's party. Can I ask you something, Lottie?"

"Shoot."

"People like Avery and you: do you reckon you could be capable of ordering someone to be murdered?"

She giggled: "What an odd thing to ask! Oh dear. Well— Not I, for sure; why would I ever need to think of killing anyone? As for Avery, I doubt it. I can't think of any reason he would do such a thing. Then again, come to think of it, there's his ex-wife—But that, as they say, is another story."

Lombard sighed and they fell silent again, until Charlotte Lottway remarked pensively to herself:

"What a strange question that was."

"It was?" he asked.

"Well—What do you think?"

"I don't know."

"Why do you ask it?"

"Huh—Small talk between strangers, I guess."

"Huh!"

A little later still, Lombard asked what she planned on doing with the 'consensual consensuality' statement she recorded on her phone.

"Delete it. Why? Are you having second thoughts? I can send it to your phone first if you wish."

"It's not necessary," he said.

"You're right," she agreed; "Besides, when you stop to think of it, it's all stupid really. Consenter one minute, consenter's remorse the next—Or by way of reciprocity: consented-with one minute, suckered the next."

Lombard silently agreed, but now also felt loose enough to play: "We're likely being filmed anyway."

"What?"

"I do a fair amount of travelling in my line of work—Got

acquainted with a few hotel managers. I have it from them that most hotel rooms are rigged with surveillance devices these days. For protection against potential litigation."

"I can't believe that. Hotel rooms—No way!"

"Yes-way. 'X' checks into a hotel. 'Y' visits their room, later alleges impropriety from 'X' and sues hotel for having provided both space and opportunity to 'X' to misbehave by renting them an enclosed unsafe unmonitored space to commit their crime."

"Never. I don't think any such scenario's ever happened."

"But it could—It will. Soon, any space where an unlawful act can possibly be committed will be monitored. Either that or they'll stick a chip inside of our eyes. You can never be too careful, right?"

"Ah," Charlotte Lottway let out, vindicated; "I knew you were having me on. Anyway, it would be touted as a deterrent if they had cameras watching us in hotel rooms. They'd let us know. Imagine—"

"I would prefer not to," Lombard sighed.

What followed was a flawless hush, and soon Lombard could tell from the girl's deep slow breathing that she was sound asleep. He feared to move for waking her, was released from the lassitude that had claimed him for most of the day, as if the girl resting on his chest truly was a tonic. How long passed, he failed to notice, but in time the moment was intruded on by a notification from his phone which he'd left in the inside pocket of his jacket hung on the back of the chair near the desk. Normally, such a summons would have remained unheeded – never mind at such a time as the present – but the notification sound was Ali's, which was unexpected as he knew her to be in the United States completing her previously interrupted recital tour. Neither she nor he ever contacted the other for the purpose of small talk. This was one of the rules that defined their relationship. Ali only ever got in touch when she was home or about to return from being away with time to spare for the two of them to meet. So, guessing she had to be on her way back to England, compelled, he gingerly pulled himself from under Charlotte Lottway's head to retrieve

his phone from his jacket. The screen lit up and he read:
   'Are you going to desert me, Xavier?'

And the muscles in his body drew tight. He stared at the words on the phone's lit-up screen for a moment, took a deep breath, conjectured as to their meaning, glanced across the shadow to the bed where Charlotte Lottway breathed peacefully in her slumber, and back to Ali's words. With one sentence, she had just transgressed not just their rules but his understanding of her. More than words, what she'd sent was a tide. A grim tide. An ill tide. Ali never pleaded. Never let him think she needed him or anyone else. Briefly, he wondered whether she could be drunk, but just as soon dismissed the notion; she knew how to handle her drink. He pondered whether she could have returned from the US sooner than planned, had stopped by his place without first getting in touch and, finding him away, guessed he was out in company. But, in all their time together, neither of them had ever visited their disappointments, or expectations, on the other; this was another of their tacit rules: no questions, no deceptions, no false promises. At last, after another glance at the bed with its sleeping girl, he made for the bathroom, softly shut the door, pushed down the toilet seat cover and sat down.

His mind went through many alternatives, puzzling over how best to respond. It took some while. All the replies he could think of at first seemed over-concerned, which he feared may betray the fact of his current situation at The Beaumont. In the end, he reckoned he was probably overreacting on account of his immediate circumstances. Ali, as always, would turn out to be the better of them.

He settled on the most non-committal response he could construct.
   'Hello Ali. Just got your text. What's happening? X.'
The reply came too fast:
   'Forgive me, Xavier. Should never have texted. Don't know what came over me. Delete my last message. I hope I didn't wake you. Hope you're good. Soon xxx A'

It wasn't necessary for him to look at her first message again to know this second one was a lie. This was wrong. More than breaking rules, Ali would never – would any woman? – never ask a man 'Are you going to desert me?' on a whim. Ali could never be owned, but all the same it wouldn't do to try to keep her through deception.

'No lies. What's going on, Ali?' he sent back, with a sense of foreboding that he might lose her.

This time the reply took a long time to come, so long he was about to call her when it finally arrived:

'A toddler mistook me for his mother earlier today; got me all tender and pity party. You're right, Xavier. Lousy; sought a shoulder to cry on and then got over it. Had no right to visit my silliness on you. You never asked and I thank you for it but since I started this I suppose I ought to finish it. We need no precautions not because I came into the world this way; I was spoiled by vandals, made a fool of myself and got over that too. Every once in a while though… There! Please do not call or reply. And promise not to bring this up when I'm back (couple of weeks). Hope to see you then. Wild with Xpectation as always. xxx A'

Lombard remained in the bathroom. There had been occasions when he'd wondered about Ali's lack of precautions – but he'd never asked, reckoned it was hers to tell. Now, one way or another, he would have to find out. He was wanting to call her, to hear her voice, but could think of nothing to say to her, his mind frozen instead with the single thought that he would now endeavour to find out what was what and, if at all possible, do what would need to be done. He'd have to be cautious, extract details in fragments; ease them out of Ali. He was skilled at that. Then, with Monroe's infinite resources, he would do what was right.

Charlotte Lottway was still sleeping soundly when, much later, he stepped out of the bathroom. He watched her for a moment, a warm breathing slumbering prize, the wages of ill-gotten gains which all at once had the quality of confiscated plunder. He quietly stole one of her cigarettes, smoked part of it standing on the spot where she had stood earlier in the open window, flicked it away half-smoked towards the street down below and went to lie flat on his back on the sofa, his eyes open towards the ceiling. He was still awake when Charlotte Lottway got up not long after the sun rose to bring light into the darkness. He shut his eyes as she tiptoed towards him to softly call his name. Then, he listened to her busying in the bathroom, the sound of water, the rustling from her clothes falling against her skin, and her light footsteps as she took her leave. When he rose, much later and long after she was gone, he found that her scent still hung in the air, was everywhere, on his skin, a whole raw musty universe. She had left a note on the bed:

'Bonjour, Monsieur Lagarde. No time for breakfast. Will be back at 3pm to fetch you for party. Be good, Lottie.'

"Mind how you go, Lottie," he sighed between his teeth.

NINETEEN

The whole thing!

Long ago, Lombard had come to think that a graph encompassing the gamut of all possible variations within the human character called for the simplest of diagrams – a short horizontal line, which for all intents and purposes needn't stretch more than, say, four or five inches. One end point of this line – it matters not which one – should be marked: 'Overt Narcissists: winners, leaders, high achievers etc'. The other end: 'Covert Narcissists: serial killers, rapists etc'. And the midpoint between the two: 'The Timid'. Thus completed, the line would provide for all human deviation on either side of 'Timid', which, by virtue of being the midpoint between the other two, represented the gentlest most unassuming souls, and, on that account the most ill-treated people to inhabit an imperfect world.

He still held this to be true today.

Charlotte Lottway made quite an impression when she swayed all shimmering and all of half-an-hour late into The Beaumont reception in a hip-hugging gold and turquoise sleeveless Egyptian-style mid-thigh-length satin gown with matching gold earrings and mid-heeled gold Cleopatra sandals. Her face was free from make-up today, her wondrous smile unspoiled by lipstick; she escaped no one's attention. Having made her mark, she kissed Lombard on both cheeks when he stood from his seat to greet her. After their night, he'd opted to drop the discomfort of his 'casual-provincial' uniform and go to battle in his own style.

"I like the suit and cufflinks, Xavier. Anyway—Here I am! You actually gave me the idea last night when you mentioned dreaming of Egyptians," she beamed, all lustrous lips while taking a step back to twirl in elegant delight to show off her dress; "I hope your escort meets your satisfaction."

"Ravishing," he said, unable to recall commenting on dreams or Egyptians.

"Good. I'm sorry I'm late; I'd mislaid my phone. But it's okay, I called Avery to let him know we're on our way."

Her mere appearance functioned as an irrepressible tonic again, which was as well, for Ali's words had left Lombard wavering as to whether to persevere with his current masquerade. He had not slept, felt brittle, adrift, febrile even, could hardly have been more indifferent to Jane's or Maude McGinnis's lots on this day. Earlier, he'd walked back to his Mews, considered checking out of The Beaumont and calling Charlotte Lottway to claim that unforeseen events meant he was required to put his plan on hold as he was to leave London at once. Only, he'd gone to *Monsieur Chose* for a late breakfast, realized that the storm within his mind welcomed the distraction afforded by his browsing the day's papers for news of Alan Winston. Other than a short piece in The Paragon stating that the authorities remained confident the runaway was still in hiding in Madeira – next to news of the Mayor of London's decision to extend the low emission zone to the whole of greater London; "Clean air for all of greater London's children is no longer a dream!" – he found none. Yet, this was enough to remind him of the river up on the plateau, and the pool and the donkey, which somewhat eased his mood. This was not a time for idleness, he figured, looking to book a flight back to Funchal at once. But there were no seats available until the next day, which swayed him to make it to Avery Weyland's mother's party after all. If he couldn't leave, distraction had better be the order of the day. Any doubt that remained vanished the moment Charlotte Lottway appeared to adorn the day, a reconciling grace to his steel eyes. The girl had approved of his suit and cufflinks, and now casually offered that she thought he'd look better and

296

younger for getting rid of his days-old stubble.

That aside, this afternoon Charlotte Lottway had reverted to her professional self; conscientious honeyed voice, coquettish and adroitly brushing against him as they settled side by side in a black cab she'd had waiting under the blue sky outside the hotel. Neither of them brought up the previous night, as if it had never happened. She explained they were going to Highgate. "You'll find Avery's mother's modest London pied-à-terre quite the thing," she laughed; "Most exciting. This do of hers is really a private launch party for her latest book of photographs of the high and mighty. 'A-plus' list—So we must all be on our best behaviour. Anyway, Xavier, I thought some more about our project and requested Monty's solicitors prepare at once a provisional Assignment of Rights agreement for you to have a look at with your niece's fiancé. I'm truly excited about this project—I'm also delighted to know it will help you vis-à-vis your niece if we can make it happen." And then she just went on speaking favourably of the many ideas she had about the script, alluding to actors and directors she strongly believed would be assets to "our team", and by the time they reached their destination a mere fifteen or so minutes later, the hitherto blue sky had turned the colour of lead, looming, and a fine drizzle had started to fall. Charlotte Lottway pulled a light black astrakhan coat over her shoulders and climbed out of the cab:

"Welcome to Never-never Land, Xavier."

Evidently, aside from her voluble display of enthusiasm for "our project", the girl had been playing with him. Avery Weyland's mother's "modest pied-à-terre" emerged as the last in a row of porticoed mansions lining a leafy private Cul-de-Sac sheltered behind a security barrier flanked by a manned gatehouse. 'Clement House' read a plaque on the gold and black eight-foot-high gates. Beyond, the drive overflowed with gleaming luxury cars of all kinds attended by a couple of uniformed guards armed with small submachine guns who casually exchanged words about the weather with Charlotte Lottway before letting them through large open double doors that led into a galleried hallway with twin staircases. "Oops.

Silly me—We seem to be more late than I thought we were," she giggled, leading the way under high ceilings across marble floors between walls adorned with art works, past an open room where chauffeurs and other staff stood at rest over drinks and a buffet, and back outside into a vast parterre garden that stretched away towards the woods and meadows of Hampstead Heath beyond. Here, with yet more security guards patrolling the perimeter lawn, a great white marquee the size of a small circus tent throbbed with light and noise under the light rain. Inside, over a hundred guests in smart informal wear stood or sat at tables between huge black and white portrait photographs that lined the marquee's sides. Most people were provisioned with beverages or plates of food, while white-shirted staff walked between them presenting trays of drinks and canapés. A great many faces were all attention, turned towards a couple who were speaking into microphones in front of a small silent ensemble orchestra. "Oh! Let's wait here and listen," Charlotte Lottway commanded as soon as they stepped inside the marquee among the guests, grabbing hold of his arm and hanging on to it. "That is Avery's ex-wife and Jake Marsh-Davani, her new husband—He's a writer and poet," she announced, restlessly.

The place smelled of alcohol, perfume and spices. On the dais, Avery's ex-wife made a tall fair figure in a crimson chiffon dress, while he who was her husband amounted to a lanky bespectacled fellow with a mane of long dark wavy hair pulled back from his forehead.

"This one is called 'All That Love Should Be Fourth Time Trying'," declared the crimson chiffon woman. "Saffron, Marjoram, Cumin, Coriander, Cinnamon," the mane-of-hair-man began to declaim; "And seminal fluid!" interjected the crimson chiffon; "Star of Anise, Nutmeg, Angelica, Turmeric, Paprika, Cardamom," continued the mane-of-hair; "And paraurethral juices!" added crimson chiffon; "Ginger, Cloves, Vanilla, Dill, Pepper, Sesame Seeds," mane-of-hair went on; "And jissom!" spewed crimson; "Liquorice, Mint, Fenugreek, Tarragon, Sweet Basil."; "And sweet spunk!" "Rosemary, Thyme, Sumac, Chili, Mustard Seeds, Juniper.";

"And vulva flower seeds!" "Fourth time trying we all find our way in the end," concluded mane-of-hair; "To the labia labyrinth", concluded crimson chiffon.

Charlotte Lottway laughed, ecstatic, squeezing Lombard's arm against her body. Most of the gathering appeared amused, some clapped, some smiled, others shrugged. During the poem's recitation, both Charlotte Lottway and Lombard had accepted glasses of Champagne from trays presented to them, and started to drink. Lombard also noted that the mounted photographs around them displayed famous faces, of whom some were present in the flesh within the assembly, such as a former Prime Minister and other politicians, actors, singers, sport personalities and fashion models. Now he understood the reason for the security outside. A few children could also be seen here and there, but seemed of little concern to the adults. "Just before I go—Let me tell you why marrying a fourth time is good," said the mane-of-hair man on the dais; "A man's spunk discharge and motile-sperm count considerably increases when he is exposed to a novel female!"

"Isn't Jake just brilliant!" proclaimed Charlotte Lottway as the ensemble orchestra began to play muted background classical music. The marquee came alive with the sound of conversation and laughter and, still holding onto Lombard's arm, she now took him on a tour of the chattering crowd, like a butterfly flitting from one bloom to another stopping here and stopping there, floating, universally delighting and delighted. All seemed to know her, asked of her news and she of theirs. Besides the more famous faces familiar to Lombard, the distinguished assembly turned out to comprise photographers, book publishers, literary and media agents, film producers, authors and other favoured guests like restaurant and art critics. Charlotte Lottway made a point of casually introducing everyone she convened with to Lombard, as if keen to impress him, only now and again and seemingly randomly taking the trouble to also introduce him to others. On these occasions, she'd say "This is Xavier, with whom I'm about to work on a great new project we are just putting into development." This prompted the odd "Really", "Oh", "Right," "Ah" and "Well done", but no pause or endeavour to find out more. So radiant were some among the crowd, that, soon, some of his escort's unique lustre seemed to dissipate, her lure dulled. Then again, perhaps this was on account of her drinking, for they kept being presented with Champagne which they both graciously accepted and downed as she dragged him from guest to guest around the marquee. Eventually, they came across a small group gathered around Avery Weyland's mother, a statuesque woman in a loose kaftan dress with long grey hair, big cheekbones and beady staring blue eyes who looked nothing like her son. "Hi, Ollie. Sorry I was late. Lovely party. This is Xavier. From French Guyana—He's just brought us a project that Avery and I have decided to produce. Xavier—This is Olivia Carr—Avery's mother," Charlotte Lottway said; "The person we need to hold to account for the fantastic photographs you've been admiring all around us," she went on, the image of sincerity. The blue-eyed woman considered Lombard warily, which, oddly, led to his feeling he ought not to be there. "How are you, Mrs Carr? Great photographs," he grinned. "It's Miss. What is it you do, Xavier? Are you a writer? Producer?" He was still grinning: "Not quite. Fisheries and mining. And a geologist." "Huh," the woman snorted; "Well—The best of luck. Delighted to have met you," she went on before turning to Charlotte Lottway to mutter: "What's the dear boy up to now!" Then, back to Lombard before turning away to resume the conversation Charlotte Lottway had interrupted: "Please, Xavier—Feel free to help yourself to a signed volume of my latest work on your way out. There should be a few copies left on display."

"Hurrah and jolly hockey sticks!" Charlotte Lottway declared with raised brows when they moved on; "You must forgive her—Chalk and cheese, she and Avery. Which—Talk of the devil—"

She'd just caught sight of Avery Weyland through the crowd in front of them; the man was in conversation with a small group standing near the playing orchestra by the dais. She hurriedly led Lombard his way, exchanged a few pleasantries with the producer-director and excused herself at once, leaving

Lombard in the man's company with a "See you later, Xavier."
Avery Weyland hardly seemed to mind having him to himself.
"Xavier! So glad you made it. Didn't I tell you it would be
interesting. I trust you don't get many society gatherings of
this kind in Guiana, right? My dear mother must be the most
celebrated portrait photographer of her generation—Anyone
worth their salt must have had their soul captured and
exposed by her lens; and let me tell you, I choose the word
'exposed' advisedly. Anyway, I hope Lottie's been taking good
care of you. I understand she's already got our company lawyer
working on the rights agreement we discussed. You're in good
hands. Isn't she amazing? Nothing trivial about the girl, let me
tell you—She's going places." Lombard grinned and Avery
Weyland seemed to search for someone in the crowd over his
shoulder: "Good. Have you met my wife? Well, I've got both
the ex and current incarnations here, but I seem to have mislaid
both of them. Come, let me introduce you to some of the
illustrious and not so illustrious entourage."

And it followed that it was now time for Avery Weyland to
steer Lombard around the present company. And throughout,
Lombard went on indulging in drink, unlike his host who
showed no interest in the free-flowing Champagne. The man
introduced him to "My friend Lauren—Head of Film and
Drama at one of Britain's flagship networks, probably the
most influential woman in the British Film industry. This is
Xavier Lagarde; a man of many surprises in whose company
we're on the cusp of embarking on an exciting new project.
Lauren is a formidable artistic force of nature, Xavier!" Lauren,
short, portly, suited and lip-sticked, twinkled: "Ah now, Avery
darling. Always itching to discuss seating arrangements;
would it be too much of a bore to refrain from talking shop so
as not to upset your mum's gorgeous party?" Then, to Lombard: "Delighted, ha-ha." "You're absolutely right, Lauren,"
Avery Weyland grinned with his deep voice; "My apologies.
I'm afraid some of us are just not that skilled at shooting the
breeze." "Ha-ha. You're forfeiting prudence now, darling. But
how is Vicky?" Vicky turned out to be Avery Weyland's current
wife, the comedienne, whose latest television show the two

then briefly discussed.

And in due course, Lombard was introduced to a comely actress, a chiselled bald man he was told was a renowned film producer, and others still, all good and groomed and merry, until they came across a middle-aged blazered American man who was actively engaged with his phone and with whom it was immediately apparent Avery Weyland had history. "Avery!" "Harry," the producer-director returned, stiffly. "Well—This is awkward," the other remarked; "I hoped—I thought—Well, the thing is I was in town and Ollie kindly invited me. She neglected to mention you'd be here and I—To my chagrin, it now appears—Wrongly presumed you were in China." "I'm leaving for China the day after tomorrow." "Ah—There you go then. And now here we are, you and I." "Yes. I'd have thought—This being my mother's event—Due diligence rather than merely making presumptions would have been in order," Avery Weyland remarked curtly. "Very true. I couldn't agree more. I'm glad—" the other started. "Then again, Harry," he was interrupted; "It wouldn't be the first time you'd made a virtue of being where you're not wanted." "Huh. Some things never change, I see. Now, Avery, it may be a technicality, but, as I just let you know, I was invited here—Most graciously so and by your very good mother, whose house this is. So, perhaps a small display of equanimity would not go amiss here." "I heard you the first time, Harry. It's at times like this that I feel my mother and I have an incestuous relationship; a healthy mother-son bond would have had her cast you off where you belong long ago. Still, now the party's nearing its end there's truly no need for you to feel compelled to stick around." The man shook his head: "Dear young Master Weyland. Like those bountiful Trust Funds that never run dry, some things perversely remain immutable in this turbulent universe." "Don't you just know it, Harry," Avery Weyland retorted; "To tell you the truth, I heard you were in town—Passing through on your way to Qatar, I believe. Fundraising, is it? What's the great lawyer's sham this time? 'The Twin Towers and Charles Manson were

CIA fixes!' Oh no—Too late—That's ancient news. Thousands have already beaten that drum, right?" The American made as if to reply, but then thought better of it: "It's how you want it to be, Avery. If that works for you, I'll work with it, and this being your momma's house, I'll leave it at that and be on my way as soon as I'm done doing what I came here to do. You take good care now," the man said, before throwing a "Charmed; the pleasure was mine" to Lombard as he turned to walk away.

"Not a friend, I take it?" asked Lombard, sounding more petulant than he'd intended once alone with Avery Weyland again. "There goes the great Harry Wallace: former entertainment lawyer turned The Great Revisionist Chronicler," the producer-director sneered as the man joined a nearby group of guests; "I don't suppose you heard of him?" "I don't believe I have." "Then I envy you very much, Xavier. He is to the Western world what Satan could only dream of being in the Good Book: its premier chief assassin. Specialist occupation: sample the past with a view to creating myths guaranteed to send all anti-western mobs into paroxysms of bewildered joy—Or pious hatred. Some study or interpret evidence— Harry Wallace mugs it, conspires to concoct grotesqueries of ill-gotten gains. And, can you believe it, the man used to be my father's lawyer." And on that note, now otherwise distracted, Avery Weyland felt he'd done enough for Lombard's recreation. "Oh dear. I'm afraid Lottie may be lost to you, Xavier," he reported, spotting his assistant among a group of glamourous young people surrounding a tall, dark, handsome man; "She would appear to have set her sights on Britain's current favourite and very recently divorced Formula One driver, Wilson Carrington, who's just put in an appearance. And from what I know of her, she's likely to distract the poor fellow into dissipation. I tell you what, have you got anything planned for early this evening?" "This evening—I don't think so," replied Lombard. "If you don't mind my saying, you look beat, Xavier." "I didn't have much sleep last night." "Well then, why don't you hang around for a little while—Help yourself to whatever you fancy. This do is just about to end and I'm having a few friends stay afterwards for an early supper in the summer house. Nothing fancy. A little get-together. You'd be more than welcome to join us." "Thank you, Avery. I'll think about it." "Good. Don't go far."

And Avery Weyland disappeared into the crowd.

It would be fair to say that by now Lombard had drunk more than was customary, and was well aware of it too, but as is nearly invariably the case in such circumstances, all the same felt he remained his own master and was lucid enough to take decisions. By chance, his host had left him near the dais where the ensemble orchestra was still playing, and there, among the quartet of musicians, a red-headed violinist in a loose sleeveless top with her hair pulled up in a ponytail brought Ali back to the forefront of his thoughts, cocooning him away from the noise and light and life swirling all around him. He went on observing this girl for a while, unable to avert his eyes from her, uncomprehending the dark stirrings in his chest and mind, sipping from yet another soothingly cool Champagne flute unaware of the crowd beginning to leave behind him. Then, without rhyme or reason, he pondered why he'd not come across Edward Duncan who he knew was likely to attend this sort of function, then forgot about the man, felt the stirrings again, realized the violin-playing red-head must have become aware of his gaze because she glanced in his direction a couple of times, and he swallowed hard and turned to leave. He accepted another glass of Champagne thrust at him on a tray on his way out of the marquee, absent-mindedly picked up a copy of Avery Weyland's mother's book of photographs, which, while simply titled 'Salt and Pepper', was so very large and shimmeringly glossy and weighty that he asked himself why anyone around the place could possibly be interested in a mere four million euros from a stranger from Cayenne. The sky had lifted outside, so that the garden basked in the most gorgeous early sunset. Now, had he been sober, he likely would have walked on, leaving the mansion in his wake. Certainly, had he been in control enough to pick his next poison, consideration would have led him to head for the wretched silence of the streets and face his soul rather than opt for the comforting noise and lights and stupor of merry making company. But by now, had he been asked, he likely wouldn't have been able to explain what he was doing there; only that he knew Avery Weyland a little and ravishing Charlotte Lottway a lot better, and that, for now, the great counsellor that is instinct advised him that distraction was a hundred times preferable to soul searching, the way of a man scared of the cold.

This being so, recoiling from the dazzling light of the early sunset outdoors, he opted to return to the marquee, found a freshly cleared table and started browsing through Avery Weyland's mother's book, grateful to be provisioned with yet more Champagne. He could find no reference point to form much of an opinion about the richly produced portrait photographs before his eyes, barely noticed that the marquee was near empty now, but was pleased to hear Charlotte Lottway's voice. She was leaving, she explained, and had come to wish him goodbye. "I hear Avery's invited you to his post-party get-together," she said, all the trappings of an Egyptian sunset in one gorgeous form by his side. "I believe he did." "Good. When are you leaving for Devon then?" "Devon?" he returned, perplexed. "Yes. Isn't that where you said you were going to stay with some friends?" "Oh—Devon. Right—Soon. Tomorrow, I guess." "Ok. Well—I daresay this is goodbye then; but not adieu. I have your phone number and address in Guiana. I'll be in touch very soon to send you the document we talked about." "Do." "Great," she said, and it seemed like an eternity ago now, although in fact it had occurred only the previous day, she bid him goodbye by leaning forward to kiss both his cheeks without hugging him, presenting enough flesh, scent and contact to agitate his senses again. "Thank you, Xavier. Enjoyed every minute of us working together."

"The pleasure was mine," he grinned between closed teeth, watching her limbs sway away through the leaving guests, her body enveloped in gold and turquoise.

What Avery Weyland called 'The Summer House' turned out to be a large single storey cottage within a copse of oak trees tucked away at the far end of the mansion grounds. He'd hired a Spanish pop-up restaurant, complete with flamenco guitar player, to provide his private guests with an informal 'Spanish evening' of prepared-on-the-spot Spanish hors d'oeuvres and meat and fish dishes purveyed with *cervezas*, *vinos* and *licores*. In time, the afternoon party guests and the orchestra had left. Also gone were their chauffeurs and the armed security personnel. As for his mother, she'd withdrawn to the privacy of her mansion with a few friends in tow to host her own after-party soirée.

Only Avery Weyland's party remained. Besides Lombard, there was his comedienne wife, Vicky, a big girl who towered nearly a foot above everyone else and was clearly drunk, walking bare foot but insisting on keeping hold of her shoes while occasionally cursing for no clear reason. Then there was Naomi, a short kittenish woman in a bow-dress who, like the host, was a film producer; two of her children accompanied her – one a well-known singer, Gem, the other an actor, Oliver. A tall rotund man called Aarush – a theatre director turned film director – was there by himself. Another man, David, a documentary maker, with his brother Joe who owned a major film distribution company, had also stayed, together with their glamourous girlfriends, Tessa, a famous ex-model, and Jemima, a celebrated ex-celebrity wife. Next were mother and son Ava and Daniel, she an author and he a scriptwriter. And a literary agent called Fay, together with another film producer called Steve. And finally there were Nick, who was head of the National Film School, and his pony-tailed partner Lawrence, also a film producer; and Jack, who ran a small-press publisher, and his wife Sophie, the daughter of a diplomat; and lastly "*les enfants terribles*" of the pack, Conor, author-script-writer-reporter, jack-of-all-trades, and his no less formidable wife Emma, who happened to be a Paragon journalist. All in all, not counting Lombard, just under twenty friends and acquaintances were there to attend Avery Weyland's 'goodbye meal' before he flew to China for a few weeks the day after next. Lombard was introduced to most of them, but had by now consumed so much alcohol that he couldn't disentangle their names or occupations; only that they were important if not eminent media folks, none of whom meant anything to him.

He'd long mislaid and forgotten about Avery Weyland's mother's book. The beer and the wine were poured, smoking cigarettes at the table was permitted and much enjoyed, and the conversation and the food started agreeably enough. At first, given his advanced inebriated state and sombre mood, Lombard gave a good account of himself in front of his host. Again, his fisheries and mining and French Guiana and Cayenne background failed to impress, at most eliciting the not unpredictable mentions of "Devil's Island", "Papillon", as well as, in this setting, "The Dreyfus Affair", someone by the name of "Polanski" and "the French space station". He was allocated a seat between the man going by the name Dan and the woman called Fay, one seat away from Avery Weyland whose wife, at the opposite end of the table from her husband, had fallen asleep to quietly snore almost immediately after sitting down. One thing Lombard did not fail to notice was that the long wooden table they sat around oddly resembled the one he'd seen at John Bowdion's. The beer, wine and food were effortlessly consumed. The conversation, just as effort-lessly, moved from poetry to films to a war in Asia, and much gossiping about absent people everyone at the table seemed to know. At one point, one man or the other scoffed: "Ha-ha. Indeed. I think Michael's book ought to have had a 'sensitivity warning' stating 'The views and words of the characters in this tale are their own and in no way reflect the views or opinions of the author. And it may be added that the views and words of the author in this tale in no way reflect the opinions of the author either'. Ha-ha. Who knows? He might just have got away with such crazy illiterate drivel." "Never mind 'trigger warning'—The novel should never have been allowed to see the light of day. The man's a dinosaur. And it's not necessarily a bad thing that his misguided publisher should be in trouble too." "Speaking for myself, I'd say the book can best be summed-up as a psychotic episode!" "Ha-ha!" "Anyway. Anyone know where he is now?" "The last I heard he scarpered to some island off New Zealand." "Huh! If it's off New Zealand's South Island, it may be where he belongs." "Ha-ha! He was a good writer once, though. And such a darling. It's a pity really."

And so it went, until, the one they called Conor started telling some story relating to a documentary programme about a round-the-world motorbike journey he'd recently made for charity, and how, on the very last leg back to the UK, a careless driver had crashed into his motorbike near the French city of Reims, totalling it. Now, Conor, the man telling this story, pronounced Reims '*Reams*', which in normal circumstances would have been of no concern to Lombard. Tonight, however, it irritated him, mostly on account of the fact that until now the man had made a conscious effort to convey the foreign place names coming out of his mouth correctly, and had certainly gone out of his way in this when speaking of the Spanish food and drink on offer.

"The correct pronunciation is more like '*Rance*'," commented Lombard; "Like in '*lance*' or '*France*': '*Rance*'—Not '*Reams*'."

"Oh! Really! I stand corrected," the other replied, brusquely, persevering with his story, making no attempt to correct himself.

Well, again, on account of his thoughts about Ali and being inebriated by now, this irritated Lombard greatly. And it must also be said that the man, like most of the present company, was himself rather the worse for wear. Still, when he again said '*Reams*' for Reims a moment later, Lombard found it beyond him to let the matter slide. "The correct pronunciation is more like '*Rance*'," he interjected, intentionally using the same wording as before; "Like in '*lance*' or '*France*': '*Rance*'—Not '*Reams*'."

"And so I stand corrected again," the other replied, clearly irked to be interrupted a second time, resuming his story at once.

"Well then— that being the case, perhaps you'd do well to correct yourself, don't you think?" Lombard grinned.

"Please remind me: who are you again?" the man grinned back.

"Gentlemen!" Avery Weyland intervened, smiling to defuse the situation; "We are gathered here to make merry. Ha-ha. Now, Xavier," he went on; "Please take no offense at Conor struggling with a particularly challenging French word. Besides, he's from Ireland. To get in a scrape with him would be ill-advised, ha-ha!"

"No offense taken, Avery. I assure you. It's just that I noticed your friend takes great pains to say '*bay—jing*' or '*teuh—raan*' or '*sehr—beh—sah*'. Right? Well, I thought I'd set him straight and give him a leg up on his French pronunciation, that's all. What with me being French and all."

"I'm confident such a brilliant author, scriptwriter and well-travelled man-for-all-seasons as our Conor here is well-versed in the French language, Xavier. It's just that some French sounds are beyond the bounds of possibility for a British or Irish mouth," Avery suggested, helpfully.

"Ah. I understand. A scriptwriter. I remember now, Avery: they who go far with a bit of charm and good dinner conversation—Jesters who know their place, yes?"

And Lombard winked at Avery Weyland, who smiled back uneasily while the man by the name of Conor glared back at each of them in turn. "We must abolish all borders, languages and accents!" somebody declared, encouraging laughter and levity to return. "Did someone say he was from Cayenne?" Lombard was certain he heard a voice ask somewhere to his right. "I think so," another voice replied. "Well—Maybe that explains it." "How's that?" "I guess he escaped the penitentiary". "I shouldn't think so. They closed it decades ago." "Well, maybe he escaped decades ago, ha-ha."

Lombard shook his head, attentive to Avery Weyland who he could see no longer looked easy behind his smile. Again, he tried and failed to recall what it was he wanted from the man, only that he'd offered him money he did not have to produce a screenplay by a sad man from Mile End on account of a niece he also did not have. Unaided by the drink and noise, his mood refused to lift. Rather, the alcohol helped grow a quiet fury in his bloodstream, heavy and menacing. His mind remained coherent enough to know this heralded nothing good, cast an ominous shadow, all beyond his influence. He tried to stop all noise from reaching him, the many voices chattering from all directions around the table again. All the same, the words "my nana" got through. Then some prattling about an American presidential election, and some babbling about somebody or other who refused to allow their new book to be published in Hebrew, then a voice lilting '*Do not go gentle into that good night*', giving rise to a female voice announcing she had "just bought the rights to a novel that should make a great cinematic exploration of the destructive impact of love on women." "Sounds good—Women need to be rid of the stigma brought by societal expectations; we must shake off the shackles of love as defined by patriarchal monogamous heterosexual society." "I'm one hundred per cent with you on that one: Love, as still taught today, harks back to a time when the female of the species was held in bondage by the male of the species. Indoctrinated with ideas of subordination and fidelity," someone approved. "Free women! We can't help but try," another assented. "Hallelujah! It must never be forgotten that a woman gave birth to Jesus! With no male interference!" declared another voice. "Begone the bonds of yesteryear! Celebrate the boundlessness of what women can accomplish by themselves!" a male approved. "It's exactly what Sasha was saying," another male remarked; "The technological revolution currently reordering life is bringing about a total rewrite of human history: the most breath-taking wonderful overwhelming thrilling edits ever are being commissioned. Bringing to light a new narrative in which women are free and taking the lead and reshaping perception, reimagining emotion, changing the course of interdependencies and antediluvian gender notions."

And Lombard swallowed hard and turned towards he who had spoken this last sentence; it was Oliver, the son of the film producer named Naomi; he was Lombard's junior by a good ten years, no doubt fitter for it too.

"This is wrong!" he exclaimed, banging his fist onto the table hard enough to send his and his nearest table companions' dinner plates and drinking glasses shaking and tumbling.

"What the fuck!" started Avery Weyland's wife, startled out of her sleep.

All eyes turned to Lombard, alarmed and incredulous. For some reason, at this moment he reflected on the fact that he was still wearing his suit jacket and cufflinks, while the other men present were in shirtsleeves or informally dressed.

"What's the matter with you?" a voice asked.

"Yes. What's wrong with him?" ventured another.

"Xavier?" Avery Weyland queried, conciliatory.

"This is wrong!" Lombard called out, banging his fist down again; "All wrong!"

"What is?" Avery Weyland asked.

"The whole thing!"

"The whole thing?"

"You all! Rewriting the rules!"

"Rewriting what rules?"

"Love is our only wonder! That which keeps me from hurting you!"

"Huh! You must mean man love; love as ordained by men to subjugate women," quipped a female voice.

Lombard sought its owner: she was the one called Emma, Conor's wife, the Paragon journalist.

"You are forgetting your place!" he commanded, returning the glare she cast into his eyes.

"Wow—My—Our places? Now—" she started.

"Your place! One half of this mirror of horrors!" Lombard cut her off, glaring from face to face around the table, disgusted.

"You women and your manly appendages are repulsive fools," he went on.

"Just a thought—But I'd say your new friend feels threatened by strong women, Avery," a woman stated.

"Silence!" Lombard interjected, turning to she who had just spoken, before anyone else could say a word; "Do not deceive yourself into presuming you can see the operation of my mind."

"Well—Someone here is calling everybody else fools? What does that call for? Do you see into our minds, Mr—Xavier, is that it?"

311

It was the one called Emma again. Lombard leered at her:

"Do not flatter yourself, woman—Can it call itself a mind, that which festers with such contempt for its own kind it wishes to tether its nature to that of a loveless creature? But I stand corrected. I shall not speak badly of women. Quite possibly no woman draws breath among this assembly—I suspect I am in far worse company here. Creatures so very drunk with lust, so blighted by their raw effluence they seek to turn all women into sisters! Stolid militants! A bone to pick. A bone to chew. Grit in their teeth. Bone Meal for a heart. But I get you, sisters. I too have a dream; I dream of a world in which I ought to be allowed to leave my wallet wherever I please with no one left around with a mind to steal or not return it! I get you! I reckon I do. But it isn't women you wish to mould. It is strange fruits—Bloodless vulva supernovas hanging from trees; rimmed with lush colours and squirted with radiant fragrance to deceive the flies! Dead! Festering mulch for wingless Hercules with stiffies! You aren't the first to speak of bending nature to your own fancy—To plot new religions—Hatch new Deities—To distract the humdrum inside of your mind with unrivalled dreams of thousand-year Empires. Men of your match beat you to it thousands of years ago! No! But you may well be unique in having your prey so eager to pick its poison! I'm talking about the male of the species—Specimens of which are here on display, with cause enough to be aroused by your intrigues. So, gentlemen," he went on, now scowling at the males around the table; "Rewriting the rules of love! What is to become of lover boys when lover girls shall all be sisters? Shall you all be brothers? Eclipse the old order? By which ploy or measure is it proposed to coerce brutes such as yourselves into becoming benevolent beasts starved of affection? Slaves. Please tell! What fantastic deeds are you to perpetrate on your soul and suffer in the flesh? What shall Romeo be to a Juliet indifferent to love? Do tell! And please be so good as to apply logic to your discourse! This is a business grave enough to deserve proper weight and consideration!"

"We—We're all trying to create a kinder, gentler world.

312

There's nothing wrong with that. I think you're deliberately misunderstanding what was being said. Certainly, shouting and fist-banging is not the way," the one called Oliver let out after glancing around the stunned and silent table for support.

"A kinder world!" Lombard scoffed; "That commands you to extinguish affection! Ha-ha!"

"Well now," declared a female voice somewhere; "It seems like we have got ourselves a—"

"Shut up! Let the brothers speak, Sister!" Lombard interjected.

Several "My Gods", sighs and disapproving noises rose at once while the one called Oliver looked back at him with a grimace across his face, floundering for words.

"Xavier, I think you've possibly had a few too many drinks. And I also recall you telling me you didn't get much sleep last night. You need to come to your senses. Perhaps some fresh air—" Avery Weyland appealed in his deep voice, worried but still conciliatory.

"True, Avery—I had too much to drink; but my senses are just dandy—I feel just fine. But maybe you can help. After all, not unlike Conor over there who crashed his big motorbike in '*Reams*', you're all man too. Fill us in, Avery: how is it to be done—Starve men of affection and enslave them with their tacit agreement? How is the sisters' dream to be made reality?"

Avery Weyland grinned: "I—"

Neither Avery Weyland's nor anybody else's opinion mattered to Lombard by now; he was on his own expedition, provisioning his own wildfire.

"No. Let me tell you, you pitiful fools. By way of your all-pervading monitoring personal interconnected devices, you New Masters of all you survey are to continue what has already begun: suffer the people to whimper while showering them with sweets to buy their trust, the better to grind them down with new rules, new definitions, novel social orders— Such wealth of complicated arrangements going against all instinct that even the most perceptive minds will no longer know which way is up. In this fashion mollified, unsteadied, unnerved, men and women are to be reduced to timid lifeforms; with anyone still minded not to comply silenced by the unending fear of being demonized by your purging mobs. For sure! In this way your spells will prevail over common sense; in this way you will persuade nature itself that swans quack, that sisters are best, that two-four-ten wrongs make a right—That love is bondage holding lovers captive. Were you to prevail, only two tribes would exist: sisters and brothers—Dead fruits hanging from the trees ogled by wingless cocked flies stuck fast to the ground. Not even apelike fuckery! But then again, you may be shooting too quick! Should you triumph, yet some savages live on to recall your fever in ten or a hundred years from now, what will they make of your having squared liberty with vulva supernova? Shall what will pass for children by then still gape at the Mona Lisa and praise her? Cry 'That's us there! We've arrived! We are neither men nor women nor love!' Or will they wonder at her form and ask 'What is that?' I shall not disabuse you, I know, but let me say this, you fools: a good man would do anything for a good woman—A good woman just as much for a good man, but there is no good to be found in men or women set on making politics of love. I said it: your poison isn't new—Only the means to administer it is. For myself, I shall go on drifting with the stars without desiring to be God. I shall return to where lice flee the cold eternity of death once their host perishes—To seek the warmth of new blood and a beating heart. I shall leave you to your fancies—Go home—Where puppy snatchers can be driven to murder, men to suicide and cursed women bleeding for their dead husbands can be snuffed out together with their children in the time it takes to cross a road. You needn't get up, Avery; I'm perfectly capable of finding my way out."

And he got to his feet, unsteady and staggering.

"The whole thing!" he said again, lurching towards the open door of the Summer House.

He barely heard the "Oh-my-God", "He's mad", "Well-well" and tut-tutting behind him. Or the "Fuck me! What was that?". Or the "I suppose we just witnessed what's called 'letting trash into the house'." Or the sniggering. Nor did he notice the blood draining from Avery Weyland's face when he spoke of life being taken in the time it takes to cross a road. He was too busy trying to give a passable impression of a dignified exit as he stumbled into the darkness outside. The marquee standing in the mid-distance under the stars blocked his view to the mansion, but he hardly cared. Instead, he gazed up at the sky above his head, and the stars beyond, grinning:

"That's what I'm talking about! The whole thing!" he growled.

And he lunged forward, staggering across the wet grass towards what appeared to be safety – a head-high cast-iron fence that marked the boundary of the grounds. He reached and grabbed hold of it, relieved to let it take some of the weight from his swaying legs, and started alongside it, holding fast to it. The other side was pitch dark, thick with trees. He moved forward in that manner for some time, unsure where he was heading or what he was looking for, then heard voices in the near distance behind him, his name being called, someone shouting "No, he didn't come through the house." He understood the company he'd just left were out looking for him and, to his own surprise, he grabbed hold of the fence high up with both hands and swiftly lifted his body up and over it, tumbling into the shadow of the trees on the other side. He got up, stumbled through the darkness, fell into a muddy ditch, climbed out, tripped over some brambles and fell headlong onto the cold earthy ground.

"One size fits all," he said between his teeth, passing out.

At sunrise, he came to and realized – on account of the leafy scenery, and the dog walkers and joggers on nearby paths – that he was on Hampstead Heath, not far from Kenwood house, and remembered how and why he'd come to be there. He'd given quite a speech the previous evening; said things he remembered, others he didn't, wished he'd not drunk and had kept his own counsel. When he rose to his feet, he realized his wallet and phone were in the dirt on the ground, likely thrown from his pockets when he'd fallen in the darkness. The phone's notification light was blinking. Ali had texted him during the night.

'Please and again, Xavier, forgive me, try to forget and promise never to ask questions about last night's aberration. I need to trust you on this. See you soon. As always... xxx A'

He growled – then swallowed hard – then wondered what if anything was to be made of the fact that neither Charlotte Lottway nor Avery Weyland had tried to contact him.

TWENTY

No place remained for a man wishing to live or die as his own property to go to, and soon, in all likelihood, neither will there be anywhere left for him to run to.

"Eventful night?"

Lombard's dishevelled hair and muddy suit and shoes provided The Beaumont receptionist cause for amusement, yet he was well enough trained not to probe. The man also agreed to send someone up to his seventh-floor room to retrieve his remaining belongings – the bag containing his 'casual-provincial' uniform and the 4000 Euros Charlotte Lottway had returned – sparing him the chore. He'd turned up at the hotel well before checkout time, and, despite his less than suitable appearance, the restaurant staff proved good enough to allow him to have breakfast without requiring him to change, a kind gesture he rewarded with a generous tip.

By the time he left The Beaumont to embark on the 15-minute walk to his Mews under a warm greyish late morning sky, he'd had ample occasion to revisit the events of the previous evening, leaving him in no doubt that Avery Weyland – whom he recalled had remained sober throughout – couldn't fail to have surmised by now that Mr Lagarde was likely not the man he professed to be. Lombard's closing statement about returning to where men commit suicide and women and children can be killed in the time it takes to cross a street was best described as careless beyond words. He'd given a terrible account of himself. Coming to the end of his drink-induced tirade, he ought still to have had enough presence of mind to turn his back on his dreary dinner companions without giving himself away in such a spectacular manner. His own ineptitude surprised him; he hadn't known he had it in him to be so spontaneous. For all that, he was satisfied the producer-director could not possibly know his true identity, and in any event had determined even before going to the party that, now he'd had a chance to appraise the man for himself, there was next to no chance of his having had a hand in Jane's death; on this account, he trusted they would not cross paths again; which was as well. Indeed, he found himself wondering how disappointed Charlotte Lottway must be, having learnt of his exploits and realising that her four million Euro 'sealed deal' was just a dream. Had Avery Weyland broken the news to her himself? Would she now regret having spent the night with the Frenchman from *La Guyane*? There could also be little doubt that she would now discard John Bowdion's screenplay, make no attempt to track its author, John Jones, for regardless of her musings to the contrary, he suspected she'd never cared for it. Still, just in case John Bowdion got ideas on account of his newfound confidence, it would be prudent to caution him to keep the screenplay under wraps for a good while, as was its lot before he'd agreed to 'lend' it for a fee.

Making his way along Queen Anne Street, Lombard had crossed Harley Street and stepped into Wimpole Street when he made out a campervan coming to a stop on his side of the road about thirty yards ahead of him. He heard its rear side door slide open and made out two men in leather jackets who leisurely climbed out of it to stand on the pavement chatting over a large roadmap they held between them. He paid them little attention, continuing on his way home less than five minutes away, readying to step into the road as the men with the map partially obstructed the pavement ahead. "Excuse me, sir," one called, grinning affably; "We are lost. Do you know the way to the M1 motorway from here?" "The M1?" Lombard returned, now heading their way. "Yeah. We were told to drive towards Regent's Park Zoo and then the Finchley Road and—" Now, within touching distance, Lombard paid the two men more attention. They were in their early twenties, possibly of middle-eastern origin, and it occurred to him – on account of their leather jackets, smart shoes, shirts and youth – that they were more the street than the campervan type; certainly hardly came across as tourists at sea in the middle of Central London seeking a route to the distant M1 motorway. But it was too late. He never saw how, but heard and felt the jolt of what he instantly knew to be a Taser gun discharge; his muscles locked into spasms. As he remained on his feet in pain and incapable of movement, he also knew that, unless tasered again, his incapacitation would be brief, last a few seconds, and then, while still unsteady and disoriented he would at least be able to attempt to look after himself. But his assailants were just as wise to the temporary nature of his induced helplessness. No sooner had he concluded this consideration than his chin absorbed the full force of a rising palm heel strike; his head lurched back from the impact, squeezing the nerves between his skull and the top of his spine, and he blacked out.

He was unaware of how long he'd been out when he came to on the hard floor inside the moving campervan; only that it was daylight, that his wrists and ankles were bound, that three distinct male voices were in the vehicle with him speaking a foreign language over the noise of the engine and nearby traffic. The rough motion, slow speed and street noise suggested he was being carted through London. He kept his eyes half-closed for a moment, seeing only grey mist through his eyelids, giving himself space to bring order to his circumstances. The words of the men in the van could have been Turkish, which fitted the looks of his abductors. They sounded unconcerned, their conversation casual, sports-related banter maybe, all three voices reaching his ears from the direction of travel above and behind his head. He guessed two were in the front passenger and driver seats, with the last, nearer to him, settled not more than a couple of feet away. Then he tried to move his hands and legs, carefully so as not to draw attention to the fact he was conscious; his ankles and wrists were bound alright, quite tight, but at least his hands were in front of him, so that his arms were unconstrained. Now he opened his eyes. The campervan was fully equipped and furnished, had a built-in cooker and television set, and was scattered with items of men's clothing. He lay in the middle of the floor, looking towards the rear of the vehicle where the outside light shone in through brown-curtained windows onto unmade bedsheets. He observed that his wrists and ankles were bound with cable ties – the type available in most Tool and Car Parts stores – and on the floor, not far from his knees, he saw his wallet, passport and crushed phone next to the open bag he'd carried with him from The Beaumont. By all appearances, his abductors had gone through his bag and pockets, removed the battery from his phone and broken it, and riffled through his wallet which lay open next to a couple of credit cards and his passport. He guessed they'd also come across the envelope with the 4000 Euros and pocketed it. He scanned the floor for his house keys but, failing to spot them, inferred they were still in the bag where he'd put them prior to going to Avery Weyland's party. Next, moving his head back slightly, he made out the sliding door to the side; it was less than an arm stretch away, however the opening handle was too high to reach. And now, watchfully stretching his head further back still, he caught sight of the man nearest him – he was the one who'd hailed him. He sat perched on top of a small fridge in the space between the sliding door and the front passenger seat, hugging the seat's neck support to steady himself while chatting with the other two in front, three-quarters turned-away from Lombard; somewhat bizarrely, he was wearing the Yves Saint Laurent monk-strap shoes he'd found in Lombard's bag.

Lombard moved his head forward and closed his eyes again. He had no doubt where credit for his current predicament lay: in the wake of his drunken blunder, Avery Weyland had got hold of this crew and sent them after him with the information he knew, which hardly amounted to much but sufficed all the same: a detailed description of Xavier Lagarde and his Beaumont room number. These three had lain in wait near the hotel and tailed him when he stepped out to head back to his Mews. Then the ambush had come. The only unknowns were the instructions they'd received: were they taking him to be questioned or disposed of? For the facts spoke for themselves now. He had been wrong. Avery Weyland owned a secret terrible enough to have him commit murders to protect it. Most likely, the two figures answerable for Jane's death were now with him in the campervan; and like the car used to run Jane down, this campervan just now used to kidnap him in broad daylight had been recently stolen too. It all came to just one thing: wherever they were heading, whatever fate they had in store for him, he had better try to break free before his captors reached their destination with him as bound cargo.

He took a deep breath and managed and checked his watch on his tied wrists: it was just past ten thirty. He recalled stepping out of The Beaumont a little over half an hour earlier, which, as he'd already reckoned, meant they were still in London, as a matter of fact still near to where he was abducted, which could signify busy streets on the outside. He took a good look at his bag and belongings strewn on the floor near to his knees again. The Lagarde passport, credit cards and wallet were of no consequence; fakes that could not be connected to him. The same was true of the bag, clothes and phone. Even if they'd not smashed his phone, it was encoded. But then, there were his house keys in the bag, and the phone sim card, which he would be wise to retrieve, and, come to think of it, his photo in the fake passport. He had no idea who his abductors were, but by all appearances they were unlikely practiced kidnappers. They were too young, but more than that, their binding his hands in front rather than the back of him, and their poor diligence suggested this to be so; they really ought to have been watching their catch with more attention or, if not, made certain he wouldn't wake up while in transit to what he may fear was a certain death – a man with nothing to lose. They were amateurs. Still, there could be no doubt they were dangerous, and only a fool would have trusted them to be unarmed. For now, they were casually chatting. He reckoned that, bound as he was, hauling his body onto his knees to reach the sliding door and yank it open ought to take no more than a couple of seconds, too quick for the near man on the fridge to do much about it. What was to happen afterwards would depend on luck, or circumstances.

Moving gingerly, using his knees and bound hands, glancing back now and again, he succeeded in bringing his bag close to his chest before doing the same with his phone and passport and transferring them into the bag. Then he waited for an opportune moment. With London's 20-mile-an-hour speed limit in residential streets – and his captors alert not to call unwanted attention by driving too fast – the moment came when, exiting a sharp corner to start climbing a steep hill, the campervan slowed to a crawl and, as it was gaining speed again, with the bag straps wrapped around his bound wrists, using his elbows and the palms of his hands, Lombard thrust his body up onto his knees and in one movement got hold of the sliding door's handle, yanked it open sideways and, cupping his head inside the tight grip of his arms and the bag, dived out head first into the open. Unsurprisingly, he collided head on with a parked car before he hit the tarmac and his curled-up body began bouncing and rolling down the hill, away from the climbing campervan. Then, as he continued to tumble down, hitting the cars parked along the kerb, the sound of a loud crash cracked the air. He never heard it, nor knew of it, but following his bailing out the driver of the campervan had screeched to a halt and caused the car behind to rear-end him. This Lombard realized a little later when, no longer a loose projectile subject to gravity, he'd crawled as fast as he could to conceal himself between two parked cars and shelter flat against the tarmac. His whole body was ablaze with pain, his mind unsteady, a mist through which he was prepared for just about anything to happen and primed to make enough of a nuisance of himself to alert the entire neighbourhood in the event his abductors showed up. But they never did. Instead, he heard voices and shouts coming from up the road, and when he stretched his neck out against the tarmac to look up, he realized what had happened. His three captors stood in the road by the campervan while the driver of the car that rear-ended them was shouting irately. This was unravelling less than forty yards away. The campervan occupants looked edgy; two scanned the road for their escaped prey, the third – the one he'd last seen sitting on the fridge – held his bleeding forehead in his hands, likely the result of being thrown off his perch during the accident. Then, as if responding to a signal, at once all three took off running towards the top of the road, abandoning the campervan. A handful of people were already gathering around the scene, exchanging words with the driver of the damaged car left behind, yet, mercifully, Lombard's dramatic tumble appeared to have gone unnoticed, and he remained unseen as he painstakingly sat up on his spot between parked cars.

His downhill fall had cost him a broken watch, the loss of a shoe and a cufflink, tears in his muddy suit, strains and aches and great pains, mostly from a bleeding elbow and knee. But, or so it appeared, little in the way of sprains or broken bones. It was fortunate that he'd been able to protect his head within his arms, otherwise – looking at the rest of him – he wouldn't have escaped with his face or head uninjured. And that was not all. Besides his freedom, his reckless getaway had provided him the use of his legs again; the cable tie binding his ankles had snapped, unlike the one around his wrists, which remained firmly and achingly in place. A crowd was quickly gathering at the scene of the accident up the road, passing traffic slowed down and drivers stopped to gape. Still unseen, he painfully got to his feet, made sure he could walk, and stepped out onto the road from between the parked cars to scan for his missing shoe. It was nowhere to be seen, probably lost under one car or another, and he considered his options. He was never prepared for such a contingency. Although his surroundings didn't look unfamiliar, he had no idea where he was, nor, had his hands been unrestrained, did he have the means to make a phone call. But, given that so far he'd escaped notice, he never pondered remaining unconnected to the campervan or its absconded occupants. There'd be too many questions. Like his abductors before him, for now his concern was to get away unchallenged, no easy feat given the figure he cut, even if, London being London, the streets were blessed with enough drifting characters for him to possibly go unnoticed, all torn up, bloody and short of a shoe as he had become. If need be, his tied wrists could be concealed under his bag, but it was meagre consolation in the circumstances, unless he could hail a passing cab. Before anything else, he heard the sirens of approaching police cars, and at once started hobbling downhill away from the accident scene. It was then, grimacing with pain while moving as fast as he could towards a near side street, that his eyes caught sight of the road sign reading 'Cemetery Hill, N5'.

It happened that he was on the very road where he'd dropped Mrs Raspberry only two days earlier; number 49 he recalled.

The doors on his side of the road showed only even numbers. Mrs Raspberry's, it turned out, was to be found across the street and up the hill, beyond the police who had just stopped by the campervan. He would have to wait until the commotion subsided.

It was a good thing Mary Raspberry had an intercom which allowed her front door to be opened remotely, for if the expression on her face meant anything when Lombard stepped into her hallway, she'd likely never have let him into her home had she had a chance to take a look at him before hearing his disembodied voice over the intercom and felt delighted that the gallant gentleman she'd renewed acquaintance with while visiting Mr Raspberry's grave only a couple of days earlier had decided to call on her so soon after their serendipitous meeting. Dressed in a red silk robe and slippers, she was perturbed and shocked. Hardly helping matters, Pester stood poised inside the kitchen doorway prepared to scarper but standing its ground to growl at Lombard, a low groan Lombard never heard from a feline before. "Dear-me!" the woman uttered, bringing her hands to her mouth. "Thank you for letting me in, Mrs Raspberry. Please don't be alarmed by my appearance—I'm good. I just escaped an awkward situation and could do with the use of your bathroom and a knife or some pliers perhaps," he said, showing his bound wrists.

"What happened to you?" she demanded to know, uneasy,

peering at the blood coming through his torn trousers; "Dear me—You're bleeding!"

He followed her gaze and saw the blood from his knee dripping onto the parquet floor.

"You needn't worry, Mrs Raspberry; it looks worse than it is," he grimaced trying to grin; "No need to call the police or an ambulance or anything like that. Please, if I could free my hands and sort myself out. I apologize for spoiling your floor. I'll clean up as soon as—"

"You're still a private detective, right?" she queried, unsure.

"Yes—Indeed," he lied.

"And you just found trouble? While working? Is that so?"

"It is. Then again, it would be more exact to say trouble found me. Please, I won't take much of your time, Mrs—"

"Somewhere near my home?"

"You could say that. Down the street. I—"

"Well now!" Mary Raspberry exclaimed, somewhat reassured; "I did wonder when I heard you through the intercom. I know I invited you to drop by. But the truth be told, I never expected to see you again—Never mind so soon. There I was, for a moment flattered. Now—"

"Please, Mrs Raspberry," he cut her off; "Could I use your bathroom and borrow a knife?"

"Oh! Yes—Yes! But I won't have you bleed all over my floor. I think you better head for the garden and get out of your bloody clothes before I let you through to the bathroom. It's quite safe from prying eyes and you'll find a hosepipe there. And pay no attention to Pester's truculence—He's been growling at strangers ever since my neighbour castrated him but is a real softie, really."

And, slow on her feet, Mary Raspberry led Lombard to the garden door off the hallway and returned to her kitchen to fetch a knife. By the time she joined him outside, he was down to his underpants settled at a table in the shadow of an oak tree hosing down the blood from a deep laceration on his knee with cold water; he had yet to take off his jacket and shirt, which required first freeing his wrists. It took a little time to saw through the cable tie about his wrists with the large kitchen knife she handed him and then to peel off his jacket and shirt; only then, seated, he showered himself from his head down, swallowing some of the refreshing water. His elbow too was bleeding, but nothing like his knee; the skin was broken, raw from being grazed, he had more small gashes and scratches and chaffing here and there, and soon no doubt his skin would also show many bruises. He thanked Mary Raspberry again, adding "I'm good." She smiled, stood watching him in silence for as long as she could, admiring his physique, pensive, eventually left to return with a large towel and let him know where to find antiseptic cream, plasters and bandages in the bathroom before she headed back into the kitchen to make coffee.

Seated inside her rusty cast iron bathtub so as not to spoil the bathroom floor, Lombard took his time tending to his wounds, strapped enough bandage around his knee and elbow to control the bleeding, clad himself in his 'casual' uniform minus the missing Yves Saint Laurent shoes and pocketed his house and car keys, which, as he'd hoped, were in his bag. Thereupon he returned to the garden to gather his wet clothes and one shoe, stuffed the lot into the bag, insisted on cleaning the blood from the hallway floor – an offer Mrs Raspberry gladly accepted – and, all this done, settled in the woman's kitchen.

Mary Raspberry served him a mug of filter coffee she'd been keeping warm on the stove, and, as if walking on pins, settled across the table from him. He grinned on noticing a bottle of whiskey and another of Cognac together with a couple of glasses between them.

"Better?" she enquired.

"I'll live," he said.

"I much preferred you before; even all messed up," she remarked.

"I'm sorry."

"These don't suit you," she said, nodding towards his tweed jacket and linen shirt.

He sighed.

"Help yourself to some whiskey or Cognac. You look like you could do with a stiff drink. And pour me the same. It's not often that old Mary gets so much excitement these days."

"Thank you."

He poured them both a generous helping of Cognac, gulped his down and refilled his glass.

"Hair of the dog," he said; "Thank you for your help, Mrs Raspberry. I'm afraid in all my trouble my phone got damaged and I need to make an urgent call. I was wondering if I could trouble you further by using your phone?"

"Help yourself—I have two phones: one landline and one mobile," she replied; "You're welcome to either."

"Thank you. Either will do just fine. Do you happen to know the number for directory enquiries?"

She did, by heart, and he thanked her again and followed her directions to her landline phone in her sitting room – which he noted was rich with thick fabrics and shelves of books – and called directory enquiries. They had no contact number for Jane McGinnis, but had a landline number for a Joseph Aratoon, and Maude McGinnis answered when he called. "How good to hear from you now, Xavier," she said, making out his voice at once; "I was actually thinking of calling you, you know. We are probably going to leave London late next week and—"

Lombard was relieved to find she was well, and to learn the same of her elder daughter and Jane's two surviving girls. "I'm somewhat busy at the moment, Mrs McGinnis," he said casually, so as not to worry her; "But I need you to leave Jane's place at once. It's important. All of you. Pack some clothes and whatever you need for the day and leave the house. Go to a café or a park or anywhere you like until I call you again later. Can you give me your mobile number again? Are you still using Jane's phone?" Naturally, the woman, sounding very much worried, wished to know more, but he merely repeated himself, although opted to satisfy some of her under-standable curiosity against his better judgement by adding: "It looks like you may well have been right about the movie man, Mrs McGinnis." The revelation had a positive effect. Maude McGinnis agreed to his request. "Have you spoken about the man to your daughter or anyone else?" he now queried. "Why would I do a thing like that?" she replied. "Good—Keep it that way. It's important. Tell your daughter any story you like about why you need to be away from the house but don't make any mention of him."

"Come on now, Pester; you needn't be such a pussy! Mr Lombard is a good man," Mary Raspberry called when her cat took off growling with its ears down when Lombard returned to settle at the kitchen table to finish his coffee. He barely felt his aching body; his mind was thundering, running bedraggled with disagreeable thoughts, dark forebodings against his temples and forehead. But at least Maude McGinnis and her family were safe, for now.

"You look haunted," Mary Raspberry said.

He swallowed hard: "I guess I do. My apologies."

"I don't suppose you would entertain this old lady with your adventure? Who knows—Many a man has found solace sharing their misery with Mary."

He grinned, without thinking, spontaneously, grateful, then shook his head:

"This man has been a fool, Mrs Raspberry. Maybe he deserves his misery. But at least he's alive. I guess he's lucky."

"Lucky? Do you really think so?"

"Well—Had I been spared my current trouble, I'd never have enjoyed your warm hospitality," he smiled.

She frowned: "What's coming next, Mr Lombard: are we going to say grace, perhaps?"

"I'm sorry," he agreed.

"I know they say it isn't the same for men, but were you ever twenty, Mr Lombard?" she asked.

He nodded, confused.

"Then you're wrong, Mr Lombard. A handsome human specimen, you most certainly still are—But lucky you are not. I have lived—Probably twice as long and as much as you have—Lived the gruelling process of living, and can tell you that had you been lucky you'd still be twenty. *Tengo veinte años—J'ai vingt ans, Monsieur Lombard*. That's the way it is: had there ever been even a ghost of a God on this forsaken

328

earth, they'd have made me twenty forever. For their sake and the feasting of all creation. The world was eating out of my hand when I was twenty. That's being lucky, Mr Lombard. And had you met me when I was twenty, then you too would have been lucky. What happened to you today is not being lucky, but merely surviving."

With these last words, she'd turned stiffly towards the windows, eyeing the garden in the day's grey outdoors light. Lombard studied the deep lines carving her ancient skin, her razor-thin dry lips, her spare grey hair and deadwood-coloured brittle hands sticking out of her red silk robe. There was no arrogance emanating from her. Rather, proud modesty. In other circumstances, he may have pried, questioned her about "being twenty", instead he asked:

"I wonder if I could bother you for one more favour, Mrs Raspberry: you wouldn't happen to have men's shoes anywhere in the house I could borrow. One of mine is missing and I'd rather not go out looking—"

First, she said she did not, then thought and recalled there may be some working boots in the garage, among her husband's equipment. "Did I tell you my husband was a tree surgeon and died on the job? Never mind—It's of no importance. I haven't set foot in the garage for years, but it wouldn't surprise me if you did find some of his old boots down there. I keep meaning to tell Jack—My gardener—To help himself to anything he may need from it but it keeps slipping my mind."

A dark cavernous space doubling as a large workshop, the garage emerged as a dusty stale-smelling and cob-webbed tree-surgeon's Aladdin's cave. The walls were lined with well-arranged worktops and decked out with cupboards, shelves and hooks that accommodated chainsaws, handsaws, axes, ropes, harnesses, climbing gear, ladders, hand-tools, high-visibility reinforced protective suits, helmets, boots and yet more safety, rigging and tree felling equipment. It also contained gallon-sized jerricans and plastic containers, together with all kinds of accessories, from battery chargers to a wheeled engine-crane. Here was a tower of tyres and rims, next to a wheelbarrow, a leaf-blower and a medium-sized trailer. There stood a heavy-duty wood chipper, and finally, nearest to the door, sat an old four-wheel-drive Subaru Brat pickup truck with a two-seater cabin and aluminium-canopied back; it had to be a good thirty if not forty years old. Certainly, Lombard would have been at pains to recall the last time he'd come across one of these small pickup trucks. He grabbed a pair of thick leather boots, checked them for size; Mrs Raspberry's husband had been a big man, they were at least two sizes too large. Still, although mildewed, they would do; and he was about to exit this cocooned utilitarian cavern with his newly booted feet when a thought occurred to him. He paused, approached the pickup truck, opened the passenger door, found the release handle he was looking for under the dash. He heard the bonnet pop and made his way to the front. As he suspected, the engine pre-dated modern electronic sensor-fuel-injection systems, was powered by a simple single carburettor feeding four cylinders, an arrangement not all that different from his Saab's. The pickup had sat in its spot so long the tyres were flat and cracked beyond use, but a rudimentary inspection revealed the spare tyres and rims next to the wheelbarrow fitted it and were sound enough to be of service once inflated. The brake fluid reservoir was full, the brake and clutch pedals firm and springy, the gear stick travelling smoothly through its four-gear and reverse positions. It would have been futile to check whether the brakes were seized, or the battery so dead as to be beyond help, or the fuel in the tank and engine so old and stale it wouldn't fire; these were givens. But they were minor matters he knew he could see to with the help of the myriad tools and equipment at his disposal. The pickup truck was so old it was serviceable. Taking into account the functional rims and tyres, presuming the truck ran when last parked, all else being well it could take as little as a couple of hours to bring it back to life. He found the ignition key on a nail next to other keys hanging from a board by the door, satisfied himself that the fuel in the jerricans was stale, and returned upstairs to Mrs Raspberry who smiled on seeing her husband's old boots on his feet. She confirmed that the pickup was her husband's, and was last driven sixteen years earlier. "Marion was very fastidious about his equipment— Kept all his work machinery in tip-top condition. So I can't think of any reason why the old thing shouldn't be roadworthy if it can be made to start." "Would you sell it?!" "Sell it? Who on earth could possibly find use for such an old truck?" she returned nonplussed. "I would." "Well—Like I said: I keep meaning to tell my gardener to help himself to whatever's down there. It's doing little more than taking space and gathering dust. So you're welcome to any and all of it for all I care. But why on earth would you want such an old truck? You have a perfectly good old car already, I recall—Did the events that brought you to my door also cost you your car, Mr Lombard?"

The idea was still taking shape, wanting form and direction, too vague even for him to articulate coherently inside his head. But it concerned Avery Weyland, the Mayor of London, Transport for London, the police and countless private and public operators of surveillance devices and cameras used to monitor everything and everyone crisscrossing the city's roads and pavements. The very breathing space everywhere was being commandeered, committed to the recording of all for all time. No place remained for a man wishing to live or die as his own property to go to, and soon, in all likelihood, neither will there be anywhere left for him to run to. Yet, as hazy as it was, *dans la mesure du possible*, the idea forming in Lombard's head already warranted the provision of unrestricted movement – the task ahead would demand stealth. He was no wiser now about what lay behind Avery Weyland's actions than he had been at the beginning of this affair. All he knew was that – for reasons understood only by Avery Weyland himself – at some time in the past the producer-director had transferred relatively modest sums of money into Joseph Aratoon's bank account, more recently likely ordered Jane's murder, and just now nearly succeeded in getting him abducted – plausibly, for the purpose of having him killed too. This much he knew, or trusted he knew. For he had nothing, no evidence to connect the man to any crime, not unlike Jane before him, who it seemed had died for no good reason, unless sketchy clues centring on a couple of phone calls, a receipt for a map and a typed note were to be regarded dangerous information that called for the murder of a pregnant mother of four. Lombard had already considered the matter more times than he wished to: logic and common sense dictated that Avery Weyland would never risk his glittering existence to cover up what had to be at worst a somewhat minor deception. It made no sense. He certainly could not be held responsible for Joseph Aratoon's public suicide. As a matter of fact, were the producer-director ever made to come clean about the cash transfers into the dead man's bank account, it would cost him nothing to explain them away as just about anything that took his fancy: loans, gambling debts, gifts, cash for favours. And it would all go away. Yet Lombard was now left in no doubt the man was to blame for Jane's murder and his botched abduction. And even more perturbing perhaps, he also trusted the producer-director had no clue as to his true identity, or occupation, or what he knew or didn't know; only that, while drunk, he'd spoken of places where "men commit suicide and women and children can be killed in the time it takes to cross a road." It begged the question: what kind of a man gets himself involved in the business of abducting and killing strangers on the strength of such slim pickings? What was this one so frightened of? Was there anyone the producer-director was not prepared to visit his fear upon? Hurting others seemed to come easy to him.

For all that, for the time being only a fool would bet against his next setting his sights on Maude McGinnis. Having brought about the demise of one daughter and two granddaughters, there would be little to stop him doing the same to the grandmother were he to learn or even suspect that it was she who had set the man from *La Guyane* on his trail? Essentially, the man had now insured that Lombard was no longer free to let him be. Avery Weyland had secured his attention, and would be made to account for himself. The only taxing question regarded how to proceed. He knew the producer-director was leaving for China the next day. He knew that if anything were to happen to the man – were he to disappear or be found dead – it would take no time at all for his previous evening's dinner table company – not to mention Charlotte Lottway – to cast suspicion on 'Xavier Lagarde', the uncouth stranger from Cayenne who'd come from nowhere and seemingly disappeared into nowhere. Bearing in mind London's monitoring of all that moves, in an echo of Al Winston's fate, his photograph would then make the news, either as a 'suspect' or 'person of interest'; after all, like Maude McGinnis had herself pointed out, Avery Weyland wasn't just anybody; his story, were anything unseemly to happen to him, would get traction, be as newsworthy if not moreso than that of the Paragon reporter.

No. Unless he was prepared to let the man leave for China and wait for his return in a few weeks – but to what end and who could say what may happen in between? – Lombard had better come up with a plan to lay his hands on him now while avoiding further incriminating himself. This way, in the event that he found the means to spare the producer-director's life, he just might be spared the disruption of needing to 'disappear for good'. Were such a settlement to prove impracticable, 'ceasing to exist' would then become his only option, but still, to do so without also carrying the label of 'murderer' would make for less unpleasantness.

This is where Marion Raspberry's old Subaru pickup truck came in. Whatever he did next would have to be done without his driving his Saab, hiring a car or using public transport; for once his picture was broadcast and they who thought they knew him were to come forward, his every recorded action on or around the day of Avery Weyland's undoing would be scanned, analysed and evaluated.

It was just past twelve o'clock when he limped out of Mrs Raspberry's front door to get a cab from Highbury and Islington Corner to his Mews. He made a passable impression of a stowaway wise to uncertainty drifting on board a ship headed into the unknown, Mary Raspberry thought to herself. "I should be back in about an hour or so," he told her, after she agreed he could return to work on the pickup truck whenever he so wished.

TWENTY ONE

I guess it's a pity I rescued you.

In the event, he proved quite accurate; it took him a little under an hour and a half to make his way back to Highbury. And he put every minute of this time to use, proceeding in good and timely order. His bruised body hurt but not half as much as his ego, which was a good thing as he had work to do and little time to do it in.

First he showered and saw to his wounds, noting with relief that the bleeding from his knee and elbow had come under control. He dressed them with fresh bandages, made some coffee, retrieved the sim card from his broken phone and inserted it in an identical spare to call Charlotte Lottway. Since he'd thwarted Avery Weyland's plans by escaping his abductors, it was imperative that the man not panic, so that he would not carry out more mischief or go into hiding for fear of his escaped victim's retaliation. Lombard also needed to know his whereabouts. In view of her behaviour, it seemed doubtful whether Charlotte Lottway was implicated in his deadly endeavours, but regardless, he figured he could still take advantage of the producer-director's cluelessness as to his identity.

The girl could not entirely conceal her surprise on hearing his voice. She sounded reticent, yet intrigued enough not to hang up or be too unfriendly. She'd heard of his previous evening's performance. "Yes—I was never one to handle the demon drink," he said; "That is partly why I'm calling, Lottie—To apologize. I'd call Avery but I haven't got his number. In any event, I'm afraid there's another reason for this call. I was mugged—Well, kidnapped—Earlier this morning and—" "Oh my God! Kidnapped! Is that what you said?" "Uh-huh. Three men in a campervan. They must have followed me from my hotel—They Tasered me, threw me into their van and robbed me. But I'm good—Made my escape with barely a few bruises and reported them to the police." "Oh my God! This is terrible. Are you alright?" "I am. Thank you, Lottie; it's good of you to ask. But I'm afraid it has changed things somewhat. That is the other reason I'm calling. I won't bore you with the details, but this unfortunate episode means I must leave the UK at once and need to call off our project for now. Force majeure, as they say. I'm very sorry." She took the news well, made no attempt to feign surprise or disappointment, sounded pragmatic; evidently, as he'd guessed, his drunken performance had put a damper on things. "I'm very sorry about that," he said again; "If you'd be so good, I'd very much like to apologize to Avery in person. Do you know how I might get hold of him? It was so kind of him to invite me to his mother's, I—" Tactfully, she avoided giving him her employer's number, willing only to get across that the man was busy in meetings all day, while promising she would pass on his "news and apology" when they met later that afternoon before he left for home to pack for his trip to Beijing the next day. "You mean his home in the New Forest?" he probed. "Ahem—No. Here, in London," she said, uneasy. "Right." He told her he understood, apologized again and thanked her.

Now, he went online to study the street view of 'The Orchard' in Downshire Hill, the producer-director's listed Georgian London home. Predictably, it turned out to be a well-presented three storey property. It was set far back from the road behind a lush front garden beyond high cast iron railings. A similarly lush but much larger garden lay at the back of the property. Of particular interest was the fact that the house stood fully detached, with access to its back garden via a narrow passage to one side and, to the other, a gravel driveway. Also, the green front garden was presided over by what he made out to be a large sweeping Magnolia tree, and the plan which had begun to form in his mind back at Mrs Raspberry's place now came together, the parts falling into place, effortlessly.

To track down a working Subaru Brat pickup truck identical in all but colour to the one in Mary Raspberry's garage from an online Classic Cars for sale site took little time; in the case of the one that piqued his interest, the owner had even found it pertinent to provide a film of the pickup being driven along rural lanes to demonstrate its roadworthiness, thus conveying the likelihood it was currently insured; test certificate and road licence needn't be of concern given that it was old enough to be exempt from both. It also proved simple enough to persuade his garage of many years to agree to overlook the provision of registration papers in order to make him a set of number plates cloned from this online vehicle; whether they believed him or not, his word that the plates were to serve to collect an old pickup just purchased online also nudged them to agree to send them to him at once by taxi; there were still places where years of loyal customership counted for something. With these matters seen to, he became free to turn his attention to the task of packing the few possessions he owned and regarded as important into a couple of suitcases; it amounted to a few items of clothing, the encoded phone, fax machine and laptop used to communicate with Monroe, his personal laptop, a few bundles of currencies, three sets of fake identity papers and credit cards, together with the paperwork relating to Jane and Joseph Aratoon which he decided to put in there for no other reason than that he'd failed to get rid of them. This was not the first time he'd had to prepare for the eventuality of never returning 'home', and following the pattern of previous occasions, freshly suited and cufflinked, he drove the locked suitcases nearby to *Monsieur Chose*, safe in the knowledge that its helpful proprietor would transport them for safekeeping to his personal residence until further notice. Then he drove back home, parked his Saab in its usual spot, returned inside to collect a couple of mobile phones, a spare suit and shirt he'd kept, a cufflinks and watch set, two wads of cash and credit cards, his 'Lombard' passport and a spare, his Beretta, its silencer and a carton of ammunition, and left by foot for Marylebone High Street to hail a cab carrying the same bag he'd had earlier, which was large enough to also accommodate the cloned registration plates. Whatever fate had in store, his Mews home would be in good hands; he had long since transferred the deeds to Ali's name, extracting her consent for this by the candid revelation that "I'm all there is; it would be a shame for such a place to pass to the British Crown were anything to happen to me." For now though, he would hang on to his house and car keys for a while longer. It would have been premature to post them to her Cumbrian address. He'd already determined that, were his undertaking to get the old Subaru to come to nothing, he'd return for his Saab.

He could have made it back to Highbury even sooner than he did had he not requested that his cab driver detour via a garage to purchase a car battery and a gallon jerrican of petrol before being dropped off around the corner from Cemetery Hill, leaving it to him to haul the fuel, battery and full bag to number 49, a considerable ordeal at the best of times, the slow painful paying of a ransom price in his aching condition. But it would prove unnecessary to return to retrieve his Saab. Once back in Mary Raspberry's garage, all in all, it took him about another hour and a half to drain and refill the Subaru's coolant and fuel systems, part-dismantle and clean its carburettor, loosen and refit the calipers and brake pads, sand the brake disks, check the lights and indicators, swap the flat cracked tyres for the spares in the garage, and get the truck to come to life and smoothly move back and forth a few inches, sounding as good as it must have the day it was last driven. Only now did he loosen the bolts securing the truck's number plates, although not yet ready to swap them for his newly-acquired clones – Mrs Raspberry needn't be implicated in his coming foray were he to be caught on camera driving out of her garage – and it was also only now that he turned his attention to the cargo bed beneath the truck's aluminium rear canopy. It was dark and quite busy in there. His eyes swept over a

'Man at Work' sign, some axes, handsaws, ropes, a couple of chainsaws and yet more loose equipment along with work boots, gloves and a crumpled and stained high-visibility tree surgeon's protective suit. The jacket seemed intact but one trouser leg was visibly slashed around the thigh area. He guessed the staining was old blood; that this was the work gear Mrs Raspberry's husband wore the day he died. The emergency services had stripped him at the scene to give him first aid and some of his workwear ended up tossed into the back of the pickup, forgotten. Somewhere in there also lay a bright orange helmet with a full-face protective black nylon mask and ear muffs. He considered emptying the cargo bed, but then opted to remove only the stained jacket and trousers, folded them over the back of the only chair in the garage and replaced them with a spare kit noticed earlier. The protective helmet had just given him an idea.

In her private way, Mary Raspberry expressed concern when he returned upstairs. This was sparked by her failure to locate the Subaru's logbook. She'd heard the sound of the engine from her sitting room, but now feared she'd caused Lombard to waste his time bringing it back to life. He reassured her it was unimportant, that being over forty years old it could legally be taken on the road without road tax or test certificate. "But how are you going to insure or prove it belongs to you without the registration documents?" "Well, we're going to sign a sale agreement stating that I agree to purchase the pickup today 'as-is', without registration document. Leave it to me, Mrs Raspberry." "If that's what you want—But I shall go on looking for it. You'll have to call me or come again in a few days, when I've had more time." "That's fine. Will do, Mrs Raspberry. Here—"

She would not accept payment for the truck, adamant that she had no use for it, nor need for money, that to know anything from the garage which had belonged to her husband would be of good use again was recompense enough, making it clear that to importune her further on this would be futile and cause for exasperation. In that manner he deferred to her wish, kept his money and refrained from mentioning the items in the back of the pickup he'd hoped to retain.

"Well," she said, peering at the clock on her mantlepiece; "Well done you! Not even four o'clock yet! Early enough to sort out that sale agreement over a farewell drink. I'm afraid longhand's become such a gruelling chore for my poor hands these days that I'll have to ask you to write it. And keep it short. I do like your company, but duty calls—I need to prepare for my five o'clock commitment."

He was in some hurry himself now, his mind racing ahead, yet reckoned he owed it to her to spare her a few minutes as she slowly shuffled to the kitchen table they had settled at earlier. She pointed him towards some paper and a pen while pouring Cognac into their glasses, noticed Pester was nowhere to be seen and whispered "Poor Pester".

Lombard attended to the sale agreement as soon as he joined her at the table. He kept it short:

'This is to acknowledge that on this date (____), I Mary Raspberry of 49 Cemetery Hill, London N5, gifted the Subaru Brat (reg No: ____) previously owned by my deceased husband Marion Raspberry "As-Is" without logbook or any warranty implied or expressed to Mr Xavier Lombard.'

"When mercy seasons justice," she said to herself, wistful while observing him writing.

"Sorry?"

"I guess it's a pity I rescued you," she remarked.

"Is it?"

She grinned, with a hint of sadness:

"Is it not?"

He frowned:

"Why should you think such a thing, Mrs Raspberry?"

She took a deep sigh:

"You're all mended and pleasantly suited and going away now—Leaving old Mary to her dreaded dreary daily dying battles."

He grinned, for the first time noticed how glazed and dark and sad her eyes appeared:

"Here," he said, sliding two copies of the agreement across the table; "One for me—One for you. If you could sign both."

She smiled, put her glasses onto her nose and signed with a heavy hand, saying:

"Do be an angel before you leave, Mr Lombard—When you drive the van out, I'll need you to come back in to double lock the garage door from the inside."

"Of course," he said, already online on his phone to see how to buy temporary insurance cover for the Subaru.

At 5 p.m. sharp, decorously rouged, in a clean blue silk robe, Mary Raspberry settled in her high-back leopard-skin armchair, rested her hand on Pester who had already assumed a curled-up position on the crimson velvet vanity stool, and looked out her bay window across the road towards number 54.

"Poor pester," she said; "Mary had a lot of excitement today and you had none. You didn't like it, did you?"

A few minutes earlier, in Hampstead NW3, kitted out in her husband's old tree-surgeon's protective suit and helmet, Lombard had double parked on Downshire Hill in front of 'The Orchard'; prior to this he'd also stopped in a secluded spot near the Heath to switch the Subaru's original registration plates for the clones.

Never before had the girl who opened the door holding a grubby toddler on her hip seen anything that resembled Lombard; the bemused expression on her pretty face said it all. Likewise, nor had the toddler in her arms, who stared wide-eyed at him, bewildered and perplexed, as if at a frightening creature from another world. More than by way of the two-sizes-too-large reinforced high-visibility full body outfit he wore over his suit – which lent him volume in addition to a ragged officious look – the effectiveness of his disguise was truly down to the large dirty chainsaw hanging from his hand – minus his wedding band – and his begrimed face inside the nylon-masked and ear-muffed protective helmet

340

which concealed most of his head. Indeed, for all her surprise, rather than feeling distrust or seeing immediate and present danger, the girl appeared reassured that anyone so generously noticeable and dangerously equipped could only qualify as safe and trustworthy. And his contemplating the great Magnolia tree which commanded the front garden, together with the pickup truck with its flashing side-lights double-parked on the road just outside the railing fence completed the illusion. Then again, the conspicuous alarm box and three security cameras at the front of the house would have afforded her a sense of safety whoever or whatever had come to her door.

Lombard was prepared for several scenarios; anything from no one being home to coming upon Avery Weyland's wife could have followed from his ringing the doorbell. The only given was that, if Charlotte Lottway could be trusted, Avery Weyland would not be home. He wasn't. And when the girl asked "How can I help you?", Lombard put on some exaggerated generic foreign accent to say he was there to fell the Magnolia tree. "The tree is dangerous. Health and safety and all that, yes? Is the home owner Mister Avery here?" Now, the girl looked alarmed, peered at the Magnolia tree which could hardly pass as dangerous, at his chainsaw, and revealed she was the au-pair and that Avery was not expected until later and his wife even later than that. "Okay. It is okay if he is not here. He asked for it to be cut down so. I will cut the tree now, yes?" "Oh—No! Wait! I don't believe—Are you certain you have the right place?" "The Orchard? Downshire Hill? It is here, no?" She confirmed it was, but remained dubious anyone would wish the lush Magnolia to be felled and advised she knew nothing of the business and had better call the owner of the house at once. A moment later she returned to the door, still holding the toddler, and handed a phone over to Lombard. Avery Weyland was at the other end, his deep voice betraying his outrage. "Hello?" said Lombard; "I am Ricardo. You are Avery?" "I am indeed," came the reply; "What the hell are you doing at my house, Ricardo? With a chainsaw! Intent on cutting down our Magnolia, if I understand correctly! Is this a joke or—" "Oh no, Mister Avery—It is not a joke. I am here."

"Then you must have the wrong place." "The Orchard? Downshire Hill? Mister Avery? It's right, yes?" Lombard declared calmly. "Yes." "Good. I have the paper in the car that you requested for the tree to be felled, Mister Avery. Health and safety issues—Correct?" "What?—How?—You must have the wrong address or be out of your mind, man!" "There is no need to be rude, Mister Avery. I'm sure we can sort things out in a civil manner. I am only doing my job. In fact this is my last job of the day." "I'm not being rude—Who sent you? What company do you work for?" "Arborist Care Tree Service, Wimbledon." "Wimbledon! What would I—I never even heard of Arborist-whatever-it-is! Can you give me your boss or office number so we can sort out this ridiculous story?" "For sure. But it is past five o-clock, Mister Avery. The office is closed. Everyone is gone home. I work until six and then I go home too." "Then give me your boss's mobile number. You must have a number for him in case of emergencies." "My boss is a she, Mister Avery. And I'm afraid I'm not allowed to share her private number. I have to cut the tree now or—" "No. Do not touch the tree, you hear! Do not touch it. Go home now and whatever fuckup this is, it will be sorted out tomorrow, okay? I'm warning you, I'll send the police to my house if you don't leave at once or if you touch my tree, you understand! And sue you and your outfit." "Look, Mister Avery. I am told you want the tree down. You say you do not. How—" "I am not Mister Avery, by the way. I am Mr Wey-land." "Oh! Then I'm speaking to the wrong man. Mister Avery is the person I need to speak to." "I am Avery Wey-land!" "Right. So you say I am speaking to the right person—Mister Avery?" "I—I don't fucking know! But I'm telling you again: I don't know what this is all about but do not touch my tree, you understand?" "Look, Mister Avery, if you can give me something in writing that you have changed your mind about the tree, I would be happy to go home, okay? It is a beautiful tree really. But now I am here, if I leave not doing the job they are going to dock money from my pay and charge me for—" "I can send you something by phone." "That is not good, Mister Avery. I need a signature and—" "For fuck's sake—Where do you people—Just stay there," Avery Weyland cut him off; "Can you wait fifteen minutes?" "I guess I can." "Good—Just stay there. Don't touch the fucking tree, all right!" "Okay. If you are the house owner and that is what you want I will wait, Mister Avery. But do not be too long, please."

He heard the man growl 'Fucking idiot!' before he hung up.

"Mister Avery sounds like an angry man," he said to the au-pair, handing her back the phone; "He says he is coming. I cannot park here. Tell him I will be waiting for him around the corner in Willow Road, yes? Can I leave my chainsaw here by the tree until everything is sorted?"

The girl shrugged, unsure, and he left the chainsaw under the tree and drove the pickup around the corner to park on a yellow line along the kerb in Willow Road, no more than five or so yards from Downshire Hill. He stepped out onto the kerb, opened the cargo bed tailgate, retrieved some equipment from under the aluminium canopy, including a thick tarpaulin and ropes which he put out on the tarmac, set up the 'Man at work' sign behind the pickup, made space along the length of the cargo bed, returned the tarpaulin to it, stretching and flattening it out over the floor, and, keeping the nylon-masked and ear-muffed helmet on his head, strolled back into Downshire Hill to settle about fifty yards from 'The Orchard'.

Some Londoners who can afford it, prefer the comfort of taxis to driving or using public transport to get around town, and it made sense that Avery Weyland would be one of them. In consideration of the fact that a Mercedes and a Land Rover sat in 'The Orchard's driveway, Lombard indeed guessed that, unless the producer-director used a bicycle, taxis likely provided his chief means of transport when in town, leading him to anticipate that the man would turn up in such convenience. He was correct; less than ten minutes after parking the pickup, he caught sight of Avery Weyland climbing out of a black cab that pulled up across the road from 'The Orchard'. By all appearances, the man was livid, had come in such haste he was in shirtsleeves with nothing but a phone in his hand. Presently, Lombard waved and called before the other could make it across the pavement to his front garden. In the grey light of the late afternoon, Avery Weyland could not fail to see the large helmeted figure in a high-visibility outfit waving at him, and called back at once:

"Ricardo?"

"Yes, Mister Avery! Hello!" Lombard called back; "It is me! Please come. I am parked here around the corner on a yellow line with the paper for you to sign," he went on to direct the man, turning back at once to disappear around the corner into Willow Road before the other could object.

A moment later, he stood poised by the open tailgate of the pickup with a pen in his hand as a frustrated Avery Weyland stomped towards him, booming in his deep voice:

"My God, man! Honestly! Talking of nonsense. I really wish you'd not made me come all the way here. I have better things to do, you know!"

"I am only doing my job, Mister Avery. I do not want no trouble," Lombard said inside his helmet; "Here," he went on, offering the pen which Avery Weyland involuntarily accepted, a man on auto-pilot in a hurry to bring an unpleasant business to a close; "If you sign here for me, you keep your tree, yes?" he added, pointing at nothing on the open pickup tailgate.

"Sign what? Where—" Avery Weyland said, leaning slightly forward, peering at nothing on the tailgate, now all flustered puzzlement.

And, before he knew what was happening, Lombard grabbed him by his belt and shoulder and brought him down to slam his forehead hard on the open tailgate, twice, then hoisted his inert body off his feet and shoved it onto the open tarpaulin under the cargo bed canopy. It happened so fast, had any onlooker been nearby, they'd probably have noticed none of it; only a whirl of movement. In the next moment, jumping to his knees on the cargo bed, Lombard strapped the man's arms and legs behind his back with one of the climbing ropes, shoved a glove deep into his mouth – which he secured with more rope – wrapped the trussed-up body in the tarpaulin, shoved this package deep in the shadow under the canopy and crawled in to tether the whole to a hook on the back of the front cabin. A minute later, anyone peering into the back of the pickup would never have guessed that a man lay tied up beyond all the tree-cutting equipment in there. Lombard picked up and switched off the phone the man had dropped when he knocked him unconscious, and returned to double park in front of 'The Orchard' to retrieve the chainsaw from under the Magnolia tree. When the au-pair opened the door to enquire what was happening, the toddler was still in her arms:

"Did you see Avery?" she asked.

Since the man had never made it to his door, it appeared the girl was unaware of his coming.

"No," he said; "I trust Mister Avery is a very busy man. But it is too late for me now," he went on, picking up the chainsaw; "So no more issues. For now the tree lives, ha-ha," he laughed inside the protective helmet.

The girl smiled: "Oh! That's good."

"Yes. Everybody is happy. What is your name?"

"My name? I'm Louise," she blurted out; "Why?"

"And is that beautiful child in your arms Mister Avery's?" he went on asking, ignoring her.

"Yes."

"Good. It was nice to meet you, Louise. Take good care now."

"Ahem—Yes. You too."

When he stopped in a quiet street off the Finchley Road soon afterwards, he shuddered, briefly, swallowed hard and took a few deep breaths. His mind had flowed into absolute lucidity, a trick he fancied had to be that of a conjurer in the middle of performing his greatest illusion. The time for improvisation was over. Hitherto purpose had partly relied on improvisation. From here on, arrangements depended on aforethought. He had a good idea of what would ensue once Avery Weyland was declared missing. Questions, confusion, presumptions, speculation; the predictable calls to hospitals and friends and family. Before long though, all would be focussed on just one thing: the tree surgeon's apparition in Downshire Hill at around the time the man was last seen and heard, and his phone had gone offline. The ever-dependable eagle-eyed Mayor of London's and many other monitoring devices would pick up the Subaru, and track it, and not without justification after it was noted that it was fitted with cloned registration plates. Thereafter, the odds for or against a link being established between the helmeted tree surgeon, the man from Cayenne and, ultimately, Lombard, would be pure conjecture. But Lombard knew enough of wheels turning, procedures, tedium and density to trust it would be at least the next day before the story developed to that point, reckoning this gave him a twelve hours head start, enough of a window for what he needed to do.

He checked his watch: it was nearing 6 p.m. First, he removed the sim and battery from Avery Weyland's phone. Then, mindful to keep his helmet on, climbed out of the pickup to check on his captive at the rear, reaching under the canopy to bump the tarpaulin with an axe. The man inside thrashed about, sent out a high-pitched squeal through the glove in his mouth. There were a few things he thought he might say to him, but he opted for silence; it was now Avery Weyland's turn to be tied up in a moving vehicle not knowing what lay in store for him, which was guaranteed to have him well scared, for he had no idea who his abductor was, and unlike Lombard earlier that day, was not dealing with amateurs affording him means of escape. Next he made his way back to the driver's seat and took off his helmet. He switched on his phone to make an anonymous call to the estate agent of the Dawlish property he'd visited nearly two weeks earlier; it remained for sale. Then he checked the map, estimated a four-hour drive would get him there. Then he reviewed the train timetable between London and Exeter and called Maude McGinnis, who answered at once in an anxious voice. Unsurprisingly, she'd been waiting for his call all afternoon. He let her know that it was now safe for her and her kin to return to Jane's house, but before she could ask questions added that he wanted her to catch the 21:04 from Paddington to Exeter, where he'd be collecting her when she arrived at 23:45.

"Be there. It's a one-time chance for you to possibly find out what happened to Jane, Mrs McGinnis. Keep this phone with you at all times so I can reach you if need be. And make no mention to anyone—And I mean absolutely anyone, you understand—of where you are going."

"You mean today? Tonight?"

"Indeed, Mrs McGinnis. I trust I'll be seeing you later."

And that was it. He felt calm if not a little weak when he turned the Subaru's ignition on again. He realized he'd eaten nothing since breakfast at The Beaumont, and promised himself he'd get some food when he stopped to fill up at the next petrol station.

"Thank you, Mrs Raspberry," he said, listening to the pickup truck engine purr before pulling away; "And Mr Raspberry," he added.

If not for his nearly getting lost in the darkness along the flat featureless country lanes lined with caravans and holiday parks that environed his destination, the drive proved thankfully uneventful, enough so that while still on his way his mind had relaxed enough for him to mull over whether – contingent upon the events about to unfold and subject to other provisos – whether to replace his Saab with the Subaru Brat. It had only four gears, comfortably reaching just about 80 miles per hour, but it struck him as practical, dependable and sturdy, to say nothing of its test, road tax and emissions-charge exemption; a steadfast donkey to a steed. On this account, thoughts of the Madeiran donkey visited his mind again; such tricks the head plays when no longer occupied with pressing questions.

TWENTY TWO

It would appear that the both of us are now people in
need of rescuing, Xavier.

Under the starlight, the property with its eight acres of
land was much like he recalled: a long rough private track
left the road to lead between paddocks and past trees and a
large pond to the isolated two-storey stone cottage and its
side garage. His was the only car around when his wheels
crunched to a stop on the loose gravel in front of the cottage's dark windows. He knew the place was free of security
paraphernalia, all the same he gave it time before climbing out
of the pickup to make his way to the back of the building
where he broke in through a window. He used his phone as a
torch, not wanting to turn the lights on; he was alone.

Avery Weyland's trussed up body hit the ground with a
thump when he yanked it from the cargo bed and let it drop to
the garage floor among Mrs Raspberry's husband's equipment.
By now, he'd discarded his protective outfit and boots, was
much the lighter for it in his suit and shoes. In the way that
no country Lombard had ever visited had really come out the
better of its geography, few if any men he'd ever come across
had proved the better of their place in society. For the present,
Avery Weyland had been robbed of his place in society, and
nothing good was left of him. In the light from Lombard's
phone, he was hog-tied, too numb to move, had soiled himself
and clearly been crying. He groaned, tried to speak behind the
glove dripping with blood and saliva stuffed in his mouth,
managed only a sorry nasal bleat. The sight of him made it

hard to imagine that so wretched a lifeform had ever been the better of anyone or anything, and Lombard found it necessary to look away from the man before grabbing the length of rope between his wrists and ankles to drag him groaning and whining across the flagstone floor into the nearby kitchen to tether him to the Aga he knew to be there. Then he went to look out the window and, satisfied he was still alone, pulled the curtains and turned on the light.

"You're a fool, Avery," he said standing some way away from the man who winced against the sudden brightness of the electric light; "You should have let me be. We'd never have met again if you'd let me go on my way this morning. Now, you might say that I've taken you up on it: kidnapping. Only, unlike your friends, I'm not going to let you get away."

Avery Weyland twisted his neck to look up in his direction, and for all his upside-down sorry state, still managed to look aghast on seeing Lombard. Evidently, the call 'Xavier Lagarde' had made to Charlotte Lottway stating he believed himself the victim of a chance mugging and was leaving the country had hit home; the man must have experienced relief that he would not be held to account for his botched kidnapping, come to think that he'd worried unnecessarily about the man from *La Guyane*, quite possibly had even berated himself for having been so mistaken as to react in the manner he had.

"Uh-huh, Avery. It's me. You see, Jane Aratoon was an old acquaintance of mine. She asked me to look you up when she caught on to you—Your note and cash donations to her husband. She suspected you of bad things. And to tell you the truth, I thought she was crazy. I mean, a man like you mixed up with the likes of Joseph Aratoon—Let alone so possessed as to have his wife and children murdered? You could have fooled me and let me go, Avery. But—Like they say—Like the dog who returns to his vomit, so a fool repeats his folly."

Again, the man tried to speak through his glove, wide-eyed and shaking his head. But Lombard cared nothing for what he had to say.

"Take it easy," he went on; "I may not hurt or kill you. It will be God's pleasure to decide your fate. What I mean is that

I shall give God's work a chance before I do the Devil's. So, if I were you, I'd start thinking how to give a good account of myself."

And he checked his watch – it was just past eleven – switched off the kitchen light and made his way back to the Subaru in the garage. Once settled in the cabin under the pale glow of the courtesy light, he called Maude McGinnis who, providing she was on her way, wouldn't be arriving for another half hour.

She answered in a worried but sober voice. He was glad she was on the train. He paid no attention to her questions, told her to get a taxi from Exeter Station to Sandhills Holiday Park on the Exeter Road and request to be dropped at the park's entrance. "Don't go in—Once there, start walking along the road; it doesn't matter what direction. If the taxi driver asks questions before dropping you off, say you've come to spend time with caravanning relatives. I'll be waiting for you. Call this number if you have any problem."

Sandhills Holiday Park was a ten-minute drive from the cottage. He'd spotted it on his way in, full of caravans busy with late-night holiday makers and, from what he could make out, a camera-free gateway. A rudimentary survey of the roadside also suggested an absence of cameras between the Park and the cottage; but it was dark and he was driving, so there was no telling. But he wasn't even sure if any of this mattered. For now, via his phone, he thought to use the time he had left alone to book a one-way ferry ticket from nearby Plymouth to Santander in Spain leaving late afternoon the next day, which called for the perusal of the spare passport in his bag; he would be Mr Gabriel Bleich from tomorrow on. And this done, he inspected his Beretta, made sure it was loaded, fitted the silencer to the barrel and returned it to the bag, which he took outside through the open garage doors and hid under some brush by a tree a short distance from the cottage. He got hold of some mud from the edge of the pond, smudged the pickup's registration plates just enough to make them nearly illegible, and drove off shutting the garage doors behind him after making certain Avery Weyland had remained put tethered to the Aga.

In this way the mystery of Joseph Aratoon's money and the death of his wife, two of his daughters and his one unborn child was about to be resolved. And how the revelation would come about, and with what consequence, would largely be due to Maude McGinnis's own faith and resolve once Lombard afforded her the remedy of seeking the truth, even though this remedy is one she would never have adopted of her own free will. Yet, once it was furnished, it is also true that she found herself unable to pass up the opportunity, both as a mother and a Christian. Lombard had always made it his business to know human nature when it came to the basic instinct for retribution ingrained in the human spirit.

He was already waiting in the darkness by the side of the road when Maude McGinnis started walking uneasily away from the bright lights of the caravan park entrance as instructed. She made no attempt at small talk when he cruised beside her so that she could join him in the pickup's two-seater cabin, but rather behaved as befitted a woman mindful of and dreading the as-yet undefined unpleasantness she guessed awaited her.

Like the previous times they met, she wore her mourning like a storm, all black dress, black coat, handbag, shoes and rings under her eyes, and gleaming crucifix against her breast. It struck him that she looked the part he had in store for her to play. He hardly cared for what he was about to do, but had told no lie when advising Avery Weyland that he would give God's work a chance before his doing the Devil's. He was so bone-tired of everything that, had the present and the future belonged to him alone, he'd have skipped God's part. All and sundry were more than welcome to God! Still, he trusted Maude McGinnis had broad-enough shoulders to be both God's soldier and her own master.

"Xavier," she sighed.

"How are you, Mrs McGinnis?" he greeted her; "Any problems on the way?"

"Well now—Jane, you said—" she commented, sighing heavily

351

again, unsure what else to say in such strange circumstances, or possibly hinting that since he had caused her to come so far so late by way of pledging she would learn what had happened to her daughter, it was really for him to speak.

So he did speak, and to the point, while heading back to the cottage nearby, but only after requesting that she hand over Jane's phone and confirm she carried no other communication devices, had used no other phone to contact him, and had spoken to no one of him or Avery Weyland or where she had come to tonight. He removed the sim card and battery from Jane's phone while driving.

"You were right, Mrs McGinnis—That movie man Avery Weyland is responsible for what happened to your daughter. I'll be brief: last night I inadvertently let on in his company that I knew of Jane and her husband and this morning he attempted to have me kidnapped—And I suspect killed too, if I hadn't got away. Now, I have no idea of the whys or hows—Know no more than what you and I have already discussed. I have nothing concrete to implicate him in Jane's murder, which means the police could and would do little if you were to seek their help. Besides, as you said, he is not just anybody. For all that, I'm positive he is the person responsible for your daughter and grandchildren's deaths, Mrs McGinnis. He was in Venice at the time, so I suspect he hired others to do his work, probably the same lot who snatched me this morning."

"How can you be so sure of his guilt if—"

"Because, like I said, he came after me when I let on I knew of Jane. Trust me, Mrs McGinnis. Somehow it's all tied up with the money in your son-in-law's account. For reasons only he knows, this man's prepared to stop at nothing because of it. His actions are that of a frightened man—A very frightened man. There's got to be a very good reason why he was terrified enough of your daughter to want to silence her—And then came after me when he realized I knew of her. Now ask yourself, what's to stop him coming after you or the rest of your family tomorrow if he suspects you too may be a threat? Still, you needn't worry. He's not in a position to hurt anybody.

He was due to fly to China in the morning but I kept him from leaving. Right now, I have him all tied up waiting for you."

"What?" she exclaimed, dismayed.

"You heard me."

"But—Why would you—"

"Because I made it so. Because I thought you'd want a chance to have him tell you the answers to your questions, Mrs McGinnis?"

"Me?"

"You."

"How? Where?"

"Here!"

"Here! But how—"

"Your words, Mrs McGinnis: get him to tell you the whole story. And you're going to tape him telling it too. And if you do well, you'll have the confession you need in order to deliver him to the police and let the law take its course. And just in case he proves uncommunicative, I'll have you have a gun to either kill him or convince him otherwise—Or both. And if he proves uncommunicative and it also proves beyond you to kill a man who murdered your daughter and grandchildren, I will put you safely back on the train to London and as sure as I'm talking to you I'll kill him myself for what he did to me this morning. And if it comes to that, in a day, or a week or a month or a year from now—Trust me on this too—You or part of you will thank me for it. Do you understand, Mrs McGinnis?"

No reply came, so he went on:

"Well—I'm sure you do understand, so I will take your silence as a 'yes'. Now all you need to think about is how you wish to proceed. Then again, if you so wish, we can turn around and get you back to the station now—But that would do nothing to spare him from my killing him," he concluded, veering off the road onto the track to the cottage.

"So what's your pleasure?" he asked, finding the place as quiet and dark as he'd left it when he came to a stop in front of the garage doors; "And let me add one more thing in case it helps sway your mind one way or another: I've gone to a fair amount of trouble to give you this opportunity."

In the darkness of the now silent car, Maude McGinnis turned to peer at him as if he was madness, and she was his mayhem, too stunned to speak. They were so close to each other in the small cabin that he could see that, deep beyond her trepidation, she was thinking, quietly weighing her desperate options, holding fast to her handbag with both hands as if to a life vest.

"He's here. In the cottage, Mrs McGinnis. What's your pleasure?" he asked again.

She turned away to stare at the cottage:

"If—If you are right—If she died because—Then I am to blame for sure," she said, perturbed; "I am to blame."

He'd anticipated this; it had always been guilt that had led her to come knocking at his door to commandeer his help: "The greatest gift is God Himself—Right, Mrs McGinnis? Like we discussed already: Jane was always going to do what Jane wanted to do; with or without you. By the way, I believe I forgot to mention that if you did kill him, I'd also take you back to the station—And take care of the leftovers before disappearing myself. So, what's your pleasure?"

The woman never answered. Instead, she turned to look out her passenger window, then, after keeping him waiting for a good while, she started inspecting the cabin around her:

"My husband used to have a truck just like this when we met", she muttered to herself, and presently she climbed out of the cabin to make her way across the gravel to a nearby corrugated shed where she started to pace to and fro with her head down, her hands still clasped onto the rim of her handbag; no longer a storm, but a quiet dark temple of torment in the starlight. It would have been wrong to rush her, so Lombard gave her time, remained in the pickup in front of the garage, wondering what would happen were she to ask to be taken back to the train station. The last train to London was long gone by this late hour. Like he'd had to the time he'd visited this part of the world, she would have to book into a hotel, lie the night awake with her thoughts enveloped in the peculiar silence of provincial towns. He ended up closing his eyes. He would give her five minutes to fight her wars, then drive off, if need be leave her alone with Avery Weyland.

It had seemed an eternity but he would realize at some later time that Maude McGinnis had needed no more than a couple of minutes to make up her mind, and she also surprised him somewhat when she spoke again after climbing back into the cabin beside him:

"Are you sure about this?" she asked.

"Are you asking me?"

"I mean—Are you sure you wish to go ahead? Whatever the outcome?"

Indeed, her voice was all determination now, but she still looked very much dark and dismayed when he took a moment to scrutinize her. And she may well have been crying too.

"Why do you think I got you to come all the way here?" he replied.

"Will I be alone with him?"

"Uh-huh."

"He's in there?" she asked, running her eyes over the cottage.

"Yes. I must warn you, though—He's had a rough time; he looks a sorry sight."

"I'm a country farmer's wife and daughter, Xavier," she returned.

"Right. So I assume you may also be familiar with firearms."

"If it has a barrel and a trigger, I am indeed."

Lombard suddenly fell prey to a sense of déjà-vu, but this was not the time to dwell on such triviality. He thought of telling her he was talking about a handgun, not a rifle, but there would be an opportunity to attend to this subject when making the Beretta available to her.

"Where are we? Is this his house?" she asked.

"You don't need to know. What you do need to know is— He's going to appeal to your good nature; to God; tell you about his children and beg and plead with you to let him go and let him be."

"I wouldn't expect anything else."

355

"Right. But don't even think of it, Mrs McGinnis. Don't turn on me. Just so we're clear: the only way I won't kill him is if you kill him first or get his taped confession. We're clear about this?"

"We are," she replied, nodding; "It would appear that the both of us are now people in need of rescuing, Xavier."

"Well, I can't speak for myself, Mrs McGinnis—But I'm sure that in your case, rescue shall come."

"Spare us from idle words now, please."

"Words spoken in earnest, Mrs McGinnis. Does the Lord not favour those who stray from the path over the righteous? I'd have thought that you of all people ought to know the story of the shepherd and his hundred sheep; how when the one went astray he abandoned the rest of the flock to search high and low for the missing one. You'll be alright, Mrs McGinnis."

She raised her thin brows, as if rattled by Lombard's familiarity with this story, and heaved a sigh.

What then followed went like this. Lombard asked Maude McGinnis to wait in the car while he made his way back into the cottage kitchen to free Avery Weyland from the Aga, cut the rope that bound his wrists to his ankles, and heaved his body up and into a sitting position on a chair facing the middle of the room, tying the man to the chair and the chair to the Aga. Avery Weyland's numb limbs so pained him while he was being manhandled in this manner that all he could do was moan and cry; Lombard did not unwelcome the fact that his discomfort prevented him from speaking when he removed the glove from his mouth. He then returned outside, retrieved the bag he'd hidden in the nearby brush, joined Maude McGinnis still sitting in the pickup, showed her how to operate his spare phone as a voice recorder and how to fire the Beretta with its silencer – which she mastered forthwith – and then watched the woman make her own way towards the cottage door after he'd let her know where she could find the bathroom.

As previously stated, in this way the mystery of Joseph Aratoon's money and the death of his wife, two of his daughters and his one unborn child was resolved. Maude McGinnis acquitted herself well on the mission, although at what cost to her own mind, faith and constitution, only she could know. When the time came for her to reappear at the cottage door with her arms crossed over her big breast holding her chin in the palm of one hand and her handbag and the Beretta in the other, the first light of dawn was breaking over the far horizon partially visible between the birch and willow trees around the grounds. She'd returned from her ordeal looking ravaged, wholly consumed by what had occurred. It took her some time to spot Lombard lying flat on his back with his arms behind his head on an old wooden bench not far from the shed by which she'd come to her decision a few hours earlier. She couldn't know that the moment she'd left him he had set out to clean the pickup cargo bed and the garage before going to toss all of Marion Raspberry's tree-surgeon equipment – except for the tarpaulin and a set of ropes – into the pond; most, like the chainsaws and ropes, sank, but other items, such as the high-visibility suit and protective helmet that had proved so helpful, floated, and required retrieving and burying in soft ground among the brush and trees. Only then, after listening to the night while quietly pacing under the stars for a little while, had he settled down on the bench, finding it situated far enough so as not to hear voices from the cottage but with a clear view of its lit kitchen window.

Maude McGinnis rid herself of the Beretta on the passenger seat of the pickup and started in his direction, marvelling that anyone could find sleep in the circumstances. But she presumed wrong. For the last hour, Lombard had been heeding to the local birds' morning chorus, lulled by its clamour, without a whisper of a thought in the compelling peace that comes from waiting for the unravelling of grave events beyond your control. Now he was mindful of Maude McGinnis's weighty heels crunching across the gravel and rough ground, and – not without agitation – sat up to pull himself to one side of the bench, thereby inviting her to sit beside him without them exchanging so much as a look. The truth be told, the woman made a bleak and disheartening sight as she let her body slump onto the bench with a long sigh; he'd expected little else, yet delayed looking at her too closely for fear the sight would stir trouble inside of him.

They sat side by side, she silent and he silent, although he was wanting to ask about his Beretta, for it was nowhere to be seen in her hands or handbag which he could see resting on her lap; he'd not heard her toss it away in the pickup. Now he saw that she was picking at a thread from her dress, absent-mindedly playing with it between her thumb and forefinger.

"He said he never meant for Jane and the little ones to die," she said at last; "They were only meant to scare her. It was never meant to happen."

Lombard swallowed hard:

"Where is my gun?"

"Oh—In your car."

He nodded.

"He also said that it upset him when Joseph killed himself; that he needed him, and Joseph had no need to fear him," she went on.

"Needed him for what?"

"He killed his father. That is why this—It all happened."

"Joseph killed his father?"

"Certainly not! Him—He killed his own father. He needed money—To expand his film business. He had an American company interested in buying his father's novels for films but his father wouldn't sell. So he killed him, making his murder look like a burglary and arson. And got away with it."

"Right. But how does this concern your son-in-law?"

"When Joseph bought the map from him online—Well, it was his elder son's map, he was helping him sell it. For sure— He recognized his name and trapped him with the money he put in his account. Poor Joseph. He spent that money and so let himself be blackmailed into doing small acts of vandalism across London—All so that he would be led to do the same to the father's house one day and could be set up as a potential suspect if the father's murder had gone wrong or the police become suspicious. They never did and Joseph never even knew."

Lombard didn't understand:

"He recognized his name from where?"

"School."

"School?"

"Don't you remember? Jane finding out they were at the same school? Different years but same school. They never ever spoke, he said, but he remembered Joseph being bullied. The whole school knew of him, he said. He was always so timid and good natured, he was, Joseph."

"So I've been led to believe," said Lombard.

"He was. So when he came across his name and cheque as the buyer of the map—He started putting money into his account and threatened him with fraud when he—Anyway," she sighed; "When Jane called him the second time on his landline, he thought she knew things—Would make trouble. But he assured me he never meant to have her or the little ones killed—Just wanted to scare her off."

Lombard could still only make partial sense of her words, but, all the same, it seemed the tale that had cost many lives and nearly his own related to greed and fear; in other words, belonged to – as do most murder stories – the tedium of the mundane.

"Ok," he said; "If the payments to your son-in-law from years back were front money to fit him up as a potential murderer's scapegoat, what about the more recent instalments? What did he need him for now? Another murder?"

Maude McGinnis sighed:

"I—I don't think I thought of asking him that."

Not without reason, it was clear that, for now at least, Maude McGinnis was incapable or disinclined to provide a more detailed account of the things she'd heard. In any event, it no longer remained Lombard's preoccupation to bring order to this mystery. But he was curious to find out about his failed kidnappers.

"Did he tell you who he got to kill Jane?"

"He did—He did: acquaintances of his younger brother who is in prison in Turkey on a drug smuggling charge. He said he never met them. Only spoke to them on the phone. Even after they killed my Jane by mistake."

If Jane's murder was truly an accident, it struck Lombard as odd that Avery Weyland had proved so keen to call on the same lot of incompetents to deal with him; for he'd thought that the campervan three were indeed from Turkey.

"And you have recorded it all?" he asked.

Maude McGinnis produced and handed him the phone he'd given her earlier, and he finally took a good look at her. She made as woeful a sight as he'd imagined, yet came across as resigned and stoical in her turmoil and pain.

"Good," he said, before taking a moment to peer at the low rising sun through the trees; it hadn't escaped his attention that up to now she had spoken of Avery Weyland in the past tense, used 'said' rather than 'says'.

"Did you use my gun?"

She sneered, then shook her head, a movement he caught from the corner of his eye:

"I told him I would."

He frowned; this was no answer.

"You did?"

"I did. And he believed I would. And I am not sure I didn't believe I would myself."

He nodded, took a moment to grin at the sky:

"Good. Good."

"Good that I didn't use it or good that I wasn't sure I wouldn't use it?"

"Both, Mrs McGinnis. Both."

"Huh!" she went.

"In any event, you may well have just saved me a hell of a lot of trouble by giving such a good account of yourself tonight, Mrs McGinnis. I don't know whether to thank you, but you may just have done me a great service," he said, reaching down to wipe mud from his shoes with a tissue from his pocket.

"I trust you did me a great service too, Xavier. And I too am unsure whether I should thank you for it."

He grinned:

"I understand."

"What happens now then?" she asked.

"Well, unless you object, what I had in mind was for you to deliver Mr Weyland and his recorded confession to the authorities. This very morning."

"So you're not going to kill him?"

"Do you want me to?"

"Certainly not. What you suggested sounds good."

"You do realize that you might find yourself in trouble when he talks to them and—"

"I do. But it doesn't matter at all—He said enough to be put in prison for his crimes. They'll understand and let me go when they hear the tape, or I swear there never was a God in the firmament."

Lombard lent back on the bench:

"I don't know about the firmament, Mrs McGinnis. Given the down-to-earth nature of the problems ahead, I'd focus on the good people for now."

"I am."

"Good. Because to help the both of us, you're also going to have to lie to the police—Can you lie to the police, Mrs McGinnis? Can you commit such an abomination?"

She bit her lips:

"Up to a point, I sure can. Up to a point, Xavier. What would you have me lie about?"

"Nothing much, in the circumstances."

And, as the sun slowly rose beyond the trees and the stars vanished and the sky began to fill with colour, they went on speaking in the shadow of their bench, and agreed that, within the next hour, Lombard would drop her off along the road together with Avery Weyland. He returned to her the phone on which she'd recorded her night's ordeal, and, should it reveal anything incriminating, also handed her Avery Weyland's phone. With regards to lying, she readily agreed, for it was all to be done for his protection and, to a degree, her own too; lie one: she had never heard of him until a few days

361

ago when he'd introduced himself by phone as an old friend of Jane's looking into the circumstances of her death; lie two: she knew him only as 'Xavier Lagarde', not 'Lombard', as did Avery Weyland; lie 3: they'd met face to face for the first time the previous night after he called telling her to come to Devon if she wished to find out about her daughter's and grand-daughters' murders; lie 4: she had no idea where they'd spent the night but it was far from where he'd picked her up – which also meant that she had better refrain from watching the road and environs when they left – and couldn't remember what sort of pickup truck 'Xavier Lagarde' drove.

"If it all goes well, we shall never see each other again, Mrs McGinnis."

And there they remained, on the bench, silent again, in the shadow, watching the sun rise until its rays finally found them. Only then did they leave the bench, she to head to the bathroom, he to collect Avery Weyland. The man tied to the chair had had time to reflect on the events of the last twelve hours while they were outside; still pitiable, he had grown mean and angry for it. "Who do you people think you are!" he yelled when Lombard stepped into the kitchen; "*To whichever of my sons the Sultanate may be granted*," he intoned, "*It is proper for him to put his brothers to death to preserve the order of the world*. This is the way of the world, you delu—" He never completed his sentence as Lombard shoved him forcefully backwards – such that he hit the back of his head against the Aga behind him – and leant over his body to replace the glove in his mouth. Then he freed him from the chair and trussed him up by his wrists and ankles like before and dragged him back along the flagstones and outside across the gravel to hoist him onto the back of the pickup and bag him up again inside the tarpaulin. All that now remained was to wipe the kitchen and bathroom clean and take their leave. Maude McGinnis, who'd tidied her hair, touched up her face and arranged her dress, had returned from the bathroom with pomegranate lipstick on her sunken lips, and, as advised, kept her head down when they drove away from the cottage, never looked up or spoke all the time it took to reach a deserted bus stop along a quiet rural road on the outskirts of a village north of Exeter. Still not a word passed between them when he yanked Avery Weyland's hog-tied body down onto the roadside and into the bus stop. Then, he emptied the Beretta's magazine, wiped the gun and its silencer clean and handed it to her.

"Why?" she asked, taken unawares.

"He saw it—Will tell them about it. It will serve us better if you give it to them; put paid to the idea that a dangerous armed man is on the loose in England's green and pleasant land."

She nodded, reached for the gun and stuffed it in her handbag.

"Mind how you go, Mrs McGinnis," he said.

"Goodbye for now, Xavier," she said; "May the Lord bless you and keep you."

Her chest heaved up and down against the crucifix on the black dress under her black coat, and the last he saw of her in the pickup's side view mirror as he drove away, was the splash of her pomegranate lipstick against the pale skin beneath the dark rings under her eyes, and her hand waving goodbye.

It was one of those looks men give one another. In the ordinary course of events, Lombard would have abstained from engaging with the male receptionist. But this morning, reticent discretion seemed the unwise option in a budget chain hotel a stone's throw from the Plymouth ferry terminal. He'd removed his cufflinks and jacket and rolled up his shirtsleeves in a bid to appear indistinguishable from the crowd.

"Will that be just the one night, Sir?" the receptionist asked.

"Yes."

"Right. I'm afraid we only have standard double rooms, Sir."

"Double it better be then."

"Good. Who knows? It might come in handy—You never can tell what good thing might come your way during a short stay in our great city of Plymouth, Sir."

This was when the man had given him one of those looks men give one another, and he'd indulged the other rather than merely flash his grin.

"Well, to tell you the truth, if things go the way I plan, I won't need any room of any size in your hotel tonight, if you know what I mean."

The man gave him another look, smiling knowingly, understanding whatever he wished to understand from this.

"I don't suppose you provide an ironing service?" Lombard went on.

"We do have a laundry, ironing and dry-cleaning service, Sir. But overnight only. You can leave what you need taken care of with instructions here at reception before 4 p.m. today and it will be ready for you by 10 a.m. tomorrow."

"Ah. Thank you. The thing is, it would be good if I could press my suit and shirt before tonight. Like I said, I'm meeting a special—"

"Oh. Yes. I understand. We do have an iron we can lend to our guests for emergencies."

Later that afternoon, freshly shaved and dressed in the newly pressed suit and shirt he'd folded into his bag on leaving his Mews, his wedding-band where it belonged on his finger again, he embarked on the Ferry to Santander and saw the last of England. He'd discarded his phone and purchased a new one in a local store. The cloned registration plates used on the Subaru Brat were buried somewhere in the Dartmoor national park; now, once again displaying its original plates, the pickup sat in a long-stay car park in Plymouth. He'd avoided watching the news, trusting that, were they already on his case – which was, as yet, unlikely – the police would have put all efforts to find Avery Weyland on hold after the latter's bus stop reappearance in Maude McGinnis's company early in the morning.

He'd not forgotten to post his house and car keys to Ali's Cumbrian address before leaving England's soil for possibly the last time.

TWENTY THREE

"Having wandered some distance among gloomy rocks, I came to the entrance of a great cavern—Two contrary emotions arose in me: fear and desire—Fear of the threatening dark cavern, desire to see whether there were any marvellous things in it."

There could hardly be imagined a more retiring guest than Mr Gabriel Bleich within any of the 300 ocean-facing rooms of the VistaMar Hotel that overlooked the port of Funchal. He was discretion incarnate. To the hotel staff, he volunteered the information that he was a recent widower who'd absconded to Madeira seeking peace and introspection, at once securing their goodwill and generosity; his forbearance deserved it, and his vagueness about the length of his stay did not warrant the raising of uncompassionate questions. Four days after stepping ashore in Northern Spain, now fully re-covered from the wounds and tumult of his last forty-eight hours in England, Lombard was his own again: pain-free, suit, wedding-band, cufflinks and easy grin; all mended, a man he trusted came across as intimidating but with clean hands, of a laconic disposition and possessing the right amount of allure to get his way. The bearer of a new name, prudence called for him to steer clear of the places he visited on his recent stay on the island. In this respect, the large VistaMar Hotel with its hundreds of guests passed muster, affording an ideal setting in which to melt among the tourist crowds, even though as broadcast by the British press the news from England suggested that, for now at least, such measures remained unwarranted.

Maude McGinnis, or 'Batwoman', as she was now labelled

within sections of the information superhighway – Lombard surmised this sobriquet was meant to impart the vigilante nature of her known actions – had become public property. Her 'abduction' of Avery Weyland had been leaked, and the account of her 'in-person delivery' to the police of the bound and tarpaulin-bagged eminent producer-director whom she suspected had murdered her daughter and grandchildren had found its way into humanity's many particular communication devices. For now, rumours and opinions were rife, but the details scarce, so that neither the name 'Lagarde' nor 'Lombard' nor mention of a Subaru pickup truck appeared in any report. Lombard reckoned that, owing to the nature of the case and Avery Weyland's standing, the police had probably elected – hitherto effectively – to withhold information, yet trusted that sooner or later a photograph of him from either The Beaumont or Avery Weyland's mother's party would make the news. Come what may, as things stood, while Avery Weyland was left to recover from his ordeal in hospital, Maude McGinnis was being held in custody for the offense of 'kidnapping and threatening with an offensive weapon in a public place', and so looking at a lengthy sentence. Of course, the producer-director denied all allegations of wrongdoing, had recanted his taped confession, claiming it was extracted under duress, that he was coerced, had been coaxed to tell some lies while constructing some more of his own on the spur of the moment to try to control an unhinged woman pointing a gun at him. Still, the overall tone of the reporting of the affair appeared to suggest that Maude McGinnis had public opinion on her side, all the moreso for her harrowing losses and taxing circumstances, and already there were calls to release her on bail on compassionate grounds; no less than the Irish Prime Minister had already promised to "look at what can be done for poor Mrs McGinnis."

Perhaps all this bid fair, in that, all things weighed and measured, it conveyed that the authorities were not completely unfavourably disposed towards Avery Weyland's abductors, for regardless of the silence about 'Mrs McGinnis's French accomplice', Lombard had little doubt that Avery Weyland had

had lots to say about him. In connection to Alan Winston, there was no more news, even in The Paragon; he remained missing and presumed-in-Madeira; already, the wanted posters for 'O Assassino Inglês' were hard to come by, few and far between amid the island's public places and spaces.

It took Lombard all of three days of marking time among the heady smells, dewed green grasses and flushes of petals by the dappled bejewelled rock pool in the plateau's ravine before, midway through the fourth, the donkey at last returned dressed in its rich coat of brown and grey dyes. By now, accustomed to the setting's tropical rains and rugged terrain, Lombard knew to come equipped with a waterproof coat and hiking shoes in addition to provisions enough to last from dawn to dusk. For the first three days, mostly in the glare of the sun burning in the sky overhead, not content to merely sit by the bracing enchantment of the waterfall pool, he'd retraced his steps along the stream's banks of lush trees and shrubbery and grasses, further down the ravine to where the water flowed into a dammed pool that fed the stone irrigation channel which went on to water the distant farmlands, and then back upstream to the pool, always exploring both banks for signs of the creature. An online survey of the area had revealed a dozen or so isolated farmsteads and dwellings amid the hills and wilderness within a 3-mile radius of the plateau, but caution was called for. Already, the local police were on the lookout for Alan Winston; had Lombard taken to probing the wider countryside and properties in search of the donkey, it hardly required imagination to predict what the locals would have made of a stranger lurking about. The undertaking would have been reckless, called unnecessary attention to himself, when, in all his time in the ravine he'd yet to have an unwelcome encounter.

"Hello partner," Lombard grinned, when the object of his endeavour at last came into sight from the shadow of the nearby copse of laurel trees; "I sure am pleased to see you." He gently patted the animal, then rubbed its coat behind its ears, inciting it to lower its head and shut its eyes, and as had occurred on their last encounter, both briefly united in ecstasy, until the donkey pulled itself away to go and graze the fresh grasses by the pool, which evidently was what drew it to venture to this spot. Again, like the previous time, Lombard sat on the grass among the wildflowers and set about eating, disposed to wait for the hour when the light would begin to fade and the temperature would drop fast with the onset of dusk, which is just the time the donkey selected to conclude its grazing and head back along the stream into the copse of laurel trees; albeit, on this occasion, Lombard set out to follow a few paces at the rear.

When the mystery was revealed, his mind was somewhat eased by the finding that it was hardly a wonder he'd failed to locate the animal's route into the ravine; a good twenty minutes downstream from the pool, concealed behind a thicket of shrubbery and willow trees, a precipitous passage – effectively a steep trench-like gully – branched off the ravine, all shadow and too narrow to walk two abreast. It ran down for about twenty yards into a small wood of twisted trees with twisted branches shrouded in mist, beyond which lay a rich open valley hemmed in by sharp green covered cliffs and ridges. Enough daylight remained for Lombard to make out he was standing on a track on the edge of a sheer cliff with a commanding view of a large farmstead below, looking down and across fields of sugar cane, tomatoes and a vineyard sectioned with straw fences, with, dotted here and there, out-buildings of various sizes. The fresh evening air was alive with animal sounds, mostly coming from dogs, sheep and birds, together with the faint echo of a radio or television which rose from an old two-storey yellow ranch-like house with lit-up windows. It stood in the mid-distance, the largest structure around, with a couple of cars and a small tractor nearby. While Lombard stood taking in this scene from his vantage point, the donkey never stopped, all the time carried on down the steep track into the valley below to end its journey in an open barn by a meadow where it was greeted with a great deal of braying by yet another donkey. Lombard also noted that now and again the valley noises were drowned by a rooster's crow. Counselled by great persuasion, swayed by the advantageous appeal a place such as this afforded to a fugitive on the run with no safe haven or property to his name, he considered following the donkey, heading down into the valley to explore the farmstead. His instinct called for it. This had to be where Alan Winston had come to from the pool, either because he was aware of the place's existence, or, in all probability, on the heels of the donkey, like he himself had just done. Of course, he could be long gone by now, but to what alternative; it was hard to imagine a more accommodating haven for a lost soul. Lombard knew; he'd seen his share of havens, and it went contrary to reason that even a cook from London would have failed to realize this much.

The light was fading fast now, and, having come this far, instead of turning away to make it back to the plateau before nightfall so as to return the following day, he succumbed to the temptation to hurry along the track all the way down the cliff and across the fields and meadows below to the yellow house where, wary of a couple of large dogs dragging from their necks long metal chains secured to tethering stakes in a messy front yard, he silently went round glancing into the lit-up open ground floor windows. He counted four people in all; an elderly couple busy with domestic chores in an old-fashioned kitchen, and two young teenagers, a boy and a girl, one involved in some game device and the other on the phone. It was nearly night when he left the farmstead in the valley behind him. The last sound he heard in the distance while nearing the top of the cliff and heading into the small misty wood of twisted trees with twisted branches was that of a crowing rooster again.

When he made it back to his vantage point atop the cliff at sunup the next morning, he found the occupants of the yellow house already up; not only was the radio or television on again but boisterous voices reached up from the open windows, and a car absent the previous evening sat in the front drive. In the stark morning sunlight, the hemmed-in lush valley was all dew, glowing greens and reds and luscious shadows and fragrances. The farmstead appeared smaller but also more chaotic and unkempt than it had at dusk. Most of the outbuildings and sheds were in a poor state of repair, the fields of sugar cane and tomatoes and the vineyard nowhere near as neat or clear of weeds as they must once have been. In three different meadows dotted about the land, besides the donkeys and dogs he already knew about, were a horse, a goat, sheep, chickens, pheasants and ducks, all free to roam outside the wicker fences protecting the fields and vineyard. The tractor and one of the vehicles near the house were rusty wrecks. Yet, by the look of it, the house had not long ago benefited from a fresh coat of bright yellow paint, gleaming white bedsheets wafted in the breeze of a long washing line, and it was plain – as revealed by the well-looked after donkey that had led him there and was now grazing with its companion next to their barn – the farm was not only being tended by its occupants but well-managed enough to sustain a large family and more.

Once again, a rooster's crow rang out, and then rang out again while Lombard decided to wait for things to happen at the yellow house before heading down. Presently, a youngish woman together with the teenagers – now in school uniform – that he'd spotted the previous evening stepped outside and into the nearby car and drove off along a track into the woods on the farmstead's far side. By now, Lombard had determined that the rooster he kept hearing crowed about once every fifteen minutes with all the regularity of a ticking clock, and by the time the white-haired couple which he knew to be in the house came out dressed in overalls with a playing radio and a number of shallow plastic buckets between the two of them, he reckoned to have heard it brag half a dozen times already. It would have been preferable if the old folks had left after the teenagers and the woman before them, but instead they leisurely made their way to the vineyard where, bent and with straw hats to shield their heads from the sun, they proceeded to attend the vines, transferring the grapes they picked to their plastic buckets.

It now seemed clear that Lombard would not have the place to himself, not any time soon at any rate, and so, mindful to remain unseen, he resolved to head down the cliff and, stealing across fences, fields and meadows to avoid raising the attention of the elderly couple or the dogs chained to their stakes, he crept into the house through the wide open front door. As expected, he found the rooms quiet, empty and modestly presented; some features here and furnishing there told of a journey from an affluent past to a utilitarian present. He opened every door, quickly toured the whole house, including the attic, until, satisfied that hospitality sheltered Alan Winston nowhere here, he returned outside to search one outbuilding after the other, from a garage near the house to the donkeys' barn, with half a dozen more in between, at all times attentive to the dogs and grape-harvesting couple. Soon, the only structures left to merit inspection were a shed near the vineyard and a couple of small stone outbuildings some way up the surrounding steep wooded hillsides; one was in the shade of a grove of chestnut trees, and the other in a laurel forest beyond a field of ripe tomatoes – this single shed and two stone out-buildings were the last constructions large and sound enough to accommodate a man against the rains and the cold of the night. Getting to the shed near the vineyard unseen would have to wait until the elderly couple left their work to make their way back to the house along with their playing radio, which, trusting the ways of hardy country folks, Lombard guessed would be to break at midday for lunch. It was just past 11 a.m., and so he turned and made for the tomato fields – picking a couple for refreshment – and, by now unsure which of pragmatism, doggedness or possibly grandiose narcissism motivated him, started uphill through the laurel forest.

A minute later, without words forming in his mind or much of a sense of vindication – or, for that matter, satisfaction – he experienced the agitation that comes from the realisation that it is right for a man to trust instinct and common sense. He had found his prey. And, before all else, thought it was dead.

Alan Winston – who'd confounded all including Lombard

himself by not getting caught in good time after landing in Madeira – had found refuge in a ten-by-four-foot windowless drystone cabin with a cracked red wooden door and a moss, lichen and grass covered tiled roof. It stood half way up the steep hillside, amidst the humidity of the laurel forest, about fifty feet above the field of tomatoes. A rivulet of clear water flowed out from an opening constructed at the bottom of its front wall, just by the side of the red door, and at the back, another opening halfway up the wall let water in from a stone waterway atop a ramp; it led water from a spring a little further up the hill into the drystone cabin. Long before Lombard cautiously pulled the rickety door open, his nose and throat alerted him that something, or someone, very likely dead, was to be found inside; the smell of decaying flesh hung everywhere. What he heard and saw within the cold shadow inside while still standing in the doorway were the buzzing hum of flies and a broken-down wooden wheel with metals cups and water trickling down from half-way up the rear wall into the channel that led to the opening near the bottom of the door; by all appearances, the cabin had once housed a crude and now abandoned water wheel electricity generator. Then, satisfied all was safe, he took a step inside and caught sight of Alan Winston lying in a foetal position on a rusty sheet of corrugated iron against the dirt floor. Oddly, the youth was dressed in a long black woman's skirt and an open black cardigan, had bare feet and legs, and never moved or made a sound as Lombard inched towards him, pinching his nose not to retch from the putrid stench within the semi-darkness between the windowless walls. He stayed put for a while, observing the inert body at his feet, giving his eyes time to adjust to the dim light, and gradually made out the full form and details that were Alan Winston. He identified him on account of his hair and what could be seen of his face, or he thought he did, for now he saw that he could not possibly have recognized the youth, but rather had assumed it was him. All the same, he was right: the form teeming with flies and cockroaches on the corrugated sheet was Alan Winston. He'd lost enough weight to be mostly bones and sinews, and his hair and face were dirty and caked with all kinds of things. He was missing several fingers from one hand, which was very swollen and raw and dark, the appearance of a balloon engorged with drying pus. The skin of his arm showing outside his cardigan sleeve was also discoloured, and putrescent with festering blisters, as was that of one of his bare legs, which exhibited a fractured shinbone. It very much looked like Alan Winston was dead, however, the pus slowly discharging from some of his wounds, the slow-leaking lesions on his skin and the sweat on his grimy face said otherwise – that what there was of him was in the grip of the fever that comes from putrefying alive. Lombard squatted down, swatted some of the flies away and carefully peeled the cardigan away from the youth's infected arm and shoulder. The infection from the hand with the missing fingers had spread all the way to his neck and torso, where the skin looked patchy, discoloured and blistered, and the same was true of his injured leg, where the infection from his broken shinbone had spread to his hip, and further up still into his gut. He closely observed Alan Winston's rib cage, became certain that he saw, through the flies, a heart beating between the bones beneath the fleshless skin, eventually caught on to the shallow wheeze of his breath passing through his split lips, then gently pressed the flesh around his shoulder with his thumb; it made a strange creasing sound, as if air was being displaced from an inner pocket. "You've seen better days," Lombard whispered to himself, swallowing hard; "Haven't you, Alan?"

"Fucking rooster!" the other replied in a faint raspy voice.

Still squatting, Lombard looked at Alan Winston's face; the eyes remained shut, and presuming he was able, he had yet to make a movement.

"What was that?" he queried.

"Fucking rooster," the other breathed again; "Driving me mad, the bastard is."

Lombard understood he meant the tireless time-keeping local rooster; by now its crowing had become background noise to his ears, yet, in spite or perhaps because of his wretched state, or the length of time he must have spent alone within the dank walls of the stone cabin, Alan Winston's mind was clearly alert to it.

"How are you, Alan?" he said.

He saw that the other had heard him, in that a thoughtful frown formed on his grimy emaciated face. Evidently, surprisingly, Alan Winston was lucid, and when he opened his eyes to look directly up at Lombard, what Lombard saw in him, through the fever and the pain and the fear, was the defiant keenness particular to youth, the irrepressible spirit of nature, eyes that don't miss a thing.

"I know that voice," Alan Winston rasped, trying to grin; "Huh. I know you. You're the tick, right?"

"The tick?"

"Yeah—The bastard who hounded my arse about the puppy."

"Oh. That's right, Alan—I am he."

Alan Winston shut his eyes again, as if it was too painful for him to keep them open and smile at the same time; for, somehow, he managed a smile:

"Well, if I'd known you were coming I'd have made tea— And put a pie in the oven."

"I'm not sure I'd have liked that. But thank you."

"Jesus, man—You're like the old bad penny, aren't you? Showing up at the end of the world like this. Thing is—I still haven't got your fucking puppy."

"I'm not here on account of the puppy, Alan."

Now Alan Winston opened his eyes again, searched Lombard's face, fresh with pitiful defiance:

"If you've come to get me for murder, you're too late— Alan's got all scabby and got no time or place to go no more."

"I'm not here to arrest you, Alan," Lombard said.

Alan Winston showed surprise, knitted his brows as if trying to make sense of what he was hearing:

"Kill me?"

"No."

"You don't say. Anyway—Killing—Talking of killing —I've been thinking. Deep. Very much so. And I don't think it has to do with the Hebrews."

"The Hebrews?"

"Mile End-Johnny Boy's mates, you know?"

Lombard presumed he was speaking of John Bowdion:

"Right."

"Yeah. I blamed them at first. They got a name for causing mischief, don't they?"

Lombard stayed silent.

"But I worked it out," the other went on; "I've got no quarrel with them. And they should have no quarrel with me."

"Good."

"Yeah. It's the one I did in that caused it—Calling me a loser. Fucking frauds, the likes of him."

"How's that, Alan?"

"Muddying next door's doormat to distract from their own. I worked it out, alright—Scumbaggery. You tell him now."

"He's dead, Alan."

"Yes—Of course he is."

Lombard watched him, unsure what to make of this, waiting for what would come next, but Alan Winston shut his eyes just as the rooster made itself heard again:

"Fucking rooster. Driving me mad, he is," he wheezed, softly, keeping his eyes shut.

And he sighed and lost consciousness, no longer responding to his name being called. Lombard reached down to feel his forehead, found it to be burning, got to his feet, tore a section of his shirt-tail which he soaked in the water trickling down the back wall, swatted the flies from around Alan Winston's face and proceeded to wipe his lips and skin clean, leaving the soaked fabric on his forehead – a futile gesture meant to help soothe his fever – before he left him to return outside the cabin and into the fresh air of the laurel forest basking in the balmy afternoon sun. Down below, the elderly couple were still tending their vines, and a few steps away from the cabin, the air alive with the sound of their radio and the calls of birds and the farmstead's animals smelled sweet again.

Lombard wondered whether Alan Winston was aware of the pertinence of his comment about having "no time or place to go no more". He knew what was wrong with the youth, had seen the same before. He had advanced gangrene, which had progressed from his limbs to his body, too far to be treatable by means of amputation or otherwise. His high fever was a sign that his body was still fighting, but his condition was such that his organs were likely already being attacked, about to fail anytime now. To suffer terrible pain and slip in and out of consciousness until his heart gave out was all he had left to look forward to. Lombard gave him a few hours at most, a day at a stretch. All of which left him in an unenviable position: should he alert the old couple working among the vines below of his presence and get them to summon help – and all that this would entail – or was he to let Alan Winston die in the cabin? Certainly, there was nothing he could do for him, and besides, he reckoned the youth was beyond being moved; he was rot, lifting him from his rusty corrugated sheet would cause agony such as would send his body into shock, the strain kill him. Long consideration of this predicament was cause enough for disquiet, but the outcome was never in doubt: the severity and finality of the situation meant the decision ought to belong to the interested party; Alan Winston's plight too ought to be left to his own pleasure.

Back in the putrid stench and dim light of the cabin, he squatted by the youth's side again and squeezed his good hand in an attempt to bring him back to consciousness, trying not to hurt him. It worked, in that the other opened his eyes and grabbed hold of his hand and immediately pulled it towards him not letting go.

"You stayed," he wheezed, looking into Lombard's eyes, fearful at first, then grimacing with pained grace; "Thank you. It's not easy being all alone, you know."

Lombard grinned, tried pulling his hand away, but the frail fingers holding it still possessed enough strength to cling onto his own.

"Are you lucid, Alan?" he asked, deciding to allow his hand to be owned for now.

"Well, I was just having a profound dream," Alan Winston replied; "Does that mean I'm lucid?"

"Seriously, Alan," Lombard returned.

"Seriously. Listen: you know all the digital info we give

away and they steal from us on all that gear we pay through the nose for? Well, in my dream, the information was used to digitise our soul and keep it alive forever in digital format in some virtual real estate they own. The thing is, they also got us to pay for it—All the years we're flesh and bone they charged us upfront for it. Even gave receipts. How lucid is that, uh?"

"It's edifying," Lombard replied, deciding it would do. Besides, for the youth to cling to his hand so determinedly suggested he was capable of thought and willpower.

In this manner, speaking candidly, he told him what he thought of his situation and options – "Although I must stress I'm not a doctor," he added.

Alan Winston listened, then remained pensive, and when Lombard reiterated that there were only two options open to him – "Dying in this cabin or, if your body can survive being peeled off this metal sheet of yours, dying in a hospital bed." – he never seemed to doubt the truth of what he was hearing. "What would you do if you were me?" is all he asked, after another long moment's thought. And when Lombard declined to answer, he requested more time to think and, having made use of this time, began to weep, quietly:

"Beyond amputation; a day, two at the most?"

"Uh-huh. But, again, I'm no doctor."

"Then I'll die here. Fucking free. But I need you."

Lombard swallowed hard, and Alan Winston now squeezed his hand with all the strength he was still capable of mustering:

"I don't want to be alone. Please. You say it won't take long so—"

And he slipped out of consciousness again before any more words were spoken, releasing his grip. Lombard, free for now, once again cooled the youth's burning lips and forehead with the freshly soaked rag he'd made earlier.

Perhaps there is something to be said for the oft-proclaimed complaint that life – like love – is not fair. Had Alan Winston been older, or obese, or uglier, or altogether a more reprehensible character, it is just about possible that Lombard would have forsaken him to his fate; certainly, only the two of them would ever have known about their time in the cabin, and it could justifiably be reported that, during his well-spent life, he'd done much worse than leave a dying man to die alone. Be that as it may, under the circumstances, it would have amounted to some sort of crime to abandon a poor fellow who, after all, beyond his recent bad decisions, was in the prime of youth and, prior to his present misfortune, had displayed spirit and qualities that made him worthy of nature, a doomed volatile butterfly. Thus, he stayed, trusting in his own prediction.

The next time Alan Winston came to, Lombard was sitting in the cabin sheltering from torrential rain that pummelled the slate roof above his head. The old couple in the farmstead below had long returned to their yellow house, and he'd kept the cabin door ajar in an attempt to ease the stench created by Alan Winston's body. The other made no attempt to conceal his pleasure at finding him still there by his side, couldn't repress a smile, and, quite possibly on account of the refreshing rain, looked more animated and less feverish than previously. "There's a wet cloth on your forehead," Lombard said, seeing him awake: "I suggest you put it between your lips and suck. Then try eating—Slowly. I got you some tomatoes. It will help." Alan Winston ignored his advice, never looked at the tomatoes Lombard had left on a flat stone beside him: "Don't you just like the sound of the rain?" he remarked instead, before asking Lombard to help him onto his back and drag him a few inches towards the wall so that he could partially sit up. He groaned, moaned, screamed, shuddered and displayed such agony while being turned – which took all of several minutes – that Lombard thought he'd die there and then, and when he didn't, rather than attempt to drag him to the wall as the other wished, made a bundle from his waterproof coat and jacket which he gently placed behind his head, so allowing him to speak with his head up rather than with his cheek against the cold metal sheet, as he'd done up to now. It seemed an opportune time to try to find out what had brought about his predicament. He proved willing and able to talk, starting with the sentence "What a fine fucking mess I got myself into, uh!" On account of his faint voice and the rain continuing to fall on the roof above their heads, Lombard moved close to him to hear him speak. "The bastard dying on me like that; never was meant to be—Just meant to hurt him," he said.

By the time he lost consciousness again, much was explained. The killing of the Paragon reporter had weighed heavy on Alan Winston's mind, aroused such confusion and self-loathing that death had seemed preferable to going on living, or prison. "The shine was gone. It's like I wasn't me no more; just another grey anybody, you know what I mean." By then, he explained, he was also tired of trying "to keep one step ahead" of Lombard. He'd come to Madeira on account of the pool on the plateau, which had lived on in his thoughts as "the secret Garden of Eden" after his short stay on the island. "If you gonna end it, it may as well be in Heaven rather than in grimy old London. I mean, have you seen the pool?" Once at the plateau, he'd swallowed eighty paracetamol tablets – "I read that thirty-two would do but thought I'd play it safe" – stripped himself naked, burned all his belongings and stepped down into the pool as night fell, confident the drug and the cold would "turn out the light" while he lay in the water face up looking at the stars. But hours later – he couldn't tell how many, only that the night had passed and the sun shone above him – he was still "switched on" and, by then, decided he wished to live; "It hit me, there in the water: if dying's any fucking good, why don't all the wily bastards top themselves?" Helplessly weak and numb with cold, he'd dragged himself out of the pool to collapse on its grassy bank. Whether because of the drug or prolonged exposure to the cold, his legs weren't "working", he had the shivers and believed he would have died if a donkey hadn't turned up. The animal had allowed him to lift his body up onto its warm back, hang on to its bristly mane – a feat he'd only just managed – and given him a ride back to the farmstead, and the next he knew he'd woken up in the animal's barn, still naked, still shivering, much bewildered and still barely able to stand on his legs. That was when, after stealing the dress and cardigan from the washing line near the yellow house – "That's all there was and I was cold." – he had made his way up to the disused cabin, thinking it was a safe place to hide in, being in the shadow of the laurel forest. He'd also picked some tomatoes and grapes on the way. He thought he was onto a good thing. The farm provided food and water, the people in the yellow house acted as if his cabin didn't exist, and even the police, when they came – which he guessed may have been on his account – left after the most cursory look around the place. His aim was to stay put until he was strong enough to decide his next move. Only, far from getting stronger, as the days passed, he grew weaker, prey to constant fever and shivers, especially in the cold of night. That was what had led him to try breaking into the yellow house to steal matches or a lighter – so he could light a fire – together with some more suitable clothes, and eggs from the chicken coop in the garden; he'd heard of the virtues of protein, and knew eggs were rich in it. He'd waited until the coast was clear, got hold of matches and clothes but, on the way to the chicken coop, had misjudged the length of the chains tethering the dogs and was savaged by both animals. When he made his escape back to the cabin, he'd lost three fingers to one dog, dropped both matches and clothes and broken his shinbone stumbling into a deep water ditch while running bleeding for safety as fast as he could. It still surprised him that he'd remained undiscovered after this episode, and wondered whether it wouldn't have been preferable if he'd shown himself to the farm people instead of returning to hide in the cabin, for that was the last time he had been well enough to venture outside. The next day had found him much sicker, and feebler, hardly able to move, and the rot in his hand and leg had set in. He had no idea how long it was now, how many days or nights he had lain on his corrugated sheet against the cabin floor, his sole nourishment the water trickling down its wall.

As was to be expected, the effort involved in recalling these events left Alan Winston much exhausted. He fainted, and from this point forward slipped in and out of consciousness, never to remain lucid or coherent for more time than it took to say a few words. Now and again, he would also whisper sentences while seemingly unconscious: "Get on your knees and pray"; "How do they call you, Mister?"; "Who can dream these kinds of things?"; and "We picked fruit and pulled up lettuce"; or "A shimmering matador of pink, silver and gold fucking brocade; a better son."

With sundown approaching and the rains gone, Lombard stepped outside again, seeking relief, and stretching his legs in the laurel forest. The windows of the yellow house in the low mid-distance were all lit-up, and the farmstead humming to the sound of life. He remained quite certain of Alan Winston's prospects, but pondered a scenario where the other would take as long as two days to die. He was looking to end this quickly, had little desire to spend the coming night or the next day in the stench of the cabin next to a dying man. In the course of the past weeks, death, it seemed, had visited him more times than he cared to remember, and here he was now keeping it company without good reason or purpose. He knew – without knowing how – that there were no dangerous predatory animals in Madeira, for a while wondered what if anything there was to make of this piece of information, then determined that he was reaching for the void, seeking to provide himself an alibi, to put himself in another place. He wondered how Ali was, whether she was still in America, whether she was still thinking about the text messages they had exchanged a few nights earlier; how long would it take to prise out of her the things he would need to know? Would she even see him again after her revelation, or would she drift away, to protect her secrets in order to go on living comfortably every tomorrow? He shuddered, felt terribly tired, in dread of all things, of all people and of himself, wished he was elsewhere, wished his mind at peace. He stopped walking under the canopy of laurel trees, let out a groan, and then swallowed hard. He peered at the cabin in the descending shadow. What if Alan Winston came to now and died alone thinking he'd abandoned him? What of it? Would it make a difference to his dying, to anyone?

The rooster crowed and he returned into the darkness of the cabin, patted the other's forehead with the freshly soaked rag again, and found the skin under his fingers no longer burning.

"Fucking rooster. Driving me mad, he is," Alan Winston whispered.

"How are you, Alan?" he asked.

"I'm mad. I will never feel love anymore. But I'm glad not to be alone," the youth whispered; "Tell me, is it night yet?"

"It's dusk."

"Dusk. Yes. Are there stars in the sky already?"

Lombard had no idea; he'd not looked at the sky through the canopy of trees. But since it wasn't raining, it was likely that the sky was clear.

"There are. Do you want me to take you outside, Alan? It will hurt you very bad. But I'll be quick. And then you'll be able to see the stars through the trees for yourself. And it will be very beautiful. Would you like that?"

"Outside is not far away," Alan Winston said after a moment's silence.

"That's right."

"I had wings once. I could spread them—Never knew I'd not have them one day."

"No one knows these things, Alan."

"All the little things they forget to whisper in your ear, uh."

Now, in the little light that was left in the cabin, Lombard watched Alan Winston open his eyes. He stared up at the dark ceiling, smiling, as if looking at wondrous things.

"I think it's night now," he said at last.

"You do?"

"Yes. I can't hear the rooster at night; driving me mad, he is."

Lombard sighed.

"My father was in the Gurkhas, you know," he heard.

"Uh-huh."

"Yeah—For real."

"Uh-huh."

"Huh. I wonder: what about all those better days that have

yet to come?"

And Lombard knew Alan Winston was about to exhale his last breath.

"Yes, I want to spend it with you," he heard him say softly. And the other died, not at once, but not long after that, in a whisper, eyes open.

Lombard observed him for a moment and winced:

"Mind how you go, Alan," he whispered.

If not for his body having been transformed overnight into a scavenger insects' dominion, the following morning Lombard found Alan Winston much the way he had left him, face up lying on his rusty metal sheet inside the cabin. He himself had spent the night fast asleep on the cold ground outside, quite some way from the cabin's stench, and was surprised to find it was well past ten o'clock when he awoke under the laurel canopy shading him from the sun. He'd remained there overnight after deciding against attempting to make his way back to the pool in the dark.

Down in the farmstead, the grey-haired couple were once again busy tending their vines, their radio was on, and across the valley the invisible rooster was reliably slicing time into fifteen-minute sections. He freshened up, dipping his head and washing his face and hands in the water channel feeding the cabin's old waterwheel. He was in shirtsleeves, had proved loath to slip back into either the jacket or waterproof he'd placed under Alan Winston's head. He sat for a while, observing the grape-harvesting elderly couple below him, watching them tidy and place each bunch they picked in their shallow plastic buckets. He waited until lunchtime, when he knew they would head off with their radio, only then made his way down to retrieve a spade from one of the outbuildings he'd explored the previous day, and grabbed a bunch of ripe grapes to enjoy on his way back up.

An hour later, Alan Winston lay buried in his black dress and cardigan, still stuck to his metal corrugated sheet under three feet of earth about twenty yards above the cabin.

Lombard had considered leaving the body in the cabin for someone to discover, or possibly leaving a sign to alert the old couple or local police to its presence, but in the end thought it better for all parties – including Alan's Winston's family – if no one were to know of his fate.

When he arrived back at the pool in the afternoon, all rumpled with his bundled jacket and waterproof hanging at the end of his arm, he found the donkey had preceded him along the black and silver stream flowing through the emerald canopy of trees to the fresh grasses by the water. He went to pat it and gave it a good scratch behind its ears, but said no words and kept it short. He felt exhausted, could think of no reason not to pause to sample the bracing water, heady colours and fragrances around him; for it had to be said, the place was truly enchanting. He took off his shirt and shoes and socks, kneeled on the boulder he had kneeled on once before to splash his face and nape. Now he rolled up his trousers and settled down on the boulder with his feet in the soothing water, letting out a sigh containing the particular and singular pleasure that only absolute relief provides. He thought he'd remain there for a short spell, listening to the water falling from the plateau splash and spatter, indulge his senses, this time without his eyes becoming transfixed by the rustling white water catching the light from the sky above. And they didn't. He just enjoyed the moment, never overwhelmed by a sense of utter emptiness, as had occurred before at this very spot on this very boulder. Perhaps he was just too tired. Or, for now, Alan Winston's death had dried up and soothed his agitations. Or perhaps it was on account of his mind's musings on certain inevitabilities in human affairs, the impermanence and vicissitudes of civilisation. For, the previous night, finding sleep hard to come by in the cold damp outdoors, he had sought the distraction of his phone, acquainted himself with the latest news from England. The police had decided to let Avery Weyland go. He was free. No evidence was found to corroborate his recanted taped confession. But so was Maude McGinnis. There could be no underestimating the director-producer's acumen in matters of public relations and marketing. He knew his business; had weighed public opinion and got his solicitor to release a statement letting it be known that "As a gesture of goodwill and in consideration of the poor, much-afflicted woman's understandably grief-stricken mind-set", he had decided to forgive and not press charges. Accordingly, to great choruses of approval on all sides, Maude McGinnis had been let go pending further investigation, and allowed to return to Ireland. There were dissenting voices though. Some people clearly thought Avery Weyland was guilty, were crying foul, screamed bloody murder. The word 'privilege' was much used by many communities. Across all sorts of communication platforms voices were congregating, calling for records of his work and his name to be deleted from all that counted, and his past awards to be rescinded and redacted from all that mattered. For this was the time at which this tale took place.

Lombard took a deep breath and sighed:

"You are my witness," he breathed between his teeth, observing the donkey in its rich coat of brown and grey dyes. And he grinned, wondering why neither his name nor his picture had made the news yet, and dipped his jacket and coat into the pool to wash them clean of the smell of death.

The End